THE FORGOTTEN MOTHER

A spine-chilling crime thriller with a heart stopping twist

DETECTIVE ARLA BAKER SERIES 3

ML ROSE

Table of Contents

PROLOGUE

Sixteen years ago

Near Nottingham

He winced as she pulled on his arm, tugging him forward.

"What are you doing here?" she whispered between pressed lips. He can tell she's angry. Her jaws are clamped tight, and her nostrils are flaring.

The room is almost dark. The reading lamp on the table has a T shirt draped over it, reducing the amount of light. The wardrobe in one corner casts a deep shadow over the bed. Posters on the wall curl at the edges, blank faces on them staring forward.

The boy is scared. He looks up at the angry face and stammers. "I...I heard you get out of bed so I came to...to see."

She shoves him back against the wall, letting go of his arm. Her tone is scathing, yet very low. "Why can't you just mind your own business for a change, you stupid idiot!"

He says nothing, staring at the worn carpet on the floor. She closes the door softly, wishing for the umpteenth time her door had a lock. She walks over to the table, sits down, and resumes putting makeup on her face. She raises the T shirt a little to make sure she can see herself in the pocket mirror.

The boy slides against the wall, moving forward. He's in his night pyjamas, and the carpet feels cold under his feet. So does the rough wall against his hands.

"Where are you going?" he whispers. She doesn't reply, busy with the foundation brush.

"Is it to that house?" he says. She stops and turns. Her eyes are like slits.

"What are you talking about?"

"You know, that house you went to last week from school."

She leans forward, eyebrows knotted. "You *followed* me?"

He shrugs, then licks his lips. "I saw you getting into a car I hadn't seen before. So yeah, I followed." He's ten years old, and quick on his bike.

She closes her eyes for a second and shakes her head. She goes to say something, thinks better of it, then goes back to her make up. She works fast, then zips up her bag and puts it inside the shoulder bag. She picks up her high heels and chucks them inside the bag as well. She's wearing trainers.

The boy can smell the cheap perfume on her. She leans over him, holding a finger up to his face.

"Say one word about this and you're dead. Got that?"

He swallows. She's hurt him before, but not like what his step-dad does to both of them. She can be scary as well, especially when she's like this. But he also knows she looks out for him, protects him when she can. He just wishes she was more friendly to him.

"You're going there again, aren't you?"

She grabs his flimsy night shirt and pushes him against the wall. Her knuckles hurt his chest.

"Ow," he whimpers.

"It doesn't matter where I'm going. You're just a little kid. Keep your nose out of it. I'll be back in the morning. And this time, I'll look out for you. Do you hear me? If I see you anywhere on the road, I'm calling him." She points to the room where their step dad is sleeping.

He stares at her with big eyes. He knows she wouldn't dare give herself away by calling him. But he stays silent.

She lets go of him and turns the light off. In the pitch black darkness, he watches as she squeezes between the table and

10

window. She fiddles with the latch, then raises the window. She sits on the ledge, dangling her legs over the wall. Right below her, it's the flat roof of the kitchen.

He can feel the cold air rushing into the room, freezing his body. She is wearing a heavy coat and tights over her skirt. She balances herself one last time, then jumps off the ledge.

He shuffles forward. The cold is biting, turning his face numb. The silvery wash from a half moon shows the girl running across the small roof, then lowering herself to the garden. She climbs over the waist high fence, then starts to walk.

He makes his mind up in a second. He scurries into his room next door. He pulls on hooded top, coat and pants, socks and trainers. He can hear the snoring of his obnoxious step dad. Too much booze and he snores louder than usual. But at least it means he's passed out. When he's asleep, he can't touch him, or his sister.

The boy jumps down to the flat roof and races across it. He's much faster than his sister. He grabs his bike from the shed, hauls it over the fence. Yellow hazes from the street lamps shows his sister's figure, getting smaller as she walks rapidly. He gives herself another ten seconds, then starts pedalling his bike.

CHAPTER 1

The man lay very still, his face hidden by a ski mask. Only his eyelids blinked. The grass around him was brittle with frost. He was watching the row of houses opposite him, his attention focused on the middle residence. Light scattered around the drawn curtains of the Georgian windows. The house was terraced but large, typical of the Edwardian terrace mansions built in the nineteenth century. They were never cheap and now sold for several millions.

Jonty was his name. J to his friends, of whom he didn't have many. Jonty wore lycra running gear from head to toe, and a tight, black ski jacket, the same colour as his mask. Precision gloves, allowing full movements of his fingers, covered his hands. He was glad of them. His hands would have frozen by now. His running shoes were black too, and gripped well.

A full moon floated in the sky like a round, silver balloon. Clouds around it were touched by a blue fire, suffusing them with bright, otherworldly shades. The forest Jonty lay in was quiet. Occasionally a squirrel rushed in the undergrowth. His ears were attuned to the silence of winter, a dead calm that claimed the movement of grass, leaves. But he was anything but calm. His heart thrummed against his ribs, breath fluttered against the nylon material of the ski mask.

Tonight was his night.

He had watched and waited for the last two months. He knew what the owners of the house did most evenings. In particular, their pattern on a Thursday evening. He glanced at the green dial of his watch. Seven pm. Any minute now.

The front door opened, throwing a shaft of light on the landing. Four stairs led down to ground level. A woman emerged, wearing a green coat and scarf. The security lights didn't come on, which made him smile.

Jonty watched the woman get into a BMW convertible and drive off. The lights remained on inside the house. He knew who was inside. Without making a sound, Jonty stood. He tightened the straps of his backpack, then set off at a brisk jog.

Even the city that never slept seemed quieter, holding its breath. Only one car passed him by as he ran, invisible in the dark cloak of night. He got to the edge of the forest and leaned against a tree. Above him stretched electric cables. He could see them swing across the road to a wooden post, from where several lines originated. Each of those cables ended in a house, supplying telephone and internet traffic.

Jonty grabbed the lowest branch and heaved himself up on the tree. He was incredibly fit, he ran two marathons a year. With five minutes, he was near the top. He rested his back against the main trunk and removed the bolt cutter strapped to his waist.

He uncoiled a harness and looped it around his waist, then tied to a sturdy branch, to take his weight in case he fell. Then he leaned forward, the bolt cutter's sharp jaws open. He could reach the cables from here. With several snips, he cut the cables, watching them fall to the ground.

He kept an eye on the road. It was a quiet one by South London standards, but if the falling wires hit a passing car he was in trouble. They didn't. The tension in the cables whiplashed them to the black asphalt, emitting small sparks of electricity. Then they moved to the edges of the road, dragged by the recoil. Silence returned to millionaire's row.

Jonty climbed down the tree slowly. Rushing down a slope or tree was dangerous, he knew, being an avid rock climber. Once his feet touched ground, he was fast as a hare. He crossed the road where the streetlamps didn't shine. Keeping to the shadows, he came up to the house. The large, thick red door faced him.

He rang the brass doorbell. After a while, he heard sounds from inside. His heart rate quickened. He took off the ski mask and patted his hair down. He pressed himself closer to the door, so his face blocked the view from the eye hole on the door.

"Who is it?" A muffled voice came from inside.

"Sky TV. Are you having a telephone and internet outage currently?"

The voice said something, then there was a rattle of chains. The door opened. A man stood there, wearing a dressing gown and sandals. He wore glasses, and was in his late fifties. He stared at Jonty in confusion.

"Who…"

He didn't finish the question. Jonty kicked the door hard. The man stumbled backwards, falling against the wall. Jonty was inside in a flash, and without turning around, shut the door with the heel of his shoe.

CHAPTER 2

Cherie Longworth shut the door of her BMW convertible and beeped the car shut. Her heels crunched the pavement as she walked briskly up to her house. The lights were still on, which meant her husband was at home. She had spent a few hours with a girlfriend who was going through a messy divorce. David, her husband, stayed at home on weekday evenings, looking through scripts.

Cherie went up the steps to the porch and stopped short. The heavy front door was open. Not wide, but a crack, a narrow opening that most people wouldn't notice. But Cherie knew. The light in the hallway was off, but the windows spilled light into the frozen evening outside. The darkness in the hallway was ominous.

Cherie could feel her heart thumping loudly. She swallowed and strained her eyes.

"David?" she called. "Are you there?"

Silence. Cherie looked behind her. Across the road, lay the expanse of Clapham Common. It looked lovely in the summer, but now it was dark and foreboding. The tall trees hunched together like a beast of prey. Ready to lunge at her. Cherie shivered. It had been David's idea to live here. She had never liked it, for precisely this kind of reason. Had the house been burgled?

"David?"

Cherie called out again. Not a sound came from inside. Cherie grabbed her phone. She was getting ready to dial 999 when she suddenly felt a little foolish. There could be a simple explanation. David could just have popped to the neighbour's. They were friends with the Patel's who lived two doors down. Or maybe he had meant to pop outside then forgotten something in his study.

The six bedroom house was massive, more than enough for her and David. She could get lost inside, and David's study was on the top floor. Yes, that must be it, she thought. David couldn't hear her.

Gingerly, Cherie pushed the door. It fell open on smooth hinges. She called out his name again as she stepped inside the dark hallway. Her fingers groped for the light switch. When the LED spotlights came on they made her blink. She crossed to the right and peered inside the living room. The lights were on but the room was empty. The room on the right was similar.

The staircase stood to the left against the wall. Straight ahead lay a smaller hallway and beyond it, the kitchen and dining room. She heard the sound as she got closer to the stairs. Muted voices. She listened hard, trying to quell the rising beat of her heart. It sounded like the TV was on somewhere. Maybe in David's study, as that was at the rear?

A light was on upstairs, but at the back of the property. The three bedrooms at the front, including the master bedroom - were sunk in darkness. Cherie stepped up, then stopped and looked at the kitchen. She had shut the front door already, should she check the rest of the ground floor? For some reason, she didn't feel like doing it by herself. A sharp knife from the kitchen drawer on the other hand....and what would she do with a knife? Stab an intruder?

She held her phone still, thumb poised over the green ring button. She climbed. Mouth dry, chest heaving, she reached the landing, then the upper floor hallway. The sound of the TV was louder now. It came from the study. The door was shut and light seeped out from the bottom.

Cherie frowned. Fear dissolved, replaced by irritation. What on earth was David up to? This was ridiculous. Locking himself up in his room, leaving the front door open...

She flicked on the lights in the upper floor and stormed towards the study. She yanked the door open, poised to give David a piece of her mind.

She froze. Two camera lights, the type used in David's studio, were placed on the floor. The beams illuminated a ghastly sight. David was hanging by the neck from the steel curtain pole. A belt was wrapped around his neck. His tongue hung out from a swollen face, rapidly turning purple. He was naked. His bowels had been sliced open, and the contents of his gut streamed out to the floor.

It took Cherie's brain a few seconds to process the scene. Then she gave a strangled cry and fell on the floor outside, vomiting.

CHAPTER 3

It was cold out, but warm within. Arla Baker snuggled up to Inspector Harry Mehta's warm body, her right arm around his wide chest. Her knee was draped across his torso, and she moved it up and down gently.

"Yes," Harry said. "Right there."

It was past midnight, and past their bedtime, as tomorrow was a working day. But one drink after work had led to a few more, as it frequently did in the Metropolitan Police Force, or Met, as it was called. While drinking together was common practice for the Detectives, fraternising was a different issue. One that Arla was acutely aware of. Her higher rank and career ambitions made sleeping with Harry a potential time bomb.

But she had learnt to take happiness when it came her way. Life was a road and Arla was forever thumbing a ride. The car called happiness barely stopped for her. Now that it had, she was going to hitch a ride. Damn the rest.

Besides, she had worked with Harry a long time. He knew the rules better than anyone. And for what it was worth, she trusted him. She didn't know how far this was going to go, but she believed Harry wouldn't use this to push her into a corner.

Arla's eyes were used to the dark. She could make out his Adam's apple, bobbing up as he swallowed, then groaned softly. She kept up the gently rubbing with her thigh, feeling him respond. They had just made love, but clearly, it was time for some more.

A loud beeping sound came from the table next to her.

Arla sighed. It was her work phone.

"Ignore it," said Harry. He lowered his hand and reached for her. Arla pushed it away.

"Come on," he complained, sliding his warm, long finger down her belly. She fought with the urge to go with it, but the phone kept ringing.

"Harry, stop." She rolled over, much to his annoyance. She grabbed the phone and put it to her ear.

"Detective Chief Inspector Baker."

"Lambeth Switchboard connecting you to murder crime scene in Clapham. Do you copy?"

Instantly Arla was awake. She folded her knees and sat up in bed. With one hand she brushed her hair back.

"Yes I do. Connect me please."

A deep male voice came on the phone. "Constable Sergeant Jackson speaking."

"Andy, this is DCI Baker." She knew the uniform Sergeant from the Clapham Met Station, where they both worked.

"Hi Guv. Sorry to bother you so late at night."

"Don't worry about it. What's going on?"

"Homicide. Victim lived opposite the Common, but on the Wandsworth side. White male in late fifties. Killed in his own home, by someone who's…"

Andy's voice dried up and Arla felt a knot in her guts. "Who's what?"

"You better come here and see for yourself, guv. It's not a pretty sight, I'm afraid."

Arla hung up and slid out of the bed. She turned the bedside lamp on and picked up her underwear from the floor. She put them in the laundry bin and took fresh ones out from the wardrobe. Harry was up on one elbow, eyes hooded.

"You should walk around like that more often."

"Shut up Harry. Go back to sleep."

"Sounded bad."

"Think it is. Andy was flustered."

"Want me to come?"

Arla got dressed, not answering. She didn't have to. Harry knew the drill. She was his boss, that was complication enough. She didn't need him to be there when all she wanted to do was focus on the job. He got that, and kept himself away, unless they were working a case together. Which was often.

She buttoned up her white shirt, then tucked it into the black trousers. She brushed her hair back hastily, then tied the black tangle into a ponytail. It would have to do. No time for makeup. She stuffed the warrant card and badge into her belt.

"It's not your case, Harry. Not yet, anyway. I'll be back soon."

She glanced at him, aware he was sitting up with his back on the headboard. His chestnut brown eyes were melting soft, and his floppy hair fell over his forehead in a boyish way. The chiselled hard line of his jaws contrasted against the slight pout of his lower lips. Harry loved sulking when he didn't get his own way. Arla stifled a grin, and the warm rush in her heart, like the waves of a tropical sea.

"I'll be fine, don't worry."

Harry nodded, but looked unhappy. Arla went out into the corridor, got the keys of her Ford Mondeo, and locked the door shut gently.

From where she lived, Tooting Broadway, south London, Clapham was four miles on a straight road. A road normally clogged with traffic and the endless rush of London's colourful, diverse inhabitants. The myriad of twinkling neon shops flew past now as she pressed on the accelerator. The streets seemed naked without the perpetual throng of people. But night was also the time she loved. When she lay down, the faded, distant swell of traffic was like waves crashing on a beach, the sound lulling her to sleep.

Sleep she wouldn't be getting tonight. The frequent traffic lights kept stopping her, and after the second one, she decided to put the siren on. Legally, she could jump the lights, but that wasn't enough warning for the occasional pedestrian, often drunk, swaying across the road.

Wind roared in her ears as she drove, the harsh cold evaporating the last dregs of slumber in her mind. The address was on her sat nav, and she slowed down as she entered the exclusive road. A beautiful row of terraced mansions sat opposite the dense canopies of the Common. The road was in Clapham, but the common they looked belonged to Wandsworth, the adjoining borough. Across the trees, opposite millionaire's row, lay the hallowed halls of HMP Wandsworth Prison. Arla made a mental note of checking if there had been any breakouts.

The flashing blue light reflected off the black mass of the trees. Arla screeched to a stop and jumped out of the car. She caught sight of Sergeant Andy Jackson, who strolled over to her. His thumbs were hooked inside the straps of his chest rig, and his face was ashen.

CHAPTER 4

"Scene of crime arrived?" Arla asked as she strode towards the house. The front door was open. She didn't bother asking Andy what it was like inside. She could guess, and was steeling herself for the worst.

"On their way, guv. By the way, the wife's over there."

Arla stopped. Andy said, "She discovered the body. Called 999." Andy pointed towards the open door of an ambulance, where a paramedic had wrapped a blanket around the shoulders of a blonde woman.

"Thanks Andy." Arla walked over to the woman. The paramedic was kneeling in front of the blanketed figure, and they both looked up as Arla approached.

"DCI Baker," Arla said, flashing her warrant card and badge. The woman was late forties to early fifties, Arla guessed, with dark rings below her eyes, and smudged mascara from tears. A pretty face, and in one corner of her mind, the woman vaguely reminded her of someone. Arla pushed it to one side. She softened her tone.

"I'm sorry about what happened, Mrs Longworth." Arla had taken the name of the victim from Andy already. She knelt to face the woman. Her sea green eyes gazed at Arla directly, then she lowered her eyes.

"I know you've given a statement. I'm going to take a look inside and maybe we can have a little chat after?"

A uniformed officer appeared, holding a cup of steaming tea. Cherie Longworth reached for it gratefully. Arla nodded at the uniform constable, then walked to the porch. She was handed white overalls, gloves and shoe covers. Fibre floor plates that looked like duckboards had been laid on the floor and up the stairs. Arla ducked underneath the white and blue police tape and stepped carefully on the floor plates. She hated them. Once, instead of the usual flats, she had worn shoes with small heels, and the darn thing had slipped underneath her. Harry caught her as she fell, but she heard no end of it later on at the pub.

Arla composed herself and climbed up the stairs. The boards squeaked and she balanced herself without touching the bannister. A uniform was waiting at the landing. The wide hallway was large enough for an elephant to walk through. Mini chandeliers hung from the walls, adorned with original art canvases. At one end, to her left, a door was open, and another uniform was standing outside. His face looked positively green, she decided. Some of it was due to the stench that was afflicting her nostrils. She knew what it was. No, not the smell of money. The victim must have emptied his bowels at some point. It was a grim thought.

Arla pressed her lips together. One bright spot tonight, she mused, perhaps the only one, was that she could survey the scene without Scene of Crime Officers (SOCO) or forensic guys being there. An almost virgin crime scene. Arla smiled at the uniform contable, who looked like he was going to throw up any minute.

"Go downstairs. Get some fresh air," she said.

"Yes guv." The man bolted, relief obvious on his face.

Arla looked inside the room and her insides contorted into a sudden spasm. She was no stranger to dead, mutilated bodies. But this shook her to the core. It wasn't just the dead body, with guts spilling out to the floor. Or the pool of blood at this feet, turning black already. Nor the ghastly swollen face, turgid and purple, tongue protruding.

It was the painstaking way the killer had set the scene up. The camera light lit up the body in a sickening glare. Green and red filters on the lights made the body glow in a weird, grisly manner. The curtains had been neatly pulled to either side, framing the body against the long window like it was some sort of painting in a psychotic canvas. The hanging figure cast long shadows against the walls, courtesy of the lights.

Arla turned away, momentarily revolted. The constable at the landing was standing discreetly to one side, perhaps he saw her hesitate at the doorway. Arla was glad she wasn't being observed. She exhaled, then turned and went inside. The smell was horrid, and she edged past the body, and lifted the window latch. She opened the window pane a fraction only, not wanting rain drops, if they arrived, to tarnish the crime scene.

The cold air was refreshing. Ignoring the body, Arla stared at the floor and walls. Had the victim put up a fight? He wasn't the biggest of men, although it was difficult to judge his height as he was strung up. She stared at the chair and table in the room. Photos of smiling men and women were on the wall, a glamorous woman with pouting lips having signed one with her name. Her face was familiar from both TV and the big screen. For a study, the room wasn't small, easily, twelve by fourteen feet, Arla calculated.

Two sofas were arranged on either side of the body, and a chais lounge was pulled to one side. Arla guessed it must have been by the window.

Why had the victim not struggled? Had he been subdued already? Or was he in the study working when the killer surprised him? Even then, he would have resisted, surely.

There was a sound from downstairs that got her attention.

CHAPTER 5

"SOCO are here, guv." Andy shouted from downstairs.

Arla walked out to the door, balancing on the boards. "Send them in," she shouted back.

She transferred her gaze back to the floor. Something about this scene was odd. Yes, it was clearly staged for maximum impact. But she was missing a lot, and it was gnawing at the back of her mind. She knelt by the doorway. The carpet was a deep shag pile, light cream coloured. She found a small area that was ruffled and looked closer. It was sticking up, and she wondered why. She looked down the hallway. Another small area caught her attention. She hadn't seen this on the way up. She was going to observe closer, when the slightly stooped and silver haired figure of Dr Banerji, the state pathologist, appeared on the landing.

"Hi Doc," Arla said. Inwards, she was was relieved it was him, and not some other random pathologist doing the night shift. Banerji was in his sixties, but like her, he obviously had no life apart from attending to those from whom life had departed. Well, someone had to do it.

The older man's lips split into a genuine smile. "Well if it isn't my favorite detective. Something told me you'd be here."

"Don't tell me. Pathologist's intuition."

Banerji strode his way nonchalantly across the boards that Arla found hard to navigate. "Something like that." He leaned over to give Arla a peck on the cheek. His smooth cheeks reeked of aftershave. His grey Marks and Spencer suit was rumpled, but his tired eyes had a glint in them.

"Are you OK?" he asked Arla. The two were friends, having worked on numerous cases together over the last decade. Banerji was one of the few people in her close group of friends who knew all about Arla, and her dysfunctional family. And about Nicole, her sister.

"At work, so can't be too bad."

He lifted a finger. "I was joking earlier. There is a time for play, and a time for work. Hope you're taking time to play."

Arla studied him. There was nothing sly to suggest a double entendre to his words. As far as Arla knew, no one was aware of her tryst with Harry. She wanted to keep it that way.

"I am," she said. "Victim's in there. Fifty eight years old, died in a horrible way as you will see. I'll leave you to it for a while shall I?"

Banerji nodded. He came to a halt on the study doorway. "Good grief!"

"Exactly what I thought," Arla said drily. She headed down the hallway, and crouched near the staircase on the landing. Another tuft of the deep pile carpet was raised. She knelt closer to it, and looked down the carpet with her cheeks almost touching it.

Now she could see it. A line that stretched from the all the way to the study. Not one. Two lines on the carpet, and both were smoothed down deliberately. But two spots were missed. It could only be the imprint of two feet. Like a body being dragged across the carpet, held up by the armpits. Maybe that's what happened. The killer knocked Mr Longworth unconscious...where? downstairs?, then dragged him up the stairs.

In which case...her thoughts were broken by the sound of more footsteps. The long, thin face of Gus Parmentier, the head SOCO came into view.

"You like it stylish, dont you, DCI Baker?"

"What time do you call this?" Arla shot back. "Thought I was taking over your job for a while there."

Gus shrugged, a briefcase hanging from each hand. "I had DNA to extract from a dead body. So I almost DNA'd. As in Did Not Attend." He gave an impish smile and Arla rolled her eyes.

"Well you're here now so get started." Arla said. She pointed at the carpet with her pen. "This area might have been touched by the perp's hand. Sure he was wearing gloves, but some hair might have fallen off him."

Gus bent down to her level. He was in his mid forties, two kids in late school years and he was going bald.

He pointed to his scalp and said, "You know what they say, Arla. Hair today, gone tomorrow."

"With that sense of humor you should work for the BBC."

Arla stood, and stared at the carpet on the stairs with renewed interest.

CHAPTER 6

Arla stopped at each stair, stooping over the carpet. Her bum kept brushing against the wall. The carpet didn't extend the entire length of the stairs, and dark wood was visible for about six inches before it hit the bannisters.

She imagined the killer dragging the body up the stairs, sweating with the effort. Was Longworth dead already? Banerji would have a time of death. The temperature in the house was comfortable, and the door being open had made it colder, ideal for stalling the body's decomposition. Arla walked down to the spacious landing, stepping to one one side for another SOCO. On the spacious hallway, she checked the wall carefully. She was looking for anything unusual, out of place. It was so subtle she almost missed it. A graze on the wall. It was to the left of the front door as she walked in. Arla glanced at the door. She retraced her steps when she came in.

Open the door, step inside...and shoved against the wall? The mark was at more or less the right spot. But the mark could be due to anything. It might have been there for years. There was nothing to suggest a fight or tussle here. Arla opened the door and the freezing cold air rushed in, numbing her face. She went out on the porch and checked the door. She saw a mark near the bottom right corner. It was the top half of a shoe mark.

Excitement clutched at her guts. She turned and spotted Andy Jackson with a notebook, writing something, stood in front of the shivering Mrs Longworth.

"Andy!" she called him over. When he came up the stairs, she pointed at the mark. He squatted and stared at it.

"Kicked by a boot," Andy said.

"The print is only partial," Arla said. "But maybe we can send it to the database?" There was a national police boot-print database. It was surprisingly useful.

Andy grimaced. "We can try, guv."

Arla stood. The flashing blue lights from one of the patrol cars was lighting up the houses in a garish blue halo. It caught her in the eyes. "Turn that thing off, for God's sake," she said. "Have you taken a statement?"

"Halfway there."

"I'll do the rest."

Andy called her as Arla turned away. He said, "By they way, guv, you know who the deceased was right?"

Arla stopped and turned. Stupendous wealth lived next to simple working class masses in her area of London. Actually the whole of London was like that. Drab grey cement council block apartments would suddenly give to wide lawns of white brick glamour and splendour.

The name of the deceased had been circulating in Arla's mind ever since she heard it. It sounded vaguely familiar.

"No," she said. "Who is he?"

"Famous film director. You know, he did films like *The Last Train* and *Goodbye my Valentine*. Back in the nineties."

Back in the nineties. Gosh that made her feel old. Nineties wasn't that long ago, was it? But the memory hit her. Those films had been raging hits, about the time when *Four Weddings and a Funeral* type films were doing the round.

"He did shows on the Broadway as well, and in the West End. Just googled him. Got his photo there and everything."

"Great," Arla said, shaking her head. Her eyes swivelled from side to side. In at least one house, she saw the curtains parted. It dropped when she stared at the dark window.

"Do me a favour, Andy. When you're done with the print, please tell the uniforms to do a door to door and request the neighbours not to ring the tabloids. This will hit the fan anyway, but the longer we can keep the media out of it the better."

29

"Sure thing guv."

Arla strode down to where Mrs Cherie Longworth was just finishing her cup of tea. She didn't look up when Arla stopped in front of her. Arla squatted.

"Mrs Longworth, have you got anywhere to stay for the night? Your house is a scene of crime now, and be best if we could help you look for alternative accomodation."

The woman lifted blank sea green eyes and Arla could see from her expression that she hadn't given this much thought. Cherie Longworth had been beautiful once, it was obvious. Despite the rings under her eyes, wild curls of blonde hair, and large, expressive eyes dulled with pain, there was a vivacity in her that shone through. Arla wondered what she was like fully dolled up, red carpet ready.

"I haven't...I don't know."

"Any family around?"

"My son. He lives in Wimbledon."

"Any chance of you being able to stay with him for a few days?"

Cherie glanced at Arla then looked down again. That was answer enough. Arla gave her a few seconds, then said, "Maybe you could ask. See what happens. If not, there's always a BnB we-

Arla stopped just in time. Where we put our witnesses just sounded crass. "...Just a BnB we know. You could stay there while things get sorted out."

Cherie nodded and sniffed into her handkerchief.

"Now, please tell me where you were this evening before you came back home."

Cherie swallowed. "I went to see Jill, my girlfriend who lives in Dulwich. She's going through a messy divorce."

Arla scribbled on her notepad. "So your friend, Jill, can vouch for you?"

"Yes."

"When you came home the door was open?"

"Yes."

"Did you see anything unusual *before* you left to see Jill? Anything outside the house? Anything odd about your husband?"

Cherie closed her eyes tight. Then she opened them and shook her head. "No. Can't say I have."

"It can be difficult to think right now." Arla stood. She beckoned towards Andy who strolled over.

Arla asked, "Is family liaison on their way?"

"Any minute now."

"Good. Check Cherie into a BnB or hotel, wherever she wants to go. Keep a uniform and patrol car outside the place for tonight. Make sure she's safe. Got it?"

"Yes guv."

One of the other uniformed constables came up to them. The name tag in white letters, sewn into his black chest rig, said Marlowe. His cheeks were red and nostrils flaring.

"Found something interesting guv. You wanna see this."

CHAPTER 7

Arla followed the constable down the road. The neighbourhood had woken up. More yellow lights in the tall, handsome windows. Arla saw two constables walked to the end of the row, mount the porch steps and ring the doorbell. She was glad they were doing it only in the houses that had lights on. It was an awful time to be woken up by two coppers at your door.

Marlowe came to a stop and pointed at the ground. "Here, guv."

At first, Arla couldn't figure out what she was looking at. She saw a collection of wires lying draped over the bushes at the side of the road. She followed their course up the wooden pole and it hit her.

"What on earth?" she muttered to herself. She took a step closer to the wires. They were cables really, black and thicker than what they looked like from a distance. She bent down to take a closer look.

"I wouldn't touch them, guv," Marlowe's voice rang out. "Could be live still."

Arla said, "Electric cables run underground. These are telephone or internet cables." She looked up again. "Even they're dug under these days. I think this was a small extension, and cutting up the ground wasn't worth it for the cable company."

Arla straightened. She tried to stifle a yawn and failed. The halogen lights cast a hazy, tepid orange glow from above, the light diffracted by swirling molecules of mist. Arla stared at the crowd of hunched trees opposite, dense, whispering secrets. She shivered. What was it about the Common at night? It gave her the creeps.

She pointed at the pole on the other side, from where the cables had been cut. "Inform the cable company. It's their property, they need to fix it. But send a team up there at first light." The Met had access to fire engine platforms that could be raised up. Not the easiest of jobs for the forensic team but it was worth a try.

They headed back. Arla was glad to see the curly haired, chubby Family Liaison Officer, Emily Harman step out of a car. She waved at Arla who nodded back, then indicated the still, seated figure of Cherie Longworth. Arla left them to talk, and went back inside the house. Banerji and Permentier, with another SOC officer had put the body down on the floor. Arla looked at the face. It was still bloated, but less mauve now. Instead, it was turning a shade paler.

Parmentier handed her a surgical mask similar to what he was wearing. Arla tied it around her nose and stepped up till she was peeking over Banerji's shoulder.

"Anything to report?"

"Yes," Banerji said without turning. He pointed to the head. "Evidence of blunt trauma to the parietal section of the scalp. Hard to kill someone by hitting in that place though. Skull is at its thickest. But there is a depression in the bone, so it was a hard blow. Might have killed him before the strangulation."

Arla couldn't help a surge of triumph. "So, he hit him then dragged him upstairs?"

Banerji turned and adjusted his horn rimmed glasses. His face looked so much like Colombo, including his mannerisms, she tried not to grin.

"What makes you say he was dragged upstairs?"

She told him about the marks on the carpet.

"Interesting," Banerji mused. Parmentier said, "I've taken samples from the carpet already. If there's anything we'll know tomorrow."

Arla asked, "Any signs of sexual assault?"

Banerji said, "Nothing in the anal passage. No signs of trauma there either. There are smudges on the neck which I'm sure are from being throttled."

"Yeah, but sure he wore gloves. Time of death?"

"Ambient temperature right now is less than 18 degrees C, according to my thermometer. But I'm guessing it was warmer indoors when he died. Regardless, I don't think it had too much of an effect. His eyelids and jaws shows signs of early rigor mortis, and as you know-

"Rigor mortis starts in the smaller muscles then moves to the bigger ones. Yes I know, doc."

Banerji grinned. "Good girl. Going by the advanced state of mortis in the jaw, eyelids, neck and the early stages in the hands, I would say about six hours. The colour on his cheeks, and abdomen, the livor mortis, backs that up."

Arla checked her watch. "It's almost two in the morning. So that makes it 20.00 hours last night."

Banerji said, "He wasn't fat, nor was he thin. Thin bodies lose heat quicker. His rectal temperature is now actually 17 degrees C, so very close to ambient."

"Are you confident of the time of death?"

"I need to put all the numbers into the spreadsheet tomorrow and see if it give me a more precise time. But between 19..00 to 21.000 definitely."

"Thanks Doc. See you tomorrow?"

Banerji stood up slowly, putting his hands on his knees. He grimaced. "Don't get old, Arla. Tomorrow? No way. I have two drug overdoses and you know how long toxicology takes to come back. The poor families are waiting for closure and its actually the Met who have kept the cases open. I wanted to give a cause of death and close the investigation."

Arla sighed. "Doc, do you know who this guy is?"

Banerji's eyes were guarded. "David Longworth. What about him?"

Arla told him and Banerji whistled. "Right, I see the urgency now. You're worried about a media circus, right?"

"Exactly."

"I can't make promises, Arla. What we need is funding for another pathologist. When will that arrive?"

She shrugged. It was something she had raised time and again with her boss. Another pathologist or medical examiner would speed up a lot of investigations. But that discussion was for another time.

Banerji shook his head. "I'll try, but don't hold your breath."

CHAPTER 8

When her alarm went off for the second time, Arla didn't even hear it. Luckily, Harry had left the bedside light on. The combination of the glare as she turned her head and the infernal noise finally woke her up. She slapped on the red dial. It didn't stop so she chucked it against the wall - that didn't work either.

Nothing worse than an alarm that doesn't go off in the morning. Arla groaned, then flung the duvet off her body. She picked the alarm up and managed to shut it off. She stumbled to the bathroom. The light sneaking in past the curtains was stronger than the zero watt, feeble early morning rays. It was past 8am. Arla hated early mornings. Almost two decades of waking up early hadn't changed that notion.

Harry always left before her if he stayed the night. She did the same if she stayed at his. They had been seeing each other for the last 6 months. She was still finding out about Harry. They had been good friends before they started dating. But intimacy was slowly bringing them closer. She didn't know where this was headed, but she was grateful to lay her head somewhere at night. Besides, Harry, infuriating as he was, happened to be quite adept in bed. The thought brought warmth to her cheeks as she stared in the mirror.

Arla finished getting ready, and left. The journey to work took less than twenty minutes, one of the reasons why she lived in Tooting Broadway. Like most of London, this working class enclave was becoming expensive. A Starbucks and other coffee shops had opened up, displacing the greasy cafes and old Irish pubs. Arla walked past the yummy mummies with prams, feeding their babies organic mash from plastic spoons. Their husbands worked in the city, and their pay packets meant government employees like Arla would soon find the rent here unaffordable.

Arla dodged the old bum who was at his usual spot outside the tube stop, and joined the regular parade of commuters. It was refreshing to get off the train and walk down to the station. She should have taken a cab really, but the walk helped her to think about the case.

Who would murder a famous director like that? How did the killer know when David Longworth would be home alone?

A lot about this case didn't fit. Arla sprang up the steps and walked in through the double doors. The desk sergeant was a tall, wide shouldered black man called Toby. He nodded at Arla and reached underneath the counter for the buzzer. The heavy bullet proof metal doors swung open.

"Boss wants you," Toby said as Arla went past.

She stopped. If Wayne Johnson, her ambitious boss, had left instructions already, it wasn't good news.

Toby said, "His room. Told me to tell you as soon as."

"Thanks Toby."

Arla sauntered into the green lino floored corridor. A couple of the detectives walked past her and they exchanged greetings. Arla glanced inside the open floor office space. Her room was still shut, at the extreme left end. She caught sight of the blonde curls of Detective Constable Lisa Moran, staring at her screen. Harry's jacket was draped on his chair but the man himself was absent.

Arla went up the stairs to the third floor. This floor had carpets, designated as one of the admin departments of the South London Command Zone. Framed photos of Commissioners and politicians hung on the wall. It was fitting that Detective Superintendent Wayne Johnson would have his office up here. After all, his promotion to Commander was all but assured. The ink was merely drying on the contract. Johnson was a slick office player, fully aware that who you know is much more important than what you know.

Arla knew the man well, having worked with him on and off since she had been a DC and him a DI. Deep inside, his heart was in the right place, but that didn't mean she trusted him.

The brown oak door held his name and title. Word was out that a new name badge and uniform was being tailored currently. A Commander rank meant Johnson was one of the big boys in the London Met. Arla knew she had to step carefully. For her own career, which had stuck as DCI for more than five years now. If Johnson was moving up, with her high prosecution to case ratio, so should she. After all, she had solved far more complex cases than Johnson ever had in his career.

Arla knocked and a loud voice told her to enter. Wayne Johnson was in uniform,and his elbows rested on the immaculate mahogany table. It was clear he was waiting for her. Another man sitting opposite him and Arla caught her breath when she realised who it was.

Harry.

"Sit down, DCI Baker." Johnson's voice was cold. His grey eyes followed Arla as she sat down next to Harry. Her questioning look at him was answered with Harry slanting his eyes towards Johnson.

The DS said, "You must be wondering why I called you both to my office."

"Thought crossed my mind sir," Arla said. "Is it to do with last night's case?"

Johnson leaned back in his chair. "Yes it is. DI Mehta doesn't know anything about the case as yet. I want you to be the SIO, and he can report to you."

Arla nodded. That much she had expected. But from Johnson's manner, she knew there was something else.

He asked, "Do you know who David Longworth was?"

"Well known film director. Did those popular rom coms in the nineties."

"Hmm yes. And as you know, his death will stir up a lot of public interest. Has anyone told the media yet?"

Arla shook her head. "I informed the staff on duty last night sir. If the media gets to know, I'll know it's one of them."

"They're well scared of you, guv," Harry deadpanned. Arla shot him a look, but he was staring at Johnson.

"Good. We need to move fast on this one. You know how it is with these media types, news will spread fast. The last thing we want is reporters camped outside."

Putting you in the spotlight, just before your blessed promotion, Arla thought to herself.

"Thought you would like all the attention, sir." It came out before she could stop herself. She bit her lip. Harry lowered his head very fast, hiding the grin that split across his lips.

Johnson's nostril flared, quivered. A patch of red moved from the tip of his nose to his upper cheeks.

"Shut up, Arla," he said, his voice very quiet. His piercing gaze held Arla captive when she looked up. "Don't make this hard on yourself."

"I'm sorry sir. Came out the wrong way."

Johnson put his large paws on the table and lifted himself off his high back leather chair. He clasped his hands behind his back and stared out at the grimy buildings, drowsing in the cold mist and rain.

"Longworth was high up in the chain at the BBC. He was a non executive member of the Board. I've had a phone call from the Secretary of State already, who appears to be a personal friend. His wife, Cherie Longworth called him last night."

Bloody hell, that's all we need, Arla thought.

"Needless to say," Johnson continued. "Longworth was well connected. He was a big donor to the Conservative Party as well. Along with his distinguished career in Hollywood and here at home, we can expect a great deal of interest in this case. I need to know," Johnson turned around and stepped forward. He fixed his eyes like a laser on Arla. "That you are capable of solving this case, Arla. This is a biggie. Not many coppers get one like this in a lifetime. This could make or break you. Do you understand?"

Arla stared back at him. She was being put to test. That was obvious. But what did Johnson mean by make or break? He was aware of her career ambitions, she made no secret of it.

Arla had never been the shy type. Quite the opposite. Her bluntness, and fiery temper, had incurred the wrath of many a senior police officer, all of them men.

"Could you clarify what you mean by make or break sir?"

"I mean every senior police detective dreams of a case like this. Provided they can bring the perp to justice of course. If you can, great. If not, you will forever be known as the copper who didn't catch Longworth's killer."

CHAPTER 9

The incident room was full. Harry was next to the whiteboard, where David Longworth, his wife and son's photos were arranged in a line. The victim was in the middle.

Lisa Moran and Rob Pickering, Detective Constable and Sergeant respectively were standing next to Harry, partially hidden by Harry's long frame. Arla nodded at them, noting that Harry barely glanced at her. It had become their routine while at work. No one knew, hence acting as normal as possible was paramount.

Arla faced the rows of detectives and uniformed police officers. The hubbub of voices softened.

"Right people, you know who the victim was by now, I'm sure. I don't have to remind you this is being kept from the media as long as we can, and the boss just informed me - no loose tongues. Word will spread anyway, neighbours talk etc, but we keep it schtum."

She looked around the room and met their eyes. Several heads nodded. She caught the eyes of Andy Jackson. He looked bright and sparky, despite the late night she knew he had. She gave him an encouraging smile.

Arla told them about the manner of death and that they were still waiting to hear back from Banerji.

"While we wait, we work with what we have. Any news of the wife?"

"Yes guv," Harry cleared his throat. "She spent the night in the Clapham Premier Inn. She will stay there as well for the time being. Her story checks out. She does have a friend called Jill Hunter in Dulwich Village and I called her this morning. Left a voice mail."

"That's good for the alibi. So, the wife, Cherie,left home at just after seven, and came back close to midnight. Long time to have a chat with a friend?"

"Unless they went out to dinner etc," Harry said. "But she was driving so wouldn't have drunk too much."

"Good point. See if we can cover all bases on the wife. Until we can, she remains in the picture." Arla took a sip of her coffee. "My problem is, the sicko who did this is good. He wants to make a statement. He made the study look like a film set. Has anyone come across a killer with the same MO? I'm talking about cases anywhere in the country, or a cold one."

Arla didn't have to tell the assembled detectives the serial killers often went quiet for a few years, then embarked on a killing spree. But they were far off still. One kill didn't a serial killer make, unless there were cold cases.

From the blank look on everyone's face she guessed no one knew. "Make that a priority. I want reports on my desk if there are similar cold cases."

Harry said, "The son. His name's Lucas Longworth. Followed in his father's footsteps and is a film director himself. Does some TV shows, tried his hand at films but not worked out. Going to see him this evening."

Arla said, "When I spoke to his mother she seemed reluctant to live with his family. Might be something there to look into."

Harry made a note. Lisa Moran peeked out from behind Harry. "I called Emily, the family liaison. She will bring Cherie Longworth over at 11.00."

"Thanks." Arla said. "I want the victim's telephone logs, laptop data, his social calendar, everything. Has the wife signed those off?"

Rob Pickering cleared his throat. "She will do when she arrives here, guv."

"Thank you Rob. I want a door to door on every house in that row, with a statement from each. Ditto within a five mile radius. I know its the Common area, but someone must have seen something."

The door open and the tall form of Johnson strode in. "As you were, DCI Baker," he said gruffly. Arla cleared her throat.

"Telephone cables were cut too. Not sure why, but we have to assume that our perp had a role in this."

Andy put his hand up. "Sky got in touch this morning guv. They're sending a team down. Myself and a SOCO willl piggy back with them."

"Good. Make sure we get prints from the poles and run them through Ident1. Any word from SOCO as yet?"

Harry said, "Only a very brief preliminary report. No prints were found. The place was squeaky clean. They're still running tests on the carpet and the body."

A knot tightened inside Arla's guts. Only a professional would leave a scene that big without any clues.

"No prints on the body? Hair or DNA?"

"None that they found boss." Harry said. Arla suppressed a smile. She felt thrilled when Harry called her boss.

"In fact, the body was wiped down with Betadine, a surgical spirit."

"That's important," Arla raised a finger. "I dont know why, but its specialist chemical used in a hospital, right? Let's make a note of that." Arla wrote it down on her notebook swiftly.

"Anything else?" she asked Harry and Lisa.

"Nope."

"Then get busy. Call me when Cherie arrives. Rob, I want a file on her. On my desk before she gets here please. We meet back late afternoon."

Johnson raised his voice as chairs were scraped back. "Before you go. David Longworth had connections. One government minister has already called about him, and more might follow. Clear the deck for this, people. We need to catch a killer."

CHAPTER 10

The studio was busy. The glow in the middle of the floor was offset by dark corners that hugged the huge converted warehouse floor. A cluster of bodies thronged the stage and huge lights trained down upon the three actors in the middle of the stage.

The man known as Jonty stepped up in front of a camera with a clapper board.

"*The Eternal Nameless*, Act 2, Scene 1, Take 3." He slapped the board shut and there was a pregnant pause as the actors were still, the workers seemed to hold their collective breath. Only the hum of machinery filled the silence. The director's voice suddenly rang out.

"Lights, camera, action!"

The camera started rolling. The actress put one hand on her hip and said, "Is this what you call arriving fashionably late?"

One of the actors responded, but Jonty had already moved backwards silently. He found watching the scene as it unfolded excruciating, terrifying. Movies always did that to him. When he sat and watched the screen, it seemed the characters came alive and spoke directly *to* him. True, watching the movie being made kind of spoiled the glamour of it all. But the skin and bones of it were fascinating as well. The circus performers who worked as stuntmen. The actresses and their hundreds of outfits. The mobile make up parlours. Jonty had worked in various studios and he was fascinated with all of them. Now, in Pinewood, he had found his home.

He slipped out into the darkness, and walked down a hallway towards the exit door. He came out into the sunny but cold day and stretched. The tepid warmth felt good on his face. He crossed the road, one of many in the huge complex of Pinewood studios, the largest TV and film studio in UK. He was headed for the cement and glass building that housed the management, where his boss had asked to see him.

Jonty knocked on the door that said Darren Finch, General Manager. Darren was the manager of Block 4, where Jonty worked. He entered and stood in front of the large desk. Darren was in his thirties, unmarried, and by all accounts, a womaniser. There wasn't any dearth of wannabe actresses who arrived in Pinewood Studios, lured in by so called talent scouts. True, Darren didn't commission any films, but he was close to the producers who relied on him for studio space.

He looked up as Jonty stopped in front of him and murmured a greeting. His fingers flew over his keyboard. "You've had two weeks of sick leave now, Jonty. Have you got a doctor's certificate?"

Jonty produced one he had received from his GP. He had learnt that his doctor was sympathetic to his claims of depression. Getting a sick note wasn't difficult.

Darren read the note with a look of distaste on his face. "Depression?" he said eventually, curling his upper lip. "Every time I see you, you're happy as Larry."

Jonty made a sorry face. "It affects me sometimes."

"Are you on medications?"

"Yes." That was true. He had found the tablets helped, and he intended to continue with them.

Darren opened the drawer and shoved the sick note inside. "Ok, fine. But it will come off your pay."

Jonty stiffened, but kept his face impassive. "You told me if I had a sick note…"

"I know what I said," Darren interrupted, raising his voice. "But things have changed. Not running a charity here. Can't make allowances for you when unauthorised leave is deducted from everyone else's pay."

Jonty stood still for a while. A pressure that began in his chest slowly spread down his limbs, filling him with a tingling sensation. He felt light and airy, and hot blood danced in his veins.

"OK." he said. He turned on his heels and left, but didn't miss the word Darren muttered under his breath.

"Weirdo."

Jonty didn't pause. He shut the door with a click. His eyes fell on the woman sat on the bench outside. She was dressed to the nines, in a coat that fell to her waist. A short skirt suit hugged her body and she wore high heels over her leggings. But what drew Jonty's eyes were her face. Her eyes were almond shaped and slate grey. She was beautiful, but in a vulnerable sort of way.

Innocent, Jonty thought to himself. That's what she is. Innocent.

The door opened and Darren emerged. He saw the woman and smiled widely. Then his eyes fell on Jonty.

"What are you doing here?"

"Just leaving."

Darren scowled at him, and ushered the woman inside. JOnty walked down the deserted hallway, till he got to the elevators. He stopped and looked back. He went over to the staircase and looked down. No one coming up. Jonty went back into the hallway, crouched and ran like a hare till he reached Darren's room. He put his ears to the door. The sound of panting and gasps came from inside. A man' voice groaned.

Jonty sagged against the door. Bile rose in his mouth and blood surged into his face. Waves of nausea hit him, and a burst of colours exploded against his skull. Images from another life surged into his mind then receded like an oceans restless current. A scream rose inside his throat and he rammed his fist inside his mouth, biting on it till he tasted metallic blood.

He wanted to leave, but the compulsion inside him wouldn't let him. He listened with morbid fascination as Darren's voice became louder and louder. When it was done, Jonty picked himself up slowly. He felt sick, he felt alive. It was always this way.

CHAPTER 11

Darren Finch put the key in the lock of his ground floor apartment in Uxbridge. It was past eleven pm, and he was shattered, but in a good way. The new girl had proved insatiable. After the couch in his office, he had taken her back to the hotel room and had spent another busy two hours. That, coupled with the gram of cocaine he had snorted, had kept him in a good mood the whole night. Now he needed some sleep.

In his drug addled state, he didn't notice the figure, dressed entirely in black with a black ski mask over its face, lying in the grass, behind the hedges. As soon as the key turned in the lock and the door opened, the figure sprang up. It rammed into Darren, bundling him inside the apartment. Jonty shut the door, and put a hand over Darren's mouth. He brought the perspiring man's frightened eyes closer to his. He liked to see them close up before he killed them.

Two hefty blows to the face almost felled Darren. He wasn't light, and fought back, but Jonty overpowered him. He dragged Darren's body into the living room and left the unconscious figure on the carpet floor. He stood on a chair and took the light fitting off the cable from the ceiling. He pulled on the wire. It was strong. Jonty slid the backpack off his shoulders. He took out the black belt and tied it around Darren's neck. He tightened it till the veins stood out on Darren's forehead. As breathing became harder, Darren started recovering consciousness.

Jonty put a knee on his chest, pushed down and pulled the belt tighter. His biceps bulged underneath the black nylon. Breath rapsed against the ski mask. Darren came to, lifted his hands and tried to grab Jonty's face. It was no use. With a soft crack, the windpipe popped. Darrens eyes widened till they became fixed and dilated.

Jonty worked swiftly. He lifted Darren on the chair and hung him from the cable. He left the chair in place. He took out the piece of white paper from his backpack and scribbled on it with the felt tipped pen, writing in large letters.

"AS YOU SOW, SO YOU REAP."

He stuck the paper on Darren's chest, then spent the next thirty minutes cleaning all the surfaces and making sure he left no trace of himself. He watched the dead man hanging from the ceiling.

A light, tingling feeling was coursing through his body. He felt elated, alive. His life had meaning today. He wanted every day to be the same.

Jonty breathed heavily as the overwhelming feeling of power came over him. His fists came up, bunched tight. He felt strong, invincible. He swallowed, trying to control his breathing. He watched the street outside for a while, then went out the door, shutting it with a soft click.

CHAPTER 12

The interview room at the station was designed to be stark, bare. The same green lino floor continued, and the metal chairs were screwed to the floor, same as the table. Arla and Harry were sat inside already when Cherie Longworth was shown in. She sat down slowly, her eyes moving from Arla to Harry.

Arla noticed she wore no makeup. Her hair, frizzly last night, was now tied back in a ponytail. The black rings under the eyes remained, pronounced if anything. Swollen eyelids suggested further lack of sleep. Arla couldn't blame her. Her blue jacket was spotted with rain, and crumpled. Arla felt a twinge of sympathy, but once again, her large eyes, sharp nose and high cheekbones held her attention. Even in grief stricken times, her features were remarkable.

Cherie said, "Do I need a lawyer?"

"No," Arla said quickly, feeling bad that she hadn't been briefed already. Harry would get in the neck later. "This is a formal statement, and will be taped and recorded. However, you are not under suspicion, and not being arrested. Therefore, a lawyer is not necessary. However, if you want to have one, then no problem, we can get one for you."

She sidled a glance to Harry, who nodded. Cherie considered for a while, then sighed.

"Guess it can't get much worse than this anyway. Come on, let's get it over and done with."

Harry pressed play on the audio and DVD recorder. "Mrs Cherie Longworth present at interview conducted at Clapham Police Station on 18th November 2017 at 10.30 hours. DI Harry Mehta and DCI Arla Baker present."

As Harry read, Arla noted Cherie turned her face upwards to look at the camera.

Arla asked, "Mrs Longworth, could you please state your full name and relationship to the deceased, for the record."

When she had done, Arla continued. "Please tell where you were between 1900 and 2100 last night, 17th November."

Arla wanted to give the woman a smile of encouragement, but resisted. This was a murder investigation, and she had to treat all witnesses equally.

"Like I told you, with my friend Jill Hunter, in Dulwich Village."

"You didn't go anywhere else?"

"No."

The response was very quick. Cherie's hands were clasped underneath the table, where Arla couldn't see. But she was trained to observe the small things. Often it was the neck that gave suspects away. After a lie, the neck muscles could stretch, often the suspect swallowed. They also blinked more, whether they held eye contact or not.

Arla let the silence run for a while, as she stared back. Cherie shifted her upper body slightly, another giveaway, and there it was, the swallow. Arla dropped her stare and made a point to deliberately write something in her notebook slowly.

Was Cherie hiding something, or was she just nervous to be in a police station? Her file had shown no previous convictions.

When Arla looked back up, Cherie had her mouth open like she wanted to say something. Arla raised her eyebrows.

"I meant to say, we, I mean Jill and I, did go out to eat somewhere. But that was all."

"I see. So you did go somewhere else."

"We went out to a restaurant called Zizzi's on Dulwich High Street. It's a chain. Just for food. I was driving, so I only had one drink."

That made more sense, Arla thought. She wrote Zizzi down in her notebook and circled it.

"So what time did you get back home?"

"After half eleven I think. Can't remember the exact time."

"You spent a long time with your friend."

Cherie shrugged. "Like I said, she's going through a bad time. We've been friends for a long time."

"What was your maiden name before you got married?"

Arla's sudden change of subject had meant to startle, and from the expression on Cherie's face, achieved precisely that.

"Uh, Reeves."

"And how long had you been married for?"

Cherie paused for a few seconds, longer than what a woman needed to think of an answer to a question she should know well.

"1 year."

"Were you married before?"

"Yes."

When Arla merely stared back at her, Cherie got the drift. "Oh, my previous marriage lasted almost eight years. Before that, I was single."

Arla did some quick mental maths. That meant Cherie had been single almost till her forties.

"Who were you married to before?"

"Gus Percival." She smiled wanly. "He was also a film director, as it happens."

Harry leaned forward. "Were you in the same line of work?"

Cherie nodded. "Yes. I was an actress. Mostly small parts in TV serials and a few advertisements. Never hit the big screen."

Harry continued. "Is that how you and David met?"

"Yes. It was at a film inaugural party organised by a common friend."

Arla asked, "Was the marriage going well?"

Cherie shrugged. "Same as every marriage. We had our ups and downs. But more ups then down, definitely. We hadn't been married for long."

An inscrutable look flashed across her face, a spasm of pain. It was tough for her, but she was holding it together. Arla lowered her voice and wondered where the hell her son was.

"I understand this is a difficult time for you. But anything you can tell us will be of help, I can assure you."

Arla glanced at Harry, who took over. "How long have you lived at that house, Mrs Longworth?"

She sniffed. "Ten years. Before that I lived in Wandsworth, with my ex-husband."

"Do you have the address?"

Cherie told Harry, who made a record. "Did you have any children with your ex-husband?"

"No."

Arla stared back at Cherie, who reached for the glass of water in front of her and took a sip. Arla asked, "Hope you don't mind me asking, but what caused the marriage to dissolve?"

Cherie sighed. "What causes any break up? We decided that we didn't love each other any more. Hence we went our own ways."

There was silence for a while. Arla made a note of the ex husband's name and circled it.

"Where is your son today?" Harry asked.

She paused again, dropped her eyes and seemed to search for an answer. "I did tell him last night. Left a message on his phone and texted. He called me this morning, but I was on my way here so missed the call."

You had time to ring the Secretary of State but not your own son? Arla thought to herself.

CHAPTER 13

Lucas Longworth, or Luke, as he preferred to be called, stared out the window. Wind and rain kept up a soft drumming against the pane, drops arriving and sliding down the glass endlessly. The houses opposite were smudged by the rain, low bellied, iron grey clouds gathering force in the sky, like phalanxes of an army determined to stage a watery onslaught.

He ignored the bead of moisture hovering in the corner of his eye. It blinded him, till he didn't know if it was the weather obscuring his vision, or the difficult memories of the man he called his father.

Had called father.

Luke looked at the phone screen again. There was no mistaking it. Cherie had tried to call several times, and sent texts. The last one said simply:

He's dead. Someone broke in and killed him. Call me.

Luke's finger hovered over the green button. He knew he had to press it. A simple motion of his thumb would connect him to Cherie. But it wasnt that easy.

His hand sagged downwards and the phone remained silent. Deep down, Luke had known this day would come. It was inevitable. He didn't feel any remorse. He hadn't done anything wrong. Still, he couldn't explain the choking sensation in his throat, the frustration gnawing at his fingertips.

The mode of death wasn't surprising either. He had known it would end this way. There was nothing he could have done to stop it. His dad would never have listened and besides...father and sons don't talk to each other that way. They don't have a heart to heart like mother and daughter. Not after a certain age, anyway.

After his teenage years, Luke had learnt most of what was hidden from him. He wanted to leave home. He knew it was an illusion.

His father was barely there and Cherie...well, she was just a human doll. She performed her functions and kept her mouth shut. He didn't even call her mother anymore.

It was odd, he knew. To have been surrounded with comfort from day one, but not know any love. Most wouldn't understand what that felt like, and would call him a spoilt brat. A hypocrite.

But Luke knew the truth. His childhood had twisted his soul, like a tree deprived of light, but forced to grow by artificial chemicals. Until he could satisfy his urges, living was like walking around wearing underwear that hurt. He couldn't share the pain with anyone, but the material dug deep into his skin, gripped his testicles. Odd, how long he had lived like that for.

And the man to blame for it was now dead. But that man was also his father.

Where did that leave him?

Luke turned away from the window and paced the living room. Now what? He was sure the police were involved. Sooner or later, they would come knocking. He wondered how much Cherie would tell them. The stupid bitch would crack probably. She was a softie. She would tell the cops everything just to get them off her back.

Would the police suspect him? Luke blinked. He had to do something. Somehow, he had to find an alibi for last night. If he couldn't, he was in deep, deep trouble.

CHAPTER 14

Arla was watching Cherie closely. She asked, "Mrs Longworth-

"Please call me Cherie."

Arla paused as Cherie held her eyes. It was fair enough. Every mention of her married name must be torture for her.

"OK, Cherie. Don't you find it a bit strange that your son has not called you back as yet?"

"Like I said, I think he might have tried already. But I was on the tube so maybe I missed him."

"What sort of a relationship did Lucas have with the...I mean with his father?"

Another pause that was noticeable. Another shift of the body and a tensing of the arms which probably meant under the table she was gripping her hands tightly.

"You could say..." her voice trailed off.

It was silent for a while, then Harry said softly, "Go on, Cherie."

Her face had lost some colour when she looked up. "David was a busy man. He was away a lot. That affected Luke. But David loved him and Luke knew that."

"Are you saying they weren't close?" Harry asked.

"No, they were. We went on holidays together. David was there at his graduation. You know, all the normal things that parents do."

Arla said, "I sense a but."

Cherie shook her head, but avoided their eyes. "There isn't. Ours wasn't any different to any other family. We had our moments, but it worked out in the end."

She looked up and stared at Arla in the eyes. There was a vulnerable, almost scared expression in her face. Arla leaned forward.

"Cherie, if there is anything you want to tell us, now is the time to do it. It will save you a lot of trouble later."

"I have nothing more to say, Inspector. Am I free to go now?"

Harry said, "Of course. Anytime. But before you go, a couple more questions about David. What was his daily routine like? Had he been abroad recently?"

"As he got older he spent less time shooting abroad. He was in more of a mentorship role at the BFI and BBC."

"What's the BFI?"

"British Film Institute."

"Did he get many visitors?"

Cherie shrugged. "Every now and then. If you're asking me if he had many visitors recently, then the answer is no."

Arla and Harry exchanged a glance. Cherie said, "Look, I am tired. I have a lot to sort out as well. Can I leave?"

Arla nodded. "Of course. But if you can think of anything at all, please give us a call." She handed a card over, and Harry did the same.

Harry spoke into the microphone. "Interview terminated 11.15 am."

They got up and followed Cherie out of the room. Arla let Harry see her out at the main desk, and went back to her room.

She stopped by the desk of Lisa and Rob, who sat opposite each other. Lisa was on the phone, her blonde curls shaking as she nodded. She glanced up at Arla, holding up one finger.

"Sorry," she said, putting the phone down. "My mother's not well, just spoke to the doctor."

"Oh," Arla said, concerned. "What's the matter?"

"It's cancer," Lisa sighed. "Started in her bowels, and now spread to her liver. Poor thing doesnt have long, apparently."

Arla gripped Lisa's shoulder and saw the younger woman's eyes moisten. "Are you sure you're coping?"

Lisa lowered her head and sniffed. She took out a hanky and blew her nose.

Arla said, "Because if you're not, I'd rather you took leave now. Work will only get busier over the next few days."

"I'm fine, guv, I really am. I go every evening to sit with her. Not much I can do now. She's on this thing called a syringe driver which pumps morphine into her. She has a bed in the Palliative Care Home, where they care for people like her. Half the time she's asleep."

"I'm sorry."

Lisa shook her head. "Don't be. To be honest work is keeping me going right now. I need the distraction, if that makes sense. If something does happen I will let you know."

"Promise?" Arla smiled. "I mean it. You can go off anytime you want."

"Thanks boss."

Rob came around the desk. Rob was rotund and short, shirt chafing at his pot belly. He dressed smartly enough, and looked older than his thirty years due to his balding head.

"Everything OK?" he asked, looking at Lisa.

"He knows," Lisa told Arla.

"OK," Arla said. "Back to work. Cherie just told me she went for dinner at Zizzi in Dulwich High Street. Can we check CCTV please? And any CCTV images from the Longworth house?"

Rob shook his head. "No guv. It's the cross between Clapham and Wandsworth Common so there's no CCTV there. All woodlands, I'm afraid, with one road bisecting the two."

"Bring up the map," Arla said. She leaned over the desk as Lisa brought up the maps."

The road was called BelleVue, and it was one of South London's most sought after residential addresses. Not far from the tube and train stops, yet exclusive and private. Arla saw the prison behind the bulge of Wandsworth Common.

"HMP Wandsworth," she said. "I know its a long shot, but can we just make sure no inmates escaped from there last night?"

"Talking about me again?" Arla half turned to see Harry standing behind her. His light coffee coloured cheeks were smooth and his chestnut brown eyes danced. The tie was a perfect windsor knot, and the tips of his black Loake shoes gleamed.

Arla said, "Yeah, because you look like a jail bird who just broke out."

"I can be crazy when the situation demands," he smiled. She wanted to retort, but relented. Things were different between them since they had started seeing each other. An awkwardness still prevailed at work, where secrecy was paramount. But Harry still riled her with his jibes, and she was happy enough to give it back. Only now, she held back more, because she knew he did too. They had gone from being sparring partners to lovers, and although they joked around, she had to admit it was getting serious.

She had feelings for Harry. And it wasn't just because he brought her to toe clenching, whole body shuddering orgasms. *Well, that helped.*

But he was also a mature and discreet man, a responsible adult who hid his seriousness well behind his jokes and Ralph Lauren suit. He judged people well, and gave Arla sound advice. He was her harbour in the tempest.

60

"So," Harry said, cocking his long neck to one side, "What's going on folks?"

CHAPTER 15

Arla folded her arms across her chest. "Just making sure insane people like you aren't roaming the streets." She turned to Lisa. "Check with the HMP Chief Warden please. And the CCTV from Dulwich."

She asked Harry, "What did you make of Cherie Longworth?"

"She's hiding something, that's for sure. Have we checked her maiden name, Cherie Reeves for any PNC's?"

"No," Arla said. "But we can do that now." She walked towards her office and Harry followed.

"I got that report guv," he called out, loud enough for Rob and Lisa to hear.

Arla stood by her desk and Harry shut the door, then came over. Arla wrinkled her nose.

"What aftershave is that Harry? God you smell like a tart's boudoir."

Harry grabbed her wrist. Arla's cheeks flushed hot. She gave him daggers with her eyes and whispered, "Let go, Harry. Not in the office!"

Harry didn't listen. He hooked an arm around her waist and held her against him. She felt the taut muscles of his abdomen, the warmth of his legs and her mouth opened. A knot of desire untangled itself deep in her guts. Harry lowered his face towards her.

"No," she whispered, but her voice was weak. He breathed heavily on her neck, and God, she wanted to feel his lips on hers.

"Still think I smell like a tart's boudoir?"

He nuzzled her neck with his nose, breath hot and tight on her skin. Arla gasped. She was getting aroused.

"Harry, please-

His voice was low and throaty, his grip still tight on her wrist. "All I want is an apology."

Despite being caught between desire and duty, she almost grinned. "No fucking way."

His tongue started to lick her neck and he ground his hips against her.

"God, Harry…"

There was a knock on the door. They separated instantly. Harry moved near the door and took his phone out. Arla sat down at her table, breathing heavily. She opened up her laptop and pretended to look at the screen.

She cleared her throat. "Come in."

Lisa walked in. She held a piece of paper in her hand. "I got the warrant for the Longworth house." She put it on the table. "And I called Banerji. He's done a miracle. Worked through the victim early this morning."

"Thanks Lisa. Leave the door open, in case I need to shout for you something."

"No worries guv."

Lisa glanced at Harry as she left, a look Arla didn't miss. She picked up the warrant and read through it.

Harry said, "I'm calling Cherie." Arla didn't reply. She smoothed her shirt down, stood and left the room.

She was in the rear car park when Harry arrived. The tension between them was palpable. Harry walked to the black BMW 7 series that the Serious Crime Squad had as a fleet car. He checked it over once, much to her annoyance. He treated that car like a precious object.

They drove out of the station into the serpentine narrow streets of inner city Clapham. Tall council block apartments, housing low income and ethnically diverse families sprouted all around them. It was less than five miles from the glamour and wealth of the manors on the Common side, but several lifetimes away in reality. London's nexus of great wealth and its welfare state funded chronic poverty never made much sense to Arla. Especially when most of those mansion were empty half the year. But she had more important matters to deal with.

She saw Harry take the opposite direction to the BelleVue Avenue. "Where are you going?" She asked with a frown.

"The hospital mortuary. Thought you would like to stop by to meet Banerji on the way."

That much was true, she definitely would like some clarity from the pathologist. Harry knew the way she worked. Hell, the man could read her thoughts. For a few seconds, she felt that warm, fuzzy feeling in her chest, the sense of belonging. It was tempered by cold reality. Everything in her life ended in disappointment and heartbreak. Why would this be any different?

She was emotional, headstrong. She opened her fat gob and said things without thinking. Sexy gob, Harry called it. But she was who she was. After all the tragedies involving Nicole and her family, she had lost hope on matters of the heart and hearth. Maybe that was why she loved her job so much. It made up for loneliness.

It made her angry. Another part of her messed up mental state. *Why me? What have I done to deserve this?*

She hit the side of the window with her fist, jaws clenched in sudden frustration.

"Hey," Harry said, glancing over. "Look I'm sorry about the office. I got carried away-

"Shut up!"

She closed her eyes and her head sank back in the seat. She felt angry with Harry too, and felt bad because of it. This emotional torpor was present often these days. Arla had been with men before, but none had made her feel like Harry. No one knew her like Harry did, not even her sole surviving, dysfunctional relative, her father.

Harry drove in silence. Arla murmured, "I'm sorry."

"Don't be." He gave her a sidelong look. "You OK?"

"Bloody brilliant."

Wisely, Harry refrained from further comment.

CHAPTER 16

Arla showed her badge at the entrance of the mortuary and they were allowed in. An elevator took them down to the three basement levels, one of them on the same level as the medical school dissecting rooms. A gaggle of white coated students entered on the last level. Looking at their eager, fresh young faces, Arla felt a twinge of melancholy. She had never looked forward to life the way they did. She never would. It was scary to think that the spark of happiness in her life currently was Harry. It would be good while it lasted. Because she had no doubt, like everything else in her life, that spark would never become the flame of a candle, lighting up the darkness of her life. Harry would leave. Once he had a proper look into her scarred, bitter soul, he wouldn't stay. She knew it, and it made her unbearably sad.

The elevator doors opened, the students poured out and dispersed down the corridor, laughing and talking. Arla rang the bell to the mortuary and Chen, Dr Banerji's assistant opened the door.

"Hi Chen," Arla said. They were ushered in, and through a narrow corridor, entered the large hall that made up the mortuary's main floor.

Banerji was leaning over a dead body. He was dressed in surgical gown, with a mask over his face. He saw them, left the gurney, got rid of his gloves and mask, and walked over.

"Thanks for doing it this early," Arla said.

"No problem," the pathologist said. He shuffled over to another gurney with a covered body, smoothing down his white hair as he did so. Harry walked ahead with Arla following behind.

Banerji put a pair of gloves on, then flung the covers off. Arla tried to keep her eyes off the white, taut face of David Longworth, but with Banerji in full flow, it was virtually impossible.

"First, the skull." Casually, Banerji lifted the shaved head by putting his hand underneath it. "As you can see here, there is a contusion. It's where a blunt object hit his head. Must be a hammer of some sort. Left quite a dent." Chen helped to rotate the head so the others could see.

"That made him unconscious, right?" Arla asked. "But did it kill him?"

"Loss of consciousness from head trauma is not as easy as you think. The whole point our skull has evolved to be thicker than the rest of our bones is to protect the soft brain. But this blow was hard enough to cause a depression. That's important, as it hits the the blood vessels right underneath the skull."

"Causing a bleed?"

"Exactly. This portion of the skull that we sawed off," Banerji spoke as Chen lifted a square piece of bone off the skull. She adjusted the light, till it shone at the black, congealed mass inside the hole.

"That is a clot. A subdural hematoma if you want the medical term. Once the clot is formed it presses on the brain, causing various malfunctions."

"Hang on," Harry said. "Isn't this how that Hollywood movie star's wife died? It was a ski injury. And it took a while to form, so she was fine for a while then just dropped dead?"

"Had your weetabix this morning, Inspector?" Banerji quipped. "Yes, very good. A subdural hematoma is often undiagnosed. Why? Just as you said, the clot takes time to form. It can be a killer, but not for a day or two."

"So this didn't kill him?" Arla asked.

"I didn't say that," Banerji said with a crafty look in his eyes. He went to the head of the body. He pointed a green-gloved index finger to a jagged line at the hairline. Arla understood. As Banerji gripped the skull with both hands, she averted her eyes.

With a squishing sound, the skull came off. Arla stepped back to find Harry reassuring body. He rubbed her back discreetly and she was glad. When she looked again, Banerji was beckoning them to come forward.

The pale pink convolutions of the naked brain seemed to be made of bubble gum. Banerji said, "That blow caused some of the arteries to rupture. That created a clot sure, but at the brain level it caused a massive bleed."

Arla glanced at the place. She felt strangely detached looking at the brain. Like it didn't belong to the body. For the first time, she understood how pathologists worked. To them it was just a collection of organs, not a human being.

"See this black stuff inside the brain?" Banerji lifted up a small slick on his finger. "That's blood."

"So," he said, "The blow caused a subdural hematoma. That alone might have killed him in a day or two. But the massive stroke he had from the bleed killed him much sooner."

There was silence for a while. Eventually Arla said, "Are you saying he was virtually dead, but then the killer hung up him like that…." her voice trailed off.

"Just to make a point. Sick bastard," Harry muttered behind her.

"Yes," Banerji said, his voice now low. "I looked all over the body. There are no foreign hair fragments or skin cells. I think the killer wore a mask, and his hair must have been covered."

"This can't be the first time he's done this," Arla muttered.

Banerji said, "The entire body was washed with betahistine as well, as you know. Hence the slight brownish tinge to the skin."

Arla asked, "Are you confident of the time of death?"

"Yes, very. Between 19.30 and 21.00. If you ask me, the killer made one mistake. The heating was turned off, and he didn't switch it back on before he left. Heat would have decomposed the body further and played havoc with determining time of death."

"So the cause of death is…."

"Blunt trauma to the head, causing haemorrhagic stroke. Secondary cause, strangulation."

"Good work, Doc," Harry said.

Banerji beamed. Then he paused and snapped his fingers. "Ah, I almost forgot."

CHAPTER 17

"What?" Arla asked.

"Those parts of the carpet you asked Parmentier to look at. Remember?"

Arla's face brightened. "Where I thought the body had been dragged. Yes, of course."

"Nothing to do with me, but he called me to ask for a match of the DNA he found in the carpet."

"And?"

"We found the victim's, sure. But there was another set of skin cells this time. The DNA didn't belong to the victim."

Arla felt a surge of excitement. " Parmentier must have run it through the database. Any hits?"

"Sadly none."

Arla glanced at Harry. He nodded, taking out his phone and walking out of the chamber. It was high time SOCO offered some feedback. Harry would get on the case.

Arla thought. She should have taken a DNA swab from Cherie when she was at the station. Unless of course, Parmentier's team had done it already last night. Cherie's DNA would be all over the carpet. If this DNA was hers, they were back to square one. But at least, they had some DNA now. Any future suspect would be checked against it.

"Anything from the rest of the body?" Arla asked.

Banerji moved down to the chest. "Some bruise marks in the throat and upper chest where he was gripped when attacked, but nothing else."

He lifted up a hand and held one finger up. "Nicotine stains on the nails of the right hand. He was a smoker."

He looked at Arla and shrugged. "That's it, really. Toxicology tests aren't back yet, they take time, as you know."

Arla tapped her fingers against her leg. "Have you checked the nails of both hands for DNA? I'm wondering if we can find the same DNA in his nails as on the carpet upstairs."

"Good point."

"The prosecution will like it to prove that the victim was attacked by the same person."

Banerji raised his eyebrows. "Jumping a few steps aren't we? You have to find this pyscho first."

"When we do, we can't let clever lawyers wriggle him out free. Best to have the case ready, doc."

The buzzer sounded and Chen left to open the doors. Harry came back. "SOCO will broaden their search. But it's a needle in a haystack. I told them we have a warrant and they'll meet us at the property."

"Good," Arla said. She turned back to Banerji. "This is a violent MO, right? Likely to be a man."

"Yes."

"I'm thinking about the weapon. A flat, hard object like a hammer. One good blow can kill. But it must also be light, or he wouldn't be carrying it around with him."

Harry said, "A knife would make more sense. But maybe his mind is more attached to a hammer. Killers like him have fixed behaviour patterns."

Arla said, "Exactly. Doc, can we see if there are any metal fragments left in the skull? Or anything, really."

Banerji sighed in resignation. "Arla, I have other jobs as well..."

"Please," Arla said. "We have pressure on this. Mr Longworth had friends in high places." She stepped forward and smiled at Banerji.

71

The older man smiled tolerantly. Arla knew Banerji made concessions for her, and his attitude towards her was one of fatherly fondness. He had no children himself, but she knew he was married. She often wondered if she filled a small portion of his heart that must be empty.

"How about I call you later tomorrow evening? Once I have done my other chores."

"You're a star."

Arla and Harry left swiftly, and soon Harry was driving down the traffic congested streets of South London. Rain arrived, with the steel grey of threatening clouds banked on the horizon. Apart from the wipers swishing there was no other sound inside the car. The silence lay heavy between them.

Arla stared at the rain slicked pavement rushing past, commuters with umbrellas walking fast, hunched against the rain.

Harry was the first to speak. "Are you OK?"

Arla had her face averted from him. She squeezed her eyes shut, then opened them. It wasn't Harry's fault. He was only being himself. But she didn't owe him an explanation. After all, she could also only be herself. Trapped in her own world.

"Yes, I'm fine." She turned and tried a smile. "I forgive you for your transgression."

From his raised eyebrows, she knew he liked the response. Harry liked nothing more than a verbal joust. Arla didn't let him get there. For now, she needed her mind on the job.

"Any new questions for Cherie?"

Harry pursed his lips together. He had full, sensitive lips and she liked looking at them.

"Well, we need to dig deeper into her relationship with her son, definitely. Something's not right there. Trust me, men dote on their mum's. If something like this happened at my home, I'd probably be guarding my mum 24/7."

Arla thought about that. "Family dynamics are weird, no doubt. Which makes me wonder about her relationship with her husband. I mean, she said it was fine, but I don't believe she was telling us everything."

"Me neither, guv."

In a while, they arrived at BelleVue Road. The white SOCO van had arrived already. Blue and white police tape cordoned off the entire row of houses. For the first time, Arla saw a woman arguing with one of the uniformed officers. Must be on of their neighbours, she thought. The woman was clearly raising her voice, and gesticulating with her hands.

CHAPTER 18

Arla ducked beneath the tape and walked towards the woman. Another uniform officer had arrived, and the woman was haranguing both of them. Arla caught snippets of the conversation as the woman shouted.

"I've had enough. I see the police take out a body bag, but no one tells us anything! You knock on our doors asking us questions if we saw anyone..."

The woman broke off to look at Arla as she joined them. The woman was in her late forties, with scraggly chestnut hair that fell to her shoulders. It needed a comb. She was dressed in dark slacks and a brown jumper and wore jogging shoes. Arla held up her badge and warrant card.

"DCI Baker. I'm in charge of the investigation here. Can I help?"

"In charge, are you?" She pointed at the two parked squad cars at either end of the row, and the SOCO van that was unloading equipment. "You call this being in charge? No one knows what's going on-

Arla disliked the woman's sneering, superior tone immediately, but kept her thoughts to herself. "What do you think is going on, Miss-

"Mrs Parker actually."

"OK Mrs Parker we are in the middle of an investigation as a crime has taken place here."

The woman rolled her eyes. "Takes a genius to figure that out, right?"

"Soon we will release an official statement. But you live here, so you must have an idea of what happened." Arla lowered her voice. "As you know we don't want to alert the media, hence we haven't notified the public yet."

That mollified Mrs Parker somewhat. She sniffed and looked Arla up and down. "Like I said, a body bag came out, so someone must have died. I know it."

Typical snoopy neighbour, Arla thought. And for that reason, she could be useful. Arla took her elbow and moved to one side.

"I can tell you, but in strict confidence. This is a serious police matter. Do you understand?" Arla dropped her voice to whisper.

Mrs Parker's brow furrowed then her eyes widened. Her voice matched Arla's. "Yes, of course."

"Did you know the Longworth's?"

"Only to say hi and hello. But we did see a lot of coming and going from the house."

"Really?" Arla did her best to look inquisitive.

"Yes, they always had guests."

"Anyone in particular?"

Mrs Parker pressed her lips together. "Yes, a man in a silver Bentley. I remember because the car was fancy. Saw him quite a few times."

"When was the last time?" Arla took her notebook out.

Mrs Parker leaned forward and whispered. "About three times in the last two weeks, I'd say. Oh my god, do you think-

Arla looked up at her sharply. "It's too soon to jump to any conclusions, Mrs Parker. I'm sure you appreciate that."

"Oh, of course."

"Did you see David Longworth out and about much?"

The woman shrugged. "Every now and then. To be honest, he spent a lot of time indoors. I didn't see him much. His wife seemed more sociable."

"What did you think of Mrs Longworth?"

"Cherie? Oh, we chatted every now and then. Like you do, you know."

Arla waited. Mrs Parker shrugged and said, "She's quite bright, happy mostly. Just normal."

"So apart from this silver Bentley that came a few times in the last two weeks you havent seen anything else unusual?"

"No, can't say I have."

"I know this is a long shot, but you didn't note the registration number of the silver Bentley, did you? If it was a private number plate they sometimes have a catchy number."

Mrs Parker crinkled her botox smooth forehead. She clicked her tongue. "No, sorry."

Arla gave her a card. "If you think of anything please get in touch. My number's on this. Anytime you want." She smiled and turned to leave.

Mrs Parker caught her arm. "Hey. You didn't tell me what happened in that house."

"No, I didn't, because I can't. But I think you know, Mrs Parker, don't you?"

CHAPTER 19

Arla left the woman staring at her and went over to the SOCO van. Harry was talking to Parmentier, who was zipping up his white boiler suit.

Parmentier greeted Arla. "The study is now a no gone zone. The tent is in place. I don't want more feet trampling around upstairs."

"We'll concern ourselves with the living in that case." Arla glanced at Harry. "Where's Cherie?"

"She's inside."

The front door was open and see through plastic sheets had been rolled out on the floor. Arla and Harry walked on the duckboards till they came into the hallway next to the massive staircase. Ahead lay the entrance to the kitchen, which was closed. Arla knocked on it, and after a short while, Cherie opened the door. Her eyes were drawn inside their sockets, and her cheeks were sunken, colourless.

"Sorry to disturb you," Arla said. "But can we have a quick word?"

Cherie opened the door without a reply and moved away. They went inside, and Harry shut the door. The open plan kitchen area was large. Light flooded in from the ceiling skylights. The kitchen bar and cooking area was to the left, the rest of the space was dominated by a long dining table capable of seating more than twenty. There was also a pool table with a TV area to the right. Straight ahead, concertina doors opened into a green lawn with mature trees on either side.

Arla stopped to enjoy the view for a few seconds, then walked over to where Cherie was making coffee.

Cherie offered it to them and they both nodded.

"Over here," Cherie said, indicating one of the four sitting stools at the breakfast bar.

"Nice coffee," Arla said after taking a sip.

Cherie's face was blank. "What can I help you with?"

Arla glanced at Harry, who cleared his throat. "Have you heard from your son?"

"Yes. He called to say he wanted to meet."

"He doesn't want to come here?"

Cherie's eyes flicked from Arla to Harry. "There are a couple of things you should know about my step son."

Cherie rubbed her face like she was tired. She probably was, Arla thought. Cherie frowned, her eyes staring past them into the distance. "I'm sorry. I should have told you this earlier. But Luke and his father don't get along. They never have. He went to boarding school, and left home early."

"When you say don't get on what do you mean?"

"He thinks his father was overbearing and treated him, well, I don't really know the details you see. But David always thought his son was-

Cherie broke off and gripped her forehead. Arla and Harry glanced at each other. A few things were now taking shape in Arla's mind. No wonder the son had been evasive.

"Was what?" she pressed.

Cherie looked weary, and again avoided their eyes. "David said Luke used to steal things. Hide things from him. A few time he caught Luke forging his signature on a chequebook. That's when him and Laura decided to send Luke to boarding school."

Arla said, "Laura was David's ex wife?"

"Yes."

"What happened to her?"

Cherie looked at them with a puzzled look in her eyes. "Sorry, I thought you knew."

Arla frowned. "Knew what?"

"Laura died. Accidental overdose of sleeping tablets."

Arla cast an annoyed glance at Harry, who shrugged. A detail like this should have turned up in the searches they had done. But to be fair, Arla reasoned, it was only in the early hours of the morning that David's body was found. It had only been a few hours, and the team was going to have its first meeting this afternoon when she went back. There would be no dearth of leads to follow.

"Can you please give us Laura's full name and date of birth, please?" Arla flipped her notebook out, and Harry did the same.

"She was forty eight, I believe. Laura Longworth, sorry I can't remember her maiden name. Something with D, I think. It'll come to me, I'm sure. I don't know her DOB."

"When did she die?"

"Three years ago."

Arla twisted the pen in her fingers. "And you got married last year, right? So two years before you got married."

Cherie nodded. "Correct."

"Do you know how it happened? I mean did David call the police when he found out?"

"Yes, exactly. He called an ambulance actually, and they took Laura to hospital. She was unarousable despite CPR and life support."

Arla wrote this down on her notebook. Her mind was buzzing, like a swarm of bees in a box. There was something here, but right now, she couldn't cut through the noise.

"Did David ever talk about it?"

Cherie's eyes moistened. She bent her head and sniffed. Arla felt sorry immediately. This woman was going through hell right now. Digging up the past was making it worse. She steeled herself. It was one of the worst parts of her job as a police detective. Pressing grieving relatives for more information. As if losing the person they loved, forever, wasn't bad enough. But nine times out of ten, it was the relatives who provided the breakthrough in a case.

Arla gave her some time, then said, "I'm sorry. I know this is difficult for you. But anything you can tell us is extremely helpful, I assure you."

Cherie unfolded a tissue and dabbed her eyes. "No, it's fine. To be honest, I didn't know David before Laura died. The David I knew was a quiet, reserved man. His friends say Laura's death changed him. He used to be the life and soul of the party."

Something flickered in Cherie's eyes as she stared at Arla. Deep grief was like a river of poison that flooded the soul, Arla knew. It changed a person's mentality. It had happened to her. She wondered if the same would happen to this poor woman.

"I understand," Arla said quietly. She paused a beat. "Did Laura die in this house?"

"No. They were on holiday in Dorset, by the sea."

Arla leaned forward. "Just the two of them?"

Cherie blew her nose and shook her head. "No. It was a family thing. Luke went with them as well."

Arla and Harry looked at each other.

CHAPTER 20

The rain pattered incessantly against the windscreen. The sky was leaden grey, and Arla's breath made fumes inside the car as they waited for the heating to kick in. She held her frozen fingers against the heating grill. Harry was navigating the busy mid day traffic as they drove to the address in Wandsworth, where Luke Longworth lived. Two phone calls to his mobile had gone unanswered.

Harry said, "For Laura Longworth, if it was an unexpected death, the coroner would have opened an inquest, right?"

"Yes," Arla spoke above the whurr of the heating on full blast. "We need to contact Bournemouth and Dorset Hospitals for that. Her GP would have records if she suffered with depression."

The traffic thickened like a knot on the road ahead. Harry muttered to himself, then put the lights on and hit the siren. It took a while, and some horn beeps, but the traffic started to part. Luke lived in a residential road in Wandsworth, but the streets were narrow like many of London's old Victorian sprawl south of the river. The houses had stood the test of time, and German bombing during the second world war. Harry slowed down as they took several turns in a grid like maze of streets. The rain was heavier if anything, an absolute downpour.

"Number 34, Leavenworth Avenue," Arla shouted.

"Yep, I know." Harry saw the sign and turned into the street. There was no parking, both sides of the narrow street being taken up by residents cars. Harry stopped in the middle of the street. He had turned the siren and blue lights off long before they entered the residential area.

Arla nodded at him and jumped off. The hood of her anorak was pulled over her head and rain drummed against it. Rows of terraced houses stood stacked together. They were redbrick and brown, with white eaves and cornishes, all of them with tall sash windows. Handsome houses built in the late 19th century. Arla found number 34 and hurried underneath the porch. She rang the doorbell and waited. No lights were on inside, and the bay windows had curtains drawn.

There was no response. Arla heard a sound behind her. Harry opened the latch gate and came in.

Arla pressed the buzzer again. It sounded inside the house, loud and clear. But the lights remained off. Rain splashed into puddles outside, and on gutters above their heads.

Harry tiptoes onto the paving slabs of the front garden, then peered inside the window, between the curtains.

"Can't see jack," he called back. He swung his long legs and jumped over a small bush. It brought him to the margin of the property, where the walls of the house next door began. Harry did his antelope gait and swung back next to Arla on the porch. He wiped the rain off his forehead and brow. He was drenched, having parked further away, and water rolled down his cheek. He slicked his hair back, flinging some drops towards Arla.

"Watch it," she said, leaning back. Harry blew out his cheeks. Arla suddenly realised she had her back to the door, and Harry was standing very close to her. So close she could feel his heat. From his eyes she knew he felt it too. And good Lord, she wanted nothing more than to seek the warmth of his embrace, melt into his arms. Feel his lips on hers. Arla swallowed hard and looked down, listening to her heart slamming against her ribs, drowning out the rainfall.

She spoke with an effort. "Well, he's not here, is he?"

Harry didn't reply, and when she looked up, his eyes were burning into hers. But he stepped back.

"No," he said, his voice a hoarse whisper. Suddenly she couldn't avoid his eyes. Arla brushed past him, out into the rain, walking fast. She could hear Harry following her. He caught up with her, and then past her. He ran a few more paces to where the car was parked, down to the left, behind a van.

Arla got into the car and slammed the door shut. She knew what was going to happen, and she didn't care. His hands found hers and she leaned into him, kissing feverishly, electric sparks shooting down her spine as their lips grazed, tongues entwined. His hands moved into her chest, below her cardigan, and pulling her shirt open. She squeezed the hardness of his abs, then further down where she found him hardening. Harry moaned into her mouth as she explored him futher, her hand massaging, urging.

She was on the verge of crossing over. She wanted to move her leg over the gear shaft, drop into his lap and....

Arla stopped. She took her mouth off Harry's and cradled his head on her neck. Her hands left his groin. They were both panting. Moisture from their mingled breathing clouded the windows. She could feel his breath, hot and humid on the nape of her neck. Arla slumped back on the seat.

She felt clammy, wet. She licked her lips. Times like this she could barely control herself.

Harry said, "Next time we tow the caravan, right?"

She couldn't help grin at that, and within seconds they were laughing. She stopped when Harry leaned forward casually and touched her breasts.

"Don't-

But his mouth was already over hers. This time it was gentle and endearing. Harry withdrew and they stared at each other. She could read it in his eyes. Words were not necessary. She knew it too, and knew that words would never suffice what she wanted to say, or wanted to hear. He reached out and stroked the corner of her chin. Then he sighed and leaned back. They stayed that way, staring out at the thick drops weaving their way down windscreen.

Harry was the first to break the silence. "Time to head back."

"Yes," Arla said, stuffing her shirt back into her trousers, feeling strangely frustrated. She wanted to get her hands on Harry again, but back at home. Right now there was work to do. She took her phone out. Lisa answered at the first ring.

Arla said, "Gather the team together. I want SOCO, uniforms, everyone. There's a lot to catch up on."

CHAPTER 21

The hubbub in the incident room was loud and Arla could hear it as she walked down the corridor. Harry had stepped outside to have a quick cigarette. It was the one bad habit of Harry's she couldn't agree with. Her lungs itched for a smoke when he lit up, so he did it by himself. To his credit, he had cut down on his smoking a lot in the last six months.

The noise level died down as Arla strode into the room. Lisa and Rob Pickering were at the white board, where photos of the victim and his family were displayed. Arla swept her eyes over the assembled detectives of various ranks, the uniformed officers and the two SOCO's who had turned up, a man and woman.

Arla checked the time. 14.30. Enough time to get some answers today.

"OK people listen up. The victim's son is not responding to our calls and is not at home. We know that he had a difficult relationship with his dad. How bad this was, we don't know. But we do know that he was a difficult child, sent to a special boarding school. He could be a very disturbed young man. It's possible his father's influence and money allowed him to slip under the radar of the medical professionals."

Arla paused. "Whatever. What we do know is that he was present when his mother took an accidental overdose of sleeping tablets and died. Now his father is violently murdered, and he is missing."

Faces looked at each other and whispers began, which became louder. ""Quiet," Arla said. "This is all conjecture on my part. There could be a perfectly good explanation why he is not around. It doesn't make sense to me, especially when he is aware of how his father died."

Rupert, a detective constable who had joined last year, raised his hand. "Guv, do we know anything else about this missing son? History of violence?"

Arla looked at Lisa, who took over. "There's no mention of him in the database. Of course that doesn't mean he didn't do anything. I went back over the last twenty years and did a search."

Arla thought about Luke's age. "So you went back to when he was twelve years old. Anything in juvenile?"

Lisa looked a bit embarrassed. "Didn't cross my mind, guv sorry. Juve records are till 16 so I should have looked."

"Don't worry, do it now. And I want the name of that boarding school he went to. I want the names of his friends, girlfriends or boyfriends, teachers, their addresses and current locations. I want Luke's work colleagues interviewed, their backgrounds searched to a Category 1 disclosure."

Many in the audience were scribbling on notepads or tapping on phones. Arla turned towards the two SOCO's. She didn't know their names but the blue and white ID badges hung from their necks gave them away. Arla had seen them around the station before.

Arla leaned forward. "Sorry, can't see your names."

The woman introduced themselves. Emily and Aloke. The man, Aloke was the first to speak.

"We got the victim's laptop back from the house, but his phone is missing. His wife doesn't know where it is either. We also got folders from his study, fingerprints and DNA."

"Anything useful?"

"The fingerprints are mainly of him and his wife. There is another set of prints and DNA. We ran this through the usual checks and found nothing. However, the DNA is the same as we found on the carpet."

Arla felt an excitement inside. "And it's not his wife's?"

"No."

"Then it must be the killer's if it's in the study, and on the carpet as well as just inside the door. These are the three locations you got the unknown DNA from right?"

Aloke and Emily both nodded. Emily said, "The only family DNA we are missing is the son."

"Yes, it could be his, but he didn't visit the house much, if at all, according to the wife, Cherie. Therefore it is suspicious if his DNA is in his father's study."

Arla said, "There's something else. A silver Bentley came to the Longworth house several times in the last two weeks. I know we don't have CCTV on that road, but maybe we can check the adjoining streets? They should have CCTV."

"I'll get on the case," Rob said.

The Incident Room door opened and the lanky figure of Harry stepped in. "Sorry," he said, having the grace to look sheepish. He took his place next to Rob.

Arla said, "Any news of cold cases? Anyone we know killed in this manner?"

Lisa cleared her throat. "Rupert and myself had a look." She indicated the younger man who stood up. "Go on Rupert," Lisa smiled.

Rupert cleared his throat. "We went back to the 1980's. I figured if the murderer used force, then statistically chances are it's going to be a man, and a strong one at that. Therefore on the young side. Didn't make sense to look before the 1980's."

Arla was tapping her fingers against the table. "Get on with it."

Rupert swallowed, clearly nervous at what was his first address to the incident room. "We found several cases as expected, that involved blunt trauma to the head. But in every case, the perp had been caught, and was either dead, or behind bars."

Arla sighed. "Well done Rupert and Lisa. So, no unsolved cold cases involving this MO. Can we widen the search?"

"To what, guv?" Lisa asked, a puzzled expression on her face.

Arla was thinking. She spoke slowly. "Frankly, I don't know. Look for any *cold* cases in southwest London over the last twenty to thirty years. There won't be that many. Pull them up. See if you can connect them to this case somehow."

Jason Beauregard, one of the Detective Inspectors who made no secret that he disliked Arla, spoke up.

"Can you explain your reasoning, DCI Baker? The Serious Crime Squad is running on skeleton staff already. We can't just open up cold cases and start investigating because you have a whim."

Arla said, "The victim's ex wife, Laura Douglas, was killed by an overdose. We don't know details, but the verdict was suicide apparently. But what if it wasn't? What if, someone poisoned her?"

Jason frowned. "Like who? You can't seriously think opening up a suicide verdict of the ex wife is going to have a bearing on this violent murder?"

"Call it a gut feeling, Jason."

"Gut feeling?" Jason smirked. "No place for that in my department."

"Oh there is Jason," Arla shot back. "It's hanging over your belt. You're patting it while you're talking!"

Laughter rumbled across the room. Arla switched her attention back to the white board. She walked up to it, and tapped on the photo of Mr. Longworth

"I need a updated file on the victim, with his phone logs, emails and websites he browsed. I still don't have a mental picture of David Longworth. His mobile phone, even if switched off, will give a signal for five days. Let's work on that."

She moved on to Cherie. "I know the wife is suffering right now, but I think she can tell us more about her husband, as well as the step son."

Harry said, "She wants to move back in the house now. Shall we put a uniform team outside?"

"Yes," Arla said, indicating Andy Jackson, the uniformed sergeant in the front row. "Can you sort that out, Andy?"

"No problem, guv."

Arla rapped the photo of Luke Longworth. "Now, this man is the missing link. At the very least, we need an alibi."

Harry said, "I suggest we ask his place of work, and think of getting a warrant to search the house if he doesn't turn up."

"Good idea. Let's get cracking."

CHAPTER 22

Luke Longworth waited underneath a tree, watching his house. Dark clouds had snuffed out any light early and despite it being half past 4, the street lights were coming on. Luke turned up the collar of his jacket and pulled the hood over his head. He had left work early, knowing the police would call there. A call had come through, but he had told the secretary he was out for lunch.

He closed his eyes and breathed heavily. Emotions ran riot inside him. He needed to focus, but it was proving harder than he had ever imagined. Guilt flooded his body, regret laced with it, wearying him down. The regret surprised him. He had never thought he would feel sad about the old man's passing.

A car passed by, it's headlight lighting him up briefly. Luke pretended to pick something up from the ground. The car passed by while he stayed in that position.

He couldn't stay here any longer. This was a heavily populated area, and by acting strange he was inviting attention. He cast one last look at the cars parked near his house. Any of them could be an unmarked police car, but he doubted the engines would be off in this freezing weather. Besides, all of the parked cars looked unoccupied.

Luke swallowed hard. He walked fast, head bent low, then slowed down as he approached the house. A mother and child walked past him quickly. Luke swung his eyes around carefully. He walked past his address, then took the next left. Another row of terraced houses on either side loomed ahead. This area was called the Grid by its thousands of inhabitants. The terraced houses were large enough for families, and well looked after. No one expected any trouble here. One of the reason why he bought the house in the first place.

He slipped inside small latch gate and inserted the key in the lock. He was inside within seconds, and disabling the alarm that started beeping. He listened for a while. The house was like a silent tomb.

His own breathing was harsh in his ears. He tiptoed down the hallway, and felt his way into the lounge room on his left. It was empty, as he expected.

He checked the dining room, then the small kitchen at the back. The place was so quiet even the cat hadn't come back in. The garden was barely visible in the fast fading light.

Luke checked the upstairs quickly. It was as he had left it. He began to relax, then jumped as he felt his phone buzz. He stared at the screen for a while, then answered.

"You shouldn't be calling me," Luke whispered.

"I couldn't help it," said the male voice. "You don't understand."

Luke was silent for a while. "It's not safe. Our phones might be tapped."

The voice snorted. "You give the police too much credit. They won't figure out anything in a hurry."

Luke paced around the front room upstairs, looking out the bay windows that faced the street. "That's alright for you to say. Cherie has already told them about me. I'm sure they suspect me."

"You need to speak to the police, Luke. If you don't, its going to get worse."

Luke's voice was a whisper. "Did you do it?"

The voice was silent. Luke said, "I told you everything-

"Luke!" the reprimand was obvious. "We cannot undo anything."

Luke knotted his hands into fists. "This could be the end. You used what I gave you, right?"

"Listen to me Luke. Speak to the cops. You have to pull this off."

Luke was angry. "How? By keeping you out of it? Yeah, that works out perfectly for you, doesn't it?"

"Think of what's at stake here, Luke. We can do this. *You* can do this."

Luke gripped a tuft of his hair and pulled. "I don't know if I can."

"Trust me. You can. Call me tomorrow."

The line went dead. Luke stared at the phone for a while, shaking his head. He glanced at the road again as two cars went by in quick succession, their headlights throwing shadows against the wall.

Luke moved away, towards his bedroom. He stopped in front of a chest of drawers. He opened it and stared at what was inside.

Then slowly, he removed the black ski mask.

CHAPTER 23

Arla and Harry were standing outside Fulham Broadway tube station, protected from the rain by the big glass portico that ran across the wall. Londoners of various shape, size and colours streamed in and out of the station entrance in a bewildering maze. It was 17.00 and the commuter rush was gathering strength, like a slow moving tidal wave about to lash against London's creaking infrastructure.

"Which way, Harry?" Arla asked. Harry's face was bent over the screen of his phone.

"Straight ahead," he murmured, and without looking at her, started walking. Arla brushed past people to catch up. The car would've taken ages in the grid lock of the roads now. It was Arla's decision to take the tube, and she was now wishing she had stayed in the office. But the need to see Luke Longworth's business premises had won her over.

Fulham Broadway was a well heeled part of south London, close to the uber expensive streets of Chelsea. Many media and film companies had their offices here, in buildings by the river. Harry navigated his way to one such tall office complex. Arla was out of breath by the time they got there.

"Wait," she gasped when Harry pressed the buzzer. "I need to catch my breath."

"Not getting unfit are we?"

"If you hadn't walked so bloody fast I would've been fine!"

"It's my muscular legs, I can't-

"Shut up Harry. I don't want to hear it." Arla grimaced and pressed the buzzer herself. She kept her finger on it till a white shirted security guard came running out of a side door.

He spoke through the intercom. "Who are you?"

Both of them pressed their warrant cards on the glass door. "Detectives from the London Met." Arla didn't say any more. There was a pause, then the door slid open.

The security guard was shorter than Harry, but at Arla's height of five eleven. He stared at them warily. "What do you want?"

"Five Guys Media. Do you know what floor it's on?"

"Yes, the first floor. I need to call them. What's this about?"

"A police investigation. We can get there ourselves."

Harry found the elevators and Arla followed. The doors opened into a deep carpeted corridor with two offices on either side. A young woman opened the door of Five Guys Media and stared at them inquisitively.

"We are closed now. Who are you?"

Arla explained, one foot in the doorway. The woman, just out of college, frowned at their ID badges. "I'm sorry, but there's no one here."

Arla pushed the door open and stepped inside. "We just need to take a look around."

Harry stepped in behind Arla. "Where is Mr. Longworth?"

The woman was still frowning. "He's left the office. Look, you can't just barge in here. What do you want?"

Arla was looking around, and a sudden flicker of movement caught her eyes. It was at a door at the end of the hallway. A face at the glass panel of the door, which withdrew abruptly as Arla looked.

She moved fast. The door was unlocked and she opened it to reveal an open plan office. Most of the desks were empty, but three to four head looked up as she stumbled inside. Another set of doors at the far end was just closing.

Arla ran, dodging past the tables. She could hear Harry hard on her heels. The door gave way to a staircase landing. The window was open and it looked out into the street below. Arla glanced up and down the stairs.

Behind her, Harry said, "Here." He brushed past her and leaned out the window. Arla joined him. Beneath the window there was a flat roof that acted as shelter for the workers at the front door. A running shape attracted her eyes, moving in and out of the throngs of people.

"There" Harry pointed, shouting. He ran down the stairs and Arla followed.

"Black jacket and dark jeans," Harry panted as they burst out the front doors. "Medium height. Didn't get his face."

"You go after him," Arla said. "I'll hook round to the left, to the station."

Arla knew it was a hopeless task, given the rush hour. But it was worth a try. A car blared its horn as she stepped in front of it. The car skidded to a halt, the driver screaming obscenities. Arla ran across the road, into an alley that was crowded with people. She raced down it, then hooked a right, coming back onto a traffic filled road.

She slammed into a man and got almost knocked over. Mumbling an apology, Arla raced towards the tube stop ahead. Moped and bikes sputtered behind her, double decker buses wheezed as they came to a stop. Arla did her best, but she knew it was futile. When she got to the tube station, sweat was pouring down her face. Her shirt stuck to her body like a second skin. She struggled past the mesh of bodies and into the station foyer. She looked around wildly.

Harry's tall figure appeared, rising head and shoulders above the majority of the commuters. She raised her arm and he clocked her, then pushed his way over. He was panting, the same as her.

"I saw him, but that guy can run. Weaved in and out so quickly."

"He came this way, right?"

"Yes, but I also lost sight of him. Sorry guv."

Arla put her hands on her waist. "Don't be. It was worth a try."

Harry's phone started to ring. A second later, so did hers.

CHAPTER 24

The station number was flashing on Arla's phone. She answered immediately.

"Where are you, DCI Baker?" Johnson's deep voice boomed down the line.

"Chasing after a suspect as we speak, sir."

"I see," Johnson's tone became slightly mollified. "But I have some urgent news to share with you."

Arla's heart sank. "What is it?"

"Have you checked the BBC news website?"

Oh no.

"No I haven't had the time sir, is there anything I should know about?"

"It's out, Arla. The media have got hold of it, and TV vans are clogging up the road outside Mr. Longworth's house. The Secretary of State has been down the phone at me again, and so has the wife, Cherie. She's in tears. How the hell did this happen?"

Arla cast her mind back and came up with one solution. The neighbour. Mrs Parker. She rubbed her forehead.

"It wasn't one of our team I can guarantee that. This case is gathering a lot of interest and it's impractical to think we can keep it under wraps."

"Try telling that to the minister who fixes our budget!," Johnson raised his voice. "I want you back at the office now for a report. We need a conviction."

"A conviction? We have no idea-

The line was disconnected as Johnson hung up. Arla grit her teeth. She felt like hurling the phone on the floor and stepping on it.

She caught Harry looking at her. She shook her head and walked off towards the elevators.

*****

Arla got herself a coffee from the vending machine when she entered the station. The coffee was normally rancid, but any warmth was good now. Holding the steaming cup and wishing she could have a cigarette, Arla walked into the office space. Some of the detectives were leaving, and she caught sight of the portly figure of Jason Beauregard. He planted himself in front of her, blocking her path.

"Well, looking for cold cases was a waste of time, DCI Baker." He said the last words with an emphasis. He had never gotten over the fact that it was Arla, and not him who had got the higher rank. Arla resisted the urge to throw her coffee over his red face.

"Thinking laterally never hurt anyone, Jason." Arla made to move past him, but he stopped her.

"You're barking up the wrong tree here, Arla. If you had any sense you'd listen to me."

"I am the SIO, Jason. And right now, I dont have the time."

She stormed past him, hearing him say something under his breath. She didn't catch it, which was lucky, because she probably would've turned around and slapped him. Arla slammed shut the door of her office. Immediately, the phone on her desk started to ring, like it had been waiting for her.

It was Johnson. "Up in my office in ten," he barked and hung up.

Arla shook her head and took her wet coat off, draping it over the chair. Someone knocked on the door.

"What?!" Arla shouted.

Lisa's blonde curls appeared when she cautiously opened the door. Arla flopped down on the chair and closed her eyes. "Sorry."

"No worries, guv." Lisa came inside the room. "You OK? Heard the boss was looking for you."

"Oh that he is." She picked up her coffee and took a sip. Her eyes fell on the folder on Lisa's hand. "Got something for me?"

"Yes." Lisa beamed and Arla's heart lifted. Lisa wasn't prone to theatricals, she put her head down and got on with the job. If she was smiling, there would be good reason.

"What is it?"

"Got hold of Longworth's bank statements which were downloaded on his laptop. For the last year, in fact. A few things stand out. He was short of money. Desperately so. Looks like he had moved a lot of money last year which made him almost bankrupt."

"Moved money to where?"

"The largest transfers are to a an entity called Blue Horizon. It sounded like a company, so I did a search on the Companies House website. It has a registration number."

"Good work," Arla said, feeling calmer and more satisfied with the progress Lisa had made. "Sit down," she offered.

"No thank guv, would rather stand. Sat on my arse for three hours going through this stuff."

"Fine. What did you find out about the company?"

"Have you heard of a type of investment called EIS?"

"Given that I have no money to invest after rent, bills and food - no."

"EIS stands for Enterprise Investment Scheme. It's mainly for media companies who look to attract wealthy investors in return for tax benefits. Like, if you invest 100k into an EIS, you don't have to pay any tax on that money."

"And what return do they get on the money?"

"If the film they are investing in does well, then its bumper profits, obviously. But even if the film flops, their base amount of 100k is still protected, less 2% for admin costs."

Arla pondered. "So this is popular right? I mean rich people with money to burn can hide their money from the tax man."

"The money's locked up for 2 years, minimum. Different EIS have different rules. But you're right, it's popular. Remember that rock star who got done by the tax man for hiding money in some dodgy tax evasion scheme?"

Lisa told Arla the name. Arla nodded. "Yeah, I remember. This is the same sort of stuff, right?"

When Lisa nodded, Arla said, "So, who's behind Blue Horizon?"

"It's registered in the Bahamas. That's all I know. As it happens, companies in Bahamas are registered on our www.gov.uk website. But I need a password to access their registry."

"OK, that's going to take some time to organise. We might have to ask the NCA for help. We have no jurisdiction abroad as you know. Leave it with me," Arla sighed. One more thing for her to do. Lisa was lingering.

"Anything else?," Arla asked.

"Yes. There's another account that the victim used to send money to. 3-5 thousand at any one time, so not small amounts. This is a UK account, so I called the bank and got the name of the person."

"His son, Luke?"

"Nope," Lisa said. "It's someone called Michael Simpson. Interesting chap, he is."

Arla grinned. "You have been digging around haven't you? This gets you lots of brownie points."

"He's a hot shot film producer, it turns out. Quite well known in media circles. But from our point, it's his car that's more important."

100

Arla frowned. "His car?"

Lisa put her hands on the back of the chair and leaned over. "A silver Bentley with the private number plate of MS100."

CHAPTER 25

There was another knock on the door, then Harry entered before he was invited. "Time to go upstairs."

Arla stood, picking up her phone. "Good work, Lisa." She took the folder from Lisa's hand, just in case.

As they went up the stairs, Arla filled Harry in. He whistled. "So this Michael Simpson was getting money from Longworth, and he came to see him a few times before he died?"

"Yes, if we can believe the nosy neighbour, Mrs Parker."

"This is opening up now," Harry's voice was low and throaty, like when he was excited. She caught the glint of excitement in his boyish eyes and smiled despite herself. She felt the same way as him, and when Harry's eyes narrowed, she almost knew what he was going to say.

"Someone was expecting us at Luke's workplace. Like they knew we were coming."

Arla nodded. "It might have been Luke himself who did the vanishing act. Or could it be a decoy?"

"Distract us from searching the place? So he could escape with stuff?" Harry paused with his hand on the door handle. They had reached the top landing. "I hadn't even thought of that. What could he have in his office that's worth hiding?"

Harry swung the door open and they went through. The fifth floor had deep carpets, two tone lights on the wall and fresh paint. It even smelt different to the corridors below.

Arla said, "I wanted to surprise him by turning up. It might well have backfire. Now we need a warrant."

"Easily done. After all, if we'd caught the escape artist, he would be under arrest now."

102

Harry knocked on the door and they heard Johnson's voice. "Come in."

Arla walked in to find two men sitting opposite Johnson. She had never seen either before. Johnson stood and did the introductions.

"Detectives, this is Jeremy Melville, our new psychologist and Ken Nixon, a case officer."

The psychologist bit Arla understood. The department was trying to recruit a criminal profiler. But she didn't like the job title of case officer. She looked from the two men to Johnson.

"Case officer of what sir?"

Johnson coughed and sat down, avoiding his eyes from Arla. "From the MI5."

Arla was aghast. "Five? Intelligence agent? This is a domestic homicide sir, something we are more than capable of handling on our own."

"I know that, Arla," Johnson said, looking up at her. His features gave away the embarrassment he was feeling. No self respecting police officer wants an intelligence agency telling them what to do. But Arla knew that Johnson was looking after his new promotion. Commander Johnson. And tacitly, he was also asking Arla to fall in line, if she wanted his job in the future. With an effort, Arla contained the sense of unease that was spreading through her like wildfire.

Johnson said, "This case might be a domestic one, but it has special features that Mr Nixon can help us with."

"Special features?" Arla couldn't hide her scathing tone.

"If I can just explain, DCI Baker," Ken Nixon murmured, standing. He was a good looking man, Arla conceded. His brown hair was short, his face tanned with the hint of a stubble. Sparkling green eyes stared out over high cheekbones, and a sharp jawline.

"I'm not here to step on anyone's toes."

"The question remains if you should be here at all," Arla said and regretted it immediately. She was poor at this game of office politics. She wished she could swallow her tongue sometimes.

"DCI Baker!" Johnson's voice held a stiff reprimand.

Nixon cleared his throat. "As you know, we work closely with the Secretary of State on matters concerning national security. That can include domestic homicides." He glanced at Arla, who took a seat next to Harry.

Arla said, "The victim was a film director. Hardly a terrorist."

"I know," Nixon said smoothly. He remained unruffled which Arla liked. "But he had a lot of interests abroad, mainly in America. He was also well known to the Secretary of State personally. Which meant he was present in the minister's house at dinner parties and so on, and as a result was privy to discussions which are of a sensitive nature."

Arla said, "Was Longworth under surveillance already?"

Nixon looked surprised. "No. He was never considered a leak. But the minister has asked to take us an interest. I'm sure you can see why."

Can I hell, Arla thought to herself.

Johnson said, "So can we please have a report of what progress you have made so far, DCI Baker."

"It's only the first day of the investigation, sir. I've been to the victim's house, met the wife and then also been to his son's office. Haven't had any time to prepare a report."

"A verbal one will be fine."

CHAPTER 26

Arla didn't want to talk about an ongoing investigation in front of an MI5 officer. She knew nothing about Ken Nixon, and didn't trust him one inch. The man looked suave and dignified, and that put her even more on guard.

But she had no choice. Johnson's demeanour made that very obvious. She knew he was kissing arse, a prerequisite, Arla supposed, to rising up the ranks in the London Met. Especially if the arse belonged to a cabinet Minister.

She told them what she knew. Johnson's brows were tightly knit, a disturbed look on his face when she finished.

"So you think his son is behind all this?"

"I didn't say that," Arla said quickly. "But his behaviour is suspect. Not only does he not go to see his step mother after such a traumatic event, I know for a fact now he is deliberately avoiding us."

Nixon intervened. "As you said, he had a difficult relationship with his father. I am sure he just needs some time. It's only been a day. He could be in shock."

Arla said, "What would you do if you heard your father's been murdered, Mr Nixon? Jump out of your office window to avoid the police?"

"Now hang on minute, Arla, no one's saying that was him. Neither you nor DI Mehta identified him, did you?" Johnson barked.

"No," Arla said. "But what happened at the office was odd, you must admit."

Nixon turned to the Jeremy Melville, the psychologist. "Shock can make people act strangely, can it not?"

Melville shrugged his shoulders. He was tall and thin, with long hair at his shoulders, and glasses. With his frayed Doc Marten black boots and corduroy jeans, he looked like a nerd who was somewhat worried he was in a police station. His voice however, was not hesitant at all.

"I'm afraid I cannot comment on a suspect without seeing a taped interview or speaking to them first."

"But in your opinion-

"My opinion is irrelevant in this case," Melville said quietly but firmly. He looked at Johnson. "I have not even been briefed in this case."

Arla liked the man immediately. He wasn't flash, but neither was he a pushover. But she wasn't worried about Melville. It was Nixon that concerned her.

Arla leaned forward, elbows resting on her thighs. She addressed Nixon. "Why are you so keen on protecting Luke Longworth? Is there something I should know?"

Nixon stopped, and exchanged a quick glance with Johnson. In that split second, Arla knew. They were hiding something, and it was the reason why Nixon was here.

She frowned. Luke Longworth didn't have a police record. Not till he was 12 years old anyway. But individuals could, in exceptional circumstances, apply for deletion of records from the Police National Computer or PNC.

And if that person happened to be the son of a minister's close friend?

Johnson said, "No one is trying to protect anyone here, Arla. Our job is to catch the person who committed this crime, and everyone is open to suspicion right now. Speaking of which, what did you say about Michael Simpson?"

Arla shook her head slowly. Harry leaned forward and his face was averted from Johnson. She saw the warning flash in Harry's eyes and the NO his lips formed silently.

Arla checked herself. Johnson's sudden change of topic made her angry, and she was about to retort. She nodded at Harry, who moved back in his seat. He cleared his throat.

"We are keeping all avenues open, sir." Harry glanced at Johnson, then at Nixon. "And Simpson has just come to our attention, thanks to the hard work of our colleagues. We will follow up on him, but if you know anything about Luke Longworth, then it will help our investigation."

Harry left it at that, and a silenced formed in the vacuum. Arla breathed deeply, forcing herself to stay calm. Inside, anger roiled like a stormy ocean. Johnson was playing his usual politics, saving his face, obeying his masters. Arla wanted to lash out, get to the truth. That was her way. Headstrong, emotional, always direct.

And always in trouble.

Johnson said, "There is no other information about the suspects, DI Mehta. And DCI Baker." Arla looked up as her name was mentioned pointedly.

"I am sure the issue with Luke Longworth will get sorted out by tomorrow when he's had a chance to sleep on it. You have a tangible opening with the vicitim's bank statements and the new lead, what's his name…

"Michael Simpson," Harry said.

"Proceed in that direction. And keep me updated." The tone of Johnson's voice meant they were dismissed.

Arla rose. One last time, she locked eyes with Johnson. He met her gaze, then looked away. Melville, the psychologist rose and came towards them.

"I believe you need me to do some profiling for you?"

"Yes," Arla said tonelessly. She glared at Nixon who smiled back at her. With Harry and Melville in tow, she turned and left the room.

CHAPTER 27

Arla walked into her office and shut the door. She was fuming.

"Fuck!" she shouted, and kicked the chair. It skidded on the floor and banged against the table. She slammed one fist against another.

Harry opened the door and stepped in. He locked the door and in two strides reached out to grab her hand. Arla tried to wriggle free but his grip was like iron.

"Calm down," he whispered. "What did you expect?"

"I don't know!"

Even Harry's voice was weary. "There's always an angle in these cases, Arla. You know that. That's why Johnson's had ants in his pants from day one."

Arla didn't reply. She jerked her hand free, opened the door and strode out. Heads lifted as she stalked out of the open plan office.

She went out the back entrance and into the car park. Fleet cars lined the bays. Needle like council apartment blocks pushed up into the air around her. She took a deep breath, it smelt of diesel and damp, inner city London's fetid lungs exhaling its noxious fumes. The grey clouds hung lower today, hovering just above the rooftops, close enough to touch. Arla thought about the brown lego shapes of houses stretching all over this city of teeming millions, millions of lies and heartbreaks, tarnished dreams mingling with the diesel fumes and her breath.

And she was a part of it, her own fractal, disjointed life, walking among these lost souls, each in their own bubble of pain and rejection. She thought of her dad, and how both of them repulsed each other, despite having no other family.

Briefly, for no reason, she saw Nicole's face. Happy, smiling in the sunshine laughter two decades ago. And suddenly she was on the verge of tears. Arla blinked and stepped out into the hard black tarmac of the parking lot. She shook her head, wishing of all things, for a cigarette.

A black BMW, similar to what Harry drove, came in through the barrier. A woman and a man, both CID Inspectors, came out of the car. Arla knew them both and she returned their greeting. When she was alone, Arla had this overwhelming urge to walk away. To simply get across the barrier and keep walking till she got lost in this crappy city's maze of loneliness.

Footsteps sounded behind her. She turned to see Harry walking towards her. He stopped, keeping a safe distance, aware of the space, invisible yet congealed, dense, that lay between them. Arla couldn't explain it either. She didn't want this distance, but like the rain, it was suddenly there.

"They're waiting for you inside. The video's ready." Harry's voice was quiet.

They stared at each other for a while, saying nothing. Then Arla nodded. "I'm coming."

Harry's face was chiselled, inscrutable. But he took a step forward, if only to lower his voice. "Arla, just let it go."

"It's not what you think, Harry." She shook her head. "Just leave me alone. Tell the others I'm coming."

Harry sighed and nodded. Something chipped off a corner of her heart as she saw him turn and walk back, his head almost brushing the top of the double doors.

She didn't tarry long. It was cold and the chill was settling into her bones. When she got back into the office, Melville and the others were sitting around Lisa's desk.

Lisa said, "The recording of you and Harry interviewing Cherie Longworth." She choose the camera that showed only Cherie, and zoomed in. They watched in silence for a while.

Rob went to get some coffee. He returned with a tray and Arla clutched her mug gratefully. This wasn't from the vending machine, this was Rob's own stash from the kitchen. Arla breathed in the fumes deeply.

When they finished, Melville leaned back and scratched his beard. "Do you know the facial muscle that's hardest to hide if you're lying?"

"The neck muscles," Harry said.

"That's a big group, but yes. Problem is many women can hide their neck effectively with long hair. So several studies were conducted, from videos like these, and one muscle was the standout."

Melville paused, to make sure he had a captive audience. Then he lifted his right index finger and pointed to between his eyebrows. "The botox muscle."

"What?" Lisa frowned.

"Several muscles of the face get very low dose botulinum toxin or botox injections. But the frown line muscle gets the highest dose. It's called the glabellar and is actually a thick, tough muscle. Hence we get that "11" line between our brows after decades of frowning."

Arla said, "So what do you see in the video?"

"She has a botox smooth forehead. I mean, I have no ways of knowing of course, if she had botox injections or note. But having stared at faces for so many years, it's obvious to me."

"And that would be hiding what exactly?"

"Well, even if she was lying, the glabellar would be contracting ever so slightly. Most liars can be exposed that way. Eeven poker players cannot hide involuntary movements, no matter how hard they try."

Harry yawned. "That's fascinating, but where does it leave us?"

"In her case? It's clear she's uncomfortable. She breaks eye contact, shifts in her seat, and her legs move below the desk. So do her shoulders."

Arla said, "But that makes sense. There was a lot she hadn't told us, and it came out when we visited her at home. She told us all about her step son, and her husband's ex wife."

Melville said, "Correct. She was hiding information, which is not the same as lying. Frankly, I don't believe she was lying. I see genuine grief and shock in her face. I also expect her to divulge more information if you go to see her again. She feels safer in her home environment."

Arla looked at Harry, who nodded. Putting a security detail outside Cherie's house was the right idea.

There was a commotion behind them. Andy Jackson barged his way past several surprised detectives. His face was red and he was breathing heavily. He addressed Arla.

"Guv, I've just had a report from Darren at the crime scene. Mrs Longworth has just been burgled. Someone broke in and stole some of her husband's stuff."

CHAPTER 28

Times like these, Arla wished she could call in the helicopter. But Harry had the siren on, and the traffic parted for him like he was prophet standing in front of the Red Sea with a tablet in his hand.

It was pitch black dark now, and although the rain had relented, the cold was biting. Bellevue Avenue wasn't far, and they reached within fifteen minutes. The media vans were lying in wait, and Arla could make out their vague shapes parked opposite the house. As soon as their car was spotted, flashlights strobed the air. Photographers had this knack of identifying an unmarked CID car.

Arla was up the steps first and rapped on the heavy door. The drawn, pale face of Cherie Longworth opened it after she had verified their identity. The media was going crazy behind them now, flashes lighting up the houses like lightning. Cherie stood to one side as Arla stepped in quickly.

"I'll catch up with Darren," Harry indicated the squad car on the kerb, with the uniformed constable leaning against it. He looked a little embarrassed, Arla thought, that the burglary had happened on his watch. Harry would reassure him, she knew.

"OK," she nodded. Cherie shut the door and walked down the hallway, then up the stairs.

Arla said, "I'm sorry about this. It didn't come from us, I promise you."

"Don't worry," Cherie said. "It had to happen sooner or later. I'm not a total stranger to camera's you see."

"Sure, but this is different. These guys will throw questions at you, follow you around. The key thing is not rise to the bait."

"I know."

"The bathroom window was open," Cherie explained, "And he got in through there. I had been for some shopping. When I came upstairs, I could feel a draught. It was coming from the bathroom

112

window. I must have left it open, which was silly of me. And then I saw the bedroom."

"Your bedroom?"

"Not the master one. David had a bedroom next to the study and it has a connecting door. He slept in there sometimes when he came home late."

Cherie opened the bathroom door. The window at the back was large enough for a man to crawl through. It was open and through it Arla could see the grass of the well mown lawn, lit up by garden lights. Beyond it, lights glowed in another row of mansions.

"There's a path at the back that cuts between the next block of houses," Cherie said.

Arla walked over and checked the window sill. The scratch marks on the paint were clear, and she knew there would be others visible to SOCO. She fumed inside. It was just damning that this happened so soon, and while they had a unit outside. The burglar, whoever he was, must have known about the security and hence chose the back.

Arla looked at the bathroom floor and saw the footprints. She knelt. Two full size boot prints were visible and that was good. Would it match the partial print that had kicked the front door open?

She hoped so.

Arla stood and said, "Show me the study please. Guess I missed the connecting door."

Cherie made a weak effort at a smile and failed. "It's meant to be a concealed door, same colour as the walls and no handles. It pushes open." She walked to the study and they entered.

The room looked very different now. Bright light flooded in from the tall Georgian windows. The furniture remained the same, but the room looked bigger and strangely bare. It had been swept clean by SOC, Arla knew that. But she suspected Cherie had it cleaned after that herself. She decided to ask Cherie.

The woman nodded. "It just felt..dirty, you know?" She shivered. "I got a cleaning company and literally sterilised it." Cherie moved to the wall next to the desk and her hand pressed against a light switch. A panel next to the light swun open, revealing the door.

They went inside the bedroom, which was of similar size to the study. A double bed was in the middle, with two large bedside tables, and another desk at the end. All the drawers were open and papers lay strewn across the floor. The bedsheets and even mattress were pulled up. The carpet was lifted from the corners, and one section was cut to roll it down the middle.

"Jesus," Arla said. She looked at Cherie, who was leaning against the wall. She was shaking and tears glistened in her eyes. Arla went to her swiftly. She led her out to the corridor.

"Let's go downstairs and talk," Arla said. Cherie sniffed and dabbed at her eyes, averting her face from Arla.

In the kitchen, Arla sat her down and offered to make a drink. Cherie pointed to where the fridge was, and the coffee. Arla took the milk out while the coffee beans were ground. When it was done, she brought the two cups to the counter.

"Thanks," Cherie said.

Arla took a sip of the coffee. "Scene of crime will take a closer look upstairs. But was there anything missing?"

Cherie took her time. "David used to keep a diary. In fact, he had several diaries from when he was younger. All of them are missing."

"You know where he kept them?"

"Yes, he made no secret of it. A lot of them were journals that he would incorporate into his memoirs one day, he said. I was thinking of doing that now, you know. He had a lot to leave behind, in creative terms."

"I get that," Arla said. "But I don't understand what a burglar would want with them. Is there anything else missing?"

Cherie shook her head. Arla asked, "If this burglar was after David's personal possessions, who do you think it might be?"

Cherie stared at Arla, and Arla knew they were both thinking of the same answer. She raised her eyebrows and Cherie looked back at her coffee.

"It's possible that Luke did this. I remember once when they had an argument."

"About what?"

"Luke wanted to read David's journals. David refused, naturally. This happened in his study and the door was closed. I could hear loud voices and then Luke came out, shouting."

"What was he saying?"

"Something about David not hiding it. I dont know what he meant. When I asked David he didn't want to talk about it."

"When did this happen?"

"Almost a year ago. I had just moved in. Luke never visited after that."

A thought struck Arla, and she wondered if Harry had already asked this. "Did Luke have keys to the house?"

"No. I did ask David." A shadow passed over Cherie's face. She blinked several times. "You don't think it was Luke who…"

"At this stage the investigation is wide open. It's too early to cast blame on anyone. But Luke is a person of interest in the investigation, and we do want to speak to him without delay. Has he been in touch?"

"He sent me that text saying he would come over. That's it."

Arla changed the topic. "Do you know someone called Michael Simpson?"

She hadn't expected the look of sudden anger that swept across Cherie's striking features.

CHAPTER 29

"Mike Simpson?" Cherie hissed, her cheeks turning crimson, for the first time. Her brows were knotted together. "The Mike Simpson that David knew? How do you know about *him*?"

Her sudden animation caught Arla off guard. "You don't like him?"

Cherie shook her head, looking away from Arla. She looked like she had just swallowed something vile. "Are we talking about the same Mike Simpson here? The film producer."

Arla nodded. "I think so. A lot of money was transferred from your husband's account to Mr Simpsons."

Anger was replaced by shock. Cherie's mouth fell open. "Really?"

"You didn't know about this?"

"I wasn't privy to David's accounts. I mean, we had a joint account, of course. But I know he kept he had a separate bank account as well."

"I see," Arla said slowly. "From his laptop we located a UK bank account. In addition he had an account with you?"

"That's right."

Which sounded normal to Arla. But she wondered how many accounts David had.

"Simpson came to visit David in the last two weeks, right?"

"Yes," Cherie nodded. "They met occasionally as they worked on projects together." She looked at up at Arla. "How did you know that he was here in the last 2 weeks?"

"One of your neighbours."

"Bet you it was Mrs Parker. Old gossip bag." Cherie took a sip of her coffee. Arla tried to gauge her attitude. The manner in which

Cherie had reacted when she mentioned Mike Simpson's name was more than a passing annoyance.

"Why do you hate Simpson?" Arla asked simply. She was aware that Cherie was still a suspect, like everyone else. She was being informal with her for the time being, but soon she might have to take her back to the station. But Melville's words hung around in Arla's mind like smoke. Cherie would talk more in an atmosphere she was comfortable in, like her home.

Cherie grimaced ruefully. "I guess I made that obvious, didn't I?"

Arla waited. Cherie sighed. "He was just...smarmy. Creepy. He tried to come on to me, more than once. I told David about it the last time he was here. I said I didn't want him back in the house."

"What did he do?"

Cherie clamped down on her jaws, hard. "It's what men like Simpson are used to doing. Any woman who's an actress or used to be one, in my case, is fair game to them."

A cold numbness spread in Arla's veins. "Tell me what he did," she said very quietly.

A fire blazed in Cherie's eyes, but her lips trembled. "Oh, I'm not some 20 year old looking for a role to star in, you know? Not easy to impress any more. But that bastard, he...." She swallowed heavily. "To cut a long story short, he was waiting for me one night he came here. David was in his study. I came out of the loo downstairs and got the shock of my life. He was right outside. He literally pushed me inside and shut the door. Forced me against the wall. Said David owed him money, and he would take it...." her voice trailed off, and a tear escaped her eye, rolling down her cheek.

Arla spoke through clenched teeth. "Why didn't you report this?"

Cherie blew her nose and collected herself. "I told David. He said that was it, he wasn't doing business with him anymore. He actually rang Mike up to tell him. I was there."

"Why did David owe him money? You seemed surprised when I said money was transferred from David's account to Simpson's."

"David denied it. Said he had paid him back ages ago. He said Mike was making it all up." Cherie looked at Arla and frowned. "I'm confused now. What's going on?"

"I don't know," Arla said. "But it's time we paid Mr Simpson a visit."

Cherie collected the cups and plates and put them in the sink. Arla asked, "Do you know of a company called Blue Horizon? It appeared David was sending cash there as well."

Cherie turned around slowly and wiped her hands on a tea towel. "No, I didn't." Her face was drawn and pale again. She looked into the distance and then focused on Arla. "I don't understand any of this. What was David doing with his money?"

CHAPTER 30

There was a noise at the door and Harry poked his head in. His lips were set tight.

"Darren and the others didn't see anything," he said. His eyes flicked from Arla to Cherie. "One of the reporter's came up to me, asking for a statement." His eyes met Arla's and she knew from his face that he said nothing to them.

Harry addressed Cherie. "They'll be far less polite to you. Be ready for insults, crude remarks, anything. Just don't rise to it."

"Can't be worse than the film directors I've worked with in the past," Cherie said.

The front doorbell went and Harry answered it. Arla heard the voice of Parmentier, asking why they weren't doing a proper job. It was meant in jest, but Cherie clearly heard it. Arla bustled outside.

"Can you keep your voices down please?" She walked up to Parmentier. "For the record, the burglar came in through the back. We can't keep a watch everywhere. When you go upstairs, in the bathroom, there is a perfect set of boot prints. I want to see if there is a match with the ones from the front door."

Parmentier rolled his eyes. "Gosh, I've been told."

Harry's lips twitched,but she could see it didn't touch his eyes. He looked at her carefully, trying to gauge her mood. Arla had other things on her mind. She suddenly remembered something. She turned to Harry.

"When we went to Luke's house, do you remember if we saw any boot prints by the front door?"

Harry fixed her with a gaze. "Oh, I remember going there alright."

Despite the stiffness of their encounter in the car park, Arla felt her cheeks beginning to burn, and her eyes widened. But she couldn't look away from his melting chestnut eyes, suddenly dancing with mischief. She melted a little and had to admit, it was when he tempted her like this that she enjoyed it the most. But she would never admit that to him, and she still felt awkward. It was also too risky in front of Parmentier.

She swallowed and took a step back, pausing to flick a strand of hair away. "I would like to check the boot prints of Luke against what we have here. Can you sort that out, DI Mehta?"

His eyes continued to burn into hers. Arla looked away finally, sneaking a look at Parmentier. To her relief, he was half turned as one of the SOCO's walked in through the door.

Harry said, "Of course I can, guv. Anything for you." He added the last sentence in a lower voice.

Arla turned away to head back for the kitchen. Harry caught up with her in two swift strides.

"Did the wife see the burglar's face?"

Arla said, "No. He entered and left through the window at the back. Left one bedroom a mess though." She told Harry what he had stolen. He creased his brows.

"Odd thing to take, no? Personal diaries?"

"I know. Chances of it being the killer is remote as surely he would've taken what he wanted the first time round."

Harry said, "Not sure. The first time he came to kill. He made the effort to stage his sick show. He could have forgotten, or not known that this bedroom existed."

Arla appraised this slowly. Harry was a good cop, and she knew when to trust his instincts. Something told her he might have a point here.

Harry said, "You know the drill, guv. Most murders are committed by someone the victim knew well. This is personal, right? Otherwise why come back for the diaries? Must be the same person, or they work as a team."

They were speaking in low voices by the kitchen door. Arla dropped his voice a shade lower. "Have you asked Cherie about how she knows the Secretary of State so well?"

Another good point, Arla thought. She told Harry quickly about Mike Simpson. Then they opened the kitchen door and walked inside. Cherie wasnt at the counter, and they found her at the opposite end of the gigantic kitchen, stacking cushions on the sofa. She turned when she heard them approach. Arla asked her about James Fraser, the secretary of state.

"Jamie? Oh, he used to come every now and then." Her face brightened. "David and him were close. They knew each other from way back, from university." Her look became anxious. "He's not in any trouble over this, is he? I mean, I'm sorry I had to drag him into this, but Luke wasn't answering his phone and I didn't know who else to call."

Arla asked, " Did Luke know Mr. Fraser?"

Cherie frowned, then her face cleared. "Yes they did. How well, I don't know. But David did mention that Jamie knew Luke from when he was a child."

"Thanks. Will you please let us know if you think of anything else?" Arla took out her card, then flipped it over and wrote her number down on the back.

"This is my personal number." She gave the card to Cherie, who took it. "Call me if you need help with anything."

Cherie's expression made it clear she appreciated the gesture. Arla and Harry left Parmentier and his team upstairs, and said goodbye to Cherie. Harry went upstairs to have a word with one of the SOCO's to get a forensic team to Luke's house, to check for boot prints.

Arla opened the front door and as soon as she stepped outside, the cameras began to click. Flashlights popped in the darkness, following her as she stepped down the stairs. They were gathered like a pack of hound dogs at the police tape barrier. Three uniform officers stood at regular intervals, ensuring none of them broke through.

"Is it a crime of passion?" One of them called out.

"Was he gay?" another hollered.

The media scrum pressed forward as she got nearer to the car. Harry ran ahead, arms spread out. He held the door open for Arla as she slipped inside. Flashbulbs popped against the glass and Arla bent her neck, shielding her face with a hand. Harry reversed with a growl of the engine, then blared his horn as the BMW took off, tires squeaking. Reporters ran for cover as the car bore down on them.

"Bloody vermin," Harry breathed as he stopped at the traffic lights.

CHAPTER 31

Jonty was sitting against the trunk of a stout oak, perched a few meters above ground. He could feel the rough bark against his back, but it felt solid, comforting. Jonty liked climbed trees. It allowed him to watch people who passed all around him in blissful ignorance. People fascinated Jonty, mainly because he didn't understand why they got so worked up over things. Why they sometimes argued on the streets and honked their horns in road rage. Jonty never got angry. He never lost control.

He could see through a gap in the leaves, the house in Bellevue Avenue he now knew well. The mask was on his head, ready to be pulled down if necessary. The binoculars rested on his eyes, and he leaned forward slightly as the door opened and the female police inspector came out, followed by the lanky, wide shouldered male officer. The man stayed at the porch briefly, looking around him. Jonty could swear he looked directly at him for a few seconds.

"You can look, but you can't see me," he whispered, in tense excitement.

The binoculars moved down to the female officer. Her dark shoulder length hair was bobbing up and down as she moved quickly towards the car. The man overtook her, moving the reporters away. Flashlight lit up the female officer's face. Jonty caught his breath. She had a sharp nose, full lips and a strong chin. She looked like someone Jonty had known in a previous life.

She looked so close. He could imagine her musky odour, a flowery, lilac smell maybe? Or would it be rosewood, the lingering smell inside that house? God, he felt he could reach out and touch her. His breath came in gasps.

The man slammed the door shut and the car took off as reporters flashed their cameras. Jonty memorised the registration number. He knew it was going to Clapham Police Station. He removed the binoculars and watched as the uniform officers herded the cameramen back. Some returned to their parked vans.

The police hadn't given a statement as yet, but he always knew the Clapham station would be involved. Jonty didn't know the name of the female officer though. He slipped off the tree and landed on the ground with a soft jump. He wasn't wearing his ski gear today, save the mask. His trekking shoes squelched mud as he walked on the grass. His head moved around, eyes searching in the dark for shadows. It amazed him the police hadn't searched this part of the Common yet, looking for clues. Not that he left any. That would be losing control.

Jonty came up to the tarmac path that skirted the edge of the Common. There was two meters of bush and then the sidewalk, lit up by the yellow orange halogen streetlights. He watched for two minutes. The media vans were on the kerb, and he could see two reporters out, smoking. A man and a woman. The woman said something and the man laughed.

Jonty moved past them. He came to another van, with a satellite dish on top. A solitary man was standing outside. He bid his time, then came out on the sidewalk several meters behind the reporter. Jonty started to whistle loudly. The reporter turned his head abruptly, watching Jonty as he came out of the darkness.

Jonty knew his face was visible in the street lights, but he didn't care. "Hi there," he said, raising his hand in greeting. He stopped in front of the man.

"Terrible thing to happen here, isn't it? Such a nice man as well."

The reporter looked at him askance. "Do you live around here?"

Jonty paused for a second. "Yes, just around the corner."

"Oh right." The reporter was instantly interested. A salacious gleam came into his eyes. "Did you know them by any chance?"

"Who, David and Cherie? Yes, seen them around a few time."

The reporter came forward. "Oh I see. What are they like?"

"Very friendly, nice people. It was a tragedy this, though. Are the police any close to finding who did this?"

"I dont know. But-

"What's the police officer's name? The woman, she seemed to be in charge."

"DCI Arla Baker," the man said impatiently. "What can you tell me about-

Jonty smiled and waved at the man. "Sorry, got to go."

CHAPTER 32

Arla craned her neck back. She was exhausted. It had been a long day, and she wanted nothing more than a glass of wine. She hadn't drunk for 2 weeks, and felt better for it. Her problem was stopping after one glass. Only four glasses in a bottle of wine. Easily done, apart from the next morning's headache and regret. Harry, like most male cops, was a big drinker. And Arla had to admit, the peer pressure made most female cops drink as well, and up the banter in the pubs after shift. It was a slippery slope.

She said, "Luke sent her a text this morning, saying he would be in touch. I've got the number."

"Excellent. We can track it."

"I have a feeling he's either stopped using the phone now or destroyed the SIM. But still worth a try."

It was close to 7pm by the time they got back. Arla expected the team to have dispersed, but was pleasantly surprised to see Lisa and Rob, with Rita Patel, a Detective Sergeant who had recently joined the force from up North, and Larry Gomez, a tall, black man who was the same rank as Rita. Next to them, Rupert the new DC was also present.

"Working hard I see," Arla said.

Lisa yawned and stretched her arms above her head. "You did say to get a move on, guv."

Arla glanced at her watch. "Look, you guys have to be here early tomorrow. Take a break tonight."

Rita spoke up in her strong Yorkshire accent. She was petite, with shoulder length black hair, and a pretty face. "Feels like we're getting somewhere though. We got new stuff to feed back to you, don't we?"

Lisa nodded. Arla said to Rupert, "Are you guys hungry?" All the head nodded almost in unison.

"Rupert, would you mind ordering some pizza? Ask the front desk to put it on my tab."

"Sure guv." Rupert got up and headed out to the corridor. Arla sat down at Lisa's table and pulled up a chair, then another one to put her feet up.

Harry sat behind Lisa, looking at her screen. "Where are those CCTV images from?"

"The Zizzi restaurant on Dulwich High Street." Lisa said.

Arla hunched forward. Lisa pointed at the screen, which was divided into four boxes, each showing a black and white image, with the time and date in the top right corner.

"That's Cherie Longworth, right?" Lisa asked.

Arla squinted, then nodded. "have you got another image?"

Lisa clicked on the keyboard, and this time it was clearer. Two women were coming out from the restaurant, and their faces were visible. The woman on the right was Cherie.

"That's her alright. What time stamp does this have?"

"23.40."

"So she was leaving then. Where does she go?"

Lisa clicked through several more images, which showed the two women walking down the quiet High Street, their backs to the camera. She switched to a camera that faced them, and stopped at an image that showed Cherie getting into a BMW convertible with the roof up.

Arla checked the time stamp. "23.47. It would have taken her about fifteen minutes to drive back home at that time of the night. So she was speaking the truth."

She glanced at Lisa. "Did we follow her down?"

Lisa gestured towards Rita. "She did that."

Rita got up from her table and came around holding a laptop. She put it on Lisa's desk and all of them gathered around it.

Cherie's red BMW was visible on Clapham High Street as she crossed it, heading down to the common.

Arla said, "OK, that's her whereabouts. Did we speak to the friend, Jill, and the ex-husband?"

Rita said, "I did guv. Went over to the friend, Jill Hunter's house. Jill backs up the story. She's in the middle of a messy divorce. One daughter doing her A levels. She's fighting the husband to stop selling the house. Although they had a dinner date, they spent till about 21.00 at her home. The daughter was also there, and I spoke to her, so it's watertight."

"Cherie's ex-husband?"

Rob spoke up. "I called Guy Percival. He heard it on the news. Sounded quite shocked, really. Yes, Cherie was definitely his wife. He knew her maiden name of Ryleigh, and her DOB, down to the mole on her left forehead, her identifying mark. They didn't have children, as Cherie said."

"Where is the husband now?"

"Lives in Salford near Manchester, where he works for the BBC. He's got a new girlfriend. I checked into him. No records on the PNC."

Arla leaned back on her chair. "So the wife is clear, for now. She has no record whatsoever, right?"

Lisa spoke. "Nope. Squeaky clean."

There was a knock on the door, which sounded loud in the empty office. Rupert went to open the door and returned with a stack of pizza boxes. Harry helped him unload them on a table. Rob got paper plates and cups from the kitchen and for a while no one spoke as they munched on pizza. Arla hadn't realised how famished she was. She polished off a half slice of veggie pizza, feeling a twinge of guilt at all the carb she was stuffing herself with.

She wiped her mouth with a tissue and drank some diet coke. "OK. Those wires that were cut from the pole. The cable ones - did we get any prints from the pole?"

"No," Larry said, bottom perched on a desk, sitting straight. Arla didn't know him well, having dealt with him only once before. He had joined the Clapham station last year.

"And Sky gave some feedback. They had no repairs planned, so it wasn't a botched job on their part. They have filed a case with us for criminal damage."

Harry said, "So it was a calculated move to stop the street from getting internet or phone access."

Rita said, "He didn't want a signal in there while he was active."

Arla asked Lisa, "Any progress on this Bahamas company, Blue Horizon?"

"Nope, still searching." Lisa clicked her fingers. "But I got something else though. Almost forgot."

She pulled out a folder from one of her desk drawers and handed it to Arla. "David Longworth's mobile phone log. Still waiting for the voice data. You know how phone companies are."

Arla grabbed the folder. "Looks like I have my homework for tonight." It was past 20.00. Arla stifled a yawn. It was only the first full day of the investigation and she was knackered.

She rose to her feet, avoiding Harry's eyes. "No further word from Banerji?"

The team shook their heads.

"We need a fix on Luke Longworth's phone number," Arla said. "I take it he hasn't been in touch?!"

"Nope," Lisa said.

"This is priority now. Get the location and if he hasn't shown up tomorrow morning, I'm getting a warrant to search his house."

Arla put her coat on and turned. "See you all in the morning."

CHAPTER 33

Arla put the folder in her office, locked the door and waved goodbye. The others were leaving too. All of them drove, Arla was the only one who took the tube back home. Mainly because it was five easy stops, and the line dropped her off near her doorstep.

"Good night guv," John Sandford, the tall black desk duty sergeant said.

"Have a good one John."

Arla wrapped the scarf around her neck and pulled the hoodie of her coat over her head. The cold was biting but at least it was dry. Lights gleamed in the windows of the council block apartments that surrounded the station. Arla walked quickly, her heels clicking in the dark. The street was almost deserted. It did give her creep sometimes, but she wanted the walk to clear her head.

Harry didn't like her wandering around alone. She got that, and found his protectiveness sweet. At the thought of him, a knife twisted inside her. Where was it going? Nowhere it seemed. Like every other relationship in her life. Men and her were like ships in a stormy night. She might see their lights, but they stayed out of reach. Maybe it was her. Maybe it was them. Whatever. It didn't surprise her no relation lasted long enough for it to become meaningful.

She lost Nicole when she was twelve. Her mother at birth. A father she never forgave, and hardly ever saw.

Why would it be any different with a random man?

She couldn't deny the instant connection she had felt with Harry when he had first joined the station, five years ago now. Her heartbeat surged every time he looked at her with those huge brown eyes. So perfectly shaped. A man shouldn't have eyes so pretty. When he spoke, the angle of his jaw, the fullness of his lips commanded her attention, and she had to make a conscious effort to listen to what he was saying.

And from day one, she thought he felt the same about her. It was that passing look, the transient lingering, the feel of his eyes on her back. Like all female police detectives, she took good care to dress unflatteringly. It was only today she wore heels, because both her flats had a split in the right sole. But she also took care of herself with running, swimming and yoga, whenever she could. No, she didn't imagine the look in Harry's eyes, the first time they met. She had never felt that way about any other man.

And now…

A pressure caught at her throat then, and the power of it was almost a physical wave, stopping her in her tracks. It was the denial of hope, when it came to her broken heart. Did she even dare let a candle burn for it? Could she?

Emotion strangled her chest, settling like a black weight in her body. Harry wouldn't be any different, would he? Like Nicole, her mother and her dad, he would go away too, one day. When he realised what she was really like, he would. Her heart was made of iron, not soft flesh.

It was so easy now. When she was with him, alone, it felt like the sun was on her face. She was floating down a summer lake in a boat, Harry rowing. Her fingertips tracing the cool water. It seemed nothing bad would happen. The skies would be blue forever.

But she knew life wasn't like that. And she didn't understand people who chased happiness like it was a dream, a chimera that would magically transform their wintry, grey days to one of perpetual sunlight and laughter. Because Arla had never had the courage for a dream like that. For her, life would always be a scarred, ruinous battlefield, where grief always won.

And yet, the happiness she felt with Harry was unlike anything she had experienced before.

Arla stopped. The wrought iron railing of a house was next to her and she leaned against it. A sob erupted deep inside her, not of tears, but of bitterness, confusion. It came out like a guttural, choking sound, the same choke hold with which she strangled her happiness before it disappointed her yet again.

This was why she never showed her heart to anyone. Get her guard down. But with Harry it was like second nature. It was like seeing with a new pair of eyes. Into a new world. A world where….what? Anything was possible?

Arla leaned forward, wishing she could slide down and sit on the pavement. She felt strength seeping from her limbs, fading out into the merciless cold of the ionic, dark night.

Too late, she heard the footsteps. Approaching fast. Arla wiped her face and stood up quickly. She was foolish to have these thoughts. And even more stupid on these streets, where muggings were common.

A fearsome sight greeted her eyes. A big figure was swooping down on her, arms outstretched like the wings of a condor.

CHAPTER 34

Arla flinched, lowering her head and spinning backwards. Her right hand dived inside her handbag to get hold of the mace spray.

But she was too late. The figure was over her now, and she felt his hands descend upon her, grabbing her by the shoulder. Arla kicked, hitting the shin bone of her attacker. He yelped and went down.

"Arla, stop!"

She did, thunderstruck. She knew that voice all too well. He was on one knee, rubbing the shin of his left leg. He turned his face up, frowning. Arla knelt by him.

"Harry, I'm so sorry."

Harry grunted and stood, hobbling on one foot before testing them both gingerly. He sighed. "Guess it's my fault for creeping up on you like that. I saw you practically sliding to the ground though."

"You followed me?"

He hesitated. In the hazy glow of the streetlight, his eyes retained their glint. "I was going home but then….I guess I just wanted to speak to you about today."

Arla could read the intensity in his expression and it sparked fear inside her. Harry wasn't going to let go of this easily.

"About what?" she asked, feeling foolish even as she did so. Harry didn't speak for several seconds.

Arla looked away. "I'm tired Harry, I need to go home." It was the truth. She glanced at him, noting the fixed way his eyes bore into hers. "I'm going. Bye."

She started to walk, and felt him behind her. They walked along in silence for a while, but Arla stopped after a while, feeling the pressure.

"What do you want, Harry?"

"Just to walk you home. Nothing else."

Moments like these she realised what he meant to her. Because he wasn't lying. She could tell from the way the tension had gone from his shoulders, and the slightly sheepish smirk on his lips. He only did that, looking like a big buffoon of an overgrown boy, when he was being honest. Something fluttered inside her heart, like a butterfly rapping its wings against a closed door.

He just wanted to be there. Why?

She knew why, and her heart spoke the answer to her in a voice like whispering spring rain.

Because you want him to.

She couldn't deny it. She didn't have any answers for him and truth be told, didn't want to speak to him either. She had nothing to explain to anyone. In the end, no one can explain what lies deepest in our souls, what makes us what we are. Words do not suffice. But she knew she felt better just having him here.

Arla swallowed hard, looking at the ground. She avoided his eyes, nodded and resumed walking. Harry walked alongside, not saying a word, but the silence wasn't a solid cloud between them anymore, it was comfortable.

They got to the twinkling lights and shining bars of Clapham High Street, dodged the revellers and boarded the tube. She caught his eyes several times on the train, standing next to one another. Harry always had to bend his neck on the tube, and she used to joke it made him look like a unicorn in a suit. She remembered those days and smiled. He smiled back, as if he knew what she was thinking.

They reached the door of her ground floor apartment. Arla took her keys out and bit her lower lip. Harry was hanging back. She knew he wouldn't ask to come in.

She turned around. His face was in the dark shadow of the streetlamp behind him. Arla went to say something, but her voice faltered.

"Harry, I…"

He stood there, unmoving, but she could feel the tension in him again. He was rigid, straight, and his chest rose and fell with deep breaths.

"I…." *Damn it woman, speak,* she admonished herself.

Harry moved forward like the wind that comes with a thunderstorm. He swept her up in his arms and she felt his cool lips press down on her. She felt electric sparks shoot down her spine and she opened her mouth, giving in to the sensation. Her feet felt like they were off the ground, floating.

When they surfaced for air, Harry lowered his arms slowly. They stared at each other for a while, a dark, silent promise passing between them. Arla had never known what it was like to stare at a man till she met Harry. She could do it for ages, seeing every emotion reflected in his curious, open gaze. His hands came up to cup her face. He bent down to kiss again, and it was more gentle now, softer, exploring.

He let go finally, then stepped back. Arla was glad the wall was right behind her, because she wasn't sure her knees would remain steady.

His face was half lit now, the other lost in shadows. "I am here, Arla." His voice was gruff, like he had to claw it up from deep inside. "If you need me."

He turned and left. She watched till he walked to the end of the street, not looking back once. He turned left for the tube station, and she couldn't see him anymore.

CHAPTER 35

17 years ago

The boy was terrified. He could hear his stepfather on the rampage outside. The boy knew he was drunk and looking for the slightest excuse to give him a beating. The boy was tired of the beatings. It would start with a cuff around the head and when he told him to stop, progress to the leather belt. His wife tried to stop him, but she was drunk half the time as well.

"Who left the TV on?" the man shouted, his voice booming against the walls of the narrow terraced house.

There was a crashing sound and the TV went off. The boy could hear the woman saying something. Her voice was weak though, and he knew she was passed out on the sofa. She wouldn't raise a finger if that brute came after him.

That's why he was now hidden inside the wardrobe in the woman's bedroom upstairs. He heard the woman shout something in a drowsy voice and the sounds of an argument.

Then footsteps rattled the stairs. The whole floor shook with the weight of his feet. He was a big, fat bastard and the boy hated him. Hated his red, sweaty face and his rancid alcohol breath.

"Where are you?" the man shouted.

They boy shrank backwards on the wardrobe floor, tucking his legs inside him. He was underneath the woman's dresses, and it had saved him before, as although the man had opened the wardrobe, he hadn't bothered to part the dresses.

The light in the bedroom turned on. The boy heard his heavy breathing, like a bull snorting. Fear clutched his heart in a vice like grip. A sliver of light came in, and he could see the man's bulk passing. Then he stopped, turned back and flung open the wardrobe doors.

The boy shrunk backwards but there was nowhere to go. He started to mumble a prayer he had learnt in school. The man muttered something under his breath. His alcohol fumes filled the air. The dresses parted suddenly and a splash of light flooded the inside of the wardrobe.

"There you are!" the man roared. A ham like fist reached out and grabbed the boy's hair.

"No!" he screamed. He kicked and fought but it was no use. He also knew it only made things worse, but he didn't know what else to do. The man picked him up like a rag doll and hurled him agains the wall. He cried out as his spine cracked against the sideboard and he slumped to the floor.

The man reached for him again when the doorbell went. It was a loud sound, and the man stopped. It sounded again, and a fist hammered the door.

"Mary!" the man shouted. "Mary. Open the door you bitch." His words were slurred and he wiped saliva from the corner of his lips.

The doorbell went again, with the loud hammering. The man swore and stomped down the stairs. The boy crept up to the bedroom doorway. He heard the door open and a voice speaking. He went to the landing, then carefully, went down two steps. He leaned over till he could see who was at the door.

A figure in black barged in suddenly, a motion so quick it caught the man by surprise. He stumbled back and fell. The boy saw a sharp object appear like magic in the figure's hand. It glittered in the light as it rose high in the air. The boy recognised a knife with a long, serrated blade.

The knife came down on the man's neck with a squelch. He screamed but the sound was clogged by blood. The figure straddled him now and kept stabbing him till he was still. Then it got up calmly and shut the door. The figure vanished from sight and the boy heard steps walking up and down the lounge.

Frightened, but curious, the boy shuffled down another two stairs. Blood was pouring out from his stepfather's neck and chest wounds. The boy felt no remorse. The figure came back into view. The black jacket was covered in dark blood. The knife was held in the right hand, dripping blood into the threadbare carpet.

He looked up and their eyes met. The boy felt no fear, but a shiver passed through him, like the wind rattling skeleton branches in the winter.

Many years later, when he was a man, he would remember the calmness in those eyes as they held his.

Slowly, the figure started to climb the stairs. The boy backed up, then held the bannisters so tight his knuckles went white.. He heard footsteps around the two small bedrooms and then the bathroom. He heard the tap run.

The figure came out. The knife wasn't visible anymore.

"Come with me," the figure said. The voice was surprisingly mellow and warm. A hand reached forward and touched his cheek. The boy didn't shrink away.

When the figure reached down to hold his hand, he didn't resist. They stood up and stepped over the dead man. From the lounge, the boy could hear his useless step mother snoring.

"Where are we going?" the boy asked.

"Somewhere nicer than here," the figure said.

CHAPTER 36

Arla was at work early the next morning. There was frost on the ground, and the sunlight was bright, crisp as she jogged up the steps to the station. Sandford was still there, looking bleary eyed. He yawned and raised his hand in greeting.

"Morning John," Arla said. "Go home. That's an order. I'll tell your boss."

Sandford grinned. "Still got half hour left guv. I'll make it."

"Good for you."

Arla was buzzed in through the bullet proof sliding doors. It was 0700, and the office was empty. She went into her office, took out the folder with the phone log and sat down, sipping her coffee.

She saw similar numbers recurring in the pages, and started to circle them. One number stood out. Longworth had called this number four times the day he died. Arla opened her laptop, and opened the case file. All the numbers of interest were stored there with the names of suspects.

The number belonged to Mike Simpson. Arla searched for Luke's number on the log. She had to look back one week, but she found it. After midnight, the week before he died, David had rung his son. The call duration was less than a minute which meant his son probably didn't answer.

The other recurring number, apart from Cherie's, belonged to James Spencer. The Secretary of State. At least once or twice a week, David rang the cabinet minister. It seemed strange to Arla. Why would a prominent filmmaker want from a politician? Or were they just good friends who had stayed in touch?

She detected a pattern with Luke as well. David was in the habit of calling his son after midnight it seemed, at least once every two weeks. Each time, his son didn't answer.

Arla sank back in her seat, thinking. Luke Longworth had his demons, that was for sure. David tried to keep in touch with him, it seemed. But Luke refused. Why did he hate the old man so much?

And did he hate his father enough to kill him?

Arla's mind went back to the recent burglary. Cherie was a brave women to continue to live in the house, but she did have police guarding both the front and back 24/7. In fact, Arla mused, it would be cheaper to relocate Cherie back to the BnB.

The burglar came back for David's personal possessions. Stuff the police hadn't got their hands on as yet. The thief must have wanted them kept secret. Was there something in David's past that they should know about?

His PCN record was clean. Could he have had a different name in the past? Many criminals used that as an effective means to keep their records hidden. Thinking of David's past made Mike Simpson come into focus. Arla ground her teeth. The man sounded like a creep from what Cherie said. Goodness knew how many young aspiring actresses he had subjected to the "casting couch."

Arla frowned. Mike was friends with David, right till the end. Did something lurk in their youth? Some old, cold case?

Arla wrote down Mike Simpson and circled it with her pen. Then she put an arrow next to to it and wrote David's name. She connected both the arrows to Luke's name. Each of the three names were surrounded by a circle and she stared at the triangle, thinking.

"What are you hiding? Why don't you tell me?" she whispered softly. Her fingertips brushed the paper. The past hid so many secrets. It made Arla who she was and she felt in her bones these men also hid something terrifying. An event that had transformed their lives. Like Nicole's disappearance had transformed Arla's.

She opened her up her laptop and searched for Simpson's production company. She found it in two hits. There could only be one Michael Simpson who owned the huge Liquid Dream Media Group in Soho. The offices occupied a seven story corner block in

Piccadilly, one of the most expensive addresses in London, and the world. Even the website was a sprawling affair. Arla put the address in her phone, with the phone numbers.

Then she rang Mike Simpson's number. It went to answer phone as she expected. There was a knock on her door. Then a voice asked, "Guv?" It was Harry.

Arla put the pen down and asked him to come in. Harry entered and shut the door. He was wearing his long grey overcoat still, and he smelt of his woodsmoke aftershave. It was a nice, comforting odour. He had come straight to her office, without stopping at his own desk. He leaned against the door, hands folded behind his back.

They appraised each other in silence, two people who knew each other intimately, but perhaps didn't fully understand what they knew.

Harry spoke without breaking off his stare. "The team will be here soon, guv."

I really hate it when you call me that!, she thought to herself. She wanted him to say her name. But she also knew he was following office rules, and she respected him for that.

Arla opened her mouth to speak but Harry detached himself from the door and came forward. His long legs traversed the three meters to her desk in almost one step. He sat down in the chair opposite her. The words died in Arla's mouth. His coffee coloured cheeks were so smooth. The angle of his jaw so pronounced. The light in his eyes so directed at her.

He leaned forward, lowering his voice. "I wanted to tell you this before we get busy." He paused and breathed out slightly. He blinked a couple of times, the normally confident, cocky mask slipping.

Then he said, "I would like to invite you to my parents' house Arla." There was a fear suddenly in his eyes.

Arla caught her breath. She knew Harry's father had died. His mother lived alone. Arla didn't have any illusions. This was a big step. She tried to understand his thinking. Was this to make her feel more...wanted? To give her a sense of belonging? Harry knew all about her tragic family. She knew that in comparison, his was a normal, happy one.

Wasn't it too soon? Especially when they were going through a difficult patch. Arla's senses were suddenly so muddled she didn't what to think. But Harry sat there, staring at her intently, like he wanted an answer.

And she was scared to say yes. She was scared to say no. Because all her life she protected herself against disappointment. Against being repulsed. And when her own family did that to her...well, she had spent her life sprouting thorns against emotional attachment.

And yet, she was always emotional. She could go from normal to tearful in milliseconds.

It didn't make sense. But it was who she was.

Arla got up suddenly, feeling suffocated. She turned her back to him and stared out the window at the car park below. A Volkswagen was entering through the barrier. The clouds had gone, sunlight showered over south London's grey and red bricks. Arla rubbed her face on her hands, trying to swallow the leaden weight stuck in her throat.

She let her breath out, unable to decide and walked around the office. Harry stood up, sensing her agitation.

"I meant what I said last night. I'm here if you need-

"Stop Harry!" Arla put her hand up. "Just stop."

She hadn't mean to use a harsh tone, but it came naturally. She saw the sudden anger in his eyes. His eyebrows came together. It made her feel awful. It made her sad and angry too. A Molotov cocktail of emotions smashed against the wall of her soul, sparkling into a million fractals of tarnished hope and dreams.

Scarcely aware of what she was doing, Arla strode forward and grabbed Harry's beautiful face in both hands. She yanked him down, kissing his hard on the lips. Surprised at first, he responded slowly, his long tongue flicking inside hers like a warm, wet arousal. They kissed for a long time, then Arla let go and reeled backwards. She leaned against the table, breathing heavily.

With the corner of her sleeve, she wiped her mouth. *God that felt good.* She didn't want to stop. But she suddenly realised where she was. When she looked up at Harry, he was regarding her with a shocked expression on his face.

Then suddenly, unexpectedly, he smiled. "I'll take that as a yes, then," he drawled.

She smiled too, partly in embarrassment, partly in relief. She also felt relieved.

Something had shifted inside her.

Why should she be scared of herself? Of emotional entanglements?

Why couldn't she love and lose? So what if she had lost before - hadn't everyone else in this world?

No. She would take responsibility. She would direct this relationship, not the other way around. She didn't need Harry to be there, when she had been there for herself.

Only me. No one else.

And I owe it to my bloody self to be happy, damn it.

But she couldn't explain all this to Harry. Someday, he would understand, and she got the impression he was beginning to. At least, he was getting a feel for her, more than anyone else ever had.

"I guess it is," She said, tucking a loose strand back behind her ear.

He smiled then, a big, heartfelt smile like the sun coming out, and she melted inside. Emotion throbbed in her throat, and tears welled in her eyes. She turned around quickly, but not before she caught the concern on his face.

"I'll be fine. Just give me five minutes. Get the others ready. Here, take this." Without looking at him, she slid the phone log papers over to Harry.

He picked them up, and their eyes met again. Arla looked away, wiping her eyes. Harry nodded and left her alone.

CHAPTER 37

The Incident Room was filling up when Arla walked in. Detectives sat on the stiff back chairs with cups of coffee in their hands, and some stood leaning against the rows of printers and fax machines that lined the side. A glass partition looked out at the open plan office, and Arla spotted Lisa and Rob hurrying through.

Harry was setting up the whiteboard. He turned as he saw her. Arla kept her face impassive. Photos of the victim and each suspect were stuck on the board. Harry had the black felt tip pen out and was writing down jobs to do in bullet points.

Under Luke Longworth's photo he wrote down the cell phone and the IMEI number as well. Arla looked at the points, perching her butt on the edge of the desk.

"Don't forget the boot print match with the burglar," Arla added.

"Yes boss," Harry spoke without lifting his head.

"Just what I wanted to talk to you about," Lisa said as she strode in. Her face was flushed, with a smile.

Arla looked at her expectantly. "What is it?"

"The Boot Print Database got back to me. SOCO did find prints outside Luke's house. They are an exact match with the burglar's."

Excitement clutched Arla's guts. Harry turned around, and their eyes met.

Harry said, "That's good, but it doesn't mean the prints outside Luke's house necessarily belong to him."

Rob said, "Or it means the burglar tried to break into Luke's house as well."

Arla spoke up. "We didn't see any evidence of breaking and entry, did we Harry?"

He shook his head slowly. "None whatsoever. But the burglar could just be having a look, right?"

The incident room had filled up even more. The sound of muttering voices was growing. Arla said, "Does the database have any other records for this bootprint?"

"No," Lisa said. "And before you ask, it doesn't match the partial boot print from the front door, either."

"Damn," Arla said. "Cherie mentioned that there was no print on that door before. It had to come from the murderer. Anyway. All this just brings Luke into sharper focus."

She turned to face the assembled officers in the room. Arla rapped on the victim's photo.

"We have a body, but no motive as yet, folks." She pointed to Luke's photo next. "All we know is that he had a strange relationship with his son. A son we cannot contact." Arla moved to Mike Simpson.

"The victim was funneling money to this guy. We don't know why as yet. He was also seen in is silver Bentley, reg number MS100, at the victim's house the week before the murder."

"Flash bastard," someone muttered and laughter trickled through the room.

Arla took a step forward and the laughter died down. She put steel into her voice. "This guy is the best lead we have. If he was getting money from the victim, that gives us a motive."

Beauregard snorted and raised his voice. "Yeah, and this guy made a song and dance about the whole thing, by hanging him up like that with lights."

"How do you know he didn't?" Arla shot back. She transferred her attention back to the room. "We need statements from Mike Simpson and Luke Longworth ASAP. We also need teams positioned outside their houses, not uniform please, the less attention we have now the better."

A hand raised and Toby, a black uniform sergeant waved a folded tabloid paper. "Got the wife on the front cover, guv."

Heads craned in Toby's direction, and several others echoed what he said. Arla blew out her cheeks. "Is the Pope a Catholic?"

"Does a bear shit in the woods?" another voice said from the back and mirth ensued once again.

"Enough," Arla said. "We didn't want this to become a media circus and now it is. Nothing we can do about that but we can hurry up and get more leads."

She turned back to Lisa. "Any news from from Dr. Banerji?"

"Nope, not yet. Still waiting for toxicology and that other thing-

"Any metal fragments from the depression in the skull," Arla finished. "Right. More waiting."

"But we have strong leads now, guys. I can't prove it, but it's looking more likely that it was the son who burgled his father's house." Arla told them about the bootprints.

"So I'm going to get a warrant ordered to search his house," she said. "I want everything on Simpson. Right from his birth. If he took a leak in the park, I want to know."

She turned to Rupert, the new recruit. "Anything from juvenile records on Luke Longworth?"

The nervous smile with which Rupert stood up lifted Arla's spirits. He had something.

Rupert cleared his throat and said, "Two things. He was sent to boarding school - Burlington College in Hampshire. It was a mixed school, and he was reported for assaulting a teenage girl."

Arla's pulse quickened. "Really? Does he have a PCN?"

"That's the funny thing, guv. I had to dig this out from his GP records. It was reported, but the PCN was withdrawn. The database says Evidence not available."

149

Arla frowned. "Did you search enhanced disclosures?"

"Yes. All of it."

Murmurs spread around the room. Harry said, "Rules are different for juve's but even then, this was an assault. Was it sexual?"

"It was groping against the girl's wishes," Rupert clarified.

"So, it wasn't a full sexual assault?" Arla asked.

Rupert frowned and lowered the piece of paper he was holding. "That's what is not very clear. The GP records state the girl broke away and ran, alerting others. Then the police was called."

Harry interjected. "And the PCN records on the database are withdrawn." He pursed his lips. "Shouldn't be, if it was a sexual assault. Any other records on him - withdrawn or active?"

"Not that I could see."

"Right," Arla gripped her forehead. "Any leads from Luke's phone? We need something on this guy."

Rob stepped forward, his chubby face red as usual. He wiped his forehead. "The phone was used last night, guv. Location was in the Common."

"The Common? Large area, Rob. Can they be more specific."

"On the Clapham High Road side. Just before midnight."

Arla pondered for a few seconds. What was Luke upto? Was he hiding in the common? He must know that using his phone would get him tracked. Something didn't add up. The bootprint match meant Luke must have broken into his father's house. To get rid of evidence?

"Put on an all points bulletin with his name and description. I think we can justify searching his house under the circumstances, even without a warrant." Arla jabbed Luke's photo. "I want him arrested. Now."

150

The meeting broke up. Andy Jackson came up and put the tabloid newspaper on the table in front of Arla. The red glaring headlines declared loudly:

"Famous director meets grisly death."

Beneath it, the front page was dominated by a full length photo of Cherie, face covered in dark sunglasses and hat, barely recognizable. There was even a zoom in box showing what they could of her face. The car's registration was blanked out.

"Here guv," Toby turned the page. Arla leaned over and read. Her heart sank.

CHAPTER 38

Arla clutched the second page of the tabloid paper, her knuckles white. If fire could emanate from her eye, they would. Her jaws were clamped tight. She could sense Harry leaning over her back, reading the same lines as she was.

"Detective Chief Inspector Arla Baker was seen leaving the famous director's house. Miss Baker is the same detective who racked the notorious paedophile ring-

Arla threw the paper to the floor. "Damn it!" Heads turned from across the floor in the open plan office.

"Easy," Harry said softly at her elbow. "Go to your office."

Arla turned on him, her face red. "I want to know who did this, OK? Someone in my team.." words failed her. She walked to her office and slammed the door shut. She was seething.

Was it one of the uniforms who had taken money from the vermin at a tabloid newspaper? If so, she would find that person.

There was a knock on the door and Harry poked his head in. "Boss wants us upstairs."

"He can wait. Get a team ready to get inside Luke's house. I want SOCO in attendance. Now, please."

She lowered her voice. Harry hung his head, then nodded and went back out. Arla went to her desk and picked up the phone. The screen saver on her laptop came on - a photo of Nicole and her, taken many summers ago. Sunlight dappled their freckled teenage faces. She was the darker one, and had her arm draped around Nicole. Like she didn't want to let her go. Truth be told, she never had.

Arla sighed, rubbing her finger against the screen. She rang Banerji's number. He answered.

"Always a pleasure to hear from my favourite policewoman."

"Being nice doesn't mean I let you off the hook, Doc. Have you got anything for me?"

"Toxicology is being sped up. So far, I know he didn't have any recreational drugs in his system like cocaine, cannabis or MDMA. Trace amount of alcohol but nothing else. Waiting to hear about barbiturates, amphetamines and benzodiazepines."

"Did you have another look at the skull?"

There was a pause at the other end. "As a matter of fact, I did. I can't see much with the naked eye, or microscopy, as I told you. And you looked yourself."

"Well, I did have my eyes shut for a while as well."

Banerji chuckled. "Yeah, the skull gets most people. Anyway I took a scraping from the scalp skin at the site of the contusion. It's been sent to Cambridge. Ask me why."

"Why?"

"What do you think he was hit by?"

"Something hard. Metallic, maybe."

"Exactly. Anything else would be too heavy to carry around. Adenbrooks Hospital in Cambridge has a heavy and precious metals lab. If there's trace amounts of any metal on this scalp, we will know."

"How long will it take?"

"They know it's from us, so give it 3-4 days. Normally can take 10 days to hear back from them."

"Thanks Doc."

Just as Arla put the mobile down her desk phone started ringing. It was Johnson. "Get up here, now," he growled before hanging up.

Arla had a sense of foreboding. Johnson sounded annoyed. She bumped into Harry in the office.

153

He said, "Submitted to magistrate and got a response back. Not that we even needed it. He's a suspect."

"I know. But I don't want a lawyer or the pen pushers upstairs to make a fuss later."

They went up the stairs and knocked on Johnson's door. Arla opened the door and stopped in her tracks. Ken Nixon, the man from MI5 was sat in the chair opposite Johnson's desk.

Johnson spoke in a gruff voice. "Shut the door and come in."

Arla noticed Nixon's eyes on her. She met them coldly. Nixon attempted a smile. Arla remained blank faced and his smile slowly faded.

"The media are all over this now, DCI Baker." Johnson patted the layer of folded newspaper on his desk.

Arla and Harry remained silent. Johnson folded his large paws across his desk and leaned his tall frame forward.

"All the more reason to bring this to a swift conclusion. Have you made progress?"

Arla told him about the burglary and the boot print match with Luke. "We need to search his house, sir. He has not been in touch and it's obvious he's avoiding us deliberately. He entered the property again to remove evidence, I'm sure of it."

Harry said, "His phone was used last night, inside the Common. We know the killer was cut the cables from the post inside the Common. He might well have watched the house from there as well."

There was silence for a while. Nixon was the first to speak. "The fact that he spoke from the Common means nothing. He could have been walking through."

Arla ignored him. To Johnson she said, "I've got a warrant now to search Luke's house, sir."

She didn't miss the the quick glance between Johnson and Nixon. Her boss asked, "What about the producer, Mike Simpson? The victim had several financial transactions with him, right?"

"He's second on our list. I want to search Luke's house first, then interview Simpson."

Johnson held Arla's eyes but he looked uncomfortable. "Leave the house alone for now. Concentrate on Simpson. He's the more valuable lead."

Arla frowned. "And not the son? Whose boot print matches the burglar-

"The print in front of his door could belong to the postman or anyone, Arla. You know that. The CPS will laugh that one out of the court."

The sense of foreboding Arla had was growing stronger. "We looked into Luke's records as a juvenile. He had a sexual assault case. Records were withdrawn. That's not possible for a sexual assault, sir is it?"

Arla turned to look at Nixon. He scratched the stubble on his beard and shrugged. Arla jerked a thumb at him. "Why is he even here?"

It was Johnson's turn to frown. "Mr. Nixon is one of our colleagues and-

"No he's not," Arla said, ignoring the warning movement from Harry. He was fidgeting, which meant he wanted her to shut up. "He has no reason to be here, unless you're not telling me something."

Johnson opened his mouth to retort but Nixon spoke over him. "DCI Baker, we just want this case brought to a speedy, but fair, conclusion. As you know, David Longworth was well known to the secretary of state."

"What about Luke? Was he well known to him as well?"

Nixon hesitated, and Arla caught the way his eyes gleamed once, then faded. "Yes, he was. Luke had also been to the Secretary's house with his father on certain occasions."

So what? Arla thought silently.

Nixon appeared to read her mind. "Look, DCI Baker, we just want minimal involvement of the family. David Longworth had many friends in Westminster. No one wants the publicity. I will follow up the line of inquiry with regards to Luke Longworth."

"What?" Arla was taken aback. She fixed her eyes on Johnson. "I am the SIO in this case, sir, is that right?"

Johnson glanced between them. He licked his lips. "That is right, Arla, but as this is a sensitive matter, MI5 are involved now."

Arla shook her head in disbelief. "So you want me to disclose our case files to them? Are they running the investigation now?"

The jibe hurt Johnson, and it was meant to. The corners of his eyes narrowed and his face went a deeper shade of mauve.

"No, *we* are. And I'm telling, no, I'm ordering you to stay away from the son's house and focus on Mike Simpson instead."

"You make me the SIO because I get results. And yet now you stop me from going after the right suspect." Arla's voice was hard like a shard of ice.

"I'm only stopping you from barking up the wrong tree."

"Wrong tree?" Arla knew she shouldn't lose her temper. But she couldn't help it. "What is this really about, sir? Your friends in Westminster helping you get the Commander post?"

A vein bulged in Johnson's head. He slammed his fist down, making the table and floor shake.

"That's enough!" he shouted. The boom of his voice echoed around the room. He wagged a finger at Arla. "I'm warning you, Arla. Disobey my orders and I remove you as SIO. Is that what you want?"

Harry shifted closer to her. "Let it go," he whispered. Arla hadn't taken her eyes away from Johnson. She wasn't scared of him. She knew the man behind the bluster. He was concerned with one thing only - rising up the greasy pole.

But he was her superior. And her future rank was in his hands.

Without looking at all contrite she said, "I'm sorry sir. I'll look into Mike Simpson today."

Johnson relaxed. "You do that now, Ar...I mean DCI Baker. I want answers later this evening."

Arla and Harry rose stiffly. Without a glance at Nixon, Arla left the room.

CHAPTER 39

Harry swung the black BMW through the serpentine inner city streets. It was raining again, that grey whispering rain that slanted morosely against the brown bricks of the council blocks, an early morning dreamy landscape of hollowed hopes and forlorn promises. Ponderous, slow moving people marched to that invisible tug and pull of London's perennial life current. Arla watched as a drunk in an Army coat begged beneath the awning of a supermarket. His eyes met Arla's as they drove past slowly.

"Damn it," she whispered. "Luke's crooked Harry. I can feel it."

"I know. But you're going too hard at this. Like you do. There's a break coming, I can feel it. Don't lose it now."

Things were easier between after her unexpected outburst in her office. Arla said, "I'm not losing it. But you have to admit, this Nixon guy being there is downright annoying. I bet you it was him who leaked my name to the press."

It took them almost an hour to hurdle through the traffic. Harry parked in an underground garage opposite the massive corner plot that was Liquid Dream Media's HQ. Harry stopped as they were walking towards the elevator. They were standing in front of a silver Bentley with the licence plate MS100.

"Shall we slash the tires so he cant get away?" Harry asked.

Arla ignored him, heading for the elevators. At ground level, the crossed the busy intersection and headed to the magnificent red brick Victorian mansion style building. The ground floor was a wrap round glass affair, with sliding doors that opened soundlessly as the arrived. An immaculately coiffeured woman sat in the otherwise bare reception and she looked up as they approached. The smiled faded when Arla held out her warrant card.

"Michael Simpson," Arla said. "We know he's in."

The woman spoke furtively on the phone below the counter, turning her back to them. Harry took his chance to look around. He stood in front of a photo for ages, checking out the women in it. Arla pretended not to notice.

The receptionist turned finally and gave them directions to the sixth and top floor. The elevator doors opened into a busy office corridor. The carpets were purple, the walls yellow and the ceiling blue.

"Rainbow office," Harry muttered. Arla didn't mind it in fact. It livened up an otherwise drab space. They walked past a room with desks, chairs and a pool table in the middle. Everyone was busy at work and Arla wondered who had the time to play pool during a work day.

Mike Simpsons office door was a deep shade of pink. The name plate read *"Boss Mike."*

Arla looked at Harry and raised her eyebrows. Harry was grimacing and she guessed it was colour of the door he didn't like.

She raised her hand to knock but the door suddenly flew open. A well dressed man in his fifties, wearing a white shirt with the top three buttons undone, showing a generous amount of hairy chest. A red rose was stuck to the left breast pocket of the shirt. His skin had seen too much sun. It was leathery and hung off his cheeks. The sparse hair was long and slicked back. His eyes were dark and a lecherous smile adorned his lips. He reminded Arla of Peter Stringfellow on steroids.

"Well you must be the police officers, is that right?"

The grin didn't falter. Arla wondered if this was an act. He must know what they were here for. After all, even if he wasn't involved, surely he read the papers. And she knew deep in her guts he was involved, somehow.

They walked into the sumptious office. It was very post modern like the rest of the office. A gleaming white table rested on one round leg sprouting from the hideous purple carpet on the floor. There was a bank of screens on the wall, and most of them showed

TV channels. But Arla also noticed two camera feeds, looking out at the corridor. So, that's how he knew they had arrived.

A cloud of expensive aftershave brushed past them as Simpson walked across to his high backed red leather chair, MS embossed on it. He moved his laptop to one side. His face was now serious, the smile gone.

"You're here about David, aren't you?"

"Yes," Arla said. He was a good looking man, despite his age. She guessed late fifties or early sixties. The tanned skin made him look older. He shook his head.

"Awful thing to happen. Any idea who did it?"

"We are exploring multiple avenues in what is a fast moving investigation," Arla said, reciting a stock phrase. "And we need to ask you some questions. Would you mind coming down to the station?"

A gleam came into his eyes, and they narrowed. "What for?"

Arla decided not to waste time. She was sure he would get a hot shot Queen's Counsel lawyer, so she might as well be frank.

"You had considerable financial dealings with David Longworth, right?"

Simpson blinked. "We were in the middle of a film financing deal, yes."

Harry asked, "And you went to his house the week before he died?"

Now Simpson frowned, his early joviality completely gone. "To talk to him about the film deal yes. I've known David a long time. He was making a comeback with this film, and wanted to put his own money into it. Look, what is this about?"

In the ensuing silence, his eyes moved slowly from Harry to Arla. A scowl came on his face, then his jaws went slack.

"You must be bloody joking."

Arla said, "It would be better for you if you came to the station with us of your own volition."

"Am I under arrest?"

"No. But if you don't come with us, then we sufficient grounds to arrest you." Arla was on a fine line, and all of them knew it.

"What if I answer all your questions here?"

"They will not be recorded, in case they need to be produced in a court of law. Which they most likely will be."

Simpson ground his teeth together. "You think I did it? I killed him?"

Arla stood. "We need to carry on this discussion at the station, Mr Simpson. Will you cooperate, or do I have to arrest you?"

His leathery face turned beetroot red. He stood as well. His chest heaved and a snarl came on his lips. It wasn't that different from the lecherous grin he had earlier, Arla mused.

"You come into my office and dare threaten me? Do you know who I am?!" His last words were a shout.

Someone used to getting their own way, Arla thought. Aloud she said, "What is your answer, Mr. Simpson? The choice is a very simple one you can see. The office is full. Your employees will see you handcuffed as we walk down-

"Alright, alright, alright!" Simpson shouted. He put his hands on the table and leaned forward, head lowered. Beads of sweat trickled down his scalp.

Harry said, "We will leave now and wait for you outside the office." Arla frowned at Harry. She wanted to make this as uncomfortable for Simpson as possible.

Simpson lifted his head. "Yes, I would like that." His voice was quieter. "Do I need a lawyer?"

"As you are only giving a statement, not really," Arla said. "But it's up to you entirely."

161

CHAPTER 40

The drive back to the station was deathly quiet. Harry handed Simpson over to the duty sargent at the desk and joined Arla in the office. An excited Lisa got off her chair and walked over to them.

She beamed at them. "Rita worked hard with the Bahamas Tax Office. The NCA authorised us to be in touch with them. The Bahamas office didn't want to disclose information, but the threat of sending details of Blue Horizon to HMRC, and for the NCA top open another case for tax fraud investigation seemed to do the trick."

Rita waved at them from behind her desk, then rose, swallowing the last of the croissant she was eating. Arla beamed at her. "Well done Rita."

Rita said, "That's not all, guv. The coroner's report for Laura Douglas came back."

Arla was momentarily nonplussed. Rita said, "You know, David Longworth's ex wife. The one who died in Bournemouth."

Arla was impressed. "You have been busy." They sat down, and Rob appeared, only to be promptly dispatched by Harry to get coffee.

"Tell me about Blue Horizon," Arla said.

"Well," Rita picked up a folder from Lisa's desk and gave it to Arla. "It's an EIS, enterprise investment scheme, as we know. It's an offshore company, and the board of trustees is this law firm in the city called Cholmondeley St John."

"That's a mouthful," Lisa grinned.

"Wait till you hear who set the board of trustees up."

"Go on then."

"Mike Simpson. He's the client of the law firm and basically runs Blue Horizon. The government can't touch him as he's not directly involved."

"Interesting. What about the ex wife, Laura Douglas?"

Rita crossed her arms across her chest. "Poor woman. She was found at the bottom of a cliff overlooking the beach. Lethal amounts of diazepam were found in her toxicology reports."

Arla frowned. "Hang on. She died of an overdose or due to the fall?"

"Both. The coroner's verdict was death by overdose. The Bournemouth CID reckoned she was drugged up to the eyeballs, went wandering round the cliffs and fell to her death."

Arla sat back, lips pursed. She found Harry's eyes. He nodded slowly, and she knew he was thinking the same as her.

Harry said, "What if she was pushed off the cliff?"

Rob had returned with the tray of coffees. Lisa brought him up to speed. Rob sipped his coffee and said, "The report said Laura Douglas left the apartment and went out on her own. Her husband was in the bathroom at the time. She never came back."

There was silence for while as everyone sipped their coffee. Thoughts rose and mingled like smoke with the coffee fumes.

Arla said, "What if she was going to meet someone? Hang on," she clicked her fingers. "The son was there as well, right? Luke. Does the report mention where he was at the time?"

"Yes," Rita said. "He was out of the apartment. Apparently he went for a run. There wasn't any mention of a witness."

Arla said, "So potentially, Laura could have been off to meet Luke. Her son."

"Why," Harry pointed out, "When they were living in the same apartment. This was their holiday, right? He was with his parents.

"Don't know," Arla conceded. "But I think it's important that when Laura was out of the house, Luke was too." She glanced at her watch, then at Harry.

"Time to interview Mike Simpson."

Rob said, "Have you heard the latest about him?"

Arla raised an eyebrow. "About Simpson? No, I haven't."

Rob, Lisa and Rita exchanged a look. It was Lisa who spoke. "Simpson's a powerful figure in the film business. He produces a lot of films, and in his offices, they do some shooting as well. Media figures say he's the man who can get you a BAFTA award." BAFTA stood for British Academy of Film and Television Arts, the English equivalent of the Oscars.

Lisa carried on. "Last year, when the #Metoo movement started in America, there was a wave here as well. Two women accused Simpson of molesting them in his office when they came for an interview."

Rita said, "And that was probably the tip of the iceberg. We contacted these two women while you were at Simpson's office. Both of them mentioned they knew of other women he had molested not just in his office, but in film studios, back of cars, virtually everywhere. But apart from these two no other woman has come forward. As yet," Rita added.

Arla shook her head. "I knew he was a right piece of work when I laid eyes on him. Something icky." She shivered, thinking of his sly, knowing smile and the leathered skin hanging off his face. A dirty old man. And a powerful one.

Harry said, "Do we have PCN records?"

"Yes. Both cases were filed, and then thrown out of court by his fancy lawyers. Not enough evidence."

Arla stood. "That might change now. Let's get to it, Harry."

CHAPTER 41

When Arla and Harry walked into the interview room, Mike Simpson was sitting there with his legs crossed and his right arm draped over the empty chair next to him. The insolent smile was back on his lips.

"Well well if it isn't the famous pair," he smirked. "Come on then, let's get this ridiculous show over and done with. Shall I smile for the camera?"

Both of them ignored him. Arla faced him, jaws flexed. Simpson had recovered his composure and she wanted to wipe that stupid grin off his face.

Harry spoke for the recorder, and activated the camera. Simpson stared at Arla. He had a blue suit blazer on, but the top three buttons of his shirt were undone. Curly chest hair was sticking out and Arla felt nauseated at the sight.

"Could you please confirm that you are the owner of the EIS called Blue Horizon," Arla said in a steely voice. It had the desired effect. The smile faded from Simpson's lips.

"Oh, I get it. Remarkable police work. Very commendable. You should be up for a promotion with that, Inspector Baker, right?"

"DCI Baker actually. Can you answer the question please."

"Let me guess. You're looking into David's financials, and saw that he transferred 100k into Blue Horizon. Is that right?"

Harry said, "Mr Simpson, we are asking the questions here, not you."

Simpson gave Harry a withering look. "Oh yeah I forgot. That's why you got me down here."

"Can you answer the question please?" Arla repeated.

165

"Well, actually I don't know who owns Blue Horizon. I appointed a board of trustees, and the company is held in a trust, managed by the trustees. So why don't you ask them?"

"The National Crime Agency are interested in offshore companies these days, and they spoke to the Bahamas Tax Office about Blue Horizon," Arla said. "So let's not beat around the bush here. If you wish, we can let HMRC and NCA deal with this from now on."

Simpson yawned and stretched his head back, showing a sagging, tanned neck. "Another empty threat. Go ahead, let them investigate. All they'll find is a legit company."

Arla tried a different track. "How well do you know Cherie Longworth, wife of the deceased?"

Slowly, Simpson turned his eyes back to Arla. His face was impassive, but she could sense a stiffness in his posture. It was obvious in the tautness of his neck muscles as well.

"I knew her as David's wife, that's all."

"You didn't know her before she became his wife?"

"No."

"She worked in TV serials in the 1980's. David and you were friends at the time. Are you sure you didn't know her back then?"

He paused before he answered, like he had to think about it. "No, I didn't."

"Were you attracted to her?"

A frown appeared on Simpson's face. "What sort of a question is that?"

"Can you answer it please?"

"This isn't a court of law is it? I don't have to answer anything I don't want to."

Arla decided to go for the jugular. There was only one way to put lecherous bastards like Simpson into his place.

"Have you ever assaulted Cherie Longworth?"

Simpson's eyes widened. "What? Is that some kind of joke?"

"Answer the question please."

He pressed his lips together and his nostrils flared. "This bullshit has gone on for long enough. Instead of looking around for the real criminal here you are, trying to allege that I touched David's wife."

"Are you denying that you assaulted her?"

A look of disbelief rippled across his face. Either he was speaking the truth, or he was a very good actor, Arla thought. But she didn't believe Cherie was lying, not for a second.

"Of course I'm denying it," he said, teeth clenched.

Arla said smoothly, "What about the two women who accused you of assaulting them in your office? Are you denying that as well?"

Simpson leaned forward. His tanned, brown forehead was drawn into knots. An ugly scowl was spreading on his face.

"That's all water under the bridge. It was all a pack of lies. Do you know what damage that did to my reputation? How dare you try to link that trash talk to something like this?"

Arla leaned back in her chair, satisfied. "They say you're the man who can get young actresses a BAFTA award."

"What?" The scowl deepened. "I have no idea what you're talking about."

Arla shrugged nonchalantly. "So all these women are lying are they? You're pure as driven snow, in all your life you've never molested a woman."

Simpson shook his head. "Believe what you want. Honestly, you guys are a joke. Why dont you do your job and stop wasting the taxpayer's money? Catch the guy who did this!"

Arla said, "Cherie Longworth has accused you of attacking her in her own house. The last time you went to see her husband."

"Bullshit."

Arla raised her voice and leaned forward. "What happened, Mr Simpson? Did you have an argument with David? Was he not giving you enough money for the film? Is that why you decided to come down and assault his wife? For you, it's a power trip isn't it?"

Simpson stood up, jaws churning, eyes filled with hate. "Shut up! Just shut up! How dare you-

"And then what happened? You didn't get your own way. Not with Cherie. David told you not to come back. You drove off in a huff that day. The neighbours saw you. So you came back and killed him. Didn't you?"

"Fuck you!" Simpson bellowed. His chest was heaving, sweat pouring down his face, dampening his shirt. "You think I did that to David? I was the animal who gutted him and strung him up like a…

Simpson stopped suddenly. His face blanched white and fear spasmed across his eyes.

Arla and Harry glanced at each other. Very quietly, Arla asked, "How did you know he was strung up?"

Simpson's mouth was open. His eyes were wild and dilated. His hands were knotted into fists, knuckles white.

Arla said, "Not a single newspaper or media outlet reported on the mode of death. No one knows apart from his wife and the murderer. And we know his wife didn't speak to you. We checked her phone log, and her voice calls."

Simpson staggered back till he was leaning against the wall. He looked like he was about to vomit. His voice was faint. "I want a lawyer."

CHAPTER 42

Later that evening

Emily Harman, the family liaison officer, watched as Cherie Longworth poured two cups of coffee from the mixer. She slid one over to Emily.

"Thank you," Emily said. Although there wasn't a child involved, her presence was reassuring to Cherie. She felt sorry for the woman. She never had makeup on and her hair was always pulled in a tight ponytail. Despite that, her appearance was striking. Emily had heard that she was an actress, and had looked her up in IMDB, but not found anything. She asked Cherie about it now.

Cherie smiled wanly. "When I did those TV serials, they didn't have IMDB. But I can show you something else."

"Oh no," Emily protested as Cherie slipped off the breakfast bar stool. "You dont have to trouble yourself."

"No trouble."

Cherie went upstairs and returned with a paper box. She took the lid off to reveal cuttings from showbiz magazines. Most of them were photos, some with written pages. She showed them to Emily.

"Look, there's me with Derek Hutchinson. He was a well known film producer at the time, who later went to Hollywood."

Emily looked through the photos. Most of them were taken in film studios and photo shoots. They seemed genuine. At the bottom there was a pair of DVD's. Cherie took them out too.

"You can see these if you want. Digitally re mastered from old VHS tapes."

"Oh no that's alright. I mean, I would like to." She looked up at Cherie, afraid of being rude, but Cherie was smiling.

"Don't worry. It was a while ago and you might find them boring."

Cherie's phone beeped. She picked it up and her face went pale. Emily put her cup down.

"What is it Mrs Longworth?"

Cherie put the phone down and stared around her like a trapped animal. "That was Luke. He wants me to meet him outside."

Emily walked over to Cherie. "Outside where?"

Cherie had put the phone on the counter and the screen was blank. She picked it up and the text message appeared.

"He didn't say." Cherie looked at Emily, her eyes wide and nostrils flaring. "What should I do?"

Emily considered. She wasn't a police officer, but she had enough experience of working with distressed families to know she had to do something. If she called in PC Darren, parked at the front, then that would be warning Luke, who probably was watching. He wouldn't be texting to meet unless he was very close. This was an opportunity to grab him. Excitement gripped Emily.

"Wait a minute, Let me speak to Darren." She took her radio off the breast pocket and turned the knob. Static crackled through it. Emily called Darren who answered immediately.

"It's the son," Emily said breathlessly. "He's shown up here. No, he's not inside. But he's not far off, as he wants to meet Cherie outside." Emily listened for a while then hung up.

"Anything?" she asked Cherie.

Cherie's cheeks were sucked in, hollow. She was breathing heavily. Emily put a hand on her arm and she startled.

"Here," Emily said, "Sit down. Can I take the phone?"

Cherie hesitated for a few seconds then gave it to her. Emily said, "Is this a new number? There's no name on it."

"Yes it must be. I have his number stored on my phone."

Emily said, "Can I text him back?"

Cherie looked fearful. "What will you say?"

"Now don't get concerned. This is what Darren told me to do. I will text back as you, saying that you are going out to meet him. But you won't. You stay here. Do you have an anorak or coat that Luke might find familiar?"

Cherie frowned. "Yes, maybe. I have a red coat that he has mentioned looks nice. But that was a while ago, last year."

"Do you have still have the coat?"

"Yes."

"OK. So, I'm going to go out when he replies. But Darren and another police constable will be right behind me. We'll try to catch him."

Alarmed, Cherie grabbed Emily's hand. "No. Don't do this. You're putting yourself at risk. And I'm worried of being on my own." Her hand went to her mouth. "I don't think I can live here anymore."

"Mrs Longworth don't worry," Emily said soothingly. "There's two units of uniformed police here. Four of them in total. One unit will keep an eye on you."

Cherie sat back down. Emily picked up the phone and texted back.

Are you OK, Luke?

He answered a few seconds later.

I'll tell you more when I see you.

OK. Where shall we meet?

Tell the police you're going to the supermarket to buy food. I'll meet you in the Tesco carpark. Near the cash machine on the side.

Emily got up and showed the messages to Cherie. She nodded. "The cashpoint has a light over it but that corner of the car park is dark. The wire fence is right behind the cash point. Maybe he'll come over that?"

"We'll see. Can I get the red coat please?"

Cherie said. "Fine. But I'm not staying here. I'm coming with you."

CHAPTER 43

Luke Longworth stared at the messages on his screen. The last one said that Cherie was on her way. Luke had a handheld drone that was hovering high in the air above Cherie's house. His father's house. Even the words filled Luke with bitterness. Bile rose in his throat.

Father. How dare he call himself that.

The grainy black and white image on his hand held device showed the front door of the house open. A woman in a dark coat stepped out. Luke recognized the coat. It belonged to Cherie. She lifted the hood before he could zoom in. Luke watched as one of the policemen stepped up and spoke to her briefly. They had a long chat, and the policeman seemed unhappy.

Luke watched with bated breath. Finally, the policeman let Cherie go reluctantly. Luke released a sigh. Cherie got into the car and drove away. The cops didn't follow. So far this was going to plan. Luke lowered the drone, but kept it hovering over the house, high enough for the cops not to notice.

He was positioned behind the parked media vans, and around the corner from the house. A clump of trees hid him from the vans as well as the property. Luke was in his car, a black VW Golf with tinted windows. He watched as Cherie's car disappeared around the bend, and waited. The police cars still didn't make a move. The media van guys either hadn't noticed, or were napping.

Six minutes went by, and still the police car stayed put. Luke flew the drone over the trees, bringing it back down to his level. He got into the car, and drove in the opposite direction, following the route to the back of the retail park that housed the massive Tesco supermarket and other stores.

Luke had been here several times. It was a quiet place. Strange, as it was surrounded by roads and a busy intersection. But no one bothered about this grassy knoll that rose between the roads and the rear of the retail park. Tall trees stood at its peak, and it was bordered by a small wire fence that was easily breached. Luke had seen discarded needles and used condoms up here. Sometimes he heard sounds as well. But he kept himself to himself, slinking between the shadows.

He waited till the road was clear, then sprinted across and climbed the fence, dropping lightly to his feet on the other side. The backpack on his shoulders contained the drone. He got up to the peak, and the glittering lights of the industrial park came into view. Luke didn't activate the drone. For his plan, he needed free hands.

He scampered along past the trees and heavy undergrowth till he was directly above the cash machine. Cherie's BMW convertible was visible, parked alongside the machine. He could see her inside the car. She opened the door and stepped out. She had her back to Luke. She put the hood on and lowering her head, walked to the cash point.

Luke watched her carefully. Something about the way she walked bothered him. There was almost a spring in her step. She didn't walk as slowly like she normally did. And neither did she move the hood from her face, or look up.

Hairs stood up at the back of Luke's neck. His heart thudded faster against his ribs. He stared closely at the other parked cars, of which there weren't many this close to the cash machine. Most the cars were parked closer to the main supermarket entrance.

Then he saw it. An unmarked dark blue Volvo. It didn't look like a police car, but he guessed that was the whole point. Inside, he could see two men in the front, and another shape at the back. The two men wore chest rigs like uniformed police officers.

Within seconds, the realisation flashed through his brain like lightning. He was set up.

Cherie, you bitch…

A sudden snapping sound came from behind him. Luke didn't think, he moved. Rising swiftly, he dashed to his right. He knew the terrain well, better than those chasing him. Luke flitted between trees, then jumped over a fallen trunk as he heard a thud and muffled shout behind him.

Within minutes he was climbing the fence. He ran like a hare to the end of the road, then round the corner. He didn't pause to look behind him. He was in the car and roaring away when he allowed himself to look in the rearview mirror. The road behind him was empty.

CHAPTER 44

It was almost 21.00 hours. Arla was exhausted, and she knew Harry was as well. She drained the rest of her coffee and threw the paper cup in the bin. She came out of her office and Harry stood from his desk.

"He's ready," Harry said in a quiet voice. He meant Simpson's lawyer, QC Jermyn Hardwicke. An appropriate name for a Queen's Counsel lawyer, Arla thought to herself. Hardwicke had just finished his confidential briefing with Simpson, who had been arrested on charge of murdering David Longworth.

They barged into a red faced Andy Jackson, running in from the corridor. If Harry hadn't been walking in front to absorb the blow, Arla would have been hurt. Andy used to be a rugby prop, and was built like a beefcake.

"Whoa easy," Harry exclaimed.

"Sorry guv," Andy wiped the sweat from his head. "There's been a development. We almost caught Luke Longworth. But he gave us the slip."

Breathlessly, Andy told them the story. Arla hardened her jaws. "Where is Cherier now? I can't believe Darren allowed a civilian to be dragged into this."

"She wouldn't stay in the house guv. Was too scared. Can't blame her to be honest."

"Is she back in the house?"

"Stu and Emily are staying with Cherie. Emily said Cherie doesn't want to live in the house anymore. She wants to go back to the BnB."

Arla nodded. "That makes sense. Can you sort out the paperwork for that. I can authorize."

"Of course, marm," Andy said.

Arla frowned. "Don't call me that, makes me sound old."

When they walked into the interview room, the first thing Arla noticed was how haggard Mike Simpson looked. His cheeks were sunken, along with his eyes which had receded deep into their sockets. He sat slumped in his chair. Next to him, Jermyn Hardwicke looked the epitome of class. His glasses sat on the bridge of his nose, Savile Row pinstripe suit neatly pressed.

He nudged Simpson to sit up straight as Arla entered. Harry did the introductions and the camera came on.

At the first interview, several basic questions had not been covered. Arla blamed herself for it. She knew the historical abuse cases against Simpson weighed heavy on her mind. That made him a despicable creature, but not necessarily guilty of murder. She had to keep an open mind.

"Where were you the night of the 17th November?" Arla asked.

Simpson looked weary. "At a work do in the evening. Lots of people were there. Ask them."

"How did you know the way David was murdered?"

Simpson glanced at Hardwicke, who leaned over and whispered in his ear. Simpson sat up straighter.

"I was sent a message."

"How do you mean?"

Again, lawyer and client had a hushed conversation. "A photo was sent to my phone."

"Who sent it?"

"An unknown number. No idea who." Arla and Harry exchanged a glance. This was getting interesting.

Simpson's phone was in custody already, and a SOC team would be visiting his office tomorrow.

"Are you sure you didn't recognise the number?"

"Yes."

"Any idea why someone would do that?"

Simpson shook his head. Arla repeated her questions about assaulting Cherie and the older cases.

Hardwicke's features barely moved when he spoke. "I believe my client has answered these questions already. Can we move on please."

Arla shifted track. "How well did you know Luke Longworth?"

She didn't miss the shadow that passed over Simpson's face. It was brief, he composed himself quickly. She had asked the question deliberately.

"Cherie said you knew him," Arla said.

Simpson's voice was stiff. "He came to house with his father a couple of times. When he was younger mind you."

"So you knew him for a long time? As long as you knew David."

"I don't know him well. He's the son of a friend, not my own son."

"When was the last time you saw him?"

Simpson replied quickly. Too quickly. "Not recently."

"When, in that case?"

He shrugged. "Maybe six months ago. When I went to David's house."

Arla remembered what Cherie had said. Luke hadn't visited the house in the last year. Aloud she said, "Are you sure it was six months ago?"

A look of irritation crossed Simpson's face. "Some time around then. I didn't put in the bloody calendar."

Hardwicke interjected, moving only his lips. "I believe he has answered the question."

178

"Not really," Arla reposted, glaring back at the suave lawyer. She turned back to Simpson. "Do you have Luke's number in your phone?"

Simpson's eyes narrowed slightly. He had a quick chat with his lawyer, then answered. "Yes. Why?"

"So although you only knew him only as your friend's son, and saw him rarely, you kept his number on your phone?"

"He was in the same business as me. Occasionally he called me for advice."

"And the last time was more than six months ago?"

"Yes."

Harry nodded at Arla and leaned in. "When you got the photo on your phone, why didn't you inform the police?"

"I was going to. But I wasn't sure if it was a fake. Like a sick joke. I rang both David and Cherie but no one replied. So I forgot about it."

"You didn't think of it again when you saw the news?"

"I did. But you guys were at my office before I could speak to you."

Harry said, "How did the murderer have your number?"

Irritation swept over his Simpson's face again. "Maybe he got it from somewhere."

"Like where?"

"How am I supposed to know? Isn't that your job?"

CHAPTER 45

Hardwicke remained his cool, placid self but raised a hand to stop Simpson from speaking further.

"My client has answered the question already."

Harry put his elbows on the desk. "So, the murderer, or someone with intimate knowledge of the crime scene, took a photo of the deceased and just happened to send it you, Mr Simpson?"

Simpson hung his head and shook it. When he looked up his eyes were blazing with hatred. "If you say so, yes."

"Why you?" Harry waved a hand in the air expansively. His long arm almost reached out across the table. "I mean, why not his wife? Why not anyone else but only you?"

Simpson sat there seething, staring at Harry like he wanted to plant nails into his eyes.

Arla said, "You, who had an argument with him before you left his house, a week before he died. You, whom his wife accused of assaulting."

"And also you," Harry continued, "Who has received almost two hundred thousand pounds from him in total. The murderer decides to contact you after he kills David Longworth. Does that not strike you as odd?"

Hardwicke intervened again. "My client has replied and has nothing further to add."

Arla said, "Tell us about your family, Mr Simpson."

He was still seething, and doing a poor job of hiding it. He chewed his words out slowly. "Divorced. No children."

Harry said, "You said David was working with you on this new film project. Was it financed by your company?"

Hardwicke and Simpson had another heads down chat. Simpson said, "We had joint rights to the production."

Arla butted in. "Joint profit sharing rights?"

Simpson sucked a cheek, brows furrowed. He could see where this was going. "Yes."

"Do you have other films where you share profits with David as well?"

Simpson said, "I dont believe my business matters are relevant here."

Arla picked up a pen and wrote in her notebook, speaking slowly as she wrote. "Right, so when this goes to court, I can confirm that you had no other film profits sharing with David-

"I didn't say that!" Simpson's nostrils were flaring, his face turning red again.

Arla looked, feigning surprise. "Oh, so you did?"

Hardwicke intervened. "As my client said, his previous business deals are not relevant here."

"Even if those deals were with the deceased? You don't think the CPS will find that interesting?" Arla caught a shimmer of irritation pass over Hardwicke's face and stifled her grin.

She glanced back at Simpson, who was glaring at her. She raised an eyebrow.

Simpson spoke between clenched teeth. "We have been making films and TV productions for a long time. Longer than you knew the alphabet."

Arla ignored the jibe. "So we're talking hundreds of productions, right?"

"Yes."

"How many of them are still active?"

"About ten in current production."

She sensed Harry stretch. He asked, "Did Luke ever work in any of these productions?"

Simpson shrugged. "Not as far as I know. I'm the producer, I can't be on site all the time like the director is. If David wanted to give his son some experience he might have. Not sure."

"So the answer is Luke might be involved."

"I dont know."

"Have you ever worked with Luke?"

Anger pulsed through Simpson's features again. "No. How many times do I have to tell you?"

Arla took the names of the people who could alibi him on the night of the murder. The uniforms came in to take Simpson back to the holding bay. He would spend the night in custody and Hardwicke would arrange bail for him in the morning.

The office was deserted. Only the cleaners were present, moving trash out and hoovering. Arla slumped on a chair and put her feet up on Harry's desk.

Harry sat down opposite her. "Do you think he's guilty?"

"Depends on the motive."

"Motive could be money related. Or business. With David out of the way, he gets all the film rights and other intellectual property. That could be worth a lot of money in the future."

Arla nodded. "That makes sense. Glad I got that out of him."

Harry smirked. "Yes, that was a nice move." His eyes swept up and down her slowly. Arla felt a heat spread inside, warming her. She was tired, and curling up in bed with Harry seemed like a good plan

"Time to go," she said.

Harry stood, keeping his eyes on her. She remained seated and he took a step closer. Arla grinned.

Harry said "Shall I give you a lift?" He dropped his voice to a whisper and leaned over her. "And maybe something else later?"

Arla inhaled his scent deeply and wiggled her eyebrows. "You are so mysterious, DI Mehta. What did you have in mind?"

CHAPTER 46

The man watched the female detective and her lanky sidekick come out the rear entrance of Clapham Police Station. He had waited patiently for the last two hours, watching people come and go from the car park. He couldn't keep the engine on forever, smoke from the exhaust attracted attention. His breath made fumes inside the car and he folded his arms against his chest, trying to keep himself warm. But his persistence had paid off. He knew it would. He felt the certainty of it rising like a tide inside him, making him infallible, imperious. He would serve justice upon this world, open the eyes of the unseeing, dumb masses. No one would stop him.

Arla Baker. That was her name. He liked it. The two words rolled off his tongue easily. He didn't know the name of the tall, wide shouldered man who was with her. They walked separately and got into a black BMW. He watched the car come out and ducked as the headlights flashed. He let the BMW drive to the end of the road before he swung out quickly, headlights turned off.

He caught up with the BMW as it turned right on Clapham High Street. He let two cars in between them, then followed, switching his headlights on.

After fifteen minutes, the BMW turned into a street in Tooting Broadway, not far from the tube stop. He went past that road, took the the next right, right again, and he was at the bottom of the road the BMW had turned into. He turned his headlights off. The BMW was parking. He parked as well, and came out of the car. He pulled the hoodie of his coat well over his head, disguising himself.

He could see the female detective and her partner get out of the car. They stood close together. The man stopped walking, and pressed himself against the shadow of a doorway. Arla Baker was leaning against the man. As he watched, the man lowered his head and they kissed.

Pulse surged inside him. He opened his mouth and breathed rapidly.

The whore. He had her marked for himself and now she was....excitement was replaced by sudden, explosive anger. He had plans for Arla Baker. He would make her a symbol of his operation, his crusade to set the world right. But for that, she had to be pure. And now, she was debasing herself by mixing with another man.

Inside the coat pockets, his hands clenched tight. He would show her. Show them both.

The couple crossed the street, bodies glued to each other. He detached himself from the wall and walked towards them slowly. He didn't want to get too close. but also wanted to make sure he knew the address.

He speeded up as they went in, light from the hallway casting a conical shadow on the dark street. Number 72. He walked past it, memorising the entrance, the sash bay window facing the street on the ground floor. A Victorian terrace, probably a split level apartment, he thought. His mind turned to what they were doing inside. He imagined touching her warm, naked skin, and a feral need grew inside him, stirring his loins. He bared his teeth.

I'm coming for what's mine.

He turned on his heels and walked back to his car quickly. He would deal with Arla Baker soon. very soon. But first, he had other tasks. He drove back to Clapham, and over the Common to the long street where rows of houses sat facing the dark expanse of the now invisible greenery. He got out of his car, locked it and walked to the large terraced property he had been watching for several weeks now. Once a splendid manor for the wealthy gentry of Clapham, it was now divided into several apartments. He was interested in the ground floor. Lights were off, but he knew the old man who lived there was inside.

He had visited the old man, dressed as a postman. Started to chat with him, and didn't see any alarm keypads on the wall. He felt a

185

sense of exhilaration delivering the letters he had written with his own hand, directly to the old man. He remembered how the old hands shook as he read the name on the envelope.

He paused, and looked around him. The road was deserted, only the tepid glow from halogen lamps lighting up the frigid, desolate night. He took out a keychain and screwdriver. Within a minute, the lock slid off the latch and he was inside.

The hallway was submerged in darkness. The light of a circuit box gleamed below the staircase. He tiptoed in, stopping as the creak of a floorboard gave him away. There was no sound apart from the faint hum of snoring. The old man was sleeping, and he could tell by the direction of the snoring the bedroom was one door down.

He let himself inside the bedroom and waited. His eyes were used to the dark. The red digital keypad of a clock rested on the table next to the bed. On the bed there was a shape huddled under a blanket.

For a brief second, he allowed himself the luxury of thinking the shape was Arla Baker. He was in her bedroom and she was his for the taking. Sleeping, defenceless. He shuddered with anticipation.

Closing his eyes, he came back to the present. He took the hammer out from his backpack. Then he approached the bed slowly.

CHAPTER 47

It was Nicole. Odd, how her face hadn't changed over the years.

It was a rainy, dark night but she stood under a streetlight, and Arla could see her face clearly. Nicole stood no more than ten feet away. Rain water coursed down her face like incessant tears. Wet hair clung to her neck and she shivered. Arla couldn't tear her eyes off her sister. After all these years, she had found her.

"Here," Arla gasped, throwing her arms open. "Nicole, come here."

Her sister stared back at her , a lost, helpless look on that normally cocky, self assured face. "Arla," she whispered. "Is it you?"

"Yes. It's me." Arla stepped forward. A brisk wind creaked the corners of her broken heart. Nicole was so close to touch, after all these years.

Then she saw him. A long, hooded dark figure.. He loomed out of the darkness suddenly, behind the lamp post. His face was invisible. He was behind Nicole and she hadn't seen him.

"Nicole!" Arla shouted. "Come here, quickly."

Her sister's eyes widened. A sudden cloud of blackness poured out from the figure behind Nicole. It blew out into the rainy, windy night like a shroud, hiding Nicole from view.

"No!" Arla screamed. She ran full tilt towards the shadow. "No….."

Arla's eyes flew open. She was sitting upright in bed, breathing heavily. Her alarm was beeping, a faint sound to her right. She felt a warm hand on her shoulder and turned to see Harry. He was fully dressed, in stark contrast to her nakedness.

"Same dream again?" Harry asked gently.

Arla brushed his hand off her shoulder. She wiped sweat from her brow and tried to control her thudding heart. God, she hated that dream. *Hated it.*

She came off the bed and grabbed the dressing gown hanging from the back of the door. As she went into the bathroom, she heard the front door click shut. Harry was leaving for work. That was planned, as they made it a point never to arrive together.

In the cold light of day, her mind slipped out of slumber. She stepped inside a hot shower and got ready quickly. Today was going to be busy.

She ticked off the things she needed to do in her mind. Simpson had to be interviewed again before he left. She knew she couldn't keep him if he was granted bail. Harry had a search warrant for Luke Simpson's house, and she didn't even need it to get inside under the circumstances. There was now a police case against Luke, for resisting arrest and assaulting a police officer. Johnson couldn't stop her now.

She also needed to speak to Cherie. Luke had used a new number so they could put a trace on it. Luke had to be found. There was no time to lose.

By the time Arla got to the station, it was 9 am. The incident room was buzzing when she walked in.

Arla took her place next to Harry, Lisa and the rest of the team. She raised her voice. The room was packed to the brim today. News of Mike Simpson's arrest had obviously made the rounds already.

"OK, listen up. We have a suspect in custody, and he is charged, for now." Arla looked around the room, and caught the eyes of Justin Beauregard. He didn't seem happy but then again he never did.

"For now," Arla said, "We are keeping the charge active, but it might change. We need a tight case, and not something the CPS will laugh out of the court. So far, Simpson had the means and the motive. He also had a photo of the deceased taken just after the murder, on his phone."

Voices and murmurs grew louder in the room. Arla spoke above the din. "He says someone sent it to him. It's true but that doesn't make him any less of a suspect."

Beauregard shouted to make his voice heard "Yeah, but doesn't make him guilty though does it?"

Arla held his eyes. "You got a case against anyone else for this murder, Justin?"

"That's your job, D.C.I Baker." He paused at each letter and Arla bit back her retort. She knew he was egging her on, wanting her to lose her temper in front of everyone. Instead she smiled sweetly at him.

"Yes, it *is* my job."

He grimaced and turned away.

Arla continued. "And we are making progress. First thing today, we raid another suspects house." She gestured at Andy Jackson, who hurried up from his seat. "Get an armed team ready," Arla whispered. "Luke Longworth's house but keep that to yourself."

Andy went off to assemble the team. Lisa cleared her throat and Arla turned to her.

Lisa said, "I'm going to speak to another witness on Mike Simpson's alibi list. But the woman I spoke to on the phone confirmed that Simpson was at this party on the 17th November. She works in his office. It was a work party."

Arla heart sank. If Simpson had a line of alibi's for that evening they might as well retract their charge now. But, she was determined not to let Simpson off the hook so easily. He still had a motive - the millions in cash if he became the sole owner of the film profit rights he shared with David Longworth.

Besides, she wouldn't put it past Simpson to have a few paid alibi's just to cover his tracks.

"Make an appointment for me to see one of them," Arla said. "And see if we can get some down to the station as well."

"For Luke Longworth, we have a match with the bootprint, which more or less confirms he did the burglary for David's personal possessions. We don't have his DNA samples as yet and that's hampering our progress. We know he is trying to make contact with Cherie, the wife and God knows what he's planning for her. So it's time we got hold of him."

The meeting broke up without Arla specifying further how she was going to get hold of Luke. Harry was outside already and Andy was getting a van ready with an SFO or specialist firearms officer on board. He saw Arla and gave her a thumbs up. Arla returned the gesture and ran to the black BMW waiting for her.

CHAPTER 48

The volume on the radio was turned on full. Arla twirled the black knob anti clockwise to reduce the sound.

"Are you receiving, Andy? This is Base."

"Yes guv, loud and clear." Static crackled over Andy Jackson's voice.

"This is a densely packed residential area. I want the place on lockdown over a two square mile area. If he's inside, I don't want him escaping down any of the side streets. Over."

"That will be difficult guv. We only have two cars with us. Over."

"Then get them to drop the team off and then take positions." Arla snapped. "Do the best you can."

Harry swerved through traffic and eventually put the siren on. Their CID car didn't have flashing lights, but the ear splitting sound was obvious enough. Harry raced through and then cut the siren as they got closer. Arla's phone beeped. It was Rita.

"Guv, I have something interesting. You know the phone number that Luke used to contact Cherie last night?"

"Yes, what about it?"

"I got the phone log. One number was called on it repeatedly the whole of last week. A number that's on our records. Mike Simpson's phone."

A ripple of tension spread across Arla's scalp. Simpson had admitted to having Luke's number. But he had not contacted Luke in the last several months. Could it be because Luke had used this number instead?

Arla clutched the phone tighter. "Rita, can you check if this number was used to send Simpson the murder photo?"

"I need to run a search against Simpson's phone log, guv."

"That's fine, I'll hold."

Harry said, "Less than three minutes ETA."

Arla nodded and picked at her nails. She stopped herself. She had done her nails three weeks ago. No point in destroying them just because she was tense. Silently, she willed Rita to hurry up.

Finally Rita's voice came back on the line. "There's no match this time, guv. The number has called Simpson's phone several times but a different number sent the photo."

Arla felt deflated. Still, Luke could have more than one number. "Fine. Make sure we get the phone log for that number as well, OK?"

"The phone that sent Simpson the photo? It's out of action. I think its been destroyed. I found the IMEI number, and as cell phones transmit a signal five days after switched off I might still find something. Waiting to hear back from the phone company."

"You have been busy Rita. Good work. See you soon."

"Be careful guv."

Arla thanked her back and hung up.

Harry took a sharp right turn and stopped the car. They were within walking distance now. The road had an identical row of terraced properties on both sides. It was narrowed further by the parked cars on both sides.

It was quiet, the buzz of traffic on the main road now behind them. Arla spoke on her radio, out of breath as they walked rapidly.

"We're coming up from behind. Are you in position? Over."

Andy's voice was hoarse. "Yes guv. The cars have gone back to watch the main street exits. You want them where these roads join the main traffic, right?"

"That will do for now. Make sure we have enough for a chase if he legs it. Did you call NPAS?"

NPAS or the National Police Air Service was the helicopter search team.

"Available within ten minutes, guv. Shall I tell them to get airborne now?"

Arla looked at Harry, who was listening to the exchange. "Can't hurt," Harry said. "If he's not there, all we have to do is call it off."

Arla agreed. "Call them, Andy. But tell them to stay away. Dont want the noise warning him."

"Copy that guv."

Arla and Harry came around the corner and stopped under the shade of a trees. It wasn't raining, thankfully. Arla's eyes took in the grey door with the artwork glass panel, similar in size and shape to most of the front doors on the street. Two mothers walked down, pushing their prams and chatting. Briefly, Arla was reminded of her tryst with Harry in the parked car. She could see the spot. A movement caught her eye. It was Andy, without his jacket, staying behind a lamp post. There was no time to lose.

She looked up at the bay windows of the property, curtains separated, a dark, lightless hole visible through the glass. It was daytime but it was murky with clouds. The ground floor bay windows had their curtains drawn.

"Go," Arla whispered on the radio.

CHAPTER 49

Andy darted out from behind a car with another uniformed officer. The second guy held the battering ram in his hand. They were joined by two more officers who ran in from the sides. It happened very quickly. The burly man with the battering ram smashed the door open in two hits. Four of them barged in, Arla and Harry hot on their heels.

"Police!" Andy shouted as he ran up the stairs. Arla stayed downstairs while Harry followed Andy. The house shook as heavy boots trampled over the floor.

Arla raced into the kitchen. The back door was locked but the key was in, and she opened it to come out into the garden. The grass was overgrown and there was a shed in one corner. Arla ran down the stairs and approached the shed carefully. A uniform officer was right behind her. The shed door was locked, but she peered through the glass. Two lawn mowers, an old pool table, a couple of rusty bikes and various other junk littered the place. There was no sign of a man.

There was a whistle, and Arla turned around. Harry had opened one of the windows upstairs. He waved at her. "Come up here," he said.

Arla was resigned to the fact she wouldn't find Luke. She went back inside and up the staircase. The house was nicely decorated, she noticed. Original artwork hung on the wall, and the paint was new. The carpets were soft and her feet sank in them. Harry was standing outside a bedroom. He had his gloves on. Without a word he turned, and she followed him to the chest of drawers in one corner. The bed looked like it hadn't been slept in.

Harry had the bottom drawer open. He went down on his haunches and stared inside. Arla leaned over him. Harry pointed. The lights were on, throwing a bright glare off the full length mirror against a wardrobe. Harry had lifted two layers of clothes and when Arla saw it, her breath froze.

It was a hammer. The handle on it was short, made of a black polymer substance. LIght glinted off the metallic surface of the hammer. It looked mean, squat and ugly. One side of it had a black mark on it. Arla shuddered when she thought what it must be. Dried blood.

She licked dry lips and breathed. "Bag it," she told Harry. She put gloves on herself. This house was now a crime scene too. Arla looked around the room. It was immaculate. She couldn't help wondering what sort of a single man kept the room so clean. Harry wasn't single anymore, but his one bedroom apartment looked like a bomb hit it.

Arla knelt by the bed and inspected the carpet closely. No marks on it. She peered underneath the bed. There was a suitcase. She got Harry to pull it out. It wasnt locked and inside all they found was old clothes.

Andy appeared at the bedroom door. "Clean as a whistle guv."

Harry said, "Look what we found." He held up the bag and explained that the murder weapons was probably a hammer. Andy's eyebrows shot up.

Arla had opened the wardrobe and was looking inside. Well pressed shirts and suits hung over a few pair of shoes. Everything pointed to order and symmetry. Even the potential murder weapon was stored neatly.

Arla shivered, remembering how fastidious some serial killers could be. Had they just found one?

She turned to Harry. "The garden. Any signs of recent digging?"

He nodded and went downstairs to investigate. Arla called Parmentier, asking him to come down ASAP with a team. She called the car team on her radio. They had not seen any running figure, or anyone matching Luke's description.

Arla put the radio back in her pocket just as her phone buzzed. It was the station. She answered.

"DCI Baker."

"It's me," the cold, hostile voice belonged to Johnson. "Where are you?"

Arla gulped. "I...uh-just found evidence that could crack this case sir. I think you'll be pleased."

"Answer the question, damn it. Where are you?" Johnson wasnt mincing his words. Which meant he knew where she was. Arla sighed.

"I'm at a suspect's house sir." Before Johnson could interject, she said, "Luke Longworth's."

"Arla!" Johnson's voice boomed. "How dare you disobey a direct order. Do you know what you have done?"

"Sir I just found a suspicious-

"It doesn't matter what you found. Get back to the nick right now. We need to talk."

"But sir-

Arla broke off when she realised Harry and Andy were gesturing at her. Harry was pointing up frantically. Arla moved the phone from her ears. That's when she heard the sound. It came from the loft space above.

Someone was moving around in the loft.

CHAPTER 50

Arla hung up, cutting a screaming Johnson mid flow. She would take the fall out later. Moving on the balls of her feet, she joined Harry and Andy in the hallway. The sounds above had stopped, as if the intruder had suddenly realised the house was quiet now. Andy leaned over the bannisters of the railing and whispered urgently to the rest of his team.

Arla looked up to see the trapdoor for the loft space. Harry went back into the bedroom and came out with a chair. He stood on it, ready to unlock the door. The firearms officer, an MP5 submachine gun on his shoulder, came softly up the stairs. He crouched on the landing, pointing the gun at the loft space. Harry nodded at him, then glanced at Arla. A silent agreement passed between them. At the same time, a sudden, unexpected fear pierced Arla's heart. She didn't want Harry to be in the line of fire. It was strange, because she had been in many dangerous situations with Harry before, but never had she felt this way. Without knowing what she was doing, Arla stepped forward and waved at Harry to come down from the chair.

He frowned at her, then realized. A tender, almost sad smile crept on his lips. He winked at her and shook his head slowly. A heavy weight was lodged in Arla's throat. She found it hard to breathe. She suddenly realised that after all these years, today, she was more scared than she had ever been.

She wouldn't forgive herself if something happened to Harry. As the senior officer, she should be up there, not him.

But it was too late. Harry had opened the clasp, and the trapdoor was lowering. It was deathly still in the house all of a sudden. The trap door lowered with a creak that moaned against the walls, unnaturally loud.

Harry moved the chair and lowered the folded staircase. The loft space was dark, and the silence was unnerving. Harry put a hand on the staircase, and put his foot on the first rung. Arla grabbed his sleeve and pulled him back. He looked at her quizzically.

Arla spoke loudly. "This is the police and we are armed. We know you're up there. Come down and surrender yourself."

Her voice echoed against the walls and there was silence again. Then very softly the creaking sound came again, before stopping abruptly.

Arla said, "Luke? Is that you?"

There was no response. She raised her voice again. "Nothing will happen to you Luke. We just want to ask you some questions. Don't make this hard on yourself. Come down, now."

In the ensuing silence, the firearms officer crept forward, weapon pointed up. Arla knew he had no intention of firing, the weapon was a deterrent. They needed this person alive.

"This is your last chance," Arla said. "Then we're coming up. I'll count to five." She counted out loud. At the count of three, a voice floated down from upstairs.

"OK. I'm coming."

A few seconds later, a man's face poked out from the loft hatch. Arla gaped at him.

It was Ken Nixon.

He caught Arla's eyes and sighed. "Why don't you come up here?" He disappeared from sight, then a light came on in the loft. Harry gave Arla a look, shrugged and climbed the stairs. She followed after him.

There was a hollow feeling in her stomach, and the sinking realisation that she had got something very wrong.

Ken stood in the middle of the loft space. Another man, wearing headphones, stood next to him. Both were dressed in warm coats and wooly hats. It was colder up here, and Arla saw two sleeping bags in one corner.

The other man removed his headphones slowly, staring at both Arla and Harry. Two black holdalls lay on the floor, with wires and machines sticking out of them. A bunch of wires trailed down the floor and into the rafters, some heading into the walls. A camera and tripod was placed to one side. A radio receiver with shiny silver dials was at Nixon's feet.

"Oh God," Arla said, gripping her forehead.

Nixon was scowling. "I did try to tell you."

Arla's temper flared but she kept her voice even. "Then why didn't you? When you saw the evidence against Luke mounting up?"

"This surveillance operation has been going for weeks, DCI Baker. Not much point in us being the secret intelligence service if we tell everyone about it, is there?"

Arla felt an overwhelming urge to slap him in the face and get out of this place. But she could do neither.

"Tell me what this is about."

Nixon spread his hands. "Sure you can see? We've been eavesdropping on Luke Longworth because he is one of the largest suppliers of violent pornography."

Arla blinked. "Violent pornography?"

"Yes. The type that involves hurting people. It's illegal, and often it includes children."

"That's disgusting."

"It is. And for that reason, we are keeping a close eye on him."

Harry said, "But it's Special Branch who normally deal with cases like these. Why you guys?"

"Because he has financial dealings with overseas governments. Offshore bank accounts. That's where he keeps the money from his illegal films."

A distant thought buzzed around in Arla's head, getting closer. "These offshore accounts wouldn't be in the Bahamas, would they?"

Nixon nodded. "Yes."

Arla said what she had long suspected. "Mike Simpson and Luke are connected aren't they?"

Nixon didn't say anything, but he didn't have to. Arla spoke quickly. "And after David Longworth's death, you wanted to investigate Luke, given his interest in this violent stuff."

Nixon shrugged again, and Arla wanted to shake the man by his collar. She stepped up to him, eyes blazing. "Why don't you just tell me now, before we waste time and money on another wild goose chase?"

He shifted, looking uncomfortable, then exchanged a glance with his colleague, who nodded. Nixon heaved a big sigh. "OK. Shall we head downstairs?"

That made sense, as Arla was freezing. They regrouped in the living room, which again was nicely decorated.

Nixon said, "We have arrested two film makers already for making child pornography. But that was the tip of the iceberg. Luke is the key member of an international gang. They're global, with operations in almost every country. Very big in Africa and Asia, where regulations over these matters are not very effective, shall we say. This has been a year long, international venture and we're working closely with our counterparts overseas. We get Luke, we can shut down the whole operation."

Arla sat down heavily on the sofa. "Have I ruined it?"

Nixon blew out his cheeks. "To be honest, now that he's missing, there's no great harm in what you did. Obviously it would matter if he was living here. But for the last two days, he has only been here once. I don't know where he is. His phone is not working and he's using a new number."

Harry was leaning against the wall. "Do you think Luke did it?"

Nixon swung his eyes towards Harry. "Kill David Longworth? Possible. He's very messed up man."

"He had no motive," Arla said. "But like you said, he's disturbed."

A silent urgency filled the space between them. charging the air. Harry voiced the common thought circulating like wildire in their minds.

"We need to find Luke."

Arla tapped a finger against her leg. "What about the connection with Simpson? You said these offshore accounts Luke deals with are in the Bahamas. That's where Blue Horizon, Simpson's firm is based."

The look on Simpson's face more or less gave it away. "Money from Luke's productions do end up in Blue Horizon, among other firms. We've been keeping tabs on him as well."

Arla crossed her arms across her chest. "You cooperate with foreign governments but not with us?"

Nixon coughed. "Actually, by bringing Simpson in you screwed our investigation. Which-

"Which wouldn't have happened had you talked to me to begin with. Correct?"

Nixon clenched his jaw and stared back at her with hostile eyes. Arla returned the look. Nixon looked away eventually. He cleared his throat.

"Look, we need a way to sort this out now."

Arla smirked. "Yes, you need our help. In fact, by charging Simpson, I think we *have* helped you. He's under pressure now, and more willing to talk."

Nixon raised his eyebrows. "Who do you think sent Simpson the images of David?"

"An unknown number. A pay as you go mobile phone, which has not been used again. The SIM card is probably destroyed."

201

"Last known location?"

"Don't know yet," Arla said tersely. *Why should I share information with you when you don't do the same?*

She knew that even if they did find the location of the unused phone, by triangulation of the phone masts, the location was never a specific one. But she would get something within two to three hundred meters.

Aloud she said, "I guess it's time to get back and regroup." Harry came off the wall and opened the door. Arla's phone buzzed. It was Rita.

She nodded at Nixon and his colleague and walked out the door, phone clutched in her hand. She didn't miss the searching look in Nixon's eyes, like he was trying to gauge her next move.

CHAPTER 51

Arla and Harry rushed down the road, followed by the uniform officers. Inquisitive residents stopped and gawked at them. Arla walked close to Harry, his figure shielding her from the windows of Luke's house. The phone was in her ear.

"Rita?"

"Yes guv, I got something for you. Cherie Longworth got a text this morning. Luke put his name on it."

A fear struck against Arla's spine like a whiplash. "What did the text say?"

"You sold me out. Today, you'll know the truth. The whole world will know."

A deep sense of unease was uncoiling in Arla's limbs. Those words sounded desperate.

"Where is the location?"

"It's within two streets of High Street Kensington. From the south west."

Arla frowned. Kensington was one of the most exclusive neighbourhoods in London. Where millionaire playboys hobnobbed with royalty.

Rita said, "Thank god Cherie called us. Otherwise we would be in the dark. What shall we do, guv?"

"I'm sending one of the squad cars out to Cherie's BnB. Is she OK?"

"There's a team with her already boss. I didn't actually speak to her. Switchboard informed me."

"Good work, Rita. Listen, I'm heading out to Kensington now. Can you check if we have another uniformed unit near

203

Kensington? Please alert them. We need to lock down Kensington High Street."

"But guv that's-"

"A big deal I know. But it's necessary. When was the phone last used?"

"Two hours ago."

"He could be anywhere. Keep Cherie safe, she's number one priority as a witness now."

They arrived at the black BMW and Andy Jackson caught up with them. Arla told him and Harry what was happening.

"Andy, I want you to get as many units as you can and head down to High Street Ken. I want a lockdown over a two square mile radius. Yes, I know it's difficult. I want two NPAS helicopters scrambled, and in air now."

Arla paused. "When Luke escaped last night, Darren saw his car, didn't he? You said a blue Renault, M reg?"

"That's right guv," Andy said, wiping sweat from his brow. "Shame we didn't get the rest of the licence plate."

"Never mind. Feed that information to the NPAS. See you there."

Andy and his team ran off to their cars. Arla got into the car and Harry swung out quickly, joining the traffic, heading north for the winding grey ribbon of the Thames, which they had to cross to get to Kensington and Chelsea, the uber wealthy enclaves of west London.

Harry said, "Remember Commander Bose? The guy who helped us in the drug trafficking case last year?"

Arla frowned, then a light dawned in her eyes. Commander Bose was a high ranking uniformed officer. His remit lay over five districts of west London, and he was part of the Royal Protection Force, the secretive, little known unit of the London Met that was charged with personal protection of the Royal family members.

"Good idea Harry." She flashed him a smile. His brows were furrowed, eyes on the road. His chiselled jaw was set in a grim line, and he spoke without looking at her.

"Anytime guv."

Arla had the phone out, thumbing for Bose's number. She stopped. "Call me Arla."

"Ok, Arla." He sped past a slow car and then braked rapidly to avoid crashing into another. "Listen, I need to put the siren on. Can you please hurry up with the phone call?"

She got the number and dialled, praying Bose would pick up. He did, and his warm, baritone voice came on the line.

"Who is this?"

"DCI Baker, sir. We worked on the Bulgarian cocaine bust last year? I'm at the Clapham nick, South London Command."

Bose's voice lightened. "Ah yes, I remember. How are you doing? Arla isn't it?"

"Yes sir. I need your help with something." Speaking rapidly, Arla laid out the situation.

Bose asked, "What do you want me to do?"

"To prevent this suspect from escaping sir, I want a lockdown on Kensington High Street, the Palace and a two square mile radius, including the tube station."

"That's asking a lot, Arla. Who is authorizing this?"

Arla hesitated. In truth, it should be Johnson speaking to Bose, not her. But she didn't have the time to explain to Johnson, and she knew what his response would be. Leave it to the MI5.

She had to be honest with Bose. "I will get clearance from DS Johnson sir. But could we please get the gears in motion? You know how long these things take."

"You don't have to tell me that, DCI Baker," Bose said in a colder voice. " I need to speak to your commanding officer to get authorization on this. You know the drill."

Arla's heart sank and a tone of desperation creeped into her voice. "Sir, please. We're trying very hard to catch this guy. Even the Secretary of State is involved in this case. He was a personal friend of the deceased, and the murderer could be caught today."

"The Secretary of State? James Fraser?" Bose asked slowly.

"Yes."

After a slight pause Bose said, "Fraser has an apartment next to Kensington High Street. I know because once we had to organise a security detail for him when he visited Prince Charles at Kensington Palace."

A spasm tightened inside Arla's mind, a potent contraction that suddenly caused a domino chain of nerves firing in her brain. James Fraser, Cherie, David….what was the connection really? What had she missed so far?

It couldn't be a coincidence that Luke was in Kensington, so close to Fraser's residence. Could it?

In a tremulous voice she asked, "Is Fraser there right now, sir?"

Bose's voice was very quiet. "As a matter of fact, he is. This is the Embassy area, as you know. A number of cabinet members are meeting with the President of Egypt this morning."

Fear caught the back of Arla's throat. She didn't know exactly what would happen today, but an ominous coldness was flowing into her skin like sheets of ice. She shivered"Sir, I think we need to order this blockade and see if we can catch this guy. I have a very bad feeling about this."

"I should have known about this earlier. Have you informed NPAS for air support?"

"Yes sir I have. Two of my uniform units are on their way as well."

"OK. I will mobilise my force and the Palace Security Guards. I believe some members of the Royal family are in residence at Kensington Palace." Bose paused. "Is this guy a terrorist threat? Do I need to alert the Counter Terrorism Command?"

Arla searched her mind for a few seconds. She was hurled against the door as the Harry took a sharp turn. She steadied herself quickly. "No, sir. I don't think so."

"Right. I will inform your boss, Wayne Johnson, and I suggest you do too. And Arla?"

Her voice was dry. "Yes?"

"The Commissioner and the entire National Police Board will be in on this. This is a big deal. For your sake, I hope you know what's going on."

Arla's heart squeezed against her ribs. She swallowed painfully. Did she really know what was happening? Yes and no. But every instinct in her being was screaming this was critical.

She tried to sound confident, but her voice was croaky. "Yes sir I do."

Bose hung up. Arla knew he would now fire off emails and call secure line phones to mobilise a huge force. She had to do the right thing too. She called Johnson.

"Where the hell are you, Arla?" Johnson's voice was impatient. Arla informed him. For a few seconds there was complete silence. She had a mental image of Johnson's mouth hanging open.

"You what?" he spluttered. "You...oh my God, what have you done?"

CHAPTER 52

Luke had rented the small studio apartment above the corner shop with cash. Mr Patel, the Indian owner of the corner shop, who also owned the row of flats above it, didn't mind. Luke had chosen the apartment as it was on the second floor and gave him a direct view of the handsome red brick terraced buildings opposite. The ground floor was all swanky, expensive boutique shops selling Prada and LV, but the upper six floors were live in apartments.

Luke knew the one where James Fraser lived when he was in town. Like most Members of Parliament, he had an apartment where he stayed during the week, its cost subsidised by England's tax payers.

Luke had a camera tripod set up near the window. He had a telescopic lens attached to the SLR camera. It was aimed directly at the window where Fraser could be seen, moving around. Luke had been in position for the last two days. This apartment was now his base. He had rung Fraser's office to find the politician's exact schedule. Luke knew in half an hour, Fraser's would leave the apartment. His bodyguard would accompany him to the Egyptian Embassy opposite Hyde Park, a twenty minute walk, at most.

Fraser liked to walk the short distances, which suited Luke's plan to perfection.

A woman in a bath robe came into view. She embraced Fraser, who was dressed in a suit. His steel gray, patrician hair was slicked back with gel. Luke watched them kiss, revulsion growing inside him.

And with it, his resolve.

At Luke's feet, lay a backpack. Inside it, he had a crossbow and two knives.

After today, Luke knew he would be famous in a way he had never dreamt of. It was a moment he had waited for several years. Not that he knew what to do several years ago. That had only been recently. The answer had come to him easily. There was only one way out.

David Longworth had paid.

Now it was Fraser's turn.

Luke picked up his phone and stared at the blank screen for a few seconds. A movement on the street caught his eyes. A car rolled down, and parked on the same side as Fraser's apartment. It was the bodyguard.

Luke returned to the phone screen. He wanted to leave another message for Cherie. But what good would it do? She was the same as the rest. Maybe she didn't even know. Now, he would never find out. It didn't matter.

Luke put his eyes back to the lens. The woman was sitting on Fraser's knee, kissing him. Anger hardened inside Luke again. He knew she wasn't his wife. He had seen the wife's photo. She was old and frumpy, not a pretty young thing like this woman. The woman was getting frisky, but Fraser stood, holding her hands down.

It was time.

As Fraser smoothed down his suit, Luke opened the bag and put one of the long blade knives in his trouser pocket. It was wrapped in two layers of kitchen towels, with only the handle sticking out.

He took out the SD drive from the camera. He connected it to his laptop, then streamed all the photos to the five newspaper websites he had opened accounts.

Then he stood. His breathing was fast and heavy, anticipation burning in his heart like fire. He slung the backpack on his shoulder, then opened the door and walked to the staircase.

CHAPTER 53

Arla wrapped the coat around herself, an ill timed rain plastering wet hair to her forehead. She couldn't speak on the radio with the hood over her head and it compromised her visual field. She walked fast, weaving past the throng of sightseers at the Hyde Park end of Kensington High Street. Kensington Palace Gardens loomed far to the right. Princess Diana's old home.

Her radio crackled and she answered immediately, out of breath. "DCI Baker." Call signs were abandoned, and she was now available on multiple channels.

"Guv, this is Andy. One of the helicopter crew has spotted a blue Renault van, M reg. Vehicle fits our description."

"Where is it?"

"Christchurch Street, two streets away from here."

"Send a team down there now. You and Darren meet me outside Fraser's apartment."

Harry was listening in, and he hung up the same time as her. He said, "Luke could be anywhere. But you're right. If he's targeting Fraser, for whatever reason, that's our first priority."

"Yes," Arla gasped. She was trying to walk as fast as him, but his bloody legs were so long she was literally running. The crowd scattered as Harry bore down on them.

"I'm guessing Fraser has a bodyguard. So he has some protection. You need to stay next to me. Got that?" Harry glanced down at her, slowing his pace.

Arla squinted up at him, frowning. "I am the SIO-

"Shut up and listen to me," he growled. "If this gets rough I don't want you hurt."

Harry swallowed, his eyes flicking around the crowd. A bead of sweat travelled down his left cheek and his lips were set in a grim line. Harry was stressed. She thought she'd never see the day. His concern for her was sweet as well, and for a brief second, despite the urgency and fear knotted up like a cannonball in her stomach, a corner of her heart softened.

"Whatever." She lifted her chin, hiding her emotion. "Its number 342."

They were on the High Street. Harry swivelled his head around. "Evens on our right. Further down."

They dodged past the Arab women with glittering headscarves and the yummy mummies with prams and designer handbags. Far above their heads, Arla heard the distant hum of a helicopter's rotor blades. The pilots were instructed to keep as high as possible, to minimise warning Luke. If it was Luke, and not someone else, Arla thought grimly.

A black BMW moved slowly past them, sirens off and unmarked, but a CID car nevertheless. It followed the traffic up the road, then parked at the top, joined by another similar car. Arla prayed they didn't give the game away.

"We're here," Harry breathed. They were standing next to the glass windows of a dress shop, thousand pound gowns draped on mannequins inside.

Harry moved swiftly forward, to a narrow door sandwiched between the dress shop and another boutique. Arla stayed to one side. Harry narrowed his eyes and gestured her to join him. Reluctantly, she agreed. He offered her his elbow.

"Hold my arm. Make it look like we're window shopping."

She shot him a look, but knew it was the right thing to do. She tried to look interested, staring at the blind eyes of the mannequin, but watching the reflection of the street opposite in the glass.

Something caught her attention. A door, much like the one she was standing next to, opened across the street. A man stepped out. He was dressed in dark jeans, a black hooded top, with a backpack slung on his shoulders. He came out on the busy street and stood still, his head moving side to side. Slow, deliberate movements. Then the hooded head lifted, and he seemed to stare straight at Arla's back.

She stiffened. Her left foot nudged Harry's. He leaned closer.

"Behind me. 12 o'clock." Arla described the man to him. His features were hidden, but Arla could make out he was young, maybe less than thirty. His right hand sneaked inside his right pocket and stayed there.

There was movement next to them. The door opened, and a stocky, barrel chested man in a suit strode out. He flexed his arms, rolled his shoulders and looked all around him. He was the bodyguard. He looked behind him and nodded.

A man in a crisp, pressed navy blue suit stepped out. He unfurled an umbrella over his head. He looked to the left, and his eyes met Arla's. She had seen photos of James Fraser several times on screens but this was the first time she was seeing him upfront. He was shorter than she had imagined.

His eyes held Arla's, swept over Harry, then transferred back to his bodyguard. Arla turned around. From the corner of her eye, she had seen the young man begin to cross the street, hand still inside his pocket.

It happened very quickly.

CHAPTER 54

Arla grabbed Harry's jacket, but he was already moving. At the edge of the pavement, he bent down, pretending to tie his shoelaces. Fraser and his bodyguard had drawn abreast of Arla, and moved past her, heading towards Hyde Park Corner. Arla saw the young man cross the road in a run, his eyes fixed on Fraser and the bodyguard. He would be approaching them from behind. Harry got up and straightened, obscuring her view.

Impatiently, she moved to one side. Fear caught at her throat as she clocked the man, now running full tilt, clearly heading for Fraser. The bodyguard walked next to Fraser, but he hadn't seen the man.

Harry was striding forward, then he broke into a run as the man went past him.

"Stop!" Harry shouted, and the bodyguard turned just in time to see the man bearing down on them. The man pulled a knife from his pocket, lifting it high. Arla and Harry got to them the same time as the bodyguard moved unbelievable fast. His right arm shot up, grabbing the knife arm, and he bundled into the man, pushing him to the ground. A woman screamed, and pedestrians stopped.

The bodyguard punched the man across the face. Harry shouted at them, but neither looked up. Harry went down on the pavement, helping to restrain the man who was still fighting. The two CID cars screeched to a halt next to them, sirens whining. More uniform police arrived. All of a sudden the place was crawling with police officers, shouting at pedestrians to keep away and forming a barricade.

The man was raised to his feet. Harry cuffed him, and read him his rights. Blood trickled down a corner of the man's lips. Arla stepped closer, inspecting his now familiar face. It looked similar to the photos she had seen of Luke Longworth.

She asked him his name. In return, the man snarled and spat at her. The gob narrowly missed Arla's face and Harry shoved him to the floor again, making him kneel. He pressed on Luke's neck, forcing his face down.

"Stop!"

James Fraser stepped inside their little circle, placing himself between Arla and Luke. Fraser reached out to grab Harry's arm. "Leave him alone."

Arla said, "Mr Fraser?" She showed him her warrant card. "I am DCI Baker. This man just tried to kill you.. He needs to be taken into custody." She frowned at the politician. "Why are you trying to protect him?"

Fraser was sweating profusely. His face was beetroot red, and his grey eyes were glassy. Rain water mingled with sweat, streaming down his head. His suit was drenched.

He looked at Arla, a strange mix of fear and pity in his eyes. He whispered so that only she could hear.

"Because he's my son."

CHAPTER 55

The sounds of the busy street seemed to die down. The mingled voice of pedestrians, distant shouts, the belch of exhaust all faded into silence. A distance dilated in front of Arla's eyes, the hapless, hopeless eyes of a forlorn man coming into focus, then receding, like he was being viewed through a lens, zooming in and out. That man was James Fraser. He looked very different all of a sudden. Stooped shoulders and sagging cheeks. Sodden suit that lost colour and turned black. Not the confident, self assured politician he normally was.

From somewhere, Arla found her voice. It sounded scratchy, like an animal trying to crawl out of it hole.

"Your...your son?"

Fraser's face was pale, but his dull eyes never left Arla's face, never looked at the maelstrom around them. He came closer to her.

"Can I trust you?"

Arla was speechless. Fraser said, "Please?"

She still couldn't speak. Fraser repeated himself, and slowly, not knowing what she was doing, Arla nodded.

"OK. He is my son. It's a long story. Are you arresting him?"

"Yes, of course." Arla found her voice. A moment had passed, sounds of daily life was filtering through her senses again. The flash of uniforms. Harry's face opposite, staring at her. The whisper of rain.

She blinked, then stared at Fraser who was watching her carefully. "If this man is Luke Longworth, then is wanted for the murder of David Longworth."

At the sound of the names, Fraser winced like someone just punched him in the gut.

He said, "Your boss is Wayne Johnson, at the south London Command, isn't he?"

Arla gaped at him. Fraser said, "I've been following the investigation. David was a close friend of mine."

Arla narrowed her eyes. A lot of the confusion had suddenly cleared. Harry had lifted Luke to standing and he was barely upright, wobbling.

"Get him a medic," Arla called out to Harry. Andy Jackson pushed his way in through the barricade of uniforms. Two riot vans appeared, sirens blazing, stuck in traffic a hundred yards away. Windows were open in all the floors above them, heads poking out, several hands outstretched with phones trained on them.

Harry said, "There's a medic at the nick, guv, that might be quicker than getting someone out here."

"Does he have a head injury?"

"No. Just been punched that's all."

"OK. Put him in the car and let's go. Andy?" She turned to the uniformed Inspector, who had done so much to ensure the operation had gone to plan. She put a hand on his shoulder and gripped hard.

"Couldn't have done this without you. I sense a commendation in the offing, mate."

Andy grinned. "Thanks guv. See you back at the nick."

Arla sensed Fraser shuffling his feet. She looked at him and nodded. "Do you wish to come with us?"

He looked relieved. "Yes, I do." After a quick chat with his bodyguard, he followed Arla and Harry as he led through the melee of sirens and flashing lights. Luke was put into a van, still handcuffed, and police escorts sat opposite him. The doors slammed shut, and the van moved out, sirens blazing. Some reporters had arrived, and they lifted cameras, popping flashlights at the blacked out windows. As soon as the van moved away, one by one, their hungry eyes roved around. One of them glanced at Arla. Fraser was standing next to her. The paps reminded Arla of a pack of wolves.

"Let's go," she barked, pushing Fraser ahead of her. One of the paps shouted, and several cameras clicked at once, lights popping. Harry got into the driver's seat, and the bodyguard sat on the passenger side. With a screech of tires, the BMW took off.

In the backseat, Arla turned towards Fraser. He looked like a shrunken, defeated man. Arla had never sat this close to a cabinet member, and she gazed at him with interest. He kept his eyes downcast. Then he looked out the black tinted window.

He spoke with his face averted from her. "I guess you're wondering what's going on."

Arla said, "The MI5 are involved because Luke is your son. The fact that your son is making child porn and illegal films is a big problem, I know. He is wanted for that, but Special Branch or us could have handled that."

He nodded, face still averted. Arla waited. Eventually he turned. Colour was returning to his face, but his eyes were still dull, lifeless.

"Luke is many things, but he's not a killer." He looked up at Arla then.

She said, "Why don't you start from the beginning?"

CHAPTER 56

James Fraser took his phone out. "Do you mind if I let people know that I'm on leave for the rest of the day?"

"Sure."

Fraser rang a couple of numbers and spoke on the phone. He was a changed man when he addressed his team. The ring of authority was clearly back in his voice, but Arla could see the effort to maintain it.

When he hung up, she asked, "I'm curious. Can you actually take leave like this? I mean, say this was the French minister of education. Wouldn't they be offended?"

"I just implore someone else with a impressive title to fill in for me. Then I do that for them in return."

"You are a politician I guess."

He smiled sadly. "I suppose." He looked down at his hands, which he clasped and unclasped. His eyebrows lowered and his lips pressed together.

"I don't know what happened to David. That's the truth. I don't think Luke did it. He doesn't have it in him."

"Beginning, Mr. Secretary-

"Call me James."

Arla pondered for a while. "OK, James," she said slowly. "How did Luke get to be your son/"

"David and I went to college together. David met his ex wife there. She was my lover at the time. They got married, and life moved on. I got into politics. Became an MP. The turning point was winning my first by election."

"For your career. But how did Luke come about?"

"You need this background to understand what follows. I got married at the same time. The Party came into power, and I got a cabinet job. A junior one, but still, fantastic at my age. All those years ago."

He paused, then continued. "But my friendship with David continued, and unfortunately, so did something with his wife."

Light spread across the back of Arla's mind. "I see."

"Mary and I started sleeping with each other. It was crazy. I was putting my career on the line. But I loved her, I guess." He stopped and rubbed his face. "One day she told me. She was pregnant. It was not David's. She was sure."

He looked down at his feet. "I didn't want it. But she wouldn't get rid of it. She would tell David it was his, and they would live as a family."

Arla was listening with rapt attention. Fraser wouldn't look at her, like he was ashamed.

"She had the baby. A beautiful boy." The hint of a desperate smile touched his lips, before vanishing like morning dew in sunlight. "Mary sent me photos. My son." His voice caught suddenly and he opened his mouth to exhale.

"If I owned up as being the father, that would've destroyed my career. I wouldn't be where I am today."

In the back of a police car. Protecting the son you ignored all these years, and who just tried to kill you, Arla thought to herself.

"Feel free to judge me. I know I'm a….." He left the sentence dangling. He clenched his jaws, closed his eyes and exhaled. He went to open the window but Arla stopped him. It was safer closed.

"David's ex wife died, right?"

"Yes. Her death changed everything. But even before she died, I couldn't bear it. I had 2 children with my wife but she didn't know anything. She still doesn't. But when Luke was 10, I came clean with David."

Arla was surprised. "You did?"

"Yes." He looked up at her for the first time. "David was a good friend. I couldn't do that to him. Sounds strange, but we were like family. Luke being there actually got us closer."

"He forgave his wife?" Arla was thinking hard about how the wife died. Found dead at the bottom of a cliff. Was it really suicide?

Fraser nodded. "We were older at this point. It wasn't easy but we had to do what was right. Besides, Luke was showing signs of difficult behaviour. He was diagnosed with ADHD."

"He was?"

Instantly Arla thought of the juvenile crime record, where Luke had groped a girl against her wishes.

"Yes. Psychiatrists were involved. He was a difficult child, despite having a great family life."

Was he more like you? Arla felt like asking. She kept the question to herself.

Fraser continued. "So we kept his secret to ourselves. Telling him the truth would only upset his fragile psychology even further."

Arla pursed her lips. "So all these years, David knew. Then his wife died. Two years later he gets married to Cherie. Does she know about this?"

Fraser shook his head. "Not as far as I know. She knew Luke as his son. By then, Luke and David had drifted apart. After Mary's death, things were never the same between them."

"Why?"

"I don't know."

Fraser turned in his seat to look at Arla. She held his gaze. "This is top secret, Miss Baker. I have just handed you the greatest news scoop in England. You can make or destroy me."

The way he said the last words bothered Arla. There was a steely gaze in his eyes, and the former, softer person was falling away.

"What do you want?" Arla asked.

CHAPTER 57

Jonty was at a funeral. The cemetery was cold and damp, a leaden grey, cloudy sky above tress bereft of leaves. Jonty stood at the back of the congregation as the Vicar read out from the book.

It was the funeral of his old boss, Darren. The man Jonty had killed. A few of his work colleagues were here too. They sat with impassive faces, some even feigned at sorrow. Jonty knew they were putting up a show. Nobody liked Darren. Yet, it was rude not to come to a funeral when invited. Jonty wondered what that said about society. It was strange how everyone had to walk around with a mask on. The mask he saw on the bus, train, on the streets and at work. No one knew what lay beneath, what unspoken visions terrorized the mind inside.

Jonty closed his eyes. He had a mask on too, a face that he knew was good looking, intelligent. It worked well for his purposes, especially when he had to get close to women.

Arla Baker.

Her face floated across his eyes. All hard lines and angles, but there was beauty there too in those brown eyes. She also had a vacant, lost look in them, a vulnerability that he found exciting. He didn't even know her, but it made him feel possesive. Soon. He would get to to her know her very well.

His phone beeped. Jonty opened his eyes and looked around. It was warm inside the church, and he was comfortable. Everyone was listening to the Vicar, and no one paid attention to him. He reached inside his breast pocket and took out the mobile phone. His spine tingled when he read the text.

Are you alright, my love?

Yes I am. How are you?

I'm fine. You got this new phone last night?

Yes.

After a pause Jonty wrote, *When are we going away? For good this time.*

Soon my love. Just be patient. One more thing to do. Then we are free.

I want to leave now.

Look at the bigger picture. What we are trying to achieve.

Jonty sighed. He knew it better than anyone what they were trying to achieve.

I know.

You're my my big strong soldier. My protector.

LOL.

There was a pause. Then a new text appeared on his phone. *I thought of her today.*

Jonty's brows creased. He didn't know what grief or pain was. He saw it in others and knew it was a big thing for them. He wanted to understand it. What he felt now, this strange upheaval in the wilderness of his soul, was that grief? Or was it anger?

He wrote back. *I think of her everyday.*

There was nothing more to say after that. No further texts came and Jonty closed his phone and put it back in his pocket.

The Vicar finished his sermon, and the congregation filed outside. A young woman who worked as the continuity girl in film sets came up to him. She had a lit cigarette between her fingers. She pulled on it and shivered in the cold. Her name was Emma. She was blonde and cute in a next door girl kind of way. Not Jonty's type. She did have a habit, in Jonty's opinion, of being too friendly with men. The office rumours stated she was easy. Jonty hated that fact, a revulsion that shook him to his core, made him feel dirty. For her sake.

Emma said, "Are you coming to the inauguration of Dark Dawn?"

Jonty raised an eyebrow. "Is that tonight?"

"Yes." She seemed to hesitate, then lifted her deep blue eyes towards him. "Why don't we go together?"

Jonty smiled. "Sure. Why not?"

CHAPTER 58

Harry swung the car inside the rear car park of Clapham Police Station. The van had arrived before them, and an officer stood next to it, smoking. Luke had clearly been taken inside. When they got out of the car, she winked at Harry, who nodded back. He headed inside with the bodyguard, while Arla and Fraser followed.

Fraser kept his voice low. "As you can imagine, I want my name kept out of this."

"Of course," Arla kept her voice neutral. His request was entirely expected, and to Arla's mind, spoke volumes about his character.

"And I don't think Luke did it. Killed David I mean."

"But he did make the illegal pornographic films," Arla said. "And it doesnt matter what you think. The evidence against Luke is damning. The murder weapon was a hammer. We found a hammer in Luke's home."

"I'm a former lawyer, Miss Barker. You know as well I do that doesn't constitute evidence. Anyone can have a hammer in their house, indeed most probably do."

"He avoided contact with the police, I bet you he burgled David's house after the murder, then tried to harm or abduct Cherie. The list goes on."

She stopped as they were about to go inside. Her voice hardened. "We have to conduct our investigation fully, Mr., I mean James. Then Luke will be charged. He is not exempt from the law, and neither are you."

His next statement threw Arla completely. Fraser leaned closer and said, "You know what it's like to lose your own flesh and blood, don't you, Arla?"

She stared at him, shocked. Her eyes widened. He said softly, "What would you do if you were in my position?"

He moved past her and into the station, leaving her standing. Arla composed herself. In the end, Luke's crimes and James Fraser were not connected. Arla was sure he had an alibi for that evening and her gut told her he wasn't the murderer. She didn't trust politicians. But Fraser as the psychotic killer? That didn't fit.

She walked inside the station, and found Fraser and Harry at the front desk. Harry was introducing John, the desk sergeant, to Fraser.

She waited till Fraser was free, then approached him. "No one from my team will leak your name. Not in connection to this anyway. The fact that you were assaulted in a packed high street might be beyond my control. For all we know, someone snapped your photo already. If and when we charge Luke, your name will not come up. Unless you try to influence the investigation in any way."

He lifted his eyebrows. "Not threatening me are you, DCI Barker?"

Arla stood. "Remember what I said." She sighed. "Look, I know this is hard for you. We need to get to the truth of whatever Luke has done. He might be innocent of David's murder, for all we know."

"I appreciate your honesty."

Arla nodded and turned to leave. He called her back. Harry was waiting for her, a few meters away.

Fraser came forward and stuck his hand out. "Thank you for saving my life today."

Arla shook his hand, then left. She filled Harry in as they walked back to the office. Heads turned as they walked in, and a silence fell over the open plan office. Arla looked at no one, and went into her office, followed by Harry.

Lisa and Rita joined them soon after. Lisa's face was troubled. "Boss wants you upstairs. Deakins is here too."

Arla groaned. Deakins, the Deputy Assistant Commissioner, wasn't Arla's best friend by any stretch. Him being here with Johnson was bad news. Particularly as Johnson tried to act like his best friend, eager to keep climbing the greasy career pole.

That thought brought her own career ambitions back into focus. How long would she be DCI for? It was getting time for her to move on. A Superintendent post beckoned, but she would never get it without Johnson's blessing.

Harry leaned forward. He smelt of aftershave, cigarette smoke and stale sweat, but it felt oddly familiar, comfortable.

"We should go and face the music now. The longer we leave it, the worse it gets."

"Trust me, I know," Arla stood. "But let's get a coffee first."

She sipped her scalding coffee while Harry towered over her in the elevator.

"Keep your cool, alright?" he asked.

She looked up at him, at the swirl of grey in his chocolate brown eyes, his lips so full she suddenly wanted to kiss him. The elevator doors opened at that moment, killing any desire she had.

"Come in," Johnson barked when Harry knocked on the door. Arla could sense the quiet hostility in the room as soon as she walked in. Johnson and Deakins were sat next to each other at the table, with Nixon opposite them.

CHAPTER 59

Arla and Harry sat down, facing the two bosses. Nixon was to their right. He nodded at Arla and she acknowledged.

No one said anything for a while. Johnson glared at her, and she returned his stare.

Deakins spoke before Johnson could. His voice was calm and unhurried. "We seem to end up here a lot, don't we, DCI Baker?"

Arla kept silent. Deakins continued. "You disobey direct orders. Put an entire operation at risk by your reckless actions. An operation signed off by a joint task force of the Police and State Department." He leaned back in his chair. "And then to top it all off, you go above Johnson's head, and call up Commander Bose to shut down Kensington High Street."

"It's a good job that I did, sir," Arla said evenly. "Otherwise the Secretary of State could've been killed today."

Johnson spoke between gritted teeth, grinding the words. "He. Had. A. Bodyguard. You didn't have to disobey me and shut down a major road in central London to protect him!"

"Not even if his attacker was the prime suspect in our murder case? What would it look like, sir, if he was injured or worse and the newspapers reported we didn't do our job?"

Johnson smashed his fist down on the table and the room seemed to shake. He waggled his finger at Arla, face red and bloated. "Your bloody job was to listen to me. Can you not see the harm you've done?"

Deakins picked up smoothly. Laurel and Hardy, Arla thought to herself.

"One year's worth of work, millions of pounds, all down the drain."

Harry glanced at her nervously. Arla knew she should keep her mouth shut, look contrite and suck it up like a scolded schoolgirl.

To hell with that. They didn't know to run a police investigation, that was their problem.

She leaned forward, jerking a thumb towards Nixon. "With all due respect sir, your friend from the *Intelligence* service was floundering. He didn't have a clue. They had bugged Luke's house but had no idea where he was. No money was wasted, as Luke wasn't even there when we entered the house."

There was a stunned silence. Arla was breathing heavily.

"So I did him and his whole operation a favour. Then I went and saved James Fraser's life."

Arla sat back in her chair, jaws flexed, anger boiling inside her.

Deakins spoke in his same sombre tone. "Do you think you will get away with it this time, DCI Baker? Complaints, insubordination, it's all racking up in remarkable fashion."

Harry coughed. "To be honest, sir, we were never told why the MI5 were involved. If we had known about Operation Condor then we would have stayed away."

Johnson made a sound like a wounded animal, a curious mix of a groan and a yell. "That's why I told you to leave Luke alone, damn it!"

Arla shook her head. "Even after all the evidence pointed in his direction? How many years have I worked for you, sir? You always told me to follow my instincts."

Johnson gripped his head. When he looked up, his face was pained, and Arla almost felt sorry for him. If only he wasn't being such a...

"I told you that because you're a good cop, DCI Baker. But good cops also listen to their bosses. You don't know the meaning of the word listen!"

There was silence for a while. Deakins and Johnson exchanged a meaningful glance at each other.

Deakins said, "Under the circumstances, we have to take some action, DCI Baker." He paused, looking at a piece of paper on the table. Arla could hear her own breathing. A sense of dread was growing inside her like a tumour. She could hear a clock tick the passing seconds, the sound suddenly loud in her ears.

Eventually Deakins looked up. "You are hereby removed as SIO for this case. Now wait!" He put a hand up as Arla began to protest.

"Believe me, I have thought of harsher measures. But you and your team have done a lot for this case already. That mitigates in your favour. Hence, you are not suspended."

"But sir, I am close to finishing this case. Two of our best suspects are downstairs. One is charged already. By tomorrow we can charge Luke, and start a prosecution." Arla could feel the blood roaring in her ears. Her mouth was bone dry.

Surely they can't do this. Not now.

Johnson looked at her, mouth set in a grim line. "The person stepping in will be Inspector Beauregard."

Arla felt a sledgehammer fall on her chest from high above. Air left her lungs in a rush. She stared at Johnson.

"What?"

CHAPTER 60

No one answered Arla. Harry broke the ensuing silence. "With all respect sir, Justin Beauregard knows nothing about this case. Handing him the reins would be going backwards."

Arla was still shaking her head, trying to control her surging pulse. She turned to look at Ken Nixon, who seemed to squirm under her glare.

"Well," she demanded of Nixon. "Do you agree with this?"

Nixon shrugged. "This is an internal matter, DCI Baker. I can't possibly comment."

"Then why are you here?" Arla shot back. "If it wasn't for you, this investigation would probably be over by now, and I would still have my job."

"Leave him alone," Johnson warned, raising his voice.

Arla seethed. She was losing control. She knew it but she was helpless to stop it. Harry was leaning towards her, any further and he would drop from his chair. She ignored him. A veil popped and cracked inside her retina, distorting her vision.

She turned on Johnson. "This is about protecting James Fraser, isn't it? This whole set up. Well guess what? In the end, it was me," she pointed at her chest with a finger, "*Me* who protected him. And Harry. And now you have the gall to-

"Shut up Arla!" Johnson bellowed, rising to his feet. His head almost seemed to touch the ceiling. The walls shook with his thunderous voice. "Shut your mouth before you get kicked out of your job."

She didn't know what she was doing. It was like an out of body experience, like she was watching herself from across the room. In slow motion, she stood up as well. She raised an arm to point at Johnson, but Harry was suddenly in front of her. He grabbed her by the shoulders and shook her lightly.

Her eyes shuddered and the room swam in front of her. Harry was telling her something and suddenly she was tired, just dog tired, a lethargy creeping through her bones, claiming her limbs. Harry pushed her gently back on her seat. She was aware of sitting down, and her head sank in her hands.

She remained like that, gripping her forehead with both hands, eyes shut. Slowly, the sounds returned. The clock ticking. Her own breath, whispering out of an open mouth.

After a while, Arla raised her head and blinked. The light was suddenly harsh, strobing into her eyes. Johnson was still standing, his imposing height making him the first thing she saw. He was breathing heavily, staring at her.

Arla swallowed. "I'm sorry, sir." She couldn't look at him. Instead she glanced at Harry, who had a concerned look on his face.

He mouthed silently. *Are you OK?*

She closed her eyes and nodded in agreement.

Johnson sat down, the chair creaking loudly. Everyone was aware a line had been breached, and no one wanted to see what lay beyond. Arla certainly didn't.

Deakins spoke in his controlled voice. "We shall choose to ignore what just happened, DCI Baker. Consider yourself lucky you're not in a disciplinary meeting right now. A meeting that would strip you of your rank, and suspend you. Do you understand?"

Arla nodded. A heaviness had settled in her heart, weighing her down.

Johnson growled, "Speak."

She had to swallow several times before she could. "Yes, sir."

"Good," Deakins said. "With immediate effect, DI Beauregard will take control of the case. You will take orders from him. I hope there won't be any friction."

Arla couldn't believe her ears. "No sir," she said tonelessly.

"Good. You are dismissed."

CHAPTER 61

Arla decided to take the elevators again. Harry embraced her and she sunk into his arms, surrendering to his warmth. They said nothing. She was aware of Harry kissing the top of her head and that simple act, for some unknown reason, brought sudden tears to her eyes. She wiped them off angrily. She pushed him back and he looked at her with a mild question in his eyes. Then he rubbed her shoulders and smiled.

"Take it easy."

She sighed, wishing the dead black weight inside her would exhale through her breath. It didn't.

"Thanks for what you did up there," she said. The elevator doors opened and they came outside and turned into a corner off the main corridor.

Harry's eyes were searching. "I know this is frustrating. But look at the bigger picture. Is the case almost cracked? Yes it is. Does everyone know you did all the hard work? Yes they do. Let Justin have his two minutes of glory. Then this case is over and you start again."

She nodded, blowing her cheeks out. Good old Harry. She said, "Rarely, you do talk sense."

His jaw dropped and he clutched his chest. "How could you say that to me?"

She shook her head at the puppy dog look in his eyes. "Should be an actor, Harry. Missed your lot in life."

Together, they strode into the office. It was like turning off a switch. Everyone stopped what they were doing. In the calm before the storm, a widely grinning DI Beauregard strode upto Arla.

"I'll be taking over the Longworth case," he said. He looked immensely pleased with himself. It made Arla nauseous.

"Yes, I heard."

"And my new role is acting DCI."

Arla frowned. "What?"

Beauregard couldn't stop smiling. "It's what the boss ordered. To help me take control of the investigation."

Arla went to say something but stopped. Harry was right. Let this idiot have his two minutes of glory.

"Whatever," she said between clenched teeth.

"I'm just about to start a meeting in the Incident Room. Care to join us?" he said. Rita, Rob and Lisa rose from their desks and approached them. Behind Beauregard's back Lisa rolled her eyes and grimaced. Rob looked grim.

"Oh, here you are. Right then let's go." Beauregard breezed past Arla and Harry.

"You don't have to come," Harry whispered.

"No. I want to." She replied, a determination rising inside her. She lifted her chin up. She still had her warrant card. She could still investigate and arrest.

Harry shrugged. "I'm still part of the team. I have to go."

"I know. And without you, I doubt this case will be solved. So let's go."

The Incident Room was filling up, but it was oddly quiet. The normal hub hub was gone. Arla caught the eyes of Andy Jackson, Darren and the other officers when she walked in. She know from their faces they knew. She sat down in the front row.

Harry stood next to Beauregard, his face dark and stormy. Beauregard clapped his hands.

"OK, I;m the new acting DCI as you might have heard and in charge of this case. Inspector Mehta, why don't you give us a rundown of recent events?"

Harry did, staring over everyone's heads. When he was done, Beaurgard asked questions of Lisa and Rita. There wasn't any new information.

Arla glanced at her watch. It was almost four pm. She realised suddenly she was ravenous. And shattered.

Beauregard said, "OK. I will interrogate the Luke Longworth and DI Mehta will accompany me." His eyes fell on Arla and he gave her a shit eating grin. Arla ignored him.

"We can meet at 18.00 before we break for the day," Beauregard said. He didn't ask anyone for opinions like Arla did, and she noted no one volunteered. The normal buzz was gone. Everyone got up stiffly and walked out. Arla was the last to leave. She went up to Harry. Lisa and Rob were summoned by Beauregard to do some chores.

"The hammer we got from Luke's house. Do SOCO have it?" she asked.

Harry picked up the phone on his desk. He spoke briefly, then hung up.

"What?" Arla said when she saw the expression on his face.

"They found old blood on the hammer. It's David Longworth's DNA. And it has Luke's fingerprints. They just managed to take them now. Negative on Ident1, but it does match the prints on the hammer."

Arla sat down next to him. "Right."

"Open and shut case now. Murder weapon found in suspect's house, containing victim's DNA."

"Wait," Arla massaged her forehead. Her stomach was growling, but she had more pressing things on her mind.

"If Luke was the killer, why would he leave the murder weapon in such plain sight? It's like it was waiting to be found. Wouldn't he at least have hidden it?"

Harry nodded. He pulled up a chair and crossed his long legs on it. "What I was thinking."

"And the MI5, who've been bugging him for days, they didn't find it?"

"They might not have looked, guv."

Arla was frowning. Her previous convictions suddenly had a storm raging through them.

"And Luke used the same phone several times. He texted Cherie that evening to meet up, and then again this morning from South Kensington. He must've known we were tracing him."

"True. It's like he wanted to be found."

"Exactly."

Harry stretched his arms upwards. His shoulders clicked. "He could still be the murderer guv. Maybe he wants the publicity. You know what these freaks can be like."

Arla's brain was whirring, a millions clicks speeding through her synapses. "Remember it wasn't Luke's phone that sent Simpson the photo of David."

Harry said, "But Luke had got in touch with Simpson several times the week of the murder, and before. From the same number he used now." He turned to look at her, and she could see the glimmer in his eyes.

Arla held his eyes, suddenly excited. "With Luke, it's too neat. Too cut and dry. It's like someone is pointing us there."

Harry sat up straighter. "What are you saying?"

"The killer might be someone else. All this time we've been looking in the wrong place."

CHAPTER 62

A figure strode past them, then stopped. It was Beauregard, and he addressed Harry loudly. "Are you coming?"

Harry gazed at him for a few seconds without saying anything. Then he rose, stretching slowly, making Beauregard wait. Arla tried not to smile. Harry could be an infuriating big oaf when he wanted to.

"See you soon," Harry said. He hitched his trousers up, then walked towards the office doors, completely ignoring Beauregard. With an oath, the man followed Harry.

Arla grinned behind his back. She rose and went to Lisa's desk. The sergeant's face lit up when she saw Arla.

Arla pointed at her office door at the end of the open plan space, then waved at Rita and Rob. All nodded. Arla went to her office, and she had scarcely sat down at her desk when all three entered without knocking. Rob shut the door, then locked it.

Lisa said, "Guv, we're so sorry. How could they do this to you?"

"Don't worry." She gestured at them to sit down. "Do you know if James Fraser is still waiting?"

"No," Rob said. "His lawyer arrived. He gave a confidential statement, then left."

"OK. I want to see it. I also want to speak to Simpson again. From dealing with Luke financially, to being in contact with him, he's lied to us all this time. Can anyone trace these women who brought the cases against him?"

Lisa said, "Oh yes, guv. I know you said you wanted to go and see one of them. I managed to track one down. She's an actress actually and she wants to speak to you."

"Excellent. What's her name?"

"Tangye Gale. I can call her now and set something up this evening."

"Do that. She will have the dirt on Simpson. Whether I believe her or not is another matter, but it will open this case up."

Lisa smiled at her. "And I keep this secret from Beuregard, right?"

Arla faltered. She had to stay on the right track here. "No. If he asks tell him. I don't want him reporting back to Johnson that I'm running my own show here. But if he doesn't...."

"Got it." Lisa left the room to make the call.

Arla asked Rita, "Did we get back the coroner's report on Laura Douglas? David Longworth's ex wife."

"Yes. I emailed it to you."

Arla was thinking. She was missing something here, and she didn't like it. Laura had been James Fraser's lover, and the mother of their child, Luke. She shook her head. No wonder Luke was so messed up. She knew Laura was a big part of this. Her death was sinister, there was no doubt about it. Arla didn't buy the story - Laura went out for a walk after taking twenty diazepam pills, then dropped off a cliff. Why? Did she have medical records to say she was depressed?

Again, too neat. Too perfect. Like a story someone wanted her to believe.

She could be wrong, of course. But she had got this far trusting her instincts. She couldn't ignore them now.

She asked Rita, "Can we dig up Laura Douglas's medical notes? I also want the exact location of where she died, who found her, and where she was staying at the time of death."

"No worries, guv," Rita said, scribbling in her note book.

Arla looked at Rob. "I want to speak to Simpson. Before he disappears on bail. Can you get him to an interview room?"

"Sure, guv. Rooms three is free. Shall I get him there?"

Arla rose. "See you there in five. Make it quick." She dropped her voice. "I want it done before Justin comes back."

Rob grinned. "Sure thing."

Rob was good to his word. Five minutes later, Arla was sat in the interview room opposite Simpson. His leathery cheeks were drooping lower, and dark bags hung under his eyes. He looked haggard, an old playboy well past his prime, left to rot on the rocks of life.

He sneered at Arla. "What's this. One on one action?"

"This is not being recorded," Arla said calmly. "I want your honest answer."

"A copper being honest. Must be the first time."

Arla ignored him. "Luke was James Fraser's son. David raised him as his own, despite knowing the truth."

From the way Simpson flinched Arla knew she had a hit a spot. She leaned forward, eyes hooked on his. "You knew that, didn't you?"

"I don't know what you're talking about."

"The weapon used to murder David was found in Luke's house." Arla told him the facts. Simpson slumped, staring at the floor.

"Luke is going to get locked up for life, Mr. Simpson. He has no alibi, as far as I know. You financed his films, and he remained in contact with him till a few days ago. That makes you an accomplice to murder."

Simpson's chest heaved. Arla said, "Tomorrow, the prosecution will be filed. This will be quick. Within a month, Luke and you will be rotting in Belmarsh, courtesy of Her Majesty."

Simpson lifted his head, a snarl on his lips. He almost frothed at the lips. "You bitch."

"I'm giving you one chance to come clean with me. I can help you. But not if you keep lying."

Simpson screwed his eyes shut, like it was too much effort to keep staring. His head sunk down again.

Arla asked, "Why did Luke call you? Why did you lie about staying in touch with him?"

"Fuck off," Simpson said.

Arla scraped her chair back and stood. "Have it your way. Goodbye Mr. Simpson."

She turned to leave. Simpson said, "Stop."

CHAPTER 63

Arla didn't turn around. She could see a reflection of Simpson in the glass window opposite. Rob was standing on the other side, keeping an eye on proceedings. He tapped his watch and Arla nodded.

Simpson said, "Sit down."

Arla looked at him. His shoulders were slumped again. The fight had gone out of him.

"Luke and I were…"

Arla waited, wondering. Simpson finally said it. "We were lovers."

She frowned. "But Cherie said you assaulted her. Oh, I forgot. According to you, she's lying. Like those other girls. Tangye Gayle."

Simpson raised his eyebrows, then swore under his breath. "Alright look. Between you and me, yeah?"

Arla nodded. He said, "I like it both ways, OK? Bit of this, bit of that."

"You're bisexual."

Simpson nodded. "Luke and I were together the night of David's murder. Happy now? We were at a hotel in central London. Staff can identify me. We visited there often."

"Did you know about his films?"

"No," Simpson said with conviction. "Believe what you want, but that is not my scene. Yes, I did some financing for him. But I did financing for a lot of directors through Blue Horizon, my offshore fund."

He looked at Arla for the first time since she sat back down. "I knew nothing about his films, OK? That's the truth."

Arla nodded. "You knew about his family?"

"Yes. I know James. I went to college with him and David."

Understanding flickered inside Arla's mind. With it, a growing distaste about this washed up sad excuse of a human being. He slept with his friend's son.

"Tell me about Laura."

A sad smile appeared on his lips. "She was a lovely woman. She really was."

"Was she depressed?"

"Not that I knew of. Why do you ask?"

"The way she died. You know about that, right?"

Simpson nodded. "Yes, it was a shock. No one expected her to go like that."

"Do you know what happened?"

He narrowed his eyes. "I wasn't there if that's what you mean. I only read about it in the papers. Why are you bringing this up now?"

"Just answer me. What do you think happened?"

Simpson told her what she knew already. Arla stared at him for a while impassively. Then she asked, "You don't find that odd? A woman takes an overdose, leaves her husband and son and jumps off a cliff?"

He frowned at her. "Of course. Everyone did. But it was a tragic accident. She had a diazepam habit. What can you do?"

Arla's ears perked up. "She had a diazepam habit? Where did you hear that?"

"It was in the papers. One of her friends mentioned it."

Arla wrote this down in her diary. "What friend?"

Simpson shrugged. "I don't know. Friend's name wasn't mentioned in the paper."

Arla went in for the kill. "You don't think it's strange that Luke was also outside when his mother fell off the cliff? The mother who hid his father's identity all these years?"

Simpson lowered his brows. "Luke loved his mother. He would never do that."

"So where was he at the time? Did you ever ask him?"

"He said he went for a walk, to have a cigarette. I believe him. You can't expect a young man to be sitting with his parents all day."

A thought occurred to Arla. "When did you get to know Luke?"

He frowned again. "What's that got to do with anything?"

Arla glared at him till he answered. "Well, I had known David all his life so Luke from when he was little. But I got to know him better when he was a teeanger-

He stopped suddenly and his eyes widened. "Hey hang on-"

A sense of nausea was churning inside Arla's stomach. That horrible feeling just before a vomit. She spat the words out. "Got him young, did you? Groomed him to become your...." Arla couldn't say the rest. She clenched her jaws, anger crackling inside her.

Simpson's eyes were wild. His nostrils flared. He looked like a caged animal. "No. No, damn it. I didn't touch him as a boy. Only when he was an adult. Jesus, is that what you think I am?"

"What age?"

"I...I can't remember."

Arla slapped down her palm on the table with vicious force. The sound was like a sharp explosion in the small chamber. She stood abruptly, face mottled with blood, a vein pulsing in the middle of her forehead.

"What age, you lying bastard? What did you do to that boy?!" She was screaming, spittle flying from her mouth, rage and frustration frothing inside her soul, consuming her.

Nicole. I don't want to think about Nicole.

Arla knocked the chair back as went around the table to stand over Simpson. She pointed a finger at him, breathing heavily.

"Lie to me and I'll have you done for historic child abuse."

Simpson stood, his chest heaving. "I never touched Luke when he was young."

The door to the interview room opened and Rob stepped inside. He moved close to Arla. "Guv, let's go."

Arla took a deep breath and stepped back. She tucked hair strands behind both ears. The air shimmered, charged heavy with electric tension.

"I'll ask you one more time before I charge you. What age?"

Simpson rubbed his leathery face. He grit his teeth. "About seventeen, eighteen, maybe? He was fully grown by then."

Arla still felt sick, but she was back in control. Many missing pieces of the jigsaw were falling into place.

She indicated to Rob, and he started the camera and recorder. She asked Simpson, "Will you give a statement about you and Luke?"

Simpson sat down heavily. He stared forward, defeated and licked dry lips. His voice was low, morose. "Do I need Jeremy?" Jeremy Hardcastle, his expensive lawyer.

"Well, this actually gets both and you Luke off the hook. Now you have an alibi for the night of David's murder. Providing our checks validate your statement."

Simpson sighed. "OK."

Rob spoke into the recorder. Arla asked Simpson the name of the hotel and wrote it down.

Arla steeled herself. For her own sanity, she didn't know if she could go through this, but she had to.

"Start from the beginning."

Simpson said, "Luke was almost eighteen. Or over eighteen, I can't remember. I hadn't touched him before that, but I had tried to chat him up. I could see that he was willing. I was at their house for a film inauguration party, one that I produced and David directed. It was a summer barbecue. That's when it first happened."

As he filled in the sordid details, Arla couldn't hide the grimace spreading across her face like ripples in a pond.

"Did Luke ever seem violent to you? Dangerous?"

Simpson shook his head. "Quite the opposite in fact. He didn't like action movies or fast cars, like most boys."

Arla said, "He assaulted a girl at his boarding school. Did you know about that?"

"We talked about it once. He was confused. He didn't know if he was into boys or girls. He wanted to make it work with girls. Guess he tried too hard that time. But no, Luke didn't have a violent bone in his body."

The sight of Simpson filled Arla with visceral hate. Here was an older man who had knowingly abused a young boy. Emotionally and perhaps sexually as well. Even if the sex had been consensual - Simpson had clearly groomed a vulnerable young boy for his own base pleasures.

But as much as she hated him, he also knew Luke. Of all the witnesses, he probably knew Luke the best.

She exhaled slowly. "Children who are abused grow up to become abusers themselves. You know that?"

Simpson looked away, fixing his eyes above her head. "If Luke was psychologically disturbed, then you had a part to play in it. Did you tell him about his real father?"

Simpson swivelled his eyes back at Arla. "No. He read that from David's diaries. The ones David kept hidden in his bedroom."

Arla said, "So that's why he burgled the house. To get hold of the diaries."

"Yes. I told him not to but he wouldn't listen."

"Why is there a hammer in Luke's house with David's blood on it? We need to prove it, but I'm pretty sure that was the murder weapon."

"I don't know. Believe me. I have no idea."

As much as she loathed the man, Arla sensed he was speaking the truth. And while she had him, she had to broach the other topic as well.

"Did you assault Cherie?"

His eyes were stony. "Depends on what she told you. It's not like she never flirted with me."

Arla snorted. "Are you saying it's her fault?"

Simpson didn't answer. Arla hardened her voice. "You're in a lot of trouble already, Mr. Simpson. Telling me the truth now is only going to help you."

He threw his hands up. "Alright, alright, alright! I might have come on to her."

"She said you shoved her inside the bathroom and pressed up against her. Feeling her. Is that correct?"

The look in Simpsons eyes was undecipherable. "Yes. Yes, I did. Happy now?"

Arla asked quietly, "And what about Tangye Gale? And the other woman who brought charges against you?"

A gleam flickered to life in Simpson's eyes. It reminded Arla of a predator sensing blood. "Oh no. No, no, no. Those charges were thrown out of court. A long time ago."

"Less than two years actually. And now you have a much worse charge hanging over your head. Potential historic child abuse. How do you feel about that?"

Simpson glared at her. "You got my statement. What more do you want?"

"Justice." Arla said the word quietly, but it reverberated around the room.

Simpson's head sunk on his chest. When he looked up his eyes were blurred. "I need my lawyer."

CHAPTER 64

The door opened and Harry walked in. Rob shut the recorder. Arla cast one last contemptuous look at Simpson. He had the audacity to hold her gaze, venom in his eye. Arla curled her lips and brushed past Harry, out into the corridor. They went for a coffee, then Harry wanted a cigarette outside. It was cold and a silvery rain whispered against the black tarmac of the car park, but Arla was grateful for some fresh air.

She filled Harry in. He sucked his cheeks. "Jeez, he's a nasty piece of work, isn't he?"

"Vile." Arla kicked her shoes. "But it puts Luke in the clear, if his statement holds up."

She inhaled as Harry exhaled. "How did it go with Luke?"

Harry eyed her. "Sorry. It should be you in there, asking him questions."

"No bother. What happened?"

"He denies murdering David. Under pressure he broke down and admitted to being with Simpson that night."

Arla nodded. "So it adds up. Why did he avoid us?"

"He was planning an attack on his real father for a while. He hated both of them. After David's death, he brought his plan forward."

"Did you ask him about his mother's death? Laura Douglas."

"Justin didn't see the point, but I asked him anyway. He denies that too. Says he was in the pub, watching a football match when it happened. They were in this village near the cliffs in a seaside in Kent."

"Is he lying?"

Harry took a deep drag, then tilted his neck and blew rings of smoke of upwards. She loved it when he did that. The rings trembled and dissolved into the rain.

"Who knows. For my money, I think he's too shaken up to lie. His hands move too much, he stutters, sweats, the guy's a mess guv."

"Arla," she frowned at him. There was no one near them.

"Arla."

Arla's phone buzzed. It was Banerji. She answered.

The older man's voice was down. "I heard. I'm sorry."

"News spreads fast. But don't worry. Things are moving in a new direction. Any news?"

"Yes. The metal fragment inside David's brain is Molybdenum and steel."

"Moly what?"

"It's a precious metal used to make steel stronger."

Arla gripped the phone tighter. "Can it be used in a hammer?"

Banerji paused for a few seconds. "It's commonly used in a hammer, Arla. It will take some time for the result to come back but there is a strong chance the hammer found in Luke's house had Molybdenum in it."

"Thanks Doc. Keep in touch."

"No problem, Arla. Be careful."

They walked back inside. Harry said, "Justin is talking to MI5, filling him in. Making sure James Fraser's name stays out of it all."

"That's why he go the job," Arla muttered angrily.

"I need to tell him about Simpson's statement. He is the SIO after all. Besides, that statement changes a lot."

They were back in her office. Arla sunk in her chair, weary. She rubbed her eyes and yawned. It was close to 18.00.

"What now?" Harry asked. "The rest of the team are digging up more on Luke and Simpson. Do you want them to carry on?" He smiled. "Not that you're the SIO any more."

"Yes, let them. I want to meet Tangye Gale tonight."

"Who?"

CHAPTER 65

"The actress who accused Simpson of assaulting her," Arla said.

"Oh yes."

Arla sipped the new cup of coffee which they had picked up enroute to her office. "Is Johnson upstairs?"

Harry stiffened. "Yes. Why?"

"I should tell him about Simpson myself. We need to move in a different direction now."

"Are you sure about this?"

"Positive."

They took the stairs up to Johnson's office. He was at his desk, with Justin Beauregard opposite him. Both looked surprised to see Arla. She ignored Beauregard and addressed Johnson.

"Luke didn't do it sir. He was with Simpson the night of the murder."

Johnson raised his eyebrows. Arla could feel the tension radiate from Beauregard. Johnson said, "But all the evidence points to Luke."

Arla explained. Johnson listened with a frown on his face. By the end, he looked deeply thoughtful.

Arla said, "Both of them admit to being with each other, sir. All we have to do is check the hotel. We have the name. I can send someone now, and their alibi's are confirmed."

Justin Beauregard shook his head angrily. "We have the suspect downstairs. He's just shown evidence of his violent nature by trying to kill his biological father. Is it so surprising he wouldn't kill his stepfather? A man he loathed?"

Johnson tapped the desk. "Justin's right Arla."

Beauregard beamed like a happy puppy. "We have the murder weapon at his home. With the victim's DNA on it. I mean, come on. CPS will love us for this. Nice, easy prosecution."

"That's my problem, sir," Arla said. "It's too cut and dry. Too easy."

Harry said, "And now both suspects have an alibi."

"Yeah, each other," Beauregard sneered at Harry. "And we all know what a good lawyer will do with a hotel receptionist's statement. Rip it to shreds. How many people did they see that night?"

"Not unless there's CCTV," Arla pointed out. "Which, this being central london, there will be. Even if they used fake names to book the name under and paid in cash."

"But even if CCTV shows them at the hotel," Justin protested. "How do we know one of them didn't leave via a back entrance? One could be covering for the other."

Tiredness was driving impatience into Arla, and with it, anger. "Just because you want a prosecution, Justin, doesn't mean we take the bait the real murderer is dangling in front of us."

Johnson frowned. "A bait?"

Arla said firmly, "Yes sir, a bait. I think this killer is devious and cunning. He's been planning this for ages. He knows what Luke is like. He's thrusting Luke in front of us, hoping we grab the obvious culprit." Arla made commas in the air with her hands as she said the last two words.

Johnson steepled his fingers and rocked back in his chair. "Sure you're not overthinking this, Arla?"

She shook her head. "Simpson and Luke are lovers. Yes, they are both very messed up, but I dont think they are killlers."

Beauregard said, "And what if you're wrong? Details of this case are appearing in the tabloids every day. Imagine if we let Luke go. The press finds out about the evidence, and have a field day, laughing at us." He looked at Johnson, desperation in his eyes. "We have to think about the safety of James Fraser sir. Can we really guarantee that when we let Luke out?"

The important question hung in the air. Arla glanced from Justin to Johnson, a heaviness in her soul. She rubbed her eyes. The coffee was working, but it would wear off soon. She could kill for a double G and T.

Johnson took a deep breath, then blew his cheeks out. "Justin is right. We cannot let Luke go free, not with that evidence. Besides," he squinted at Arla, "Have you actually got another suspect?"

She found Harry's face. His lips were set in a thin line and she knew he was thinking the same as her. To hell with this. She looked back to Johnson. "No, sir."

She made fists of her hands as she heard the sigh of content that passed Beauregard's mouth.

Arsehole.

Johnson leaned forward, putting his elbows on the desk. "Justin is the SIO in this case now, Arla. I know you two don't like each other. But you need to put personality clashes aside here, and work for the case. Arla, you need to support Justin on this. Do I have your word?"

Arla looked at him with daggers in her eyes. Johnson looked uncomfortable. Arla held his eyes for a while, then nodded curtly. "Yes."

Johnson turned to Justin. "Same goes for you, Justin. Works as a team. Alright?"

"Of course, sir." Beauregard said in a nauseatingly happy voice. "I always do."

CHAPTER 66

Harry drove down the winding inner city streets of Clapham. Raindrops smudged the windscreen, reflecting the haziness in Arla's mind. Red and yellow lights from the traffic flickered like questions popping up in her brain, then dying without answers.

Harry said, "Something Lisa told me to tell you. Sorry, I forgot."

"What?" She blinked at him.

"She went through Laura Douglas's medical records. There was no mention of depression."

Arla digested this in silence. "I want to look at those records myself."

 It was a habit, she had to sit down with the sheets of paper, or screens, making notes by hand, and go through them one by one. Something, somewhere would click.

"How did Cherie sound when you spoke to her?" Arla asked.

They were on their way to see Cherie. Harry shrugged with one shoulder. "Pretty down."

Ten minutes of traffic later, they were pulling up outside the Victorian mansion house now split into apartments and a Bed and Breakfast. The BnB was a show. In reality, it was a safe house for the London Met's Witness Protection Programme.

The guard at the gate checked their ID before letting them in. The receptionist knew Arla. They signed their names and ranks, then took the flight of stairs up to the second floor. A depressing green carpet made the corridor look smaller than it was. Dark oak panelling on the walls didn't help. Arla knew some Victorian gentleman had thought it looked splendid, but to her eyes it was dull, boring.

Harry knocked on the door and said the password. Cherie opened the door. Arla's breath caught when she looked at the thin, haggard face. Cherie's cheeks were considerably more shrunken than last time, and dark roots where showing plenty in her blonde hair. Her usually bright, large eyes were glassy. But they widened when they saw Arla. Harry stood to one side and let Arla enter first.

The room was full with three suitcases in various stages of being unpacked. There was only one dresser, and Arla knew it would be full. Cherie was dressed in jeans and jumper, sans makeup. The table had a small mirror on it, and it was littered with envelopes, newspapers. The room was a mess. From a des res to this, Arla thought.

"Are you OK?" Arla asked. Cherie glanced away and her lower lip trembled. Arla stepped forward and touched her arm.

"I know this is hard for you," she said. She opened her arms and Cherie stepped into her embrace. A soft sob escaped her throat as she hugged Arla. Arla released one arm and waved at Harry. He turned and went out, closing the door.

Cherie let go, then sat down on the corner of the unmade bed. She dabbed at her eyes with a handkerchief that had CL embroidered at one edge, Arla noticed.

"Is it true? About Luke, I mean," Cherie asked in a small voice.

"Yes." Arla knew Harry had told her. "James Fraser was his biological father. Did you know that?"

She shook her head vigorously. "It's a shock to me. You see, I wasn't married to David that long. Only one year." She gripped her forehead. "I'm starting to see I knew so little. He had this whole past that I knew nothing about." She turned and stared at Arla. "I feel like such a fool."

There was no acting in this. Her eyes were sincere. Arla said, "We were all fooled by this. So don't feel bad about it."

"But I was married to him! He never told me...obviously he didn't love me, did he?" tears rolled down her eyes and she took the handkerchief out again and wiped her cheeks. "Gosh that sounds really bad, doesn't it? He's dead and I'm saying that about him."

"It's a lot to take on board," Arla said. She rubbed Cherie's forearm. "Many of us lead secret lives no one knows about. Sometimes not even the ones we love."

Cherie stared at Arla with red rimmed eyes. "Yes," she whispered.

"Thank you for alerting us about the text that Luke sent you. We tracked his location on the back of that."

"No problem," Cherie sniffed. "I wasn't even sure if I was doing the right thing. But now I'm glad I did."

Arla said, "But I don't think Luke is the killer." Gently, she told Cherie about Luke and Simpson. Cherie's covered her mouth. Shock had frozen her into silence.

"I'm sorry," Arla said. "It is possible that Luke was abused from a young age. Abused children can become abusers themselves. It's a tragic circle. That's probably why Luke made those films."

Cherie rose and went to the window that looked out into a courtyard. She kept her back to Arla and head bowed.

Arla said, "But he confessed to assaulting you. I think he's done that to many women over the years. I'm going to speak to one of them later tonight."

Cherie remained silent and still. Arla got up and went to her. "At least some good will come from this. We got Simpson. I'll make sure he ever hurts anyone again."

Cherie felxed her jaws, and when she turned to look at Arla, there was cold steel in her eyes. "Thank you."

"No problem. Can I ask you about Laura Douglas, David's ex wife?"

"What about her?"

"Did David ever speak to her about you?"

A sad, mirthless smile crept into Cherie's lips. "He never told me about Luke, what makes you think he would say anything about his ex wife?" She looked away. "He mentioned her. How sad he was when she died. It took him more than a year to get over it. It destroyed him, to be honest. I told you that before."

"I know. Can you think of anything specific David said about Laura? It could be important."

"He said she was kind and caring. A soul mate. He was devastated when he lost her." A curious expression flitted across Cherie's face. She frowned, then grimaced as if in sudden, deep pain.

"What is it?" Arla asked.

Cherie leaned forward, gripping with window sill hard. "Soul mate. Guess I was never that to David, was I?"

"That's not true. He wouldn't have married you if he didn't love you. Maybe he was waiting for the right time to tell you. Guess that moment never came. I'm sorry."

Tears were rolling down Cherie's face again. Arla rubbed her back. "Shall we sit down?"

When Cherie had composed herself, Arla asked, "Did you know if Laura had a friend? I mean did David ever mention that to you?"

Cherie thought, then shook her head, blinking puffy eyes. "No. Not that I can recall anyway. He told me about the funeral, how doing the speech was the hardest thing he did. But nothign about a friend."

Arla rose. "I'll leave you alone now. But I'm around if you need me. Just call."

Cherie also got to her feet. "Thank you so much. Really appreciate you being here."

"Has Emily been to see you?" Emily Hudson was the family liaison officer.

"Not yet. Sure she will."

"Do you have any family around?"

"I'm a single child and my parents are both dead. But I do have some friends around."

Arla lingered by the door. "Will you go back to live in the house?"

Cherie's face darkened. "I can hardly carry on living here, can I? What option do I have? I need to see the lawyer first about the will, and the money."

"OK." Arla opened the door. "Just call me if you need anything."

Cherie thanked her again and Arla left. Harry was loitering in the corridor, looking bored. He glanced at his watch.

"You know we have to get to a party, right?" Tangye Gale, the actress, would meet them at a film inauguration party.

"It's work, Harry. Not recreation."

"I bet you there'll be free drinks. Besides," he rolled his shoulders and stretched. "When they see me, I might get offered a film role. I could be England's George Clooney."

"You're more like England's Chevy Chase. Now shut up and move."

CHAPTER 67

The film inauguration party was at a large pub in Soho, the heartland of London's creative industry. Soho's narrow, cobbled streets were lined with bookshops, studios, art galleries and peepshows. Bearded bohemians rubbed shoulders with city folk in sharp suits. Warm yellow lights gleamed inside pubs packed with punters.

Harry stopped in front of a large terraced building which had a sign that said "Dog and Fox." It was a traditional pub, older than most, Arla noted, judging by its thatched roof and timber beams. Two bouncers at the front checked bags and ID before letting people in. A skinny woman with a guest list on a clipboard stood next to them, smoking and shivering in the cold.

Arla introduced herself, and they had to wait till Tangye Gale was called. A tall, glamorous woman appeared shortly after. She wore a blue camisole dress, shoulders bare. Her chestnut hair was shoulder length, and glinted in the light. She checked Harry out for longer than necessary, then smiled at him in a way that Arla didn't like. She stepped past him and held up her warrant card.

"DCI Baker," she said loud enough for all to hear. "Can we come inside please?"

Tangye's green eyes fell on Arla and her eyebrows lifted. "Sure." She gestured at the bouncers and the rope was lowered, and for the first time in her life, Arla stepped on the red carpet. It was softer than she had thought and was glad of her flat shoes. She wondered how Tangye had walked on this in her high heels.

It was dark inside, expensive looking dresses gleaming in the dim lights that moved around, flickering on and off. Tangye was the same height as Arla, and the appraised each other in silence.

Arla could have groaned aloud. *Here I am, dressed in the most ridiculous outfit for this place.*

Her dowdy black business suit. Well, she was here for work. Tangye stuck a hand out and Arla shook it, feeling her surprisingly hard grip. Arla returned it, her lips twitching at Tangye's generous, if somewhat nervous smile. Arla introduced Harry.

"Yes," Harry said, "we spoke on the phone."

"I remember," Tangye said in a throaty voice, which Arla thought, she must reserve for men. Harry was smiling like an idiot, and he was about to say something when he caught the venom in Arla's eyes.

Tangye cleared her throat. "Shall we go somewhere quieter?"

They followed her upstairs, squeezing past the skinniest women Arla had ever seen. She didn't miss the handsome men who nodded at her and smiled.

Upstairs was quieter with armchairs strewn around. Several couples were head to head in deep conversation. Tangye sat down in a chair with two empty ones opposite.

Arla got straight to business. "We have Mike Simpson in custody. He is charged with the murder of David Longworth."

Tangye nodded. Her serene eyes became troubled. "Everyone's talking about it. Nothing like this has ever happened in our industry. They were two of the biggest names. Behind the scenes, I mean."

"What do you think about it?"

Tangye seemed taken aback by the question. Her eyes flitted from Arla to Harry. She cleared her throat.

"What do I think? Well, I took Simpson to court two years ago for molesting me at his office. I can tell you I'm not the first one. It's an open secret. You have to sleep with him to get a role in one of his films."

"Then why did you go to see him?"

Tangye didn't seem perturbed by the question, but a hardness flashed in her eyes. "Don't you see your boss, detective, when you

261

want a promotion? What about a job interview? Do you expect to be told to take your clothes off at that time?"

"No, I didn't-

"Well that's what I was told to do. By one of the pillars of our industry. Like it was the most normal thing in the world. What makes me sick even now is the relaxed look on his face, like he expected me to just go ahead."

Arla waited, aware of the sudden anger that radiated across to her. Tangye said, "When I refused, he said I would never work in the industry again. He even said forget about Los Angeles. His mates in Hollywood would make sure I never got a role anywhere."

"Then what did you do?"

"Well, I asked around. You know what surprised me? How many women didn't say anything. I knew their silence was as good as a lie. That protected him. But I did find another person who was just as pissed of as I was."

"Sarah Skelton. The other actress who brought charges against him. That led to another three women coming forward, right?"

Tangye nodded. Arla lowered her voice. "You did the right thing. I know the case got thrown out due to lack of evidence. But, now, we have Simpson where we want him. I cannot tell you confidential details about the case, but you can reinstate your charges, and bring them to court."

Tangye's beautiful eyes widened. "You mean reopen the case?"

"Exactly."

"What makes you think it will work this time?"

Arla smiled. "Let's just say I have a good hunch." She became serious. "Did you know David Longworth?"

CHAPTER 68

Tangye's eyes narrowed ever so slightly. She went to say something then paused. Arla noticed the hesitation, a small warning unfurled in the back of her brain. She had never guessed the truth about Luke. She didn't know what was hiding here either.

In a neutral tone Tangye said, "I never worked with him. But of course, everyone knows about him."

Arla said, "Yes so do I and the rest of the world. But I'm asking if you knew him personally."

"No."

"Did you ever hear anything about him? Was he a womaniser?"

Again the slight hesitation, then a shake of her head, less convincing this time. "I never heard anything about him, no. Look, he was a famous film director. He was high up in the BBC. Everyone wanted to meet him." She stopped.

Arla frowned. "And?"

"And nothing. I never heard rumours about him."

Harry said, "We're not asking you to compare him to Simpson. But you're sure you never heard any stories about David?"

"No."

Harry sat back in his seat. He got up a second later. "Going to the loo," he said to Arla.

She waited till Harry had gone, then turned her attention back to Tangye. They held each other's eyes. Arla saw a toughness in her stare, Tangye was clearly a person who wouldn't be easily intimidated. She respected that.

"You can tell me," Arla said. "Off the record. No one will ask you for a statement."

"You're fishing in the wrong waters, detective. I dont know anything about David Longworth. He's clean as far as I know."

Again Arla got the impression something lay below the surface here, but she couldn't put her finger to it.

"Did you ever meet David's wife? Or ex wife?"

"No. Like I said, I didn't know David personally."

"Did you know Luke, his son?"

A shadow passed over her face. The mask slipped once more only this time, it fell lower. Arla shuffled forward on her seat.

"Luke is under arrest, Tangye. Did you know that?"

The glacial calm had cracked, and Tangye eyes were moist all of a sudden. She swallowed, her long graceful neck barely moving. She sniffed.

"Tell me," Arla urged.

Tangye looked down at her hands, and splayed her long fingers. No rings, Arla noted.

"It was Luke who introduced me to Simpson. I did a commercial for a designer wear. Luke was the director. He told me Simpson was looking for a new face."

She was silent for a while, avoiding Arla's gaze. "I regret it. I never spoke to Luke after that."

A distant buzz was getting louder in a corner of Arla's brain. What was she missing here? A shape was forming in her brain, and she just needed to make the right connection. Was Tangye connected to David through Luke?

"Where were you the night of 17th November?"

Tangye looked up like she had been slapped in the face. From her expression Arla knew exactly what she meant. Arla repeated her question.

"I...I don't remember."

"Are you sure? Maybe you need some time to think."

Tangye touched her forehead. "I think I was out with the crew after a shoot. Not sure. I need to check my diary."

She didn't ask why that date. Because she knows why.

Arla waited while Tangye thought for while. Soon, Tangye said, "Look detective, I thought this was about shedding light on Simpson. Not sure how it got me in the spotlight. I've had a hard dar, and I need to relax. Can I get back to you about this?"

Arla relented, despite the warning signs flashing in her mind. There wasn't much more she could do tonight anyway.

She thanked Tangye and stood. She weaved her way past the bodies and got to the ground floor. She walked around, looking for Harry. A waiter with a tray of flute glasses stopped her. Arla was tempted by the frothing bubbly, but good sense prevailed. She shook her head and walked on.

She found Harry in a dark corner,leaning against the wall. He wasn't alone. A striking looking woman, dressed in a long gold, figure hugging dress, stood close to almost touching him. Her skin was tanned to almost brown. A sudden weight hit Arla like a sledgehammer in the gut. She couldn't breathe. The woman clearly knew Harry well. He was paying close attention to her, head leaning close to hers.

As she watched, the woman lifted a long arm and smiling, leaned forward to touch Harry's chest.

CHAPTER 69

Arla stood rooted to the spot. Jealousy erupted inside her like a geyser, blowing apart all rational thinking. She shook in rage as the woman laughed and Harry joined her, throwing his head back. The woman was facing Arla and she caught her eyes. The smile faded from her lips. She tapped Harry on the arm, who turned. His laughter stopped abruptly when he saw the stormy look on Arla's face.

With a feral snarl, Arla twisted away. She barged past bodies, colliding with a waiter. The tray of flutes went flying. A woman shrieked, glasses smashed on the floor. Arla paid no attention. Someone shouted her name.

She threw the doors open and stepped outside. The bouncers looked surprised. She pushed past them, and one of them reached out to stop her.

"Whoa, easy there."

"I'm a DCI," Arla shouted, slapping the hand away. "Get out of my way, now."

An arm tugged at her shoulder and she turned to find Harry. He grabbed her arm and she fought him, dragging them out on the street. A car honked and swerved to miss them.

"Arla stop!" Harry shouted.

"Let go of me," she said, teeth clenched. "Go back to your friend."

She was panting, still trying to free herself from his clutch, but he was strong. She almost spat in his face. "Let go of me now before I kick you. Now!"

Harry let go of her. Breath clouded their faces. Arla shook her head, pain suddenly spearing her insides. She almost doubled over, but turned to leave. Harry grabbed her again.

"Go if you want to, but listen to me first."

"You have nothing to tell me."

She put the flat of her palm against his chest and shoved him back. He stumbled, caught his feet on the pavement and toppled backwards.

"Harry!", a woman shouted, and tottered towards him on heels. It was the same floozy he was chatting to.

"Hope you're happy now," Arla shouted at her. The woman had stopped over Harry, and helped him to stand up. She left him and walked over. Her eyes were blazing.

"What's your problem?"

Arla squared up to her. "I'll give you a problem. Listen love, I can bury you six feet underground right this second. You want to try me?"

Harry appeared to one side. "Stop it," he said.

Arla glared at him. "Fuck off."

"Arla," Harry swallowed and came forward. "Will you just listen?"

"Listen to what?"

Harry wiped rain water off his face. "She's my sister."

Arla reeled backwards, head spinning. Her mouth fell open. Embarrassment flooded to every fibre of her being. She turned her back to them, and covered her face in both hands. She felt a presence, and Harry was putting his arm around her. She buried her head in his chest. Good old Harry. Would she have been so charitable if it had been the other way around?

"I'm so sorry," she mumbled.

"Guess it looked odd, me chatting to her."

"No. It's not you. It's me." Her voice was small, and her head was still buried in his chest. His coat was damp with rain. Her words were muffled, but she sensed Harry could hear them. He could

267

reach her where no one did. For that, she was thankful. He tugged her head back gently, and she lifted her face up to him. His lips were cool and inviting. She opened her mouth and his tongue slid in softly, exploring her. Electric sparks shimmered down her spine.

"Ahem, lovebirds," a woman's voice next to them called out. "It's raining, cold and everyone's watching you snog. Do you mind?"

Harry detached with a smile. "Arla, this is my smart mouth sister, Smita. Sis, this is Arla."

Smita was pretty. Arla smiled sheepishly as they shook hands. "Guess I owe you an apology," Arla said.

"No. I can see how it would look dodgy."

"I shouldn't have flown off the handle like that."

Smita leaned closer. "Our reactions are always stronger when we care more."

Arla stared at her. It was a deep statement to make, especially when they had just met. She wondered how much Harry had told Smita about her.

"Let's go inside," Harry said. They walked back in, the bouncers giving Arla a funny stare. They went upstairs again, and Arla looked around for Tangye. She couldn't find her. Harry went to get drinks while they sat down.

"Shall we start again?" Smita asked.

Arla was suddenly tired, and she wanted a drink. Now that she had talked to Tangye Jones, officially she wasn't on duty anymore. She smiled tiredly at Smita.

"From the beginning. By the way, what film inauguration is this?"

"It's a thriller called Dark Dawn. Production company is based in Pinewood Studios."

"And you have a role in it?"

She smiled. "My role is small. A support one, to the lead role. Tangye Gale is playing it. You met her, didn't you? Harry said."

"Yes. What role is she playing?"

"A police detective."

They looked at each other, then both burst out laughing. The earlier awkwardness had melted away. Arla threw her head back and slapped her knee, mirth bubbling inside her. It felt good to find something funny.

Smita said, "Oh look there's two friends of mine." She waved at a young couple who had just walked up the steps and were standing near the landing. The woman waved back and started towards them.

Smita introduced them. "Arla, these are my friends Emma and Jonty."

Arla stood to join the rest. Jonty was closest to her, and she found herself looking at a pair of intense blue eyes. She shook the warm, if slightly moist hand.

"Hi," the young man said. "Nice to meet you."

CHAPTER 70

Jonty couldn't believe his eyes. From the landing, he had seen her in profile. The shock of recognition made his face rigid and breath froze in his lungs. If he ever needed a sign that Arla Baker's destiny lay in his hands, this was it.

Jonty had told Emma he was going home from the funeral. He would pick her up later. But Jonty didn't go home. He waited in an alleyway opposite Arla's apartment in Tooting Broadway. He itched with impatience to see her. When she didn't appear, he wanted to get inside the apartment. It wouldn't be hard. He had seen the security camera outside, it was child's play to remove it from the wall. He could cut the electric cables to take out the alarm inside.

But he did nothing. Instead he waited. Standing in that dark, wet alley, rain whispering against his ears, visions of what he would do to Arla Baker filled his mind. He played them out like a movie. He would take her while she slept. Put her in the car. Take her to his secret hideout. Strip her naked while she was tied down. Then he would teach her how to be pure.

Now, as he stared at her, those visions flooded his imagination once again. He wasn't dreaming this. It was actually happening. He had debated, for a fraction of a second, to run down the stairs. Avoid seeing Arla. But curiosity had won out. She had never seen him before. There was no need for her to be suspicious. Excitement churned in his guts and sweat broke out on his scalp.

Before he knew it, he was next to her. Shaking her hand.

Act normal. Remember she's trained to look out for unusual behaviour.

Arla nodded at him and they sat down. Smita and Emma started chatting and Jonty was silent, acutely aware of the vision of his dreams sitting right next to him. He sneaked a look at her. She was dressed in her usual attire - black business suit. Why was she here?

He ran scenarios through his mind. No, it wasn't because of him. It couldn't be. Simpson was in custody. Could it be due that? Yes, that made more sense. Simpson was an executive producer of the film Dark Dawn. She was following up a lead, chatting to people who might have known Simpson.

She looked tired as well, Jonty thought. God, how well he could comfort her. Once she did his bidding, of course. Once she was purified. Another man had touched her, that big oaf of a police inspector who hung around with her all the time. Jonty wondered if he was here. Probably. Unless of course, he thought with growing heat inside his belly, she had come alone. In which case, he could get it over and done with tonight. He could follow her back and…

"So, what do you do?"

Jonty glanced to his left. Arla was speaking to him. He looked into her eyes, the swirling brown depths almost mesmerising him. He liked her voice too, clear, direct. Shivers ran down his spine. God, he wanted to get his hands on her.

Jonty shrugged, trying hard to be casual. "I'm a lighting director. Without the right lights, you can't have a film." He smiled.

She cracked a grin as well, but he could see through it. A different gleam came into her eyes. "Did you know Mike Simpson, the producer?"

He shook his head. "Can't say I did."

"How about David Longworth?"

Jonty frowned. "He died, didn't he? Read it in the papers."

"Yes."

"Why do you want to know?" Jonty asked carefully. He needed to watch his step here. He noticed that neither Smita nor Arla had as yet disclosed that Arla was a cop. That made him uneasy. But he also understood she was doing her job.

"Oh, just asking."

Jonty nodded and thought about his next question. Then he asked, "So what do you do?"

He saw the hesitation in her face and almost smiled to himself. Now that he was in control he was starting to enjoy it. He could play with her.

Soon, you will be mine.

"I'm a police officer," she said matter of factly.

"Oh?" he made a face. "Am I in trouble?"

"No," she laughed, and her guard fell. Jonty's mouth opened as she caught the first pure glimpse of his prey. Arla Baker being her normal self. His heart thudded against his ribs. He would remember this moment. This laugh.

"Just here about something else," she said after, being evasive.

"Oh, I see." He dearly wanted to ask her so much. He wanted to know how the case was going. How hard she was working. What colour her bras and knickers were? Matching?

He thought of her in underwear only, and he could feel an erection stir in his pants. He inhaled deeply. Her scent was invigorating, he would never forget it. Her aroma made his erection stronger. Jonty looked down, flexing his jaws. He had to get back into control.

"I'll just nip to the loo," he smiled at Arla, then at the other two ladies.

In the bathroom, he looked at himself in the mirror. He took deep breaths and splashed water in his face. He was so close he could touch her. Feel her. He couldn't wait any more. It had to be soon.

When he came back, Arla had gone.

CHAPTER 71

Arla didn't sleep well that night. Harry had a few drinks, and he was out like a light after they made love. Correction, he was always out like a light after they made love. While she remained awake, skin tingling.

Only tonight, the thoughts that filled her mind were far from pleasant. She saw Simpson's red, leathery face, eyes hooded, cheeks sagging, an old pervert whose image made her want to vomit. She thought of Luke, probably awake like her, his soul twisted and scarred. Scarred enough to commit murder? Had she got this all wrong?

In the early hours of the morning, she fell into a fitful sleep. Harry woke her as he was leaving. Arla felt groggy, the few drinks she had last night enough to give her a light hangover. She got ready and once out in the cold air, felt better. She was in the office by 9 am.

Lisa bustled up to her as soon as she walked in. Her eyes were flashing. "Guv, you won't believe this."

"What?"

"An old man was found dead in his own bed in Clapham last night. Head was smashed in by a heavy, blunt object, according to SOCO who attended."

Excitement gripped Arla. "Blunt object, like a hammer?"

"Yup, hammer is the word SOCO used too. And spotlights were left focused on the body, the walls were freshly painted red, the room was staged up like a theatre screen."

"Same MO," Arla said softly. "Luke wasn't released last night?"

"Nope, and neither was Simpson."

Arla looked at Lisa and nodded slowly. The grin on Lisa's face was catching. Arla couldn't help herself.

"You were right, guv," Lisa beamed. The smile didn't last long. "The killer's still out there."

"Where's Harry?" Arla had glanced over at his empty table.

"He's speaking to Darren, who went over to the hotel this morning to verify Simpson and Luke's alibi."

The uniforms shared a different office. Arla thanked Lisa and walked down the corridor, stopping to get herself a cup of rancid coffee from the drinks machine. She spotted Harry with his hands on a table, leaning forward. Darren and another uniform sergeant were speaking to him. He straightened as Arla approached.

"Their stories check out. We have a copy of the CCTV as well, just need to check it."

"Excellent," Arla smiled. "Good work guys." She turned to Harry. "You heard of the new murder?"

"Yes. Justin's there now, checking the place out."

Arla crinkled her nose. "I want to be there."

They walked back to her office, and Arla perched herself on Lisa's desk. "Tell me about this guy. Is he in the film industry as well?"

"No," Lisa said, her eyes still on the laptop screen. "He's a retired judge, as it happens. Lived alone, divorced, no children. No family as far as we can see. He owned the apartment he lived in."

"Method of entry?"

"Break in. Wasn't hard. No alarm and the door was old."

"Let's pull up CCTV images. There must be some of the killer. He's getting bold now. What was the victim's name?"

"Stanley Mason. 79 years old."

"Pull up his medical records and employment files. Nothing on IDENT 1 or the PCN websites?"

"No guv, nothing. He was a judge after all."

"Means nothing," Arla said, getting off Lisa's table. "Come on," she said to Harry. "I wasnt joking when I said I want to be on sight."

Harry sighed. "Guv, Justin said-

"I don't care what he said. He might be the SIO, but I knew this might happen. Now let's get going."

The building was a terraced mansion block overlooking Clapham Common. Squad cars were directing traffic and the jam was building up. Harry parked on a side road and they walked the rest on foot.

Arla signed her name at the entrance, covered by a white forensic tent. She put the shoe cover and gloves on. Through a narrow corridor whose walls were covered in peeling paint, they stepped through a door into an apartment. The place was blazing with lights the SOCO had set up.

Arla saw Justin Beauregard first. His face changed when he saw Arla. "What are you doing here?" He glanced at Harry. "I told you to stay at the station."

Harry shrugged. "She wanted to come guv, what could I do?"

Arla said, "This is what I said might happen, Justin. The killer's still out there. Therefore, I think I have every right to be here."

Beauregard frowned. "I'm the SIO."

"I still have the higher rank. you might be an acting DCI but you haven't replaced me. To be honest, what the hell is an acting DCI anyway? Either you are one or you're not."

Beauregard's face turned red. He spluttered. Arla stepped up to him. She took out her phone and placed it on his chest. "You want to call Johnson? Cry like a little girl? Go right ahead."

She stepped past him, but not before she heard the snort of laughter from Harry. The bedroom was lit up with garish bright light from the SOCO headlamps. Parmentier was hunched over the body and a bored looking Banerjee was standing next to him, shoulders stooped. His face brightened when he saw Arla.

"Well if it isn't the saviour! Welcome DCI Baker."

"DCI is ok but not saviour, doc."

Banerji rolled his eyes. "You're saving me. I'm getting backpain standing here."

"What does it look like?"

Banerji repeated what Lisa said. But he looked troubled. "Anything else?" Arla asked, lowering her voice.

His brows were lowered. "There's signs of a struggle. Victim has fingerprints on the neck and small lacerations caused by nails on his neck and chest. Also on the hands."

"What do you think happened?"

"He was strangled but he fought back. The attacker subdued him eventually. He didn't have to kill him with the hammer blow."

Arla understood. "He was dead already or close to dying."

"Yes."

"Sick bastard had to leave his calling card behind by bashing his head in." Arla grimaced.

She asked "Time of death?"

"It's 9.30 now. I reckon more than twenty hours. Body is much colder than ambient temp of 18 degrees. Rigor mortis has spread to the larger muscles."

Arla pondered. That meant before yesterday evening. When she was at the pub with Harry and Smita. She looked at Banerji.

"That makes it what time? Roughly?"

"Afternoon, I'd say. Early afternoon, say between 2 and 3."

When Luke was already behind bars. Arla nodded. That made sense. CCTV would also be useful in excluding Luke being there the night before. Even if the time of death changed to earlier, there was no way Luke could have murdered this old man earlier in the morning, and then escaped to his hideout in High Street Kensington.

"The TOD won't be early in the morning? Say around ten o' clock?" She asked Banerji.

He shook his head. "No. Body would show signs of decomposing then. Definitely afternoon. I can get you a more precise time later."

Parementier got up from his kneeling position. "You want to have a look at this." He pointed at the bed.

Arla stepped onto one of the plastic duck pads gingerly. The man's legs were in view. Her breath caught. Cuts were marked all over them, both shallow and deep. Blood had seeped out and congealed on the bedsheets. The cuts formed a pattern, like the shape of a christmas tree, moving up his legs into the groins

Arla shook her head. "Jeez."

Parmentier said, "He went to town on this poor man, didn't he?"

Banerji added in a grim voice, "He took his time. This must have taken a couple of hours at least."

Arla moved up towards the rest of the body. Black marks littered the chest and abdomen, with more cuts.

She asked Banerji, "Cigarette burns?"

"Yes."

Arla turned away from the macabre sight. It wasn't often a dead body disturbed her. It was the cold hearted way this man had been tortured that made her feel sick.

Parmentier said, "He also destroyed the few belongings the old man possessed."

Arla went to where Parmentier was standing. Broken pieces of china littered the floor. With a gloved hand, she picked up one of the pieces, then the others, squatting on the floor.

"Bag all of them. It looks like a china vase. Wonder what the value was."

Banerji took one of the white pieces with blue engraving on it. "My mother in law used to collect these things. She didn't have any Ming dynasty vases, but I saw some Song and Tang era ones at her place. To my inexperienced eye, these look valuable."

Arla said, "Well, you might be the only expert we have right now. But lets get it checked, Parmentier."

"Sure. Nicer than looking for crumbs DNA."

"If they were valuable, this gets interesting," Arla said. "Almost like he bore a grudge against this guy."

She looked around at the red paint on the wall. It smelled fresh. It was just dabs of colour, flung on the wall with haphazard brush strokes. She struggled to find a pattern. They seemed like wild, angry lashings of red against a white wall.

The focus lights on the body were turned off now, but they hadn't been removed from their original position. They stood on long tripods, their black heads angling down at the body in the bed. She looked at the curtains above the bed, they were parted like a theatre screen, gathered at the sides. The curtains had also been painted red.

"It's like he's an artist, and this is his canvas," Arla thought aloud. She was reminded of looking inside David Longworth's study, that weird feeling of being a member of the audience, staring at a macabre stage of death.

Banerji said, "Well, whatever he's trying to do, he's succeeding."

Arla snapped back to the present. "He won't succeed for long, if I have my way."

A voice from the rear said, "I am the SIO." It was Beauregard. Without turning, Arla rolled her eyes at Banerji, who smiled.

Arla brushed past Beauregard and out into the narrow corridor. She headed outside, Harry behind her. Her phone beeped. It was Johnson. There was a note of resignation in his voice.

"We need to talk."

"I thought you might say that," Arla said in a dry tone.

CHAPTER 72

Cherie Longworth looked out the window of her BnB, down at the courtyard. It was raining, drops pattering against the glass. It was strange being here. She felt enclosed, encapsulated, but she could hear the sounds of traffic. She didn't have a window that opened out on the street, and could only see the empty courtyard below, ringed by the four floors of the old building.

Cherie was debating whether to go out. She had to buy some groceries. She also wanted to swing by the house. Her home, until recently. Now that Luke was behind bars, it might be OK to go back.

Her mind wandered back to Inspector Arla's questions. She didn't mean to be intrusive, but it was the nature of her job. Cherie thought back to the questions about Laura Douglas. It was weird, what the Inspector was digging for there.

Cherie took one last look at the mirror. She had put some makeup on today. Not that she felt like it. But she had forced herself to, and now that she had, it did make her feel a little better. She had more colour in her cheeks, and the mascara helped hide the dark shadows in her eyes. She needed a trim as well, her hair was getting way past the shoulders.

She took her handbag, making sure she had the mace spray the police had provided her with. The woman at the reception waved at her, asking where she was going.

"Just some shopping, then I might head to the house."

"OK," the woman said. "I'll tell a uniformed unit to be there."

"It should be safe now," Cherie said, her voice weakening. She didn't mind the police being there at all.

"It's no trouble," the woman said. "What time will you be there? They'll arrive before you."

"Maximum two hours," Cherie said.

The guard at the door nodded at her as she left. The air was cold, but it was also fresh. Distant cries of ball players in the Common reached her ears. Cherie decided not to drive, or wait for the bus. The skies were grey, but rain wasn't forecast. Like most Londoners, Cherie never trusted the weatherman anyway. She had a small folded umbrella in her handbag. It was a couple of miles to the High Street, less than half an hour walk. She felt the exercise would do her good.

Cherie glanced at her phone before she set off. She walked next to the green expanse of the Common, the bandstand visible in the distance. Come summer, the big brass band would play on Sundays, and the place would be full with people. She couldn't wait for summer. This winter was getting more dreary every passing day.

An occasional car whished past her, but the mid morning traffic was light. The smell of sodden earth and wet leaves carried to her, borne by a chilly, wintry breeze. Pedestrians were few in this part of the Common, green parkland surrounded her on both sides. She would have to walk for fifteen minutes at least before she came closer to the shops.

A bird flew over her head, startling her with its sharp cawing. A raven. She watched it swoop over something on the grass. She avoided her eyes and kept walking. The sound of her heels was loud now, echoing against the trees. The occasional passing car was now behind a screen of trees.

She heard it faintly at first. A soft, almost slithering sound. But also tapping like footsteps in the distance. It came from behind her.

Just another pedestrian like me, she thought.

Cherie didn't look back. There was no point in getting paranoid. She exhaled and kept walking at her normal pace.

But the sound grew louder. Very quickly, whoever it was, got closer. Cherie turned her head. It was a hooded figure, dressed in a black raincoat. From the shoulders, she knew it was a man.

Fear lashed against her spine, turning her mouth dry. She quickened her pace. So did the man behind her. Sweat broke out on Cherie's head. She looked around. The road ahead was a straight line with no cars on it. Trees covered both sides. In the distance, she could see the traffic of the High Street. It would take her longer than she had imagined.

Panic consumed her. She looked behind again, and he was getting dangerously close. She could make out his face, pale and gaunt. His eyes were hidden by the hood. Cherie broke into a run. Breath rasped inside her chest, and her pulse surged when she realised the man was running as well.

She reached inside her handbag and pulled out the mace spray. He was very close now, and Cherie opened her mouth to scream. No sound came out, her throat was bone dry.

In a flash, he was upon her. He seemed to know that she held a spray in her rigth hand. He grabbed her from behind, pinning her against him. His right hand clamped down on her wrist and he squeezed a pressure point till she screamed and let go. The spray clatttered on the pavement

He clamped a hand over her mouth and dragged her into the trees. Cherie was in her fifties, but she wasn't unfit. Yoga and running kept her reasonably supple. She gagged, but managed to bite down on the hand while she kicked with her back leg, aiming for his shin. She hit bone and heard him grunt.

He flung her to the soft earth with savage force, and then was upon her. He straddled her chest. Pain exploded in her head as she fell, and the pressure on her back was terrible. He grabbed her throat and pulled back. Tears ran down her eyes and she tried to scream again, but he was holding her neck tight. His face lowered to hers.

"Before you die, tell me what the police woman told you! Arla Baker." He whispered.

Cherie couldn't speak, and he relaxed the grip on her neck. She sucked air in, and started to cough. He pressed down harder on her back.

"Tell me what she said!"

"Nothing. Nothing!"

"Don't lie to me. I know she came to see you at the hotel."

His voice was low, hoarse, but Cherie felt she had heard it before. There was a sound on the road, and then the sudden loud beep of a horn. A car had stopped by the side of the road. A man got out of the car, beeping his horn again.

"Hey you!" a male voice shouted.

The pressure on Cherie's throat lessened abruptly. A weight lifted from her back and then the man jumped over her, running away. Cherie got to her knees. She saw a flash of black as the figure faded between the trees, moving fast.

"Are you OK?" Cherie turned to see a middle aged man, wearing a builder's orange high visibility vest, staring at her with concern.

She wiped the snot and tears from her face. "Please call the police," she said.

CHAPTER 73

Lisa, Rita and Rob were sitting opposite Arla in her office. Harry was leaning against the shut door.

Arla asked, "What did you find out about Stanley Mason?"

Lisa opened her file. "He was a judge at the Woolwich Crown Court for the last thirty years. Originally from Middlesborough, moved down here for university, then got married. Divorced after fifteen years of marriage. No children."

"As a retired judge he should be on a good pension. Why was he living in a one bedroom apartment?," Rob asked.

"Haven't been through all his bank statements, but the last three months show regular payments to Bet-to-win.com."

"An online gambling company," Rob said,

"Yes. He moved roughly one grand there every month. Nothing came back though. Bet to win havent got in touch with me as yet."

"So he wasted his money on gambling," Arla said. "Does anything tie him to David Longworth? I mean, we are assuming here that this is the same killer. It feels the same to me."

Lisa shrugged. "Not on the surface, guv. It's not like DL had any prior convictions or a police record. Stanley Mason was a loner. Haven't been through his emails, his laptop is still with SOCO. I'll check if he sent any emails to David or Luke."

"Or Simpson. What about his mobile phone?"

"Either he didn't have one, or the killer took it."

"Hmm," Arla said. "Must've been a loner. Was the apartment in his name?"

"Yes. No other assets in his name, I checked with land registry."

"What about his ex-wife?"

"She's been informed. She lives in Wales now, by the sea in Pembrokeshire, in a retirement village."

"He must have some friends somewhere. Keep looking. I want his whole employment history - in particular a record of all the cases he was involved in. I mean every one. The killer seemed to bear a grudge against him. Destroyed all his vases, tortured him for ages. I want to know why."

Harry blew out his cheeks. "That's a lot of work, boss. Can I remind you that you're not the SIO anymore?" His eyes twinkled with mischief.

"Shut up Harry." She turned to the rest of the team. "Look, keep this to ourselves for now. Justin will have his own agenda. But that record of cases is a must. Look out for anything unusual. A case he dealt with that left angry relatives, for instance. Or a criminal he put behind bars who's now free."

"But how does that tie in with David Longworth?" Rob asked.

Arla shrugged. "I don't know. But we need to find out, before this lunatic strikes again."

She glanced at Harry, who nodded and opened the door. Arla said, "We're going up to meet the boss. Let me know the minute you have something."

They filed out, and Arla and Harry went up the staircase to Johnson's office.

"Come in," a muffled voice said when Arla knocked. Johnson was sat in his usual seat, with Justin Beauregard opposite him. Justin avoided looking at Arla as she walked in.

"Sit down," Johnson said gruffly. He put his huge paws on the table and stood. Folding his arms behind his back, he stared out the window behind him. It looked out into the rear parking lot, a grey wash out in the rain.

"I've looked at the preliminary case report of the latest murder. MO is similar. Is that correct?"

"Yes sir," Arla said, allowing a note of satisfaction to creep into her voice.

"And approximate time of death is in the afternoon. When you apprehended Luke Longworth?"

"Correct sir."

Johnson turned around, hands still clasped behind his back. He was almost as tall as the window.

"So we know the murderer couldn't have been Luke."

Justin said, "Unless there's more than one culprit."

"With exactly the same MO?" Arla scoffed. "And where exactly did this new murderer come from? Thin air?"

Justin's face turned red. He went to say something but Johnson shut him up with a wave of his hand.

"Enough. The real issue is that we have not yet guaranteed the safety of the Secretary of State." After a pause, he continued. "We have to err on the side of caution, and accept the killer might still be out there. And that it might not be Luke."

Harry said, "CCTV images of Simpson and Luke arriving at the hotel have been obtained, sir. They came separately."

Justin said, "But there's no conclusive images of them leaving. Sir, there's still a chance that Luke is our man."

Johnson shook his head. "Luke is of interest, no doubt. But in the light of this new murder, we have to assume the killer is still on the loose."

"Not just on the loose sir," Arla said. "He tortured this poor old man. Deliberately broke all his possessions. I think he's becoming more sadistic."

Harry said quietly, "I wonder who's next?"

The question hung in the air, suspended in the silent thoughts of each detective in the room.

Johnson asked, "Are you sure there's nothing to bind the judge to David Longworth?"

"We're looking for it actively. Nothing as yet."

Johnson cleared his throat. "Under the circumstances, DCI Baker is reinstated to her post. She is also taking over as SIO." He looked meaningfully from Arla to Justin. "Is that understood?"

The anger was obvious on Justin's face, but he was a detective over and above all else. Jaws clenched, he nodded in silence.

"I want you two to work together. Bury the hatchet."

Both of them murmured in agreement. Johnson's desk phone rang. He frowned, staring at it. Arla knew he would have told switchboard not to disturb his meeting. Johnson reached over and plucked the old fashioned receiver from its cradle. It looked ridiculously small in his hands.

As he listened, his brows lowered further till they met in the middle. He said, "Is she alright? Oh, I see." He hung up.

He faced Arla, and she felt a sudden knot of apprehension tighten in her chest. Johnson said, "It's Cherie. She's just been assaulted. They took her to hospital and now she's downstairs."

CHAPTER 74

The waiting room for families was less bare than the interview rooms. Two potted plants rested on the windows, and some posters about knife crimes and community help hung on the walls. Cherie was sitting on the leather sofa, head bent and knees together, when Arla walked in. She looked up and Arla saw the fright in her eyes. Her own heart contracted in sympathy. No one deserved what Cherie was having to endure.

Harry shut the door softly and sat down behind the desk. Arla came to the sofa, next to Cherie. Cherie's eyes were fixed on the floor, lips pressed. She didn't cry. She didn't move.

"I'm sorry," Arla said. She held Cherie's hand. It was cold and stiff. Cherie moved her hand away.

She said, "I thought we had the...the... killer." She closed her eyes, like the word took a lot of effort to pronounce.

"I know this is hard for you," Arla said.

Cherie looked up at Arla then, eyes blazing. "You don't know anything. Do you have any idea what it feels like to come home and see your husband dead?"

"Mrs Longworth-

"Don't call me that." Her tone was sharp, stinging. "I hate being reminded of what a failure I was. David kept so many secrets for me. I didn't even know that his son...." her voice trailed off as her eyes took on a faraway gaze. She blinked, then became downcast again.

"Tell me what happened," Arla said gently.

"Why?" Cherie said bitterly. "What good will it do? You'll never catch him. He knows everything."

Arla exchanged a look with Harry. He was frowning. Arla said, "What do you mean?"

"He knows you came to see me at the BnB. He even knows your name."

Arla sat back, stunned. Cherie continued. "You know that I think?" She glanced from Harry to Arla. "I think he works here. Or he knows you." Her expression became pained, eyes moist. "He's keeping an eye on me. Following me around everywhere. And all this time, you guys haven't done a thing. Not a thing!" Her voice rose at the end.

"Cherie, that's not true." Arla reached out to touch her but she shrank back on the sofa. Arla made a fist and withdrew her hand. This was not going the way she wanted, but what Cherie had just told her had significant potential. Arla's mind was in turmoil.

"What else did he ask you?"

Cherie sniffed. "That's all. He wanted to know what you told me."

"What did you say?"

"Luckily the car arrived. He escaped. There wasn't any time for me to say anything."

Cherie turned to Arla again. Her eyes were wide with fear. The tip of her nose was red.

"Can't you see? He's always one step ahead of you. He broke into the house because he knew there was no one at the back. Now he knows who you are, and what time you come to see me. He knows where I'm staying. How can that be? He must know what you're planning."

Cherie looked wildly around the room. She pointed at Harry. "For all I know, it could be him. Or someone else in your office. Somone…

"Now, Cherie," Arla said firmly. It was the first time she had used Cherie's first name and it got the woman's attention. "I can guarantee you it's not Harry. Or any of the men who work for me."

Cherie sniffed, staring at Arla. Her fists were bunched tight on her lap, knuckles white.

"Really? Then how does he know where you're going? Where I live?"

"Cherie, I-

"You'll only realize when I'm dead. You know that?" Cherie's face dissolved into abject misery. Her lips trembled, nostrils flared, cheeks sagged. Her head sank down on her laps. "I'm going to die." This time she couldn't hold back. Huge sob wracked her body. She shook as the tears flowed out of her.

Arla got closer and rested her arm on Cherie's back. She murmured in her ear. "You're not going to die, Cherie. Do you hear me? I swear on my life. If necessary, I'll come and stand guard over you myself. You're not going to die."

She looked up at Harry. He moved his head laterally, twice, slowly. His eyes were burning with intensity. She felt the same burn deep within her soul.

Whoever this killer was, he was now crossing lines he should leave alone. It was time to catch him. By any means necessary.

CHAPTER 75

Arla was leaning against the wall outside the family room. Harry was next to her. Emily Harman, the family liaison officer, hurried down the corridor towards them.

"I just heard," Emily said. "Is she in a bad way, guv?"

"Yup. Look after her."

"I will," Emily promised. "Are we moving her to a new safe house?"

Arla nodded. "She stays here for a couple of hours while we sort things out. No one knows about the new safe house, OK? Even I don't know the location yet. Keep it that way."

"'Course guv," Emily smiled and went in.

Emily was a new member of staff. She had joined the force after university graduation last year. Arla watched her close the door, not moving her eyes away.

"I know what you're thinking," Harry muttered.

"What?"

They walked off, heading to the rear car park, Arla assumed because Harry wanted a smoke. She liked this easy feeling, of knowing each other's moods and thoughts without having to spell anything out.

Harry studied her after he lit his cigarette. He didn't offer her one and she was glad, despite knowing she would love one.

She looked away from him, at the almost perpetual rain clouds that seemed to hang over the city these days. Miserable, wet, cold. As English as fish and chips. And maybe she was becoming a bit mutton jeff. That was Cockney slang for deaf. She wasn't hearing the signals blinking on and off in the streets, in the tortuous, dark corridors of her mind. Dealing with the devious meant listening to her own self. She got that - twisted and weary souls looking to hurt themselves over and over again. Whose silent screams broke glass, slashed wrists. She was good at that, hearing their moans, sorting out the angles. But she was missing this. Did Cherie have a point? Could it be someone in her team?

Emily?

Darren, the uniformed PC? He was also new.

How about Larry, the detective sergeant from Liverpool? No one knew much about him.

"Don't overthink it," Harry said softly.

"Someone leaked my name to the media."

"Could be one of the neighbours. Remember that Mrs Parker?"

Arla did. It made a lot of sense too. But then why did she have this uneasy feeling, like being forced to walk with a stone in her shoe? Something wasn't right. It was close enough to touch, but she couldn't see it. Maybe it was there, surrounding her like a fog, and everytime she reached out, she was going right through it. Delicate, diaphanous, a miasma of her mind.

Because Cherie was right. How did the killer know so much?

"You think she has a point?" Arla asked Harry, wheels slowly turning in her head. Mentally, he was a reflection of her. When she tried to shine a light into darkness, it bounced off Harry like a mirror, brightening everything.

"How far do you roll that ball, Arla? Who do you keep an eye on?"

"But she does have a point."

"She does," Harry conceded. "But don't think that's the only explanation. Maybe Justin is right, this is a team we are dealing with. They're keeping us under surveillance."

The click sound in her skull was so loud she almost heard it. "We have CCTV all around the station, right?"

292

"Yes?"

"So we can search for anyone who keeps an eye on the car park. A car that's always there, for example."

Harry nodded. "Good idea. Worth a try."

He flung his cigarette away and they walked back. Arla was glad to get back into the warmth. She said, "Maybe he's in contact with someone on the inside, telling him when we go out."

Harry's head was bent so low his chin was almost touching his chest. "Yes. He can't be sitting outside all day, freezing his bollocks off."

Rita came up to them as they entered the office. "CCTV from outside Stanley Mason's apartment is ready."

"Have you been through them?"

"Yup."

They gathered around Rita's table. She pulled up four images on her screen. She pointed at the time stamp.

"If the time of death was afternoon, then we need to check the morning as well as night before. He might have got in, then hid himself."

"Good thinking," Arla said. "He tortured the victim, so we know he was there for a while."

The video played, and the top box showed a moving figure. It was night time, close to midnight. They could only see its back. The grainy image was lit momentarily by a passing car.

"Stop," Arla said. "Do we have views from the opposite direction."

"Yes," Rita said. She clicked on her keyboard, and this time they had the person facing them.

"Zoom in," Arla said, leaning forward. She squinted. The pixels became larger, disfiguring the close up. But one thing was clearly visible. The face was covered with a black mask. Holes were cut for the eyes, nose and mouth, but the rest of the face was hidden. It looked hideous and Arla shivered. Not a sight she wanted to come across at night.

Rita said, "I've sent it for facial recognition. It came up blank, but it's not like we have much to work with."

Harry said, "He also knew where the CCTV's were. He hid his face from them."

Rita played the video again. The figure stood still in front of Stanley's door for a while, then let himself in.

"There were cars passing by. Get their reg numbers, track the owners down. They might have noticed something."

"Ok, guv," Rita said, scribbling on her notebook. Lisa had joined them as well.

Arla said to her, "I want a sign outside and at each end of the road. We need more members of the public to come forward."

"What time did he leave?"

"I can't tell. No one in a mask left at any time of the day. That makes sense, because if anyone saw him in broad daylight they'd remember it for sure."

Arla sat down on an empty chair and put an elbow on the table, cupping her chin. "Bring up the afternoon rolls. Go through them slowly."

Four of them huddled around the screen as Rita played them. Arla rubbed her eyes after a while. It was tedious watching the parade of people as the rush on the streets swelled. Several people came and went from the building, it was divided into several apartments, like most of the old Victorian houses on the main road.

Rob appeared with coffee and doughnuts, biting into one happily. As did Lisa and Rita. Arla looked at one, then averted her eyes. She could do without the temptation. Only coffee for her.

"Hold on," Harry said. His long index finger was touching the screen as he hunched over Rita's head. "Back up two screens. Yes, there. Freeze it. Zoom in."

"This frame?" Rita asked. "It shows an old man and a lady with a pram."

"I want the old man."

The image showed a man stooped over almost double, leaning on a walking stick. He wore a big coat, and a peaked farmer's cap pulled low over his face. He also wore sunglasses covering his eyes.

"Go back one frame."

Now the screen showed the old man emerging from the same building. He was unsteady on his feet, using the walking stick heavily. His face was effectively hidden. Once he faced the camera, Rita froze the frame again.

"Look at his shoes," Harry said.

Arla squinted. While the old man's clothes were shabby, the black, rubber soled trainers looked brand new.

"Those are running shoes," Arla said.

"Not what an old man would be wearing. It doesn't match the rest of his gear. And why is he wearing sunglasses on a cloudy day?"

Arla nodded. "You think he's our man? It makes sense to disguise himself as an old man. If he bumped into anyone from the other apartments they wouldn't notice anything different."

"Zoom into his hands," Harry said. The flesh on his hands were bare. No rings or tattoos. Harry said, "See how tight the skin is. That's not the wrinkled hands of some old guy."

Arla said, "He's a master of disguise, right? Not easy to copy the look, posture and walk of an old man."

They sat around, eating doughnuts and sipping coffee. Arla said, "Anything more from Stanley Mason's emails or bank account?"

Lisa went to her desk, and called from there. "Yes, technicals managed to break into the rest of his emails. He had three email accounts. I'll have a report ready for you soon.

Arla took a generous sip of her coffee. "Right, two things. I want this photo circulated to every London station." She pointed to the fake old man on the screen. "Put it up on every internal website. Ask other London stations, and all over UK, for crimes with similar MO. We need to widen our net."

The team were scribbling madly, while Harry was leaning back, hands crossed behind his head, eyes closed.

Arla said, "Number two. I want a TV Crimewatch appeal for Cherie's attack. We have a statement off the guy who saved her, but others would have noted something. A TV appeal will help."

"I'll call Media Liaison now. Do we need clearance from Johnson?"

"I'll get it, don't worry," Arla said. "I have to see him anyway. Is he here today?"

Rob said, "I don't think so. He's doing interviews in Victoria."

"OK, I'll call him. But start the ball rolling with the TV appeal please. It's important."

Harry opened his eyes. "I can get an actress for you, no problem." He winked as Arla smiled.

"You do that Harry. Now, as I am the SIO," Arla rose from her seat. "I want to interview Luke Longworth myself."

CHAPTER 76

Arla was waiting in the interview room when Harry and a uniformed PC arrived with Luke. The PC took the handcuffs off Luke. Luke sat down, and Harry beckoned at Arla to come outside.

The huddled in the doorway and Harry whispered, "I told Smita and she will get us an actress matching Cherie's description. Informed Media Liaison. They're happy they don't have to hunt for an actress. Hopefully we can shoot later this afternoon."

"Good," Arla said. "Where's the lawyer?"

"Should be here any minute."

Footsteps rang down the corridor, and the suave, erect figure of Jeremy Hardcastle became visible, striding towards them.

They headed back inside, after perfunctory greetings. Arla despised the arrogant lawyer.

Luke was staring at them with tired but inquisitive eyes. He was a sallow cheeked, pasty faced young man. A shock of brown hair fell over his forehead, and a strong jaw outlined his face. In his blue eyes, angles of his cheekbones, Arla could detect a strong resemblance with James Fraser.

She introduced herself and the others for the camera. "You must be wondering why we called you back," Arla said to Luke.

"I should get bail later today. So you better ask me everything you want to, now," Luke said.

"When did you find out who your real father was?" Arla asked.

Luke looked caught out by the question. He had a whispered conversation with his lawyer. "As I said before, it was when I was a teenager."

"And I guess you never looked at David Longworth in the same light? I mean, it must've been a shock to know he wasn't your dad."

Hardcastle intervened. "Where are you going with this line of questioning?"

"Just asking. Your client's been charged already."

"In that case, there's nothing new to add."

Luke intervened. "No, it's OK." He looked at Arla, and she detected a frank appraisal in them.

"You're right," Luke said. "It was a shock. It would be for anyone, right?"

"Yes," Arla said, slightly surprised by his honesty.

"But I didn't kill him." He held Arla's gaze. "I didn't like him, but here's the weird thing. He gave my mother and me a home. He cared for us. And until I found out, I did treat him like a father."

"And he treated you like a son."

A strange expression flitted across Luke's face. A collision between rage and regret. His eyebrows twisted in pain. Emotions Arla knew well.

"Yes," his voice was hoarse suddenly. "He did."

"You loved him Luke, didn't you? Even though you didn't like that fact-

"That he wasn't my real dad?" He interrupted her. "Yes."

"But you did hate James Fraser. Your real dad."

Luke curled his lips. "He doesn't know the meaning of the word. He sacrificed me for a political career."

"So you decided to sacrifice him," the words slipped out of Arla's mouth before she could stop herself.

Hardcastle stirred. "That is provocation, DCI Baker. My client has nothing to say."

Arla shrugged. She knew that beneath Luke's calm exterior lay a deeply disturbed soul. She had to bring Simpson up. It would open a can of worms, but she had no more time. Luke would be granted bail soon. She had to do this. Not for this case, but to put men like Simpson behind bars.

She lowered her voice. "When did Mike Simpson first try to seduce you?"

She might as well have reached out and slapped him across the face. He lowered his face and Arla could sense him twisting his fingers.

Hardcastle said, "My client doesn't have to answer that. It has nothing to do with this case," he added pompously.

Arla glared at him. "It will be when I bring historic child abuse cases against Mike Simpson."

Hardcastle narrowed his eyes. He opened his mouth to say something but Luke spoke over him. His head was still bent low and he stared down at his hands.

"I was fifteen." His voice was soft, croaky, like he was dragging it up from deep within him. "I had come back from football practice. I had a ensuite bathroom and I didn't always lock the door."

There was no sound save their breathing. Every eye was focused on Luke, who remained downcast.

"He opened the door and stood there, watching me shower. I didn't see him at first. Only when I turned around. I reached for a towel. He said he wanted to congratulate me on winning the match." Luke swallowed and paused. His nostrils flared.

"This became a pattern. Whenever he came to the house, he was upstairs in my room. Watching me shower."

"Didn't you mother notice?"

"He always said we were having man talks. I had grown distant from David by then. I knew. Mum liked Mike. She thought it was good a man she trusted was my friend."

"Then what happened?" Fear caught Arla's voice.

"It progressed to him touching me in the shower. I..." his chest heaved. Eyes screwed shut, then opened. "I responded. He was good at it. When it was over, he told me this was our secret. No one can know."

Air seemed to be sucked out of the room. Words dropped like bombshells from Luke's mouth, fracturing the silence.

"So, it carried on. He brought me gifts. Made me feel special. We started meeting up in hotels after school. I told mum I was staying with friends."

Arla closed her eyes. Dark fingers were clawing inside her throat, dredging up the remains of the past she desperately wanted to forget.

"Did you ever try to stop it?" she asked.

"I didn't know what to do. Because he was nice to me, I sort of went along with it. After a few years, he began to lose interest. I remember being angry about that. Feeling lost and weird. I...." Luke broke off, shaking his head.

He lifted his head. His eyes were dull, blank. He stared at Arla. "But he came back into my life. Again, it was the same. Buying me gifts, wining and dining. I was older, and was living as a gay man by then. I didn't like him coming back, but I guess I fell for him again."

Arla brows were furrowed tightly. "I'm sorry, Luke, for what you had to go through."

"I've never told anyone this."

"I know," Arla said simply. A moment passed between her and Luke, then he narrowed his eyes.

Arla cleared her throat. "What you've told us now lays the groundwork to bring Simpson to justice. I promise you he will never touch a vulnerable boy or girl again." She rose, more to hide the storm of pent up frustration and grief inside her than anything else. "We'll take a minute's break Luke, then come back."

Harry spoke on the recorder as Arla left the room. She literally ran into the bathroom. When she emerged, she was more composed. Nothing would take the past away, and Luke's experience had been like the sliding of a gravestone. The ghosts had returned. But she had to keep them at bay. There was work to do.

They re grouped in the interview room again. Luke was sipping from a glass of water and walking around the room. Hardcastle was sitting, typing on a laptop.

When they were ready, Arla asked, "We want to know about your mother's death, Luke."

He stiffened. His expression, softer than before, was suddenly guarded. "What about it?"

"Tell us what happened."

"I was in the pub watching a football match. Spurs were playing, my team. Mum and David were in the lodge."

"How was your mother at the time?"

He thought for a while before answering. "She was quieter. Not her usual self."

"Why?"

"I don't know. She went out a lot, to see a friend."

A bulb flickered to light in the recess of Arla's mind. Simpson had mentioned a friend as well. "What friend?"

"I don't know. But I saw a car come to pick her up."

Excitement gripped Arla. "When was this? While you were in Kent on holiday?"

"Yes. In fact, I remember now." He stared at Arla, and she saw clarity in his eyes. "It was the morning she died. This car pulled up outside. I was smoking outside the window. David was in the back. I saw mum come out and get in the car. Then it drove away, with her inside. She came back an hour or so later, I think."

"What sort of car? Think Luke, this is important."

He screwed his eyes shut. "Something blue. A common make. A Vauxhall, or Ford maybe. Not sure."

"But it was blue?"

"Yes. I didn't notice the reg number."

"Who was driving it? Did you see them?"

Luke shook his head, still frowning. "No. Think it was a man in the driver's seat. Not sure."

"What was he wearing?"

"Sorry, can't recall."

"Did you tell the police this, at the time?"

Luke looked at her then. "No, I didn't. I didn't think it was important. She was meeting up with this bloke a lot those days. Guess he drove to Kent to see her."

"How did you know it was him she was seeing?"

"I don't," Luke confessed. "But I know that she went out to meet a friend regularly. She told me when I asker her. But then she would clam up. I assumed it was one of her girlfriends so never pushed it. Come to think of it, I did see that blue car near our house once. I didn't live there anymore. But once I came to visit, and the car drove off."

Luke shuffled forward in his seat, a light suddenly gleaming in his eyes. "Yes, a blue car. You know what, it was a Ford. Like a Ford mondeo or something."

CHAPTER 77

Arla hung up after speaking to Johnson. Harry and the rest of the team were gathered in her office.

"OK, we got the green signal for the new safe house, and a Specialist Firearms Officer to guard the premises. Johnson had to pull strings for that. The TV appeal is going ahead, too."

"Our actress should be calling Media Liaison any time now," Harry said.

"Good. I want to give Cherie the news myself. Is she still in the family room?"

"Yes guv," Rita said.

Arla held up her right thumb and counted up. "Number one, we get the rest of Stanley Mason's emails, bank details and his entire case load as a judge. Over his whole life. No exceptions. I need three of you to do that so we get somewhere by tonight."

"Number two, we get hold of this blue car that Luke mentioned. Check the CCTV on the main roads near Cherie's house. This happened two years ago. I know it's a tall task, but we could get lucky."

The team filed out, and Arla, followed by Harry, went to see Cherie. She was still huddled on the sofa, but Emily was sat next to her, holding her hand. Two cups of tea were placed on the table, one almost empty, the other untouched.

Cherie had more colour to her cheeks, but her eyes still had the vacant, listless stare. She didn't turn to look when Arla stepped inside the room.

Emily stood and left. Harry closed the door while Arla sat next to Cherie.

"We found a place for you," Arla said. "It's in Dulwich. You have a friend there, right? Jill Hunter, I believe her name is."

"Yes." Cherie looked relieved. "Thank you. But is this place safe?"

"No one, apart from DI Mehta and myself know about this address. No other member of my team. My boss gave it to me over the phone, on a secure line. You will be very safe here."

She saw Cherie glance at Harry. Arla said, "I can vouch for DI Mehta. He won't tell anyone."

Cherie shrugged. "If you say so."

"I do."

Harry broke his silence. "You won't be leaving via the rear car park. In fact, you will be disguised as a uniformed sergeant and leave in a police van. The van will be followed by a CID car to make sure it's not being tailed."

Arla said, "This time, if someone is after you, believe me, we will know. The safe house in Dulwich is in a prominent street corner, with CCTV everywhere. The audiovisual team will monitor the live feeds. We simply pick up anyone seen acting suspiciously."

Cherie seemed more reassured. Arla told her about the SFO as well. Cheris asked, "Is that necessary?"

"Best to be safe than sorry," Arla said.

Harry opened the door and called Emily back inside. She was instructed to take Cherie to the uniformed officers department.

Cherie hung back to ask Arla a question. "Inspector Baker-

"Call me Arla."

"Ok, Arla. I just wanted to say thank you. I'm sorry if I came across as being rude before."

"Don't worry. You've been through a few major shocks. It's understandable."

Cherie's eyes were moist. She went to say something but then thought the better of it. She followed Emily out of the door.

Harry's phone rang. He spoke on it briefly before hanging up. "Film crew are in place. Smita just turned up with the actress. Her name is Kirsten, friend of hers obviously."

"Let's go."

CHAPTER 78

Two squad cars blocked the exit to the road in either direction. Two trailer vans were parked on the pavement. A long haired, bearded man wearing a black jacket was speaking to the cameraman, who held a large camera from a rig on his waist. Several crew members were fixing lights up on tall tripods. They were fiercely bright, turning the murky afternoon incandescent.

One of the trailer doors opened and Smita stepped out. She was followed by a woman as tall as Smita, with shoulder length blonde hair. Harry called Smita's name and she turned.

She gave Harry a peck on the cheek and hugged Arla. The affection seemed genuine. Not for the first time, Arla wondered what Harry had told Smita about her.

"This is my friend, Kirsten," Smita introduced the actress to them. Arla shook hands politely.

"Any instructions?" Kirsten asked. She was stick thin, Arla noted, much lighter than Cherie. She was young and attractive, and Arla guessed the director would have some way to make her appear older.

Before Arla could speak, the hirsute man in the black jacker bustled over. He looked Arla and Harry up and down. "Are you the coppers?"

"Yes," Arla said.

"My name's Tim. I'm the director for a lot of these shoots. I need to get it done quickly I'm afraid. After this I have a commercial ad shoot for a clothing company."

"Don't let me hold you up then," Arla said.

"Any instructions?" Tim asked. Everyone laughed and he looked bemused.

"That's just what I asked," Kirsten said.

"That's actually my job," Tim said, suddenly stiff and serious. "Yours is to follow instructions, and act them out" he added pompously. He looked at Arla again. "Well?"

"Your directing better be good, Tim," Arla said in a sharp voice. "We need lots of responders to this one." She told him what Cherie had been through. Tim waved a young man over. A mask was produced by one of the crew from a trailer, and the actor put it on. It was a ski mask covering his face.

"That's the best we can do," Tim confessed.

"He was wearing a hooded top covering his face," Arla said. "It was a dark top as well, and he wore black trainers."

Tim barked out orders, and the crew member disappeared inside the trailer van again. This time he took longer, the actor inside the trailer with him. Kirsten vanished inside the ladies trailer. When she emerged, Arla had a job recognizing her. Her hair seemed shorter and she had put on at least 5 Kg in weight.

Smita leaned towards Arla. "More clothes, covered by a larger size jacket. Makes her look bigger. Plus, the camera puts on more than ten percent weight when seen on screen. That's why us actresses have to diet so hard."

"And exercise more," Arla said.

"Yup. Before a role, I literally live in the gym, drink soup and smoke."

"Smoke?"

"Yes. Nicotine reduces appetite. It does work."

Arla was dubious. "Sure it doesn't become a habit?"

"The smoking you mean? Nah, not for me."

Arla asked, "Do you enjoy what you do?"

Smita seemed surprised. "Yes, of course. You can't do it if you don't enjoy it. It's bloody hard work for next to no money. Unless you get lucky."

307

"That's the main factor."

"Absolutely," Smita agreed. "Get lucky or know someone famous."

"Like Luke Longworth," Arla said, and immediately regretted it. To her mind, Luke was anything but lucky.

She was aware that Smita was observing her. Arla put on a bland smile, but from the expression on Smita's face, she knew the actress saw through it.

"It's messed up, right? This whole thing." Smita said softly.

Arla nodded. "Yes. I can't say much more at this stage. But I am doing everything possible to bring this mad man to justice."

"Hope Harry's helping," Smita said, raising her eyebrows.

"Oh, he's a bit lazy you know, but he'll do."

Smita laughed. "Maybe he pays more attention to how he dresses. Like a peacock."

Arla couldn't help joining in. "That's him alright."

Harry turned to them and frowned, like he knew he was being spoken about. Tim's voice came over the loudspeaker.

"Take your positions please. Start rolling on my count of three. Three, two, one. Lights, camera, action!"

Arla watched as the cameraman followed Kirsten from behind as she walked down the pavement.

Nobody saw the figure on the sturdy branch of a tree, less than twenty meters away, high above the ground. He had binoculars to his eyes, attention focused on the scene below.

CHAPTER 79

By the time the shooting was done, it was past 18.00. Arla and Harry said goodbye to Smita and Kirsten, who were off home. They shared an apartment in Acton Town, West London. Arla decided to call on Banerji before she got back to the office. The pathologist was still at work.

"To what do I owe this pleasure?" he asked, taking off a green surgical gown and dumping it in the bin.

Arla tried not to gag on the stench of formaldehyde. "Any more news on the new victim? Stanley Mason."

"He's there," Banerji pointed. "Guess you want to have a look."

"Not really," Arla said. "It's late, and we still have bits to tie in at the office. Why don't you just give us a rundown."

"Come to the office. He was the first body I did this morning, and my memory isn't what it used to be."

They sat down in Banerji's small but comfortable office. Photos of the Taj Mahal, and huge temples hung on the wall.

Harry pointed to one massive temple complex, with what seemed like hundreds of conical shapes rising in the sky. "South India?"

"Yes," Banerji said, adjusting his glasses. "India's most ancient temples are in the deep south, where the Muslim invaders couldn't reach."

Arla sat down, gratefully accepting the cup of coffee that Lorna, Banerji's secretary, offered her. "Let's get to the case, doc."

"Righty ho." Banerji adjusted his glasses and pulled up a folder on his laptop. "OK, so MO is the same as you know. I got metal fragments from the skull. And yes, it's that Molybdenum stuff. Matches the hammer you got from the suspect's house."

Banerji continued. "The multiple lacerations we saw on the lower and upper limbs were done with a serrated knife, available easy in any store. The lines on them are jagged. The victim must have been moving while he was cutting him up."

Arla grimaced. "Horrible."

"He's a nasty piece of work. Time of death is the same as I told you earlier, I am glad to say. Between two and three pm, closer to two. He was half dead from the neck throttling, then he was tied up, as seen by the rope marks on his ankles and hands."

"Any DNA on him?"

"Yes, as it happens. Some hair and skin cells. Which is odd. Despite the time he had he became careless. The hair cells were on the ground, by the broken vases. No matches on the police databases though."

"Maybe he got angry and lost control this time, right? He destroyed things the old man liked. Maybe even made him watch it. Like he bore a grudge against him," Arla mused.

"Possible."

Banerji said, "And I checked the DNA against that found in David Longworth's house. There's no match."

Arla nodded. "Thanks, that ties in with what's happened so far." She told him about Luke. Banerji listened in sober silence.

"He will still get done, won't he? For those films he made, I mean." Banerji was speaking about Luke.

"Yes. And charges against Simpson will be opened again."

"That's something positive, at least. What a mess this is." He looked up at Arla. "This is someone who is manipulating us very carefully. You need to watch yourself Arla."

"I will, doc. Don't worry."

Finishing their coffees, Arla and Harry stood. They bid Banerji goodbye and headed back to the station.

Arla walked into the office to find Rob, Lisa, Rita, Rupert and Larry hard at work.

Arla said, "Is anyone hungry? It's past 7pm."

Pizza was the unanimous vote and Arla ordered it.

Lisa stretched and yawned. "Got all the emails of Stanley Mason. Makes interesting reading."

Rob and Harry returned with coffee for everyone. Arla sipped hers. "Go on then."

"Stanley was in close contact with a man whose name is only CX. Cyber crime tracked the email - it comes from the dark web. We have no idea who CX is. What we do know is he was emotionally blackmailing Stanley Mason."

"Really? How?"

"It gets strange here. About some crime Mason had committed when he was younger. Apparently he hurt someone related to CX, a woman or girl. CX writes how she is watching from hell, and will take Stanley prisoner one day."

Lisa tapped the screen. "There's pages of this stuff. He really pours vitriol on the screen, guv. This CX guy had a serious grudge against Stanley."

Arla rose and went Lisa's side. "Let me see." She pulled up a chair and sat down. As she read, her frown got deeper. "Goodness me, this is vile stuff. He talks about torturing him and everything. Just the way he was, in fact."

"And see how far it goes back. Over the last three years. This CX guy has been doing it to Stanley for a while."

The pizza arrived and they started eating. Harry said, "You're assuming this CX is a male."

Lisa wiped her mouth with a napkin and said, "He describes how he'll cut him up and so on. And that's how Stanley was killed. So, it stands to reason this is the same person."

311

"What about the blue car? The one Luke talked of?"

"Nothing as yet, guv."

"And did you see anything on the CCTV footage from outside the station? Anyone keeping tabs on us?"

Rob said, "I spent a couple of hours with the AV guys in the control room. Went through dozens of reels. There's a lot of blue cars parked on the roads around the station. Several of those cars have a direct view of the front and back. Without more details, its a needle in a haystack."

Arla swallowed a mouthful. The pizza tasted great and she hadn't realize how famished she had been.

"Rob's right. Even if we did find it, if it's a stolen car, we're back to square one." She switched to Lisa. "What about the cases that Stanley sat on as a judge? Anything there?"

Rita answered. "Still going through them. He worked more than twenty years as a judge. It's a massive pile."

"Narrow your search with David Longworth, Mike Simpson and," Arla thought for a few seconds, "James Fraser. See if they were ever in a case that involved Stanley Mason. She frowned, a new path opening in front of her. "Especially Mike Simpson. And do search for all the young female crime victim cases he dealt with."

Rita wrote everything down. "That should help a lot. Now I know what to look for."

"There has to be a reason," Arla said, "why this madman targeted David and Stanley. We need to find the link before he strikes again."

CHAPTER 80

Arla was sat in the doctor's waiting room. A toddler walked up to her, put a hand on her knee, and raised his snotty face to her. Then he grinned. His mother bustled over and grabbed him.

"Sorry, he's very friendly," the woman said. She had another baby in the pram. She took out a packet of crisps and gave it to the boy, who promptly threw it on the floor.

"Looks like you have your hands full," Arla said.

The woman bent down to pick the packet. "You have no idea." Then she gave Arla a look up and down. Arla was dressed in her usual black trouser business suit, hair in a ponytail, mascara but no make up. She knew what the woman was appraising her for.

Single. No children. Married to the job.

Well, she was wrong with the first one. Technically, she was in a relationship. One out of three wasn't bad. Her mind went back to Harry. They finished around 8pm last night, when Arla bid them goodbye. Harry went back to see his mother, and Arla spent the night alone. She missed Harry when he wasn't there. Was it the same for him? Sometimes she wondered.

The reception room was full. Children coughed and sneezed, old people sat quietly with walking sticks and walking aids. Arla had arrived at 9am sharp to attend the meeting with Laura Douglas's doctor. She hoped she wouldn't have to wait long.

It was ten past nine when the receptionist rose and called out Arla's name. She was instructed to go through the double doors and into room 4. Arla knocked and was told to come in.

Dr Griffiths was almost bald, and looked to be in his sixties. He greeted by Arla by standing and shaking her hand.

"I understand you wanted to speak about Laura Longworth." The doctor seemed intrigued. "May I ask why?"

"Well, and her husband too, David Longworth. They were both patients at this practice."

"Yes they were."

Arla already knew Cherie wasn't a patient here. She was still registered with her previous GP in Hammersmith.

Dr Griffiths said, "Are we any close to solving Mr. Longworth's murder?"

"No. That's why I'm here. What can you tell me about him?"

"A nice man. But he was depressed after Laura's death. I wanted to start him on antidepressants, but he didn't take them."

This was news to Arla. "But his medical records don't state depression."

"I know. But it does mention Bereavement reaction. It became prolonged in his case."

"Anything else you noticed about him?"

"Like I said, he seemed to just lose the zest and appetite for life. It does happen."

"Any changes after he married the second time?"

The doctor shrugged. "Not much, no."

"Did you know his previous wife, Laura?"

Dr Griffith's hooded his eyes slightly as he gazed at Arla. "You know, this is the first time I've thought about it. Maybe because of your questions."

"What do you mean?"

"Laura was depressed as well. But in her case, it took a worse turn."

"What do you mean?"

"She was addicted to diazepam tablets."

Arla gripped the handle on the chair. "That's how she died. Accidental death from diazepam overdose."

A shadow of sadness clouded the doctor's features. "Such a sad end."

"Where was she getting the diazepam from?"

"Not from me. Or from any of the other doctor's here. I only diagnosed her as having withdrawal symptoms when she came in asking for more."

"I see," Arla said. "She didn't disclose her source to you, did she?"

Dr Griffiths shook his bald head. "Nope. I had to admit her into hospital the first time she came in. She had the shakes, and I was afraid she might have a full blown fit. That's what happens when an addict suddenly stops diazepam," he explained.

"Must've been bad."

"Very bad. I couldn't believe it in fact. In the space of a few months, a normal, healthy woman was reduced to diazepam addiction."

"What do you think brought it on?"

"I have no idea. It was bizarre. I mean, she was clearly getting it from somewhere."

"Where from, that's the question," Arla spoke in a low voice, almost to herself.

"These days anyone can buy stuff on the internet. There's this dark web thing, where you can buy any drug you want. Like Silk Road, which got shut down last year."

"The dark web," Arla whispered, eyes suddenly wide. "CX."

What if this CX person had supplied Laura with diazepam?

"What?" the doctor appeared confused.

"Nothing. Did you see anything else that was odd about Laura?"

"As I mentioned she was depressed as well, which came on gradually before she got addicted to diazepam."

"What caused it?"

"I don't know. But that's what clinical depression is. There doesn't have to be a cause." His brows came together, meeting in the middle. His eyes lost focus, like a sudden memory had occurred to him.

"What is it?" Arla asked.

"Just before she got depressed, I remember Laura telling me something about David. She said David had a past that she knew of. She said she hated him for it."

Arla narrowed her eyes. Like a veil lifting slowly, a shape was slowly revealing itself. But it was vague, blurry, just out of her reach.

"Did she ever tell you what it was?"

"No. But I do remember she was never the same after that. Then came the diazepam, and she became a different person."

"What about her relationship with David?"

Dr Griffiths stared at Arla for a while. "Because both these people are dead, and you are a detective, I have provided you with confidential information. I hope you can appreciate that. Under no circumstance would I have done it otherwise."

"Of course. Believe me, your help is invaluable. If you can tell me anything more about them, I would be grateful."

He nodded. "I don't know much about their relationship after that. She was clearly unhappy. After she died, so was he. It's what you made me realise today. Both of them led happy lives, but in the end, both died miserable, sad. Shame, really."

Arla gazed back at his face for a while, digesting what she just heard. They both died unhappy. But they had remained married all these years. Something had changed. Laura had come to know something about her husband's past she couldn't forgive. Or maybe she always knew, and couldn't bear it any more.

Well, she owed David, didn't she? He still made a home with her despite Laura bearing the son of his friend. It took a certain type of man to do that. For the first time, Arla had the inkling that David Longworth hadn't been the innocent man she had imagined. Maybe he had something to hide, too. Something that Laura knew.

Each had their own secret. What did Laura tell David? I might be pregnant with your friend's child, but if you let me keep him, I won't tell the world about your past?

Was it a marriage of convenience between two guilt laden souls? Yet, they had acted like the perfect happy couple all these years, pulling the wool over everyone's eyes. But in the end it had come apart. Some event had been the trigger to start that process.

What was it? What was she missing?

Arla stood, her mind in a trance. Thoughts ran helter skelter in her brain, a racing car roaring down a narrow, winding road.

"Are you alright?" Dr Griffiths asked.

Arla snapped back. "Yes, I'm fine. Listen, doc, can I be in touch with you again? You've been very helpful. If you think of anything else about these two, will you please let me know?"

"Sure. Glad I could help. I liked the family, but guess there was a lot about them I didn't know."

"Yes," Arla said. "I'll be in touch."

As soon as she was outside, she was on the phone to Lisa.

Lisa didn't answer and Arla had to go through switchboard to get her. She waited impatiently while that call too, ran out.

"No answer from DS Moran," the switchboard operator said. "Shall I page her?"

"Yes, and also try Rita, please."

317

Rita didn't answer either.

Fuming, Arla arrived at the black BMW in the GP surgery car park. Just as she slid into the driver's seat her phone began to ring. It was Lisa.

"Guv sorry didn't answer but things have gone bonkers here." Lisa's voice had a stressed, almost emotional edge to it. Arla checked herself.

"What's the matter?"

"It's awful, guv. Harry's sister's been abducted."

CHAPTER 81

"What? Where?" Arla gasped.

"Last night, quite late. She went out from her apartment to the supermarket. She didn't come home and she's not answering her phone. She walked there. Several witnesses have come forward. They saw a black van stop, a man get out and grab her, shoving her inside the van. Then they drove off. One of the witnesses called us."

Arla gripped her forehead. "Oh god. Where's Harry?"

"He's gone to the site with a uniform squad. Do you want the address?"

"Yes, can you text it to me?"

"OK."

"I'm going there now, and then we're coming back. Gather everyone in the incident room. Arla hung up and started the car. She put the address in west London on her GPS, then hit the road. Traffic was building, and she was forced to turn the siren on when she got stuck.

Arla rang Harry several times on the hands free, but he didn't respond. She saw the yellow and black striped tape and the police cars blocking the street as she got to her destination. Curious bystanders stood staring. Arla cut the siren and pulled up on the kerb.

She flashed her warrant card to the uniformed officer who was manning the tape lines. She ducked and entered as the man lifted the tape for her. She saw Harry immediately. He was speaking to a man, taking down notes. Their eyes met and she saw the tension in his eyes soften. Arla got up close to him. She nodded at the witness.

"I heard just now."

Harry nodded without saying a word, but the pain was evident in his eyes. The skin on his face was stretched tight between cheekbones and jaw. He concluded interviewing the witness, then just stood there, the normally square shoulders stooped for once. The supermarket entrance was behind them, people going in and out, staring at them.

Arla pulled at this coat sleeve. "Come with me, please."

"No."

"There's nothing you can do here, Harry. Let this team do their job. Just come and sit inside the car. Tell me what happened."

Harry stood his ground, staring around, avoiding Arla's eyes. She stepped forward and softened her voice. "Don't make this hard on yourself. How many times do you tell *me* that?"

Harry looked at her, his face haggard. "Come on," she said. "Just for a while, OK?"

She would love to give him a hug, but it wasn't the time or place. He followed her stiffly to her car. In the passenger seat, his head sank to the chest. She held his big hand, rubbing it gently.

"It's my fault," he said eventually. "I shouldn't have got her involved in the Crimewatch shoot."

Arla said, "You're sure this is related to the case?"

In response, he took out his phone and passed it to her. Arla stared at the text message.

"I have her. Punish the real criminals. Leave me alone."

It was followed by a photo of Smita. She was tied to a chair, hands bound by rope. Her mouth was gagged and she looked terrified.

"Oh my god," Arla said, hand to mouth. She felt like she had been punched in the gut. "What do they want?"

As if in response, Harry's phone began to ring. He snatched it off her hands. No caller ID flahsed on the screen.

"It's him," Harry said, teeth clenched.

He put it on loudspeaker. Apart from the hiss of static they heard no sound.

"Who is this?" Harry asked.

"You will know my name soon. First of all, answer my question." There was a pause. Then the even toned, male voice said, "Is she there?"

Harry frowned, then his eyes burned. He locked eyes with Arla. "Who do you mean?" he asked.

"Your girlfriend."

Harry clamped his mouth tightly shut. Arla's went lax. Breath left her chest in a rush, replaced by the sudden curl of nausea in her guts.

Harry breathed heavily, then said, "I don't know what you're talking about."

"Oh really? You can fool those idiots you work with, but not me. You two are attached at the hip."

Harry's was staring ahead, grim faced. Arla was frozen. She couldn't think straight. It was Harry who spoke eventually.

"Where is my sister?"

"Right here, with me."

"Listen, you won't get away with this. I promise you-

"Shut up and listen. I want Arla Baker. Do you understand. Send her to me, and I'll think of handing over your sister."

CHAPTER 82

Arla gestured to Harry to keep him talking. She took her phone out and gently opened the car door. She planned to call Lisa and see if she could get a fix on the line,

The voice said, "I'll let you know the time and place." The phone went dead.

"Hello?" Harry shouted. "Hello?" He slammed his fist into the side of the car, making the vehicle shake. "Damn!"

They sat in silence, breath fuming in front of their faces. Arla turned the engine on.

She said, "He's been following us. He knows...maybe Cherie was right. Maybe we do have a mole."

Harry's face was made of granite. "He must've got my number from Smita's phone. Unless of course, we're missing someone on the inside."

"Any details on the van?"

"Acton station are looking into the CCTV images as we speak. Let's hope they can get a registration number."

"What did her friend say?"

"Smita left the apartment at 22.00 to get some milk. She was dressed in black coat and blue jeans and wore a beanie hat." Harry glanced at Arla. "The swine must have followed her from the shoot to her address."

He continued. "I'm going to be at the Acton station. Call me if you need me."

"Harry let them do their job-

"What would you do if this was your sister? If this was Nicole?" Harry's eyes were blazing with intensity, face lowered to within inches of hers. She didn't move. She didn't look away.

But a small corner of her heart crumbled and fell to pieces. Harry was right. She had searched for Nicole for more than sixteen years. Her lost sister. Now, by a cruel trick of fate, it seemed Harry was in the same position.

"Oh, Harry."

His head lowered in pain again, like he had been hit from behind. Arla reached out and pulled him towards her. He folded, his large head coming to rest on her chest. She could smell his hair, aftershave and faint cigarette smoke. He shivered like he had a fever.

He raised himself after a while. She stroked his hand, wishing she could do something to take this nightmare away.

"If it's me he wants, I'll go," Arla said softly.

Harry's mouth twisted in agony. "Can't you see what he's doing? He's torturing us. Just like he did to Stanley and David."

Arla frowned. She hadn't thought of it that way, but it made sense. Whoever this guy was, he was twisting the knife. The pain of others seemed to be his pleasure. Arla felt a cold chill encircle her heart. Fear numbed her insides. She had wondered who was going to be the next victim. She couldn't bear the answer that was now staring at her in the face.

She steeled herself, swallowing the heavy weight at the back of her throat. "I mean it Harry. Just find out where he wants me to go, and I'll be there. At least you'll get Smita back."

"Will I? What if this mad man decides to keep both of you?"

Arla massaged the back of her neck. "I still don't see how he's going to pull this off. But Harry," the tone in her voice made him look at her. "What I'm saying is, I don't want this on my conscience."

Harry started to say something but she put a finger to his lips. "Just listen. We'll plan something, OK? Don't do anything hasty without talking to me first. Like trying to rescue Smita on your own. Promise?"

Harry nodded in silence. "I'll see you back at the station."

"Don't be long," Arla said, and watched nervously as he got out of the car. He walked around the police van and disappeared from sight. Her phone rang suddenly and the ringtone made her jump. She hadn't realised that she had turned it on loud.

It was Lisa. She answered immediately. "What is it? Did you find anything about Smita?"

"No," Lisa's voice was hesitant. "But I did find something strange going through the case history of Mason. Sixteen years ago, he was the judge in the case of a 17 year old girl who was killed in a house. Her dead body was found floating in the swimming pool. Coroner put the cause of death due to drug overdose. He also found signs of forced sexual activity in the autopsy. No one was convicted."

"Why not?"

"No one was found to be living in the house. It belonged to a company. This is where it gets interesting. The company does not exist any more. But I rang Companies House and got the details of the directors. Guess who it was?"

"There's no time to play games Lisa," Arla snapped. "Just tell me."

"Mike Simpson. His new company Blue Horizon, now owns all of his previous assets. This house was one of them."

Arla frowned. "So who called the crime in?"

"There was a 999 call at the time. Caller ID was unidentified, but he said he was the brother of the victim."

"The brother?"

"Yes. I dug out the transcript. It's a harrowing read, guv. The boy actually says, My sister is lying there and not moving. Two men attacked her. Come and help. I think he saw the whole thing happen in front of his eyes."

Arla closed her own. "That sounds horrible. The poor boy actually witnessed this."

After a pause Arla asked, "So what happened to the case?"

"It got thrown out due to lack of evidence."

"What about the witness and the girl's parents?"

"The boy's evidence was regarded as unreliable. He confessed to following his sister around many places, and seeing her take part in similar activities. He was also caught once for glue sniffing in the classroom."

Arla frowned. "Sounds strange. Where were the parents?"

"The boy and girl were living in a foster home. Father unknown, mother was a drug addict."

"You got names?"

"Yes, and digging up the rest of their history."

"Good, I want a full report when I get back. That boy is now a young man if he's still alive and he would have one hell of a grudge against Stanley, wouldn't he?"

"Definitely."

"Get hold of cyber crimes again and see if they have any updates on this CX chap who sent the emails to Stanley. I also want to know if this guy ever contacted Laura Longworth."

"Right."

"And, I want a team to go up to Kent and get statements from those who knew Laura, or saw her last."

Arla hung up and started driving. She stopped to pick up some food, and was back in the station by midday. The office was a hive of activity. Lisa came up to see her the second she stepped in.

"Johnson's in your office. I said you were on your way back."

"Arla?"

Both of them looked up to see the massive figure of Johnson waving at them from her office. They stood in her office, and Lisa shut the door.

Johnson had heard. "How is Harry holding up?"

"Not badly under the circumstances. He's still on site." She wanted to tell him more, but bit her tongue. If the killer wanted Arla, then it was best kept secret for now.

She asked Lisa, "Did you get the names of the girl in the Mason case?"

"Yes. Sadie Cross. Her brother was called Jonathan Cross." A light began to dance in Lisa's eyes. "He's still alive. I managed to track him down. He works in the film industry at Pinewood Studios. Not sure what he does, but his CV is on a job site. I got his address as well. And he's served a prison sentence for GBH. His ex girlfriend accused him of domestic violence."

Excitement clutched Arla's guts. "It could be him. He's trying to avenge his sister, hence he killed Stanley Mason."

Lisa said, "And maybe David Longworth and Simpson were the men who killed her sister? They escaped but he obviously saw them."

"So now he comes back to take revenge." Arla bowed her head, perching her bottom on the desk. "But why now? Why wait all these years?"

"Wait," she said. "Let's not get ahead of ourselves. This could all come to nothing. We need to get hold of this guy first."

Johnson was looking confused. "So who is this guy?"

Lisa explained, just as there was a knock on the door. It was Rob, and he was waving a piece of paper.

"A background check on Jonathan Cross."

Arla took the paper off him. A dread settled inside her as she read. As a young boy, Jonathan had a terrible life. He went from care home to foster home, never staying in one place for more than a

326

year or two. But everywhere he went, his sister went with him. Arla found that touching. Had Sadie, the older sister, become Jonathan's protector?

A weight lodged in her throat, the black, leaden weight of a past she couldn't escape, and couldn't live with. She too, had lost a sibling once.

And Jonathan had probably watched his sister being…

It didn't bear thinking about. No wonder the boy had grown into a disturbed, twisted man. *If* he was their killer. Arla was getting an ominous feeling in her guts that she was right about this.

The room was quiet, and she found knowing expressions in Lisa and Rob's face when she looked up at them.

"It's him guv," Lisa said softly. "I bet you it is."

"Gather everyone in the incident room. Now."

CHAPTER 83

There was a franticness in Incident Room that superseded the normal buzz. The whole station, and some detectives from Lambeth were present. All chairs were occupied and staff lined the walls at the back.

It was Johnson who opened proceedings. His voice was grave, and it rumbled across the room.

"We have a crisis. One of our own, DI Harry Mehta's sister has been abducted. He has been notified by the kidnapper and we think," he turned to Arla, who nodded back at him, "the kidnapper is the suspect in the killing of David Longworth and Stanley Mason."

Johnson told them briefly about what happened to Smita, and the messages Harry had received. He stood to one side and Arla took the stage.

There was no photo of Jonathan Cross as yet, nor of Sadie. But his name and address were written in bold letters on the whiteboard.

"This is the person of interest currently." She told them the reason why. "I am leading the team going to his address and then his place of employment. I want a UK wide APB for this man. Please ensure we cover all major ports and harbours. Home Office is being made aware as we speak, and his passport is on its way. This guy has been in prison once for GBH. He might be armed. Approach with extreme caution."

Rob's voice called out from the back of the room, where bodies stood alongside a bank of fax and printer machines. "Got the fax of his passport page."

Rob walked up the room, brushing against people. Face flushed but smiling, he brandished a page at Arla. She took it, and Rob attached a sheet to the whiteboard. It bore the faxed photo of Jonathan Cross's face, zoomed in.

Arla frowned at the photo. It looked familiar. Very familiar. The truth hit her like a blinding flash of lightning, a blazing white jolt of electricity suddenly rooting her to the spot. She staggered backwards, feeling the earth move beneath her feet.

Rita was right behind her and Arla bumped into her. Arla didn't hear what she said. She couldn't stop staring at the photo. Thoughts tripped in her mind at the speed of light.

The night she met Smita. Upstairs, after the interview with Tangye Gale. This man came in, sat down next to her, introduced himself as….*Jonty*

Her ice cold fingertips were numb and the paper slipped from her hand, falling to the floor. She looked up to find the room was suddenly quiet, and every eye was fixed on her.

Johnson stepped closer. "What's the matter, Arla?"

She had to swallow twice before she could speak. "I know this man. He works for…" she felt like smacking her head. Of course he works for a film studio. Of course he knows the Longworth family.

"Pinewoood studios," Arla said breathlessly. "Send multiple armed units there and shut the place down."

She turned to Rob. "What's his address?"

"It's in Wandsworth. Not far from HMP Wandsworth actually."

And right across the Common, and Bellevue Avenue, where the Longworth's lived. He had probably done surveillance for many months on them, just hiking across the Common at night.

It was falling into place. Many of the jigsaw pieces were still missing, but Arla knew getting hold of Jonathan was paramount now.

But did he have Smita? Or was that someone else? Jonathan might have grabbed Smita but another person was driving the van. Arla remembered the man who came to see Laura in Kent, just before her death. The same man, in the blue car, who came to her house as well.

Arla pointed at Andy and Darren. "I want two units with me. We're going to his house. Send more units to Pinewood Studio. I want his street on lockdown."

She said to Rob, "Take Lisa and go down to Kent."

Rob frowned, "Sure you don't need me here?"

"Dont argue," Arla snapped. "Go to the address where Laura and David were staying before she died. It's near Shorncliffe, right?"

"I think so, but-

"Take photos of everyone - David, Cherie, Luke, Simpson, Jonathan - and see if the locals can identify anyone. Go to the pub where Luke used to drink - ask about him. Any information you can get on the driver of that blue car is important. Got it?"

"Yes guv," Lisa and Rob said in unison.

Darren and Andy had run out already to get the cars ready. Johnson grabbed Arla. "Take an SFO with you. If this guy is armed-"

"Sir, believe me, there is no time to wait any more." Arla ran out the door, and to the rear parking lot. She was in the squad car, sitting next to Andy. He put the siren on and tore out, leading another four squad cars in a convoy behind him.

CHAPTER 84

"Harry?" Arla said, when Andy cut the siren so she could speak.

"Arla," he sounded relieved to hear her voice, but she could detect the tiredness. "What's going on?"

Arla told him quickly. Harry's tone picked up. "So it was him! He knew Smita all this time. I'm coming over."

"What's happening with the van?"

"We followed the CCTV footage into the woods of Acton Town. The van was left there. There's no CCTV in the woods, and we lost them. My guess is they changed cars."

"Clever," Arla swore under her breath. "Keep it together Harry."

"I know. I need to see you."

His voice was hoarse, frank, strong. She felt it too, despite her mind running into knots, her panic over Smita, she wanted Harry next to her. But they both had a job to do.

"Harry, make sure you get all the CCTV footage you need. Have they looked for a blue car, like the one Luke described?"

Harry was quiet. "No. Damn it, I should've thought of that."

"Do that now, Harry. Don't rush. Andy and Darren are here with me."

Harry started to protest, but she made him see reason. He hung up. The cars cut through traffic and after an interminable twenty minutes, they had arrived at their destination. As soon as Arla stepped out she could hear the dull roar of the helicopter overhead.

This part of Wandsworth had seen better days. It was a complex of council blocks, with some terraced, two bed housing on the streets adjoining it. Number twenty, the dilapidated terraced house they wanted, had boarded windows on the ground floor.

"Sure this is the right address?" Arla whispered to Andy. Both of them were flat against the wall, peeking around the corner at the house. It was in the corner, and end of terrace building. The upper floor bay windows had curtains drawn. Arla guessed it was divided into small apartments.

"That's what we have, guv."

Another unit, led by Darren, arrived opposite them. Arla raised a hand, then lowered it. A uniformed officer, with a battering ram, ran towards the house, flanked by two of his colleagues. Arla ran behind them. The door snapped open easily, and the officers charged in.

"Police!"

Two uniform officers peeled off into the ground floor, and Arla ran upstairs, behind Darren. The narrow staircase only allowed single file movement. The carpet on the floor was threadbare, floorboards creaking under their boots. The place had a smell of damp and something else that Arla couldn't identify, a nasty, rotten odour.

Darren crouched at the landing, Arla behind him. The sounds of the officers trampling around downstairs was heavy, but the upstairs remained quiet. Arla could see three doors after the landing. One was half open and showed a bathroom and the other two were shut.

She patted Darren on the back and he went right, she did a left. She rapped on the door and shouted. There was no response. She tried the handle, the door was locked. Behind her, she heard a splintering crash as Darren kicked in one door. Arla turned into the bathroom. Mould grew on the corners of the kitchen sink, and between the grouting of tiles. The mirror was hazy with yellow spots. She could barely see her own face.

She put on her gloves and slid open the glass cabinet. Inside, she found a used toothbrush and a razor. She took out a plastic bag and put them inside. The bath tub was bare, rust claiming the tap and shower nozzle.

Darren appeared behind her. "Found the bedroom, guv."

Arla went with him. A naked bulb lit the room up in a yellow glow. Papers and folders were dumped on the floor. On the wall, Arla saw photos with posters. Darren went to the curtains and flung them apart to get some light into the room. Arla went to the wall next to the bed, heart thumping in her mouth.

She saw photos of David Longworth - cut out of newspapers,printed from the internet. In several of the photos, eyes were gouged out. Black marks were smudged on them too, and she recognized them as cigarette burns. She looked closer, some were old blood stains.

Below David, photos of Stanley Mason were stuck on with blue tack. They had received similar treatment.

Her breath wavered as she got to the last row. There was an old image of her, a newspaper cut out from last year. Arla knelt, getting closer. Her mouth was bone dry. Her image had not been tarnished like the others. Instead, four letters, drawn in blood were written next to it.

MINE.

Arla stood, shaking like a leaf in a storm wind. She turned to Darren. Words didn't come easily.

"Get SOCO here. We need evidence from this place analysed ASAP."

Her phone began to ring. Harry she thought. But the screen showed no number. He might be calling from the Acton station.

She answered. "Harry?"

"Hello? Hello? Help me, please." The high pitched voice of a scared woman came on. Arla stood rooted to the spot. Then she recognized who it was.

"Smita? Is that you?" Arla whispered, her pulse surging.

"Now you know she's alive," a male voice came on the line. "Hello, Arla Baker. How are you?"

CHAPTER 85

Arla couldn't breathe. Her chest was rock solid, like her lungs had turned to concrete. She couldn't speak either, words frozen deep in her brain.

"Hello?" the male voice said, sounding almost cheerful.

Arla made a grunting sound, like a wounded animal. She finally found her voice. "Who are you?"

"By now you must know the answer to that question. I'm guessing you know where I live, and are even there as we speak. Am I correct?"

"What do you want?"

"You." He paused. Arla shivered again, like she was naked in a Siberian wind.

He said, "Just listen. I want you to come on your own to this address. Bring anyone with you, and the girl dies. And there will be worse to follow. Get into your car and I will give further instructions. Do you understand?"

Arla cupped the receiver with her palm, averting her face. She breathed heavily, twice. She needed to get back control.

She said, "I come and you kill us both. Job done for you. Let the girl go first. Then I'll go wherever you want me to. I promise."

He gave a short laugh. "You think you can bargain with me? I know what your promises mean. I'm not that stupid. We're running out of time. What will it be?"

"I told you," Arla clenched her teeth.

"OK. I was going to hold back my trump card, but I guess there's no point." The sound of a scuffle came, and a woman cried out. Arla's thought her heart would stop beating. Scraping, shuffle, then another voice came on the line.

"Speak," a male voice said roughly. "Speak!"

There was silence for a while, then a scared woman spoke. "Hello?"

"Who's this?" Arla said, desperately trying to recognize the familiarity.

"Cherie. Is that Arla?"

Arla sank down to her knees, like she had been punched in the gut. Her vision dimmed.

"Cherie, is that you?"

"Yes. Arla, they grabbed me on the way to Jill's house. Help….help me please."

Jill Hunter was her friend in Dulwich. Arla opened her mouth to speak, but the phone was snatched off Cherie.

"I've got all the aces, detective. Go to your car, now. It's time we met again."

"Jonathan?" Arla croaked. "Jonathan Cross?"

There was silence on the other line for a few seconds. Then he said, "In an hour, I start torturing them. The young girl first. Your choice."

Then the line went dead.

CHAPTER 86

Arla was on the ground floor. She stepped outside the house, her gait unsteady. She steadied herself by leaning against the wall. A uniformed officer nodded at her as he went inside, Arla stared at him unseeingly. Her hands were bunched tightly inside her trouser pockets.

What should she do?

Alerting Harry wouldn't be the right thing. He'd probably get there before she did. There was no telling what this mad man would do. This was a massive, sick game for him. His desire to show who's the boss. His twisted, depraved need for revenge.

Her phone rang again. She answered. Before he could speak she said, "Jonathan, listen to me. I'm sorry about what happened to Sadie. I really am. But this will not bring her back."

Silence.

"Jonathan, I promise you the men who hurt her will be punished."

"I punished them already."

"Your statement said there were two men. Is the other one Simpson?"

Silence for a while again. Then he said, "Yes. And call me Jonty, since we're getting to know each other."

"Simpson is already being charged. This time, he will not escape."

"You seem to think I actually care about what you can do." He snarled suddenly, rage erupting in his voice. "When it's your pathetic system that failed my sister in the first place! Your rubbish, crap investigation. It's people like you who are to blame. Not Simpson. He's just the symptom. You're the disease."

He breathed heavily on the phone. "I'm going to cut the girl's little finger off and send you a photo. Are you ready?"

"No, wait," Arla spoke rapidly. "Tell me the address. I'm coming, now."

He gave her the address. "I'm waiting."

Arla put her GPS on and searched the address. Andy called from behind her. "Guv, you alright?"

She turned to him quickly, putting the phone away. "Yes I am. Listen, I just have to go for a meeting. See you back at the station."

Andy was looking at her strangely. Arla crossed the road and ran down the street. She called an Uber and waited impatiently for it to arrive. Luckily, it came in five minutes.

After an interminable wait, she arrived at her destination. The driver turned off the road into the dirt track. He looked at Aral in the rear view.

"You sure you want me to go here, Miss?"

"Yes, and stop."

There was a wooden fence going around the perimeter of a huge nature reserve. Arla paid the cab driver and watched him as he did a U turn and went down the dirt track. Dust rose under the wheels and soon the car had vanished from view. Arla walked up the road to a long, waist level farmer's gate. The latch was on but she climbed over it easily. She shivered, thankful for her overcoat.

She walked ahead, shoes squelching in the muddy track. The woods started in the distance. To her left lay the vast expanse of a nature reserve, fields undulating to a lake in the middle. It was cold and grey but it wasn't raining and she could see quite far. But the beauty of the view was the last thing on her mind.

After fifteen minutes of fast walking, she was out of breath, but the woods loomed closer. The dense darkness inside was foreboding. Arla kept walking till she was inside the bank of trees. It was suddenly much darker. The smell of wet earth and pines was overpowering. The ground was softer under her feet. She found a path that snaked in between the woods, just like Jonty had said she would. Walking was a bit easier now.

After another ten minutes, she saw a small opening in the trees. As she got closer a glint caught her eye - it was light reflecting off a pond. Next to the pond the outline of a hut appeared. It had a rusty, corrugated iron roof. The windows were shut, it appeared deserted. The hut faced the pond. She approached it from behind, and came up to its side. The window facing her didn't have any light peeking through.

Arla walked around slowly, heart thumping wildly in her mouth. The balcony had four rickety wooden steps. She put her feet on the first one, eyes on the shut door. The steps creaked loudly as she climbed them, puncturing the almost complete silence. A bird swooped down from the trees, making her lurch her eyes upward. She stopped and silence flowed back.

Arla walked up on the balcony and stared a the door. It, like the rest of the hut, had seen better days. She saw nothing but trees all around her. When she pushed the door, the moss on it wet her fingers. It fell open with a horrendous creak.

Darkness inside, encapsulating, like a tomb. The air was dank, wet. Arla took her torch out and flashed it inside. The beam cut through the blackness. Dust motes danced in the light. She saw some garden utensils at the back of the room. But the place was empty.

"Hello? Jonathan?"

No answer. Arla walked in, jaws clenched, knuckles white on the torch. An old table and chair stood in one corner, facing a window that looked out at the pond.

There was a door at the back. It opened when she pushed it. This time, the light beam fell on a female figure tied to a chair. The chair was placed in the centre of the room. it was Smita. Her mouth was gagged with cloth, and ropes tied her arms, feet and body. Her clothes were torn and there was an ugly bruise under the left eye. Blood had dried on her forehead, crusting over her eyes.

Smita averted her eyes in the glare of the light. Arla flashed it around around the room. A chain hung from a wooden beam, with a platform below it. Arla turned to look behind her, but a hand suddenly reached out and pulled her inside. Arla skidded on the floor, lost her balance and fell.

The door was kicked shut. A light came on, bathing the room in a yellow glow. Arla blinked. Smita was moving behind her, making muffled sounds. Arla looked up at the shape that loomed above her.

She stared at the figure till the shock hit her like a bullet train. Her insides smashed into a trillion pieces, fragmenting into the cold and silence. She couldn't look away, numbness claiming her body.

"Hello Arla," the figure said.

CHAPTER 87

Lisa slammed the door of the maroon BMW. Rita got out of the other side. The wind off the English Channel whipped their hair back, the cold, salty air refreshing. Lisa had long hair, and she reached in her pocket for a hair tie.

"Great view," Rita said, shivering. "Wish it was warmer though."

"That's why Rob stayed back. Nicer in the office."

They had parked in the visitor's zone at the top of a section of white cliffs. Below them, the wind raised flecks of white on the blue expanse of the Channel. France was a dim outline in the horizon. The wind had scoured the blue sky clear of clouds, and visibility was excellent. But it was freezing, too.

"Let's go," Lisa said. The large country pub was a hundred meters away, to their left. It was a two story country house that had been converted. Rita had got the name while on the phone with Luke. Both Luke and Simpson were out on bail, and cooperating with police.

The two women hurried along, close to each other in the wind. They were glad to reach The Eagle's Nest. Rita pulled the old oak door open and they stepped inside into warmth and light. They took their coats off and opened another glass panelled door through which the bar was visible. It was past midday and some punters were having lunch.

The ancient wooden beam ceiling bars hung low, but the floor was spacious. A ruddy faced, white bearded barman stood with his hands resting on the counter.

"Hello ladies," he said in a strong Kentish accent. "What can I do fer yer?"

"Oh hello," Rita said, "we called earlier. We've come about the lady who disappeared off the cliffs two years ago, Laura Longworth." Both she and Lisa held up their warrant cards.

The farmer squinted. "Well I guessed you was outsiders the minute you walked in, like."

"Is there somewhere we can talk?"

"Sure let's sit down here. Carl, can you manage the bar for me, lad?" An acne faced teenager came around the corner.

"My names Tony, by the way," the bartender said. "I own the place." They sat down at a side table, next to the window with splendid views of the Channel.

Lisa took out a photo of Laura Longworth. Luke had provided them with a family album, and it contained several photos of Laura on holiday.

"Do you recognize her?" Lisa asked.

Tony picked up the photo and looked closely. He clicked his tongue on the roof of his mouth. "Ah, yes, I do like. Everyone here does. Sad day for this place."

"What happened?"

"A walker saw her body on the beach. She fell of the cliff. But you know that already, don'cher?" He peered at them under bushy eyebrows.

Rita asked, "Did she come here often?"

"Yes, she did like. This is the biggest pub in the village, so it is. All of `em come here for a drink."

"So she came the day she died, or before?"

Tony narrowed his eyes. "Are you going to tell me what this is all about?"

"It's a police investigation so we can't comment on that. Anything you tell us can be of great importance. So please think. It will make a big difference."

Tony pursed his lips then ran his hands through his long beard. He stared out the window for a while. He turned away and shouted across the room to a table nearby.

"James, our kid, come here a minute, will ya."

A younger man, by no means a kid, rose from the table he was drinking at. His three companions looked at them. James ambled over, dressed in sheepskin leather coat and muddy wellington boots. He was clearly a farmer.

Tony showed him the photo of Laura. "Remember her? Lass who fell of the cliff, two years ago."

James frowned. He studied the photo and raised his eyes slowly to examine Rita and Lisa.

Tony said, "These be police women. Came to check on some stuff about the lass."

When James spoke, his voice had the same twang as Tony. "Yes, I remember. She used to sit there," he pointed to an isolated table for two, hidden around a corner. "With her friend. They only came for holidays, twice a year."

Lisa asked, "What did her friend look like?"

"Can't remember that well. She always kept a cap on her head and sunglasses on. Sat with her back to everyone else."

"Her friend was a woman?"

"Yes."

Rita and Lisa glanced at each other. Rita asked, "Can you describe this woman to us?"

James shrugged. "Only saw her back, like. She always wore dark clothes. Walked in and walked out quickly."

Lisa said, "How did they come here?"

Tony said, "I saw her," he pointed at Laura's photo, "walking. But sometimes they came in a blue car."

Lisa leaned forward, a sudden tightness gripping her inside. "A blue car?"

James spoke. "Yeah, I remember too. That was the last time I saw them, like. Both of them came off the blue car in the car park. Her friend drove."

Lisa's heart was beating loudly. "Do you have CCTV in the car park?"

Tony nodded. "Aye, that we do, like. It's digital and records 24/7. Got all me films, going back five years. So I have."

Lisa stood. "Can you show them to me? Please? Right now."

After almost an hour of going through all the image files on Tony's old laptop, and two cups of coffee, Lisa and Rita found their images. Their heads were almost touching as they focused on the screen.

The roll played and they saw the car drive in and park. The driver stepped out. It was a woman with light coloured hair, baseball cap pulled low, and large sunglasses covering her face. She kept her face down, making any view impossible. Laura was easily recognizable when the camera zoomed in. Her hair was straggly, darker, and her pasty face was lifted up in the air.

Rita wrote down the registration number of the car, and rang Rob immediately. He got back within ten minutes.

"The car is off the road and unlicensed, according to the DVLA. But I did get the previous owners name and address. It's registered to a Gus Percival. He now lives in Salford, up north."

Rita had Rob on loudspeaker, and she looked at Lisa, scowling. "Who is Gus Percival?"

Rob said, "Cherie Longworth's ex husband. His name's on my screen. I called him to check Cherie's background."

Lisa was scowling too. "What on earth was his car doing here? And who is that woman with Laura?"

"I don't know," Rob said. "But I think asking Gus is a good idea."

344

Lisa took his number down and rang him. Mr. Percival answered on the third ring. "Who is this?" he asked in a cautious voice.

Lisa introduced herself and explained the situation. There was silence on the other end. Lisa said, "Mr. Percival?"

He coughed. "Sorry, I have no idea why my car would be there. In fact, I gave that car to my ex wife before we divorced. She kept it."

A sudden hollow feeling echoed around Lisa's heart. A cold hand wrapped around her ribs, squeezing tight. She cleared her throat, mouth dry.

"Mr. Percival. Please do me a favour. Can I send you a photo? I need to show you something. It's very urgent."

"OK."

Lisa hung up and turned to Rita, her eyes frantic. "Do you have the photos of Cherie Longworth on your phone?"

Rita nodded. Lisa said, "Send them to Gus Percival and see if she can ID her. I guess Rob never did this at the beginning."

Rita sent the photos and Lisa rang to confirm that he received them. He called back almost instantly.

He sounded bewildered. "That woman is not my ex-wife. Whose photo did you just send me?"

Lisa's mouth was open, but she could barely take a breath in. "Are you sure?"

"Of course I am. I lived with Cherie for ten years. That photo you just sent me is not Cherie."

CHAPTER 88

Harry was frowning at the screen. There was a number of blue cars on the CCTV cameras, and any one of them could be the one he wanted. He passed a weary hand over his eyes. This wasn't helping. He grabbed his phone, wondering why Arla hadn't called him back yet.

His phone rang then, but it wasn't Arla. Lisa's breathless voice came on the phone. "Guv, is that you?"

"Yes. What is it?"

In jerky, fast sentences, Lisa told him what happened in Kent. Harry stood abruptly. "So Cherie is using a fake identity? What happened to Gus Percival's real ex-wife?"

"No one knows." Lisa paused, and Harry knew she was thinking the same as hi,

"Well, if Cherie took her identity, and no one heard from the ex-wife…" Harry left his sentence dangling.

"She's dead, isn't she?" Lisa finished.

Harry rubbed his forehead, a headache pulsing inside. "I can't believe this is happening."

He paced the CCTV room of Acton station, his mind frantic. "Where's Arla?"

"Don't know guv. She didn't call you? Last I heard she was headed out to that Jonathan Cross's house."

"Yes, I know that" Harry said impatiently. "OK, I'm coming back to the station. Did Arla pull the unit that was keeping watch on Cherie's place?"

"Yes, guv."

"I'm getting a bad feeling about this. Call all the uniform units that went to the Cross house. Find out what's happening. Prepare the incident room."

Harry hung up and thanked the two other detectives in the room. He ran out into the car park and screeched out into traffic, turning his siren on.

The incident room was empty when he came back. Rob hurried over to him from his desk.

"You heard about Cherie, guv?

"Yes, where Lisa and Rita?"

"Still on their way back from Kent."

"Any news from Darren or Andy?"

"Yes. Andy says he saw DCI Baker get into a cab and go off somewhere. Says she got a call from someone and went outside the house to take it. She left right after she finished the call."

"Where? Where did she go?" Harry's voice was thick with tension and he advanced on Rob. Rob stepped back, worried.

"Don't know guv. Andy didn't say."

The knot of unease deep inside Harry's guts was spreading like a poisonous flower. Nausea rose up in his mouth. He gripped the back of a chair, thinking hard and fast.

Rob said, "There is one thing to report. Cyber crime came back with the rest of Stanley's emails. We got hold of Laura Longworth's emails as well."

Harry was listening with only half a mind. "So?"

"So this CX guy, who was sending hate mail to Stanley, was hiding his IP address as he was using the dark web."

"Get to the point," Harry growled.

"Well, he slipped up. Using the dark web, he could hide his IP address, unless he accessed a website that needs Flash, or uses javascript. He did that, to buy some diazepam. As soon as he did so, that website placed tracing cookies on his IP address. These cookies can breach the dark web."

Harry turned to face Rob. "So we know his IP address now? That means we can use Webcrawler to get the GPS location of the IP address. Right?"

"Yes guv. And what's more - the diazepam he bought was being sent to Laura Longworth's address. We know because cyber crime tracked down the supplier and checked their records."

Harry's eyes widened. "So it was CX who was responsible for Laura's diazepam addiction?"

"He sent her emails under a different account. As SadieX."

"SadieX," Harry echoed. "That's the name of Jonathan's sister. The one who was killed. So, CX must be Jonathan, right?"

Rob nodded, still eyeing Harry warily as Harry's long frame hung over him, intent on every word.

"Get the geolocation of the IP address."

Harry pulled out his phone and called Andy. "Andy, its DI Mehta."

There was static on the line and Harry could tell Andy was driving. "Yes guv."

"Did you check the reg number of the uber that DCI Baker took?"

Andy faltered. "Uh, no. But it was a green Toyota Prius. I remember it being P reg, with VH the last two letters."

"Access the CCTV cameras in that area," Harry said urgently. "I'm putting out an APB for that car. Can't be that many matching cars, and it must have GPS on, if its an Uber."

"I'll get on the case now. GPS tracking might be our best bet. What's going on guv?"

Harry gripped the phone tightly. "Something very bad. Arla has gone to my sister, I think. This bastard wants them both. If you get the GPS signal of this Uber, get in touch with me ASAP."

"Roger that," Andy said.

He turned to look for Rob but couldn't find them. Two detectives walked in, and Justin Beauregard was one of them. Justin stopped when he saw the frantic look on Harry's face.

"What's going on?"

"Arla is missing, probably chasing after the real killer in the Longworth case. Have you seen Rob?"

"He was outside, heading into cyber crimes lab."

"Thanks," Harry started for the door.

"Listen," Justin called back. "Shall I get some uniformed units ready for dispatch to wherever you think Aral might be?"

Harry turned, relief etched on his face. "Thanks Justin, that's just what I need. Stand by for the location."

Harry sprinted down the corridor, and up the stairs into the first floor. Most of the tech work was outsourced to third party labs, but Clapham station had a small department that looked into phone and social media accounts. A row of analysts were staring at their screen inside the room. Harry spotted Rob in one corner and hurried over.

Rob's eyes were wide. He patted the analyst, a young bearded man on the back, and straightened as Harry approached.

"Got it guv," he showed Harry a piece of paper. "The geolocation of the IP address from where that bastard CX was sending his hate mail."

Harry grabbed the paper from Rob's hand. His forehead creased. "Brent Reservoir?"

"Up in North London, near Brent's Cross. Here look," Rob pointed at the analyst's screen.

Harry peered at the google map images. A huge water reservoir was surrounded by what looked like farm land. A green dot was pulsating in the middle of a wooded region, next to the water.

"You sure this is it?" Harry asked.

The analyst nodded. "It's there alright. There's no other laptop being used in the location."

Harry bunched his fist and swallowed. "Call air support and get as many mobile units as we have."

He ran for the door, Rob puffing after him.

CHAPTER 89

The light from the naked yellow bulb was strong. It fell on the face of the figure standing over Arla, and another light at the other end of the room illuminated it further. There was no doubt.

Arla put her palms on the floor and scuttled back, her hands touching something soft. She heard a whimper and knew it was Smita. Arla wrapped her fingers around Smita's leg and gave a reassuring squeeze. She stared in disbelief at the figure.

"Cherie." Arla found her voice at last. She squeezed her tightly shut, then opened them again. Like a domino chain, pieces of the puzzle were falling into place. But areas of darkness still remained.

Cherie's blonde hair fell around her face. Her eyes were hard, stony. The normally beautiful face was set it tight lines, thin lips pressed tightly together.

"What are you doing here?" Arla asked.

Cherie stared at her in silence for a while longer, ignoring Smita. Then she spoke in a calm and unruffled voice.

"Remember the first time we met? Outside our house, the night I found David."

She continued. "I knew all about you, of course. But I didn't know that you would come to the scene that early. It was a stroke of luck. You see, detective, you and I are very similar."

Arla's brows met. "I don't know what you're talking about."

"You lost your sister when you were eleven. Isn't that correct?"

An iron first tightened around Arla's chest, and air squeezed painfully out of her lungs. "How...how do you know that?"

"I know James Fraser, the Secretary of State. My son can hack into his emails. Sending an official request to the London Met wasn't exactly difficult."

Arla's head reeled with a twin blast of shock. She focused on the second one. "Your son?"

A creak on the wooden floor came from behind her. Arla turned quickly. A pair of legs appeared, the upper body still in the shadows. Then the man stepped into the light. He smiled.

Arla gasped. It was the man she had known as Jonty. Behind her, she could feel Smita squirming again. She made loud sounds against her gag, and Jonty strode forward swiftly. He grabbed Smita by the hair and slapped her hard.

"No!" Arla shouted, kicking Jonty in the shins. He grunted, let go of Smita, and bent down to grip Arla around the neck. He was immensely strong. Arla wasn't weak, and she fought valiantly, but his fingers were like iron pincers, crushing her windpipe.

A shroud of blackness came over her eyes, and white pinpoints of stars appeared. A voice spoke from one side, and she was flung back down to the floor, her head smashing on the wood. Pain exploded in her skull, and for a while she couldn't move. She felt her hands being dragged behind her back, and the roughness of rope tying them together.

A light dazzled her face and she winced, unable to open her eyes. She had her back to the wall now. Cherie stepped in front of the light.

"Yes, my son. I rescued him from a life of abuse in foster care."

The words floated through the slumber of pain and ache in Arla's mind. She blinked. Cherie was bathed in the halo of the light behind her.

"After my daughter died, I knew I had to do something. I couldn't help her. But there was no way Jonathan would suffer the same fate."

Arla tried to shake the heaviness from her head. It wasn't working. Despite the grogginess and nausea, she tried to focus.

"Why couldn't you help your daughter?"

"Sadie and Jonathan were taken from me when they were toddlers. I was a drug addict at the time, and a sex worker. It's not a life I'm proud of. The children being taken was my wake up call. I was in jail at the time, and couldn't stop them being put into foster care."

Arla was aware that Cherie's tone had changed. It wasn't flat and dispassionate any more. The words shook as she stopped speaking.

"I pleaded with social services to get custody rights for my children, but they wouldn't even allow me visiting rights till they were older. I watched..." her words trailed off.

Jonty spoke from behind Arla. "It's OK Mama. You don't have to do this."

"Yes I do," Cherie's voice seemed strange, ethereal, emanating from a face shrouded in darkness. "Can't you see she understands? She gets what happened to Sadie. Isn't that right, Arla? A similar fate fell on Nicole, your sister."

An ache settled on Arla's heart, and with it, a new dread for the situation she was in. She needed to buy time. She had to keep them talking.

"No one can change the past, Cherie. If it's revenge you're after, then remember it won't change anything." Arla lowered her voice. "It won't bring Sadie back."

Cherie stepped forward, the bulge of light behind her growing, expanding the strange halo.

"No. But the past changes us, Arla. You know that, don't you? It made you who you are today."

A sudden emotion caught in Arla's throat, and she was surprised by its intensity. Cherie's words had her mind reeling. With uncanny insight, this cold blooded manipulator had caught Arla's life in her cross hairs.

And for some unknown reason, tears trickled down Arla's cheeks. She shook her head angrily, desperate to caste away this spell Cherie had on her.

"You don't know anything about me. I'm nothing like you. You're a heartless, cold serpent." Arla sniffed and lifted one shoulder to rub her nose.

She said, "How did you get married to David Longworth?"

Cherie laughed for the first time, and it sent cold shivers down Arla's spine.

"Oh, I did go into acting, once I cleaned myself up. Men are easy, you see. They only want one thing. And I was good at it."

"Were you really married to your previous husband?" Arla ransacked her brain for the name.

"Gus Percival?" Cherie said. "Ah, that was a decoy. It worked so well. His wife, the real Cherie, fell for my friendship charms. Stupid stepford wife that she was." She laughed again.

"What did you do to her?"

"Killed her, of course." Cherie shrugged her shoulders casually. "She was divorced already. I simply took her name and identity, so the other stuff wouldn't catch up with me."

"Like the murder of Jonathan's foster parents?" A clarity was spreading in Arla's mind, and with it, a stark, horrible realisation she was facing a fiendishly clever, bitter, twisted character. How far did "Cherie's" killing spree extend?

"You're catching on," Cherie came forward till she was standing right in front of Arla. The light behind her was blinding again. She knelt to face Arla.

"Come join us, Arla. For Nicole's sake. Think of the evil we could get rid of."

Arla frowned deeply, bile rising in her throat. "Join you? You're an evil witch. A cold blooded killer, and the saddest thing is you can't even see it."

Jonty appeared. "Enough of this. Mama, we need to go. She's just playing for time now."

Cherie stared at Arla for a few seconds, then raised herself. She looked at her son. "You're right. My little trooper. Get the car ready."

Both of them left the room. Arla waited til the sound of footsteps had faded, then she bent her knees and leaning against the wall, managed to stand. She called to Smita, but her head was lolling over her chest. With heavy legs, Arla stumbled towards the door. The front room was empty, but the main door was open. The still waters of the pond reflected a murky grey sky.

The sound of a car engine had Arla run to the wall and flatten herself against the window. A black van appeared. Cherie jumped out of the driver's seat and Jonty ran around the passenger side, then up the porch stairs. Arla didn't have time to escape.

Jonty smiled when he saw Arla. She ran into the back room, but he was too quick. A sliding tackle brought Arla crashing to the floor. Hands still tied back, she couldn't break her fall. Her head hit the wall with a sickening thud and she cried out, crumpling down.

Dimly, she was aware of Jonty picking her up. He tied a cloth around her mouth, gagging her. Then he lifted her on his shoulders and went to the car. Cherie had the doors open. Arla landed on her back inside. The door remained open, with Cherie standing guard. Jonty appeared shortly, carrying Smita. The girl landed on a heap next to Arla. She was still unconscious.

Arla lifted her head to find Jonty staring at her with a sickening grin on his face. "Time for a swim."

The door slammed shut. The engine came to life, and the van moved towards the Brent Reservoir.

CHAPTER 90

"Hurry, god damn it!" Harry roared, his voice rising above the siren.

Darren was at the wheels, and his training in the obstacle driving course was being put to good use. He swerved and spun, flinging the five officers in side the car against the sides. He bellowed in impatience like Harry as a builder's truck blocked their way, slow to pull over to one side.

Harry's radio chirped. "NPAS unit 4 approaching location."

The helicopter was almost there, Harry sighed in relief. "Roger that," he said on the radio. "Standy, standby."

They had been on the road for more than forty minutes. Sirens filled the air behind them as a convoy of squad cars screamed down the North Circular A406 road. Darren took a hard left, leaving the road for a dirt track. Harry bounced, bashing his head against the ceiling. The cars rolled down the country lane, till on his left, Harry saw the open land of the nature reserve.

His radio beeped again. "Zero this is control." It was Rob's voice.

"Receiving Rob. What's happening?"

"The laptop is moving, guv. It's out of the woods and heading for the reservoir."

"Copy that."

Harry got on the pilot's radio channel. "Unit 4, Can you see anything?"

"Yes." The pilot's voice crackled on the line. "A black van. moving at high speed towards the reservoir."

"Stop it," Harry shouted. "You have a firearms officer on board, right?   Shoot   the   wheels   out."

The pilot was quiet for a second, the sound of rotors loud in the radio channel. Then his voice came back. "Who's giving authority for the SFO to fire?"

"Authority?" Harry almost screamed. "DCI Baker and my sister are probably in that van! Why the hell do you have an SFO if he can't use his weapon?"

"I'm sorry sir, DCS Johnson needs to-"

"Just do it!" Harry bellowed. "You're not shooting a suspect, it's a bloody car!"

"Suspect out of vehicle, repeat, suspect out of vehicle," the pilot's voice suddenly had an urgency to it. "He is- oh my god."

Harry was shoved against the door as the car lurched into the field. Andy jumped back, he had run out to open the gate that led inside the nature reserve. Darren followed a sign that said Brent Reservoir. There was no road, it was an open field. In the distance, the waters of the massive reservoir gleamed.

"What's he doing?" Harry shouted. "Speed up," he snarled at Darren. Harry was shaking, palms moist. He could see beads of sweat pour down Darren's forehead.

The pilot said, "The engine's on and the van is going into the reservoir. The suspect is now in a car and they're moving out. Towards you."

"Do something to the van!" Harry roared.

His head hit the ceiling again and he winced. Darren had the accelerator down flat, and the engine whined as the wheels churned up dust. They went past a clump of trees, and ahead, two black shapes appeared, getting larger as they sped towards it. Harry recognized the shape of the van, and a salon car speeding away.

The helicopter was hovering in the air, and it started to descend closer. A stream of yellow flash came out of the helicopter window, splattering sparks against the side of the van.

The back tires of the van exploded, then the front. The vehicle did a funny sideways movement, then lurched to a stop. The wheels sank in the sand of the reservoir, and the van started to sink into the water.

Harry saw the helicopter take off after the fleeing car. Darren drove like a madman, and they screeched to a stop near the reservoir's edge. Harry was the first out. He took his jacket off and shoes off. Then he ran towards the van, its front tilting into the water, the back settling into sand.

Harry pumped his long legs and managed to reach the van just in time. He pulled on the doors, but they were all locked. The side and back doors had no windows.The driver's seat was empty, as was the front passenger's.

"Move guv," Andy shouted behind him. He splashed into the water, battering ram raised over his head. Harry ducked, hands over his head as Andy shattered the glass of the driver's window.

The van was sinking steadily, then water level now upto the side view mirrors. Harry was up to his waist, and it was happening very quickly - the heavy vehicle losing its fight with gravity.

Harry brushed the glass fragments from his hair. He hooked a hand inside the driver's door, fingers feverishly searching for unlock button. He couldn't find it. His fingers were numb with cold, the freezing water making things far worse.

Andy broke the passenger side window. Darren dived inside the window, his body more compact. Water gurgled in through the windows and Harry heart sank. He knew they had seconds before the car sank altogether.

Darren opened the sliding side door an inch, grunting against the pressure of the surging water. Harry put a hand inside, gained some purchase and the two of them pushed with all their might. The door screeched back and water rushed inside, pooling into the floor. Harry's eyes widened. Arla scared, gagged face stared back at him. Her legs were untied and she moved forward. Darren grabbed Smita, who was now awake. Both women were bundled out of the car, Harry holding them for dear life, as more water rushed in, pushing Darren inside the van.

Arla and Smita were dressed, with shoes on, and Harry had to get them out of the water first. Feet sinking into sand, he fought his way back, holding the women by his side. There was a giant whooshing sound behind them, and shattering glass as the windscreen broke and water plunged into the van.

"Darren," Harry shouted, but his voice was weak with exhaustion.

Bubbles broke the water next to Harry and a figure broke out of the reservoir, coughing and spluttering. It was Darren, followed quickly by Andy. Both wore shirts soaked to their skin, chest rigs already discarded before they entered the reservoir.

The five of them made it back to the muddy, sandy shore and collapsed on it. Harry removed the gags from Arla and Smita's mouth. Smita whimpered and clung on to Harry, and he swallowed the emotion inside his throat, holding his sister tight against him. His eyes locked onto Arla's. She nodded, and despite all that had happened, gave him a grin.

CHAPTER 91

Commander Wayne Johnson's room was completely silent as Arla finished speaking. She stood, facing a table that seated Johnson, James Fraser, the Sec of State, Nixon from the MI5 and his boss, and Deakins, the Assistant Commissioner.

Harry was to her left, seated. The rest of the team were downstairs. Arla sat back down on her chair.

Johnson said, "Both Cherie and Jonathan Cross are now in captivity. The other squad cars blocked their escape route. They surrendered without a fight, not that they had any other option."

Fraser took off his glasses and rubbed his eyes. Arla noted how haggard he looked. The earlier polish of his nice suit and gleaming eyes were gone.

He said, "Do we know Cherie's real identity?"

Arla said, "Polly Holdsworth was the name on her birth certificate. But this was a woman who changed her identity frequently."

Fraser coughed. "I had a word with the Justice Minister. Simpson's trial for historic sexual abuse crimes will be brought forward." He looked down, closing his eyes briefly. Arla could read the guilt in his features. Luke was his son, and he had failed him in every respect as a father.

When Fraser looked up, he stared at Arla. "I thank you for bringing Simpson to justice."

She shrugged. "He was going to get it sooner or later."

Johnson said, "All of you did a great job." His eyes moved from Arla to Harry.

Deakins, the mild mannered, but cut throat hard ADC said, "And now that Commander Johnson has left his post as Superintendent, I think there might be a vacancy looming."

Fraser leaned forward. "I heard about that too." He smiled at Arla, and she felt a lightness in her heart. Expectation filled her being like sunlight. She looked at the men, coming to a stop at Johnson. He cleared his throat.

"No post has been created as yet. I am still in charge for the time being, as you know." He gave Arla a grin. "But when the time comes, all of us know who has put herself forward as the best candidate for the job."

Arla felt happiness bubbling inside her, rising up in her chest like the first spring morning of the year.

*****

The beer was flowing freely inside the pub. Harry had sneaked out for a fag, and Arla had persuaded him to let her have one. A few double gin and tonics warmed her insides and after her near death experience, she deserved a smoke, damn it.

Laughter came through the doors as they opened it and stepped outside. They were at the rear of the pub and Harry found a dark corner and lit his fag. Both blew out smoke, Arla coughing as she did so.

"You OK?" Harry asked.

"A little nicotine won't harm me. I almost drowned yesterday, after getting my head bashed in."

Harry missed the mirth in her eyes and looked away. She stared at his face, wondering. He had been unusually serious since the rescue operation. Smita was fine, despite the scars she now carried. She would pull through.

She punched him lightly on the forearm. "Hey. It's over. We did alright."

He looked at her then, his eyes large and melting and she felt the breath catch in her throat. She had never seen Harry look so serious.

"Yes we did," he said in a low, rough voice. "But I never want to see you like that again."

He took a deep breath, his big chest rising and falling as he looked away again. Arla remained silent. The quietness deepened. She was about to say something when he spoke.

"We have to take better care of you. You try too hard, get yourself into these situations. It's not right." He shook his head, throwing the butt away.

"I can take care of myself," she said in a small voice.

"I know, but if anything happened to you, I…"

His voice caught and his mouth opened suddenly, expelling air. His eyes had a strange light in them as he looked at her. The burning intensity in them held her captive.

"I…"

Arla stared at him. He faced her now, and she was aware how close they stood.

"I couldn't forgive myself if something happened to you. Because I…" he swallowed, suddenly seeming incapable of further speech.

"Yes?" Arla said, looking up at his shining eyes. "What is it?"

"Because I…" his forehead creased in an expression that was like pain, but spoke to her of tenderness, of lost hopes and dreams.

He reached out a hand to cradle her cheek. She felt the warmth of his hand, then the brush of his thumb as he gently stroked her lower lip. She held his hand in both of hers and lowered it. She stepped closer till there was no distance between them. His aftershave smelt of woodspice, and faint cigarettes.

"Tell me, Harry." Her voice was the rustle of winter leaves falling to the ground.

"I think I love you, Arla Baker."